THE THIRD BOOK OF CATACLYSM

THE PALE DEMON

G.A. Finocchiaro

ISBN: 9798989747887

First Edition September 2025

duskboundbooks.com

www.gafino.com

Edited by Cari Dubiel

Cover Design by Rachel Perciphone

Interior Design by G.A. Finocchiaro

Author Photo by Ashley Griffin Photography

Also by G.A. Finocchiaro

This story is part of the

SCALES SEQUENCE.

The SCALES Sequence can be read in order or as individual series within. You decide. Each book is marked with a roman numeral within a circle. This is where it exists in the SCALES SEQUENCE.

For more information, please go to gafino.com and click on SCALES.

1. THE KNIGHTMARES
2. QUIBBLES *(short)*
3. GRACE FALLS
4. BOGEY *(short)*
5. THE RAPTOR: Cataclysm pt 1
6. THE OMEGA: Cataclysm pt 2
7. MASKED
8. THE PALE DEMON: Cataclysm pt 3
9. SUCKERS

prologue

Someone. Somewhere. Somewhen...

There were gasps within the room.

"The following crimes will be entered into the record: The Creation of Divine Contraband. The Creation of a Cataclysmic Remnant. Crimes Against the Natural Order of Time—"

"Is the timeline not back on track?" I argued.

"There are...inconsistencies," said a voice.

"The following additional Empyrean crimes will be entered into the record: the murders of Richard Jansen, and the Celestial beings known as Eris, Carina, Sagittarii, the Archangel Raphael, the Archangel Uriel, and the Archangel Gabriel, Princes of Empyrea."

"I did not murder any Celestials!"

"That is false!"

They were right, but not about this. "You are looking for a scapegoat. You are looking to make a villain out of me. I am not the villain here! Are we all expected to be perfect, mindless automatons? We have free will! We experience joy! We experience anger and hatred! We experience love and lust! Your outdated ideology is choking us. We are more like the humans than any of you care to believe!"

Murmurs. There were many who agreed, but too frightened to speak up.

"Know thy enemy."

"But they are *not* our enemy! When the Omens rip through the Breach and storm back into this world, we will be outnumbered! We must have allies. The Demons. The Fae. *And* the Humans!"

"Sacrilege."

"We are all children of The One!"

"Sacrilege."

"We are all fighting this war! We have turned a blind eye to the treachery of the Boggleboo! The Dream Lands have been unprotected for far too long! Those kids in Philadelphia in '99? They prevented an invasion! They fight and sacrifice just as much as we do!"

"Liar," screamed someone.

"Your testimony has been invalidated."

"What?"

"Liars cannot be trusted!" said the Voice.

"I am not a liar!"

"The Raptor shall finish his testimony, and new records will be included from the Omega and the Pale Demon. Judgment will be rendered thereafter."

***

MALUS
June 21, 2013

Time.

One spends most of their existence searching for more time, while wasting most of the time they're given. There are no guarantees in life. Time is a gift—for every second spent worrying of tomorrow or ruminating on the past, we move one step closer to Death's harvest.

We all eventually die. Even immortals.

It is in our nature to want more. There was no such thing as having enough—wealth, desire, time—covetous gifts that keep us yearning. Devour, then seek to acquire more. Existence, in all forms, is to consume. We consume. We fuck. We waste. We care not for where we shit, so long as it lies behind us—someone else's problem.

Yet, when one has all the time in the world, having patience is insufferable. A year to an immortal is but a single grain of sand along a wave-swept shore. An immortal waiting for a single moment to occur is like Tantalus stretching for a sip of life-saving water—ever receding, ever just beyond reach.

Immortality can warp even the purest of things. Survive long enough, and even the best intentions can become the darkest of endeavors.

It was the Summer Solstice. Two solstices, two equinoxes, one passing every three months. A cycle of four in a calendar year—one for each of the Four Keys of Eden.

Within the girl's natural lifetime, there was only one year that matched the criteria…

"To gain what you seek," Frigg had predicted, *"you must start on the first day of a single calendar year in which the previous contained no less than two solar eclipses, two lunar eclipses, and with the rare transit of Venus across the sun."*

Twenty-*thirteen*—was it a coincidence? Or destiny?

I'd captured one key every quarter, each key leading to the next, until the final day of the year when all four would open the gates of Eden—then the Holy Dyad would be mine.

I would ascend. I would be a god above all others.

The Key of Capricorn signaled where to go, like a tuning fork striking the perfect note. A softening trill that settled into a hum when we arrived in southern China under a moonless night. High upon a cliff overlooking the Li River, the key began to pulse. The cliffs were formed like mismatched fingers reaching to the sky from the bluish green water, winding its way between narrow rocky cliffs like a tangled serpent.

Along the sheer cliff, half the distance to the water below, was a small crack in the stone face. It appeared shallow from the surface, but as it cut into the rock, the jagged edges wide enough for a man to slip through, it revealed itself as an entrance. The crack was accessible to only the most daring human, or perhaps a casual stroll for a Fallen who could bend gravity to their will.

Beyond the entrance chamber and through a narrow crag came a soft glow. That glow led into a corridor with walls of luminous crystal, and a staircase wound deep into the cliff. I lost track of how far we had descended, far below the river and into a great hall. Stone dragons of black crystal and jade crawled along the walls with lush green tapestries hung from the vaulted ceiling. It was a palace, and it was decorated with riches that would have entranced Mammon, the god of greed, or even the rotten heart of Midas himself.

The deeper we ventured, the more sour the stagnant air, entombed for centuries. There were no scents or sounds. No danger, nor confrontation. Just age. Age and stillness from every winding corridor and direction, but I knew the danger ahead.

This was the Crystal Palace of Ao Guang, the Dragon King of the East. After spending thousands of years teetering on the scale of good and evil, Ao Guang finally sought refuge within his palace and disappeared from history. He was the second of the four guardians protecting the Keys of Eden—the second key, the Key of Libra, was his ward for eternity.

What did you do, dear king, to be barred from returning home forever? And what could you ever hope to accomplish by protecting their baubles?

Pathetic.

Shadows did not exist inside the Crystal Palace. Lack of shadow made my kind tremble. To be seen was against our nature. With the crystal walls emanating light from every angle, it was our reluctant member, Nox, who dimmed the radiance around her, allowing us to pass in relative darkness. Her black hair was a voluminous wisp, twisting and drifting to surround her form, never allowing her beauty to be witnessed all at once, but in small revelations.

I admired her, but she was a threat to me.

All Fallen were powerful, but Nox was elite. The goddess of night was no fool, nor was she wicked or malicious. Nox's darkness was a manifestation of her eternal grief—a mother seeking her lost child. Her only loyalty was to her daughter.

I sensed betrayal from the moment we struck our deal, but I needed her abilities. Nox controlled the light. Without Nox, we would have never captured our prize—Jacinda Moira O'Neill—the Extraordinary Girl—the Omega.

As Nox swept through the crystal halls, concealing us within shadow, the goddess of revenge, Nemesis, scouted ahead. She flitted from corner to corner, as fast as a hummingbird, and deadlier than a viper.

Astoreth remained hidden, while Moloch paced in front, unafraid.

Dagon's tentacles lashed at the floor, anxious for grappling, while Xolotl, god of monsters, magic and mayhem, mumbled spells of good fortune from his deformed mouth.

Xolotl was a god of the new world—a rarity.

"This palace is a maze," complained Dagon—his voice an endless abyss. "It may yet become our tomb."

The Crystal Palace was an acropolis with rooms meant to confused, beleaguer, and mystify. Pitfalls and traps became more common as we descended deeper into the earth. But with the key as our guide, we proceeded without incident.

"I will not be trapped beneath the ground," hissed Moloch, clawing anxiously at his scarred chest, the mystical hooks still embedded in his flesh. "Not again."

Astoreth studied Moloch—we all collected information. Scraps that could lead to the revelation of true names. Their origins were a mystery to each other—their names legendary, but their stories were an amalgam of truth and tale.

Only I knew their histories. When I unchained Moloch from the labyrinth beneath Minos, he was all too willing to sign my contract. Crumbs of information should be guarded—one slip, and a name might come wandering through the ether of time, and out the lips of a rival.

"Quiet," warned Xolotl—his vestments, made of cryptid skin and bone, clattered. His wispy voice was like a gentle breeze as he balanced on the tips of his twisted feet.

Nemesis had stopped at the mouth of the next chamber, and her hand rested on the hilt of her blade. She removed the Sword of Peleus from its leather scabbard, a trinket she'd admittedly collected from the dead body of the great tactician, Hannibal—opting for its precision over the power of her second blade, the Sword of Methuselah.

Though I wondered, what use had Nemesis of such toys? She was protected from head to toe in the bloodstained Armor of Achilles, the Greek hero. With her power, why surround herself with mere... *trinkets?*

Divine Devices. We all had them. We were slaves to their power. Some Fallen were nothing without them and the edge they provided. Some were more decorated than others. Even I had a few: my precious ring and the sickle I carried into battle. Nobody understood the full capability of my possessions—few knew their legendary names, and from whom I had collected them. Such was the game of power—an arms race that spanned all history.

We entered the adjoined chamber in a mass of shadow, when the Key of Capricorn pulsed. The Dragon King was near—perhaps waiting in the next room—but first, the inevitable...

Puzzles. They always hid behind puzzles.

Within the chamber blocking our path was a solid mirrored wall of crystal. At its center was a small circular hole, ten men high from the floor.

It was a test.

No mere man could scale the mirrored wall, but a Fallen could. It was insurance that no human could apprehend the key. However, reaching the hole was not the test.

It seemed rather obvious—the hole was meant for the first key—a small brass hoop and stem with two bits.

With a leap, I landed next to the keyhole and knelt beside it, perpendicular to the floor.

Could it be so easy?

The Key of Capricorn slid into the hole and twisted clockwise until it clicked—preceding a rupture that split the crystal wall directly down the middle, like a jagged crack along a clean pane of ice.

However, the crack never parted.

The key could not be turned any further, and there was no mechanism to assist the stalled split. Was it broken? Improbable—unlike humankind, when Fallen built complex machines, they lasted.

What had we missed?

"Is this another trick?" asked Astoreth, as I removed the key and dropped to the floor.

Dagon slithered closer to investigate, then attempted to wrestle the wall apart with his tentacles—he was amusingly unsuccessful. The wall was too smooth to grip and much too heavy to move.

Nox drifted forward and into a black mist, attempting to slip between the crack in the form of vapor. But she too failed—the crack was airtight.

Even Xolotl used his mastery of magic—a telekinetic spell to rip the walls apart. The incantation fell on the deaf ears, resulting in nothing— not even a tremor.

One by one they tried, either by force or alchemy, but all failed.

What was I missing?

Nemesis, quiet and astute, studied her surroundings from the dust upon the floor to the ceiling spotted with ancient spider's silk.

I was staring at my own reflection through the cracked crystal façade, attempting to decipher a hidden meaning from every jagged branch. If the centuries had not sullied my features, the cost of violence had. I hardly noticed the man looking back at me, save for the eyes.

My eyes made me an outcast from the very beginning.

There had to be another way. My journey could not end here.

One calendar year. One day to retrieve each key. There were no second chances. And while I stood there, befuddled and angry, the key continued to pulse in my palm, beckoning me onward, but the wall of reflective stone was impassable.

Then, by chance, order appeared out of chaos.

Reflected in the mirror were sharp jagged edges of the wall behind me—but when viewed from an angle, it formed meaning.

Enochian letters, the script of angels.

Each character appeared as my perspective shifted.

"How does it read?" asked Astoreth, revealing herself from behind the veil and following the progression of letters. Not many Fallen had the ability to read Enochian. When we fell, our knowledge of the next world was taken.

I read them aloud as I continued to pivot, revealing the message.

"To each at birth one is given,

More acquired but never taken,

Some are mimicked, others common,

Precious the first, lest it be forgotten,

Thou arrive, the unknown stranger,

Thou may enter, a welcomed neighbor,

Open the lock and speak thou secret key,"

The words cut deep. The riddle was simple. Passage would only be granted once the keyholder's name was spoken aloud.

We were all given a true name at our creation, and we had all since acquired new names, burying our one true weakness. I was known as Malus, a name bestowed unto myself. It was never my true name. We arrived as allied strangers, but if my true name was spoken aloud, they would know me for whom I really am—thus breaking our contract.

If the only way beyond the crystal wall was to speak my true name, I was doomed.

I looked around and studied my "allies." Trust was complicated. Of them all, I trusted Nemesis most, but could I trust her with my secret? Nox and Dagon would seize any opportunity to destroy me—the others too. I would if I were them.

Though, there were always *loopholes*.

I whispered my name and the crystal wall slowly parted at the crack. A wide grin spread across Dagon's grotesque face, but it was Nox who took the opportunity.

The former Harvester spoke my name aloud, then absorbed the light to blind me. She went straight for my heart, talons bared, when the air went icy cold, freezing the light-stealing vapor. Her muscles clenched as she lashed—when a ghastly phantom grabbed her by the wrist and held her strike. The spectral apparition rippled as it wrestled her on to one knee. In life, he was my servant—in death, he was my guardian. I had bound Richard Jansen's soul to the ring when he was only a boy.

When Nox broke free of Richard's grasp, more of the dead arrested her in place, as if casting her in stone.

I laughed.

"It would never be that easy," I said, placing my face next to hers before whispering, "Nimera."

Her true name, like all the others, was signed to my contract. Once spoken, her anger dissolved into bitter fear and cold realization. My name had not weakened me. It had not given her an advantage over my magic. It had not loosened the grip I had over her angelic spirit. My name had not unbound her from the contract.

"How can this be?" she whined. "How could you know?" I smiled at her, unwilling to answer. "Signing your contract never stipulated the knowledge of our true names." She was furious, as if I had cheated—life, however, was not based upon fairness. Life was cannibalism. Life was chaos, and I was merely playing by the rules as they were allowed. "Only your true name could open this door, and yet you retain your power. How? How!?"

"The riddle asked for a given name," I said. "That name is what I gave." The sickle in my hand buzzed as it sensed death, and I freed her head from her neck. The head had barely hit the floor before the others jumped onto the body and ate her flesh. "Give the heart to me."

Nemesis handed the bloody muscle to me, and I stomped it flat under my boot, destroying the body and spirit forever.

Moloch watched. I could taste his tension. Apprehension, confusion, yet relief that it was not *he* being devoured. Another reason not to defy me.

I was now a contract short, and the stealth of our attack was gone.

Would six of my Thirteen be enough to destroy the Dragon King?

The remaining Thirteen were guarding the girl—would a choir of angels or a legion of demons eventually come for her? Breaking their vow to let Earthly affairs play as they may? I could never be too careful.

We had little time—only four hours remained in the day, and there would be no second chances.

We faced the chamber beyond the impassable crystal wall. It was a short corridor with a pair of doors at the end, carved from solid blocks of jade in the form of dragons and other ancient beasts of the sea.

Beyond the jade doors was a vault—a throne room. Black stone crustacean statues sat in each corner of the room, and a grand jade throne carved into the likeness a winding giant wyrm extended from floor to vaulted ceiling. Its head was roughly the size of a pachyderm, and easily more than two hundred meters long as it snaked its body throughout the room. Even the dead son of Loki, Jormungandr, the world serpent, would have struggled to wrangle such a beast.

The room appeared abandoned, though the stench said otherwise.

Something stirred. Slowly. Then the throne began to unwind. The great jade dragon was not ornamental. It was alive, and uncoiling.

Nemesis twirled her blades, eager to begin.

As the wyrm unwound, it revealed a dark figure seated upon a verdant throne. Our prize, the Key of Libra, hummed in tune with my own, the Key of Capricorn—it was in this very room, and it would be protected to the death.

The crab statues came alive, snapping their claws, slowly reanimated from centuries of dormancy. They crawled off their pedestals and arranged into defensive positions. Dagon laughed, his tentacles uncurled and active. Crustaceans did not often survive encounters with cephalopods.

All at once the dark figure, the key's sentry, erupted to life. Dead skin was shed, flaking away as he moved, revealing fresh green scales and golden yellow eyes. His head was crowned with horns, and his black plated armor shuffled as he moved. In each hand was a long, jagged spear with green tassel, like that of ancient Chinese warriors.

"Ao Guang," I said, "we have come for your key."

The Dragon King growled and pointed a spear at Xolotl and Astoreth—a command. The great jade wyrm shifted, then spat green fire that enveloped them and melted the crystal floor. Moloch rolled away, while Xolotl and Astoreth took the full breath of flame.

Astoreth's skin was as hard and tempered as diamond, having no effect—Xolotl, however, was freed of his contract...

The black crustaceans lashed out, nipping at Dagon's whirling tentacles as Astoreth evened the odds—two against four.

Nemesis eyed up the mighty jade wyrm, leaving the Dragon King for me and Moloch.

The Dragon King's movements were as smooth as silk, a cobra on the edge of a venomous strike. Ao Guang lived up to expectation—as fierce as he was deadly. Without a twitch, he sprang forth and jabbed Moloch with his spear, slicing through the beast's hide and spattering his royal floor in puddles of blood. The King was surprisingly fast as they danced, circling each other at a distance.

Ao Guang may have been formidable—his protectors were magnificent. However, he had no understanding of our might. He should have had an army.

Dagon crushed one of the stone crabs with his mighty tentacles as Astoreth ripped the shell off the other and scrambled its innards. The remaining crabs backed away defensively as the gods closed in.

The Dragon King fended off a coil of phantoms I slung from afar—deflecting it into Moloch, who roared as their psychic anguish gouged his hide and tossed him beneath the wyrm. I readied my sickle and smiled as the Dragon King sauntered toward me, spinning both spears—when a ball of green fire exploded like a flash of lightning and shook the entire mountain.

Ao Guang's yellow eyes lit up in fear.

The wyrm fell dead.

Nemesis had gutted the great beast from the inside. She was by far the most powerful of us. A killing machine unlike anything that had ever Fallen before. The wyrm's head ignited as she ruptured the gland that produced the flammable secretion responsible for its green flame, resulting in a powerful blast that destroyed the head.

The second key was all but ours.

I unleashed another spool of the dead while the Dragon King was distracted. The spool swept him away and pinned him against the far wall, crushing the King beneath their icy grip. The phantoms clawed at his throat and chest as they groped for his lifeforce, flaying scale and skin.

The formless dead wished only to live again. Compel them to attack, and there was no more powerful weapon. The ring I wore was a simple conduit, but its effects were unrivaled.

"Where is it?" I asked.

The Dragon King stared at me, unflinching against the agony of the dead.

"I know your name, Ao Guang," I said, and a moment of dread flickered across his scaly face. "The Dragon King of the East. Would you like me to divulge your most prized possession? To call out your name to a room full of your enemies?"

His expression was impassable. He didn't believe me.

"Give up the The Key of Libra, or I will find a way to defile you until you beg to be sent into the Unbecoming, to march into the eternal nothing as one with the Wild Hunt."

Nemesis stood over the wyrm's carcass, watching as its blood soaked the ground with viridescence. Her curiosity was perhaps one of her most useful traits.

"Yes. Yes," I hissed with approval. The king's refusal to look upon his fallen pet said all I needed to know. "Nemesis. Rip the wyrm apart."

The goddess spared no time ripping apart the flesh with her blessed sword. Within moments she uncovered a glowing membranous sack buried in the bowels and tore the cyst apart.

Within the cyst was a handful of lost mythical treasures, including the magical staff, Ruyi Jingu Bang. There were priceless gems of unparalleled clarity, and even the legendary Book of Thoth, the Emerald Tablet, said to contain the alchemical secrets and spells of the highest form within its pages—written by Thoth and Hermes, our fallen brethren, who smuggled the information out of Empyrea before the last War of Omens.

As each treasure was tossed aside, Ao Guang fought less and less against the ghastly grip my spool had upon him. When Nemesis let out an audible sigh, his body went slack.

"The Key of Libra," said Nemesis. In the palm of her hand rested a beautifully carved piece of jade. Two wyrms attached at the tail, snaking around the bow and stem. Their heads met at the bit, and their teeth formed the key's wards. She held it for all to see.

Our eyes met. I readied a spool of phantoms—trust was a mistake, and I was ready to tear her limb from limb should she attempt to keep it, but she placed it in my hand with haste. Her honor was unflinching. I wondered how and why she ever fell. She was the perfect soldier—duty above all else.

From the moment I set my plan in motion and contracted twelve earthly horrors to assist, I knew that if they ever intelligently aligned, they would destroy me and void their contracts. However, that was the beauty of their evil. All too greedy, too self-serving and selfish to work as one.

I could sense the greed, the plotting. They all wanted me dead, but none of them knew how—at least, not without voiding my power over them—not without my name.

"Ao Guang." I wrapped my hand around his scaly throat. "Urandil, I relieve you of your duty."

Then the dead destroyed his heart.

the omega

TONY
Unknown
Then.

Do you like those "previously on" segments? The ones that recap everything you need to know? I sure do. After the day I just had, I think I need one.

Previously on Tony's Fucked Up Life...

Jacinda, the love of my life, died years ago, and I blamed myself for it. The trauma left me living a half-life, drowning under anti-depressants and going nowhere, fast.

It all started at Doctor Hammond's office. We dug a little too deep into my brain on our very first session and I went spiraling.

It was a strange day—reports of a building demolition gone wrong and lightning struck a Rodin statue downtown four times in a row. If that wasn't a bad omen, I don't know what is.

I cracked. Had a run-in with a creepy fuck named Summanus who attacked me through a mirror and chased me down a dark alley. I ran and ended up in the haunted State Penitentiary across town where I was about to be tortured by unknown creatures until a band of masked misfits busted me out, saved my life, and sacrificed themselves in the process—two of them may have even been my old pals from childhood, Chris and Thaddeus, who called themselves...*the Nightmares?*

"Be seeing you, Tony Oscuro," said a mysterious voice—a phantom passing by.

I made it home alive only to be confronted by a future version of me, my Echo, who sent the present-me on a journey to find a key—a small brass key, the key to my heart—a trinket that was given to me by my deceased mom, and later given to Jacinda as a token of my love, then buried with her after I left the loony bin.

My Echo told me I was once an angel, then burst into flames and introduced me to my brain-trust; Henry, the late 19th century psychologist—Chappy, the 19th century preacher—Doshin, the 17th century Japanese samurai—Jamaal, the pop-culture addict, and late 21st century gamer—and Montoya, the Vietnam war vet and demolitions expert. All of them other versions of my angel spirit that had been shattered and spread throughout time.

But the one thing future-me didn't do, was tell me who the fuck I really was, or what the fuck I was supposed to do.

Malus, the pale haired two-different-eyed psycho and leader of the Thirteen, a collective of thirteen Fallen angels masquerading as mythological gods, were after me—and it all seemed to connect to her... *Jacinda.* The love of my life who took her own right in front of my eyes with a gun to the head inside an old, abandoned warehouse above the Grace Falls waterfalls.

My friends died. All of them. Marshall, Brad, Anne...even Amanda, who I hadn't spoken to since High School. Malus took them all out because of me. I nearly died too—Mammon, one of the Thirteen, had me dead-to-rights—until I burst into hellfire and consumed the Fallen whole. I even took his favorite coin out of the ashes as a souvenir.

With the help of my brain-trust, I journeyed back to Grace Falls and found the key buried in the frozen dirt below Jaycie's gravestone—and then the impossible happened. Jaycie came wandering out of a funerary fog…alive.

Everything I had ever hoped and dreamed for came true—but like all dreams come true, it was just too good to be so true. Something was wrong. She kept changing—looking like someone entirely different. Her red hair, her green eyes, her freckles—all replaced by a blonde hair, blue eyed stranger.

We sought out help from an old friend, Maynard, who just so happened to be some kind of occult specialist. He took us to meet some friends of his, but we were stopped halfway there by Malus, waiting in the middle of the road. Jaycie and I got out to confront him and found ourselves surrounded. Malus pulled some mumbo jumbo and took over Jaycie's mind. The brain-trust and I decided to run, survive to fight another day. So I did—I ran and got away…barely.

I managed to kill one of them with a hellfire bullet—a gun I found in a storage lot infused with my own internal fires—the fiery passion that burned inside my gut my whole life. Bacchus, the vampire god, didn't know what hit him.

I escaped, met Maynard's friends; Father Monaco, an aging priest—and Jonah Johnson, a paranoid weirdo with a good heart. They took me to another expert—my old professor, Dr. Celestine—who just so happened to be a Fallen angel himself.

There, I learned I was a Powers—a type of specialized angel that was extremely powerful, and very few ever created. We learned that I had committed a crime, was called the infamous moniker *The Raptor*, shattered, and fell to Earth—each piece living out their lives separately, and only coming together as one when Malus hunted us down to wipe out the competition.

What was the competition you ask?

Four keys to Eden, and Jaycie.

Why? What was Jaycie? What the fuck was going on?

After a series of events which brought Jaycie and I back together briefly, we survived a gauntlet of horrors—malicious ghosts, giant wolves, Fallen, monsters, goddesses and more—within Hallows Hall, a science building at Milton State University, only to have Jaycie taken once again, and Maynard and I escaping through time.

Turns out the key from my mom was more than just a normal key. It was something else. It was a Key of Eden—the Key of Capricorn, which could do some amazing things.

So, I returned Maynard then went back in time. I watched Jaycie grow from toddler to adult and saw some really fucked up things. Her abusive mom, her struggles fitting in with peers, and an ever changing reality around her caused by the persistent and ever present Malus and his Thirteen. They were after her…but why!? Why!? Why!? Why!?

Then, she showed me why…

I witnessed a timeline where Jaycie destroyed the world. Her ex-boyfriend, Rick, was a total piece of shit who did some awful things to her. I couldn't stop it. And her rage took the whole planet. It was only then that I stepped out of the Veil—the invisible world in parallel to our own, where angels and demons watched from the sidelines—that I convinced Jaycie to start over, to do things differently.

And she did.

She reset the world. She left Rick. In the new timeline, she and I got together.

But Rick wouldn't leave her alone. He kept after her.

Then one night, that night from mine and Jaycie's shared past, when Rick attempted once more to take her, I stepped out of the Veil and put a bullet in his brain.

The thing about being a time traveler was that we're not supposed to interact with our own timeline. It causes paradoxes, and too many paradoxes could destroy the world and open a breach—a tear in the fabric of reality that could allow some awful things in.

My old buddy, Sid—a mysterious entity that was more than meets the eye—grabbed me—the real me, not the past me—and gave me a firm talking to about paradoxes and killing Rick, before I decided I was done playing around. I left at once for New Years Day, 2008, the day Jaycie took her own life. But before I could do anything, a pack of crows attacked me, and sent me to the far future.

The crows that surrounded Jaycie turned out to be her angelic guard, but instead of protecting her against Malus, they were stopping me from fixing the past. Nice priorities, fellas.

We fought in the future hellscape of Philadelphia—where I was introduced to the newest member of my brain-trust—Markus, a Roman soldier from the far past—a new voice in an already crowded head. Then out of nowhere came the Prince—the archangel Gabriel—along with the last two remaining Powers, Eris and Sagittarii—my kin?

Gabriel told me this entire mess was my fault, but he wouldn't tell me why. Then he showed me a Remnant—a timeline that never came to be—where Jaycie and Rick died in a car accident. It was a timeline where Jaycie found a way to free herself from her pain. A death without Malus there to take her. A death without me...

And here we are...

Now.

"I think you know how this will end," Gabriel said.

You have no fucking idea how monumentally livid I was. I wasn't ready for...*this*...

Gabriel—Archangel Prince—powerful enough to end Jaycie's suffering by commanding an entire Host of angels to destroy Malus and put things right, stood in front of me and all but said, "welp, shit happens." That the task was entirely up to me. To put things right was my responsibility.

Fuck. You.

Yet Gabriel *could* help. He, this super-powerful, semi-omniscient, transcendent being, *could* prevent the catastrophe that would end the whole damn world—the coming Cataclysm, as he put it—he just wasn't gonna. Like a snotty kid refusing to chuck over the fucking NES controller after two dozen failed attempts in the same fucking level of Battletoads. Would Gabriel really allow me to fail and risk all existence coming undone at the hands of a fucking lunatic?

As much as I appreciated the effort he took to fill in so many holes in my swiss-cheesy past-life memory, I wanted real help. Help that came with flaming swords and a Choir of badass Angels.

That one phrase, *"I think you know how this will end,"* was like a rib spreader cranking open. I was so vulnerable, a well-placed spitball could've brought me down.

How was I supposed to do this alone? Against stacked odds? The house was holding all the cards and the bouncers were closing in.

The Raptor against Thirteen—my Echo had said.

And then, get a load of this… I asked, "What is Jacinda? What is the Omega?"

It was a pertinent question, was it not? I had spent a lifetime searching through Jaycie's past, and although I found some real fucking terrifying supernatural forces at play, I had no context to fully comprehend what I had witnessed. Jaycie had power—through her own hands, or perhaps aided by celestial beings hidden beyond perception. She seemed powerful enough to destroy the world—tearing Rick apart atom by atom and splitting the planet in two with her rage—but how? To what extent? Why?

Then he answered me.

I didn't expect an answer. I expected wordplay. I expected a politician's pivot. I expected a smokescreen, riddles, maybe even a fucking sudoku puzzle, possibly another food metaphor about a ham sandwich. But, what he said was so extraordinary, I knew at once it must be true.

"Locked within Jacinda's soul is the Holy Dyad—the Godly powers of Creation and Destruction." He paused as if what he was about to say next was even more monumentally obscene than the previous. "Tony, Jacinda is the Omega. She is the maelstrom, the coming cataclysm. Jacinda is The One. She is…God."

"Huh… *Huh?*"

The first "huh" was strictly the shock speaking. The second "huh" was an all-encompassing plea for clarification.

"I understand how difficult that may be to grasp."

You ever hear something so monumentally fucking crazy followed by gosh-darn stupid, that you blink—then blink-blink in rapid succession? Yeah, I triple-blinked Gabriel.

"You just said my fiancée is God," I explained, while continuing to watch the aftermath of a tragedy that never was—a Remnant of time that never happened—Jaycie and Rick dead after an accident involving a truck carrying cans of chicken soup.

Gabriel's face tussled, like one might do when they're deciding to split hairs.

"Jacinda is the One," clarified Gabriel. "I called her God to provide context with which you might understand. You know the One as God, but the One is more than that title. The One has infinite meaning. Jacinda is the One, and she is so much more than what you understand that to be."

"If she had died here," I said, gesturing with a shaky hand toward the flaming car wreck housing Jaycie's lifeless body a few dozen feet away—a once-upon-a-time future's past where she bought her own ticket out—the one where Jaycie and Rick died and got to rest in peace—disaster averted with a chicken-soup analogy that blew my damn mind. "Would she have been set free?"

It was my fault, wasn't it? I mistakenly changed the favored outcome Jaycie tried so hard to achieve, believing I was doing the right thing by putting a flaming bullet through Rick's skull as he assaulted her. How messed up was the world that by sparing her that pain, I ultimately inflicted worse on her in the long run?

Gabriel, with a scalp full of perfect, *Head & Shoulders*-hair, nodded twice—his celestial armor clinking with the gesture. "The Holy Dyad would have returned home, under our protection."

Shit. Shit fucking shit fuck.

"Does she know?" I asked, my brain overloaded with questions. I felt like Johnny 5 being struck by lightning with the inevitable short circuit to follow. "Does she know what she is? Does she understand what she can do? Does she know she's been altering reality?"

Gabriel apprised me for a second, as if to gauge how close I was to a paranoid break, then decided to answer in a manner that suited the recommended amount of lunacy. "There is an aspect of Jacinda that exists within the subconscious. An aspect that is fully aware of what she is and what she is doing, but it is a survival mechanism only. You were witness to the events. She used her *gifts* to make herself forget."

"The FORGOTTEN room," I muttered, and Gabriel reacted with a furrowed brow. I suppose there are some things even Gabe couldn't possibly know. I had been a visitor inside Jaycie's mind. I saw the room and the letter she had written to herself. She locked away the sad and scary things that didn't make sense and moved on. The hauntings ended up behind that door—heck, even her sister Jane ended up there—Jaycie erased Jane from everyone's memory.

"Tony," said Gabriel, noting my obvious emotional deterioration, "may I ask you a personal question?" I shrodded—I shrugged and nodded simultaneously. "You used the power of the Key of Capricorn to view Jaycie's life from birth to death. However, I noticed you avoided many important moments in her life. Some of them sad and disappointing, but many more were happy—moments spent with you at her side. Why did you avoid those memories?"

I thought for a moment, thumbing at the pocketknife and Mammon's coin in my pocket. When I spoke the answer surprised me.

"I didn't want to cheapen the memories by seeing them that way," I explained. "I lived them, and that was enough." He was an empath, examining every expression, tone, and muscle twitch, but did Gabriel know what it was like to be human? Or was I merely an emoting ape to be studied? "Why do you ask?"

"You have such guilt," said Gabriel. "Everyone suffers, Tony. You were a powerful force of good in Jacinda's life. You brought her so much joy, yet you equip those joyful moments like sandbags, dragging you down."

"How can I take joy in the happy memories when I am responsible for *this*?" I asked, waving my arms around. We were, after all, standing in a lost reality of one of Jaycie's, *apparent*, many deaths. "Would she have had this life if not for me?"

"Which life are you referring to?" asked Gabriel. "A life in which she suffers? Or this one?"

The world around us bent and shifted, and we were crammed into a crowded room that looked as familiar to me as a random face in a crowd. It took a moment through the neon violet light and the shifting bodies to understand where I was. It was the Karaoke Lounge in Mercy Point along the river walk—and there was Jaycie. I spotted her before I spotted anyone else. Marshall and Anne were there—so were Sid and Brad. For a moment I wondered where they had gone without me, until the memory caught up; the crowd cheering a familiar tune.

"Ah shit," I groaned. "Of all the nights you could have shown me."

"Sing it, T!" shouted Jaycie, her voice like a beacon.

"She leads a lonely life," I sung—though, could anyone call that singing?

Anne was laugh-crying, and Brad was eating popcorn like this was his own personal summer blockbuster.

"I must ask," smirked Gabriel, "how did this scenario come about?"

I was embarrassed for my past self, and felt a good defense was in order.

"It was no secret I went to karaoke nights with them for beers and good times, not to perform," I explained. "Marshall—*that asshole*—he set me up."

"How so?"

"His shoelace came untied all day," I said, recalling the whole ordeal. "He tripped over them multiple times, and faceplanted leaving the apartment. He whined about how he *jammed his finger* and didn't have *the dexterity to tie a proper knot*. Then after a few beers, he lured me into a bet. It was some stupid bar trick—that he could tie a napkin into a knot by holding both ends without letting go. I never saw it coming. The whole day was just a big set-up he and Jaycie had planned to get me on stage—and they let Brad pick the song."

"Ace of Base?" he questioned. "All That She Wants."

"Fucking Ace of Base," I groaned.

I met Sid's eyes in the mirror over the bar, and he nodded toward me—the actual me, not the memory—raised his glass and took a drink. That was another mystery that needed solving—I needed to get to the mysterious bottom of all that was Sid Thistle.

In the midst of listening to my own flat voice and the crowd both cheering and laughing at my expense, I noticed something I never saw in the moment as I lived it. I heard Jaycie's laughter and could taste her tears from across the room—joyful tears. There was admiration in her eyes, and a glow that made me smile despite myself.

"You brought her joy, Tony," said Gabriel. "Your love for her was equaled only to her love for you."

I turned away from the memory and could feel the flames inside roaring like a furnace. The scar along my face—the crescent moon, symbolic of Gabriel's own angelic house—itched. How could I watch her laughing while knowing what I know? How could I watch them all after dragging them into all this? They were dead because of me. I was determined to end Jaycie's torment. Yet, how would I accomplish that? They had numbers. They had weapons. They had minions...a whole lot of creepy fucking minions.

"I am sorry," said Gabriel, noting my distress. "I did not mean to bring you pain. Do happy memories not bring joy?"

"Sometimes," I said, "the happiest memories haunt the most."

I turned back and watched—her big, infectious belly laughs were one of my favorite things. I would do anything, absolutely anything, to set her free.

"Even if it means burning the world down, my man?" asked Montoya, sensing a scorched earth policy bouncing through my head.

"Especially if it means burning the world down," said Markus, the new guy. He showed up after Zephon—one of Jaycie's angel-guard—clobbered me into the future. The brain-trust apparently felt I needed a bit more brains.

"She deserves a happy ending," I said. "Can we change it?"

"Change the current outcome?" Gabriel questioned, then answered, "You can defeat Malus and return the Holy Dyad, yes. You are capable. But can you change the past to influence a better future? No. There are dates even the most powerful must submit to—even with the Key of Capricorn allowing you to exist as a walking paradox, it is not enough. Try as you might, it would never be enough."

Those last words stung more than Gabriel could ever know.

"No," I said, attempting to clarify. "Can Jaycie, or me, use the Dyad to make it right? Can we change this reality and wipe everything away? Can we start over?"

The world around us bent and shifted, and we were no longer standing inside the Karoake Lounge, nor along the side of the road witnessing the end that should have been—the end that I fucked up.

January 1st, 2007

Grace Falls

We were back at the falls, walking atop the current as if it was frozen, while the rumbling waters rushed over the side and crashed into a pool several hundred feet below. In front of us was the Jansen Family Mill, and it was only a matter of time until that trigger's pulled. The waterwheel was frozen in place—a mixture of rust and ice—and the old wooden structure creaked under a gentle winter breeze. The sun was climbing, the clock was ticking, and I was getting sick. At any moment, a younger me would come along and step inside that warehouse, then walk the familiar path to the Devil Door—and minutes later a gunshot would reboot the nightmare all over again.

"To create a new world with the Dyad, one that would replace the unfortunate results of this world, would be a fool's errand—a fallacy," Gabriel finally explained. "Something is always missed. Something is always forgotten. Like a puzzle, the creator would attempt to rebuild the interlocking pieces from memory, but without reference. There are too many details. It cannot be done without error."

"Then let's create something else," said Markus as he straightened his blood-red tunic, like he was preparing to fight. "Create something new, for just the two of you. So what if it's not the same or if it's not perfect. Is this world perfect now?"

"I am reminded," said Henry, cleaning his spectacles, "of our departed Echo."

"You will have to make a choice," said my Echo. I could still perfectly recall the words from that fateful night a lifetime ago. *"It will be a very difficult choice. I made the wrong one—I tried to end it before I was ready—but*

you, if you make the right choice, you will only be faced with another choice, and another, until you either succeed or fail."

"There are no cheat codes in life, Tony," said Jamaal. His kind round face implored me with a sympathetic grin, as if to say *don't do anything village-idiot-stupid you'll regret.*

"All we have are the choices we make," added Chappy, the early morning sun highlighting the silver in his beard. "We must live with those consequences. They should not be undone."

"Things happen for a reason," added Doshin, who stood by the falls' edge.

"Do tell," challenged Markus, glaring at him. "What reason is that exactly?" But nobody answered.

I felt a pressure building between my temples. My heart began to race. I was on the verge of a panic attack. The love of my life was about to kill herself at any moment, and I was capable of stopping it—if Gabriel and his funky bunch would let me.

The white noise of the falls let my mind wander in a thousand directions, exploring the mess that was my life. The water licked my boots as it passed, and instead of pondering how the hell we were walking on rushing water, my awe was curbed by one thought—one question that was beginning to burn a hole in my gut.

"But *how* is Jaycie, God? She can alter reality, rewind time, and destroy the world, because she has these powers inside her? How did they get there?" My question had no sooner left my lips when I received the quickest glance of frustration. I could sense Gabriel's anguish, and one very specific conclusion pelted me like a palm-licked slap of sobering reality. "It was me."

Oh, fuck me! I really was the cause of all her pain.

I felt sick. I felt murderous. I wanted to burn everything. I was so fucking monumentally naïve. How did I not figure it out sooner?

"What did I do? What was my crime?"

"I'm sorry, I cannot say," he replied.

"Why won't you help me?" I choked.

"We cannot," he said. "Free will. The Judean Accords. We can only intervene when the Fates allow it."

"The Fates?" I scoffed.

"The entire world must have perfect synchronicity between all things. From the atom to the cosmos, everything was created with equilibrium. When the world was created out of chaos, there was only one law—balance. And that balance was upheld by the Cosmic Scales. Like a mathematical equation, the Scales are the governance of constants, holding this world together by its four fundamental forces —nuclear, electromagnetic, gravitational, and alchemical. But it does not stop there. The Cosmic Scales balance all—and that includes good and evil forces, like the polarity of a magnet. The Scales are attended by the Fates—Clotho, Lachesis, and Atropis—these three waterfalls bear their names," he said, gesturing to the Grace Falls waterfalls. "The Fates are proprietors of the Loom of Destiny, upon which we all receive a single Thread of Fate. That thread holds our past, present, and future."

"You're saying there's a higher power than God?"

"The One?" he asked, correcting the human name we had given him…it…*her?* "Yes. The Cosmic Scales and the Fates exist to maintain harmony. Everything in this world, from the atom to magnetism—the very structure it is built upon—must be in perfect balance."

"Balance?" I growled. "How is torturing an innocent girl to the point of taking her own life, considered fucking balance? What about that is balanced? It's just me versus all of them! How is that fucking balanced?"

I could hear someone sloshing their way through the snow toward the mill. At any moment that gunshot would go off, ending my world all over again.

"The One did not create the Cosmic Scales—there are rules even by which The One must abide." We began to walk upstream, slowly approaching the mill, as if he wanted me to have a front row seat to the worst moment of my life. "The Fates employ the Furies—positive and negative charged beings that perform sacred duties to uphold balance."

"What happens when the Scales are imbalanced?"

"The Furies are given orders. A polarity shift to rebalance is acted upon."

"What you're saying is," I grumbled, after giving it a quick thought, "when one side becomes too powerful, the Furies help the losing side win a few rounds to put things back in balance?"

"More or less," he shrugged. "Yes."

"Who are these Furies?"

He smiled at me.

"Jaycie?" I asked.

"No," he said shaking his head. "Remember, she is The One."

I thought for a moment. The answer was right there. He should have been my first guess. "Sid," I chuckled. My old friend had big secrets.

"Sid Thistle died in 1986 at the bottom of this waterfall."

"What?"

"He sacrificed himself to save his friends against a great evil. In doing so, he was rewarded with immortality—so long as he performed his duties without compromise to the Fates."

There were a few moments of silence—only the sound of the creaking waterwheel and the hum of the falls—filling the air like television static.

"Okay," I said. "Sid is one of these Furies. Why was he here?"

"To watch over Jacinda, of course."

"Right, but how does that connect to everything else?"

"Balance, Tony. Do you know why Malus succeeded in taking Jacinda on this day?" I wanted to say Malus only succeeded because *he* wouldn't let me intervene, but instead I shook my head. "Malus could not touch Jacinda until she was thirteen years old—when her mind and body had matured enough to extract the powers of Creation and Destruction—when they could be manifested with more than just compulsion. Ever since she was born, there were eyes upon her. Good and Evil eyes, but we could not directly intervene."

"The Judean Accords," I said aloud, remembering my conversation with Father Monaco, a long, long time ago. I had watched her entire life between then and now.

"You remember it?" he asked, sounding relieved.

Was I there?

"No," I replied, "something I learned along the way."

"Free will, Tony. It is at the core of everything that was ever created within this Realm." Gabriel paused for a moment, and I continued to follow him as we paced atop the water, meandering toward the water-wheel. "Angels were created with celestial energy. That energy was channeled into whatever the One saw fit. We were each unique. Some of us with extreme power to fight, to guide, to obey, to destroy, or perform miracles, while others were more limited, specialized, like the messenger and harvester. It was our names, given to us by our Creator to guard, that became our weakness. The unknown is a powerful form of fear—and fear itself is a powerful magic.

"To know one's name is to have dominion over them, taking away the unknown that diminishes our various talents and abilities. Our names were wiped from the minds of Demons when they were cast out of Empyrea, our home. Within the Pit they were reforged and given new names by their corrupted masters. The Fallen received the same treatment—as they passed from Empyrea into this world, their wings were clipped and halos broken—like a key, disallowing them access through the gates between our realms. Only the original nine archangels are immune—our names known by all; the four of us who remained in Paradise, the three who fled, and the two who fell to Earth. Thus, balance was created."

"If names are so important, why introduce the angel-squad back there?" I asked, referring to Zephon and his band of merry jerks.

"Your halo is gone. Your wings are clipped. You are stranded and retain no memories of your true self," said Gabriel. "You bear us no threat."

"Then why not tell me my own name?" I asked—the frustration leeching from my voice.

"You committed a crime," he explained. "Like all *cruciati*, those tortured Fallen who sought redemption, dominion over yourself may only be found through penance. When *something* is created, it is given a name—like a rock or a tree. When *someone* is created, it is given a name, free will, and has dominion over oneself—a true name is the founding principle for Alchemy. It is the basis for the magic of names."

"Dominion over myself?" I growled. "You mean, I'll only learn my true name when I've adequately paid for my wrongdoing—but that I won't become self-aware until I learn my true name?" He nodded. "Fuck me, I'm stuck!"

"If your predicament was easily undone, many would have succeeded."

"How many like me—how many *cruciati*, have ever redeemed themselves?" I asked.

"None," admitted Gabriel.

Who needs enemies…am-I-right? Every which way appeared another obstacle, another roadblock.

"Free will, Tony," he continued. "When you shot and killed Rick Jansen, an ability afforded only by the Key of Capricorn, that was in your possession, making you a living paradox, it toppled the natural order the Cosmic Scales were created to prevent. You provided the Negative Furies a pass. They used that pass today, providing the perfect conditions for Malus's success. When it was all said and done, he whispered into Jacinda's ear. He promised that if she ended her life, she would be free, and you would be safe." He held up a finger, grabbing my attention. "Listen. You can hear him."

The forest was still, and the falls filled that stillness like a steady hum. I couldn't hear it at first, but then I caught a word—it was indecipherable, but it was there. Whispering, like a secret radio broadcast.

"She was tricked into killing herself?" I asked.

Gabriel nodded. "At that time, she was out of our hands. Out of our protection. Free will. Malus snatched her departed soul with his ring—and the Holy Dyad along with it. With his powerful magic over the dead, he forced her soul back into her own broken body and began repairing her flesh while mesmerizing her mind. However, there is only one way he can retrieve the Holy Dyad from her soul, as it is bound to the very fabric of her being—she must love him—heart, mind, body, and soul—and celebrate that love sacramentally within Eden."

"That's impossible," I scoffed, "she could never—"

"—Magic, Tony," he interrupted, "can do amazing things to the chemicals in one's brain." The look on his face was a warning. "Do not underestimate the scientific reality of what love truly is. Love is chemistry, and that can be manipulated."

I recalled the cold stare—Jaycie, the gun, and her empty eyes when she looked at me. In all my life, after all I've seen and experienced, her unloving glare was the most horrific thing I had ever witnessed. It haunted my dreams behind the Devil Door ever since.

"How...?" I croaked. Tears ran free. I had no more shame to hide them.

Gabriel waited for me to finish my question. When I didn't, he looked perplexed. "How?" he questioned back. "What are you asking?"

I looked at him, and everything seemed so quiet—so still. A tiny, quiet moment before the bang. "How," I repeated, "after all I've been through, do you expect me to stand here and do nothing?"

A streak of fear glanced across his face a split second before I took off running, like stealing second base—one moment I was stationary, and the next I was going full speed. I was desperate and tapping into a source of power I had only begun to understand. Within a blink, I had traveled from the rusty water wheel up the side of the warehouse, and slipped through the pane-less window on the second-floor landing—

—and was immediately greeted by Sagitarii—the red-armored angel —a Powers, like me.

"I cannot let you pass," he said. His voice was as cold as Iceland—or was it Greenland?

"Greenland," said Jamaal. "And this is a dumbass idea, dumbass."

Brad used to sing, "It's beginning to look a lot like fuck this," when he saw no other way around a confrontation, a video game, or even homework—the little guy knew when to stop giving two fucks.

It was time to promote my inner-B-Rad.

I said, "Two words. One finger," then popped Sagittarii the bird—he was unaware of its meaning—but, when I hit him with a left-handed jab to the nose that put him off balance, he got the point.

Leaping from the mezzanine to the warehouse floor, I dashed to the far end—

—and took a fist to the chin.

Eris hit me so hard, I caught a glimpse of my heels before I landed.

"You're predictable," she said as she brushed the black hair from her bright blue eyes.

"So I've been told," I groaned, recalling the confrontation with Sid, the night I killed Rick Jansen—

"You're a predictable creature, in every form," he had said.

From the floor, I swept her legs out from beneath her, and spun directly into the fist of Gabriel—

—my vision dimmed.

Though the distance traveled was more than two hundred feet, the time from impact to collision was instantaneous—all the way into the furthest corner of the warehouse—away from Jaycie.

The crash made no sound. Even as I tore myself free from the pile of rubble I had created on impact, everything was muffled—they had stolen the sound from the freakin' air to preserve *the moment.*

Why? Why was the integrity of this *moment* something that must be kept perfect? Why did terrible things need to happen? Why did this terrible thing have to play out according to some loony *space scale?*

When the rage took over, I felt nothing. No pain. No broken bones or torn muscles. They stitched themselves together as I rumbled forward. This wasn't a battle with flaming swords—this was a fist fight, a street brawl—a family squabble, and I was the black sheep.

Sagitarii blind-sided me with a left, and I countered by driving him into an old, rusty mill saw. Gabriel ripped me away, then discarded me with a flick toward Eris. She clotheslined me directly out of the air, like she was the Undertaker plucking a pint-sized jobber. My head slammed into the pavement, but I bounced back onto my feet a moment later.

Pain was an itch I had no time to scratch.

I was inexhaustible, a raging, berserker hellbent on stopping the event that ruined my life—and if these strangers, my *family,* wanted to stop me, then I would just go through them.

"Stop," pled Chappy. "Please, Tony. We need their help!" But he was just a small voice at the back of my head.

"You cannot fix the past," said Henry, equally distant. "What if it creates an even more horrific future?"

I wasn't going to stop. I wasn't going to listen.

From one wall to the next, I leapt, putting distance between us—but as I landed, they were right behind me, keeping pace. Gabriel cracked me across the jaw with a left at the exact moment Sagitarii crushed me with a right.

I nearly blacked out, but the rage wasn't letting go.

I had moments, maybe less, to stop this once and for all, and desperate men do desperate things.

Desperation changes people. Desperation makes us do things against our nature. Like running from the cops when Mr. O'Neill attempted to have me arrested when I was looking for Jaycie—

—or Roman...

When I connected my next swing—it was fueled with the desperate need to remove obstacles. I hit Sagitarii so hard, he tumbled away from me like he was blown back by the wind. Perhaps it was a trick of the eye, but his trajectory appeared to adjust as he collided with Gabriel and landed in a heap—far enough away to make a run for it. I leapt up the stairs and sprinted down the neverending hallway toward the Devil Door when Eris appeared, blocking my path.

"If you do this," she said, unafraid of me and my bloody knuckles, "you can never come home."

"She is my home," I said, and Eris's impassive, unemotional stare shattered. She looked defeated, and I thought she might even let me go...

As I slipped past her, she immediately repositioned herself to block my path and placed a warning hand into my chest. When she began to push, I slid backward, as if the old, creaky wooden floor was made of ice.

"Let me stop it," I pled, unable to gain traction—unable to prevent her from pushing me further away from Jaycie. They wanted me to let go, but why couldn't they? Why couldn't they just let me go?

"I cannot let you pass," she responded—her blue eyes were pools of tears. "You may not remember us, but we remember you. It is no surprise to me that you are here, fighting for a love you cherish, but this is not the way."

Her words felt distant, like she was speaking to me from behind a concrete wall.

"This is your chance," said Markus. "It's now or never."

"My man," begged Montoya, "is this what you want? Sure, save the girl, but at what cost?" He was almost translucent—the figments in my head were fading.

"Can you not see yourself?" cried Eris with a violent shove, "The darkness is growing. If you do not course correct, you will lose everything, including hope." There was a gloom inside me, and it was getting bigger, gobbling up the flames with something...*else*. An urgency mixed with raging desperation clouded my judgment—but I didn't care. I didn't want to care about anything—other than Jaycie.

"My everything is in that room with a gun to her head."

"I'm sorry," said Eris. "You have endured so much."

But I didn't want to hear it. I couldn't stand to hear it. Not from her. Not from them. Not from anyone. Nobody understood! Nobody could possibly know!

"JUST LET ME GO!" I screamed. "LET ME GO! FUCKING JUST LET ME GO!" The world darkened, and even though the floor was like ice, Eris was unable to move me another inch despite her effort.

When she withdrew her hand from my chest, I threw the first punch.

Eris threw the next dozen.

It was as succinct a beating as I had ever taken since Rick Jansen jumped me from behind that fateful day. She bashed my head into both walls, slammed my guts into her knee—she even hit me with an uppercut that put me to the floor. When I was down, she stood over me and said, "This was the first time I have ever beaten you."

A gunshot went off.

And Eris held me as I cried my very soul out all over again.

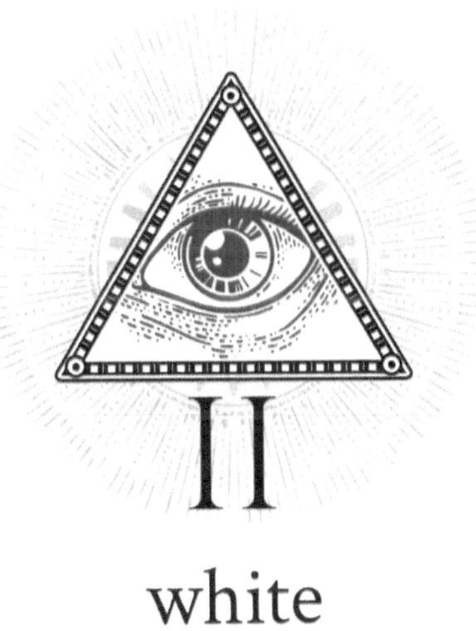

II

white

A VOICE
Long Ago...
Then.

At the beginning, there was nothing. Then, from nothing came a brilliant white light. Where there was once nothing, suddenly there was something—and the light spread far and wide. Yet, try as it might, the light could not conquer all, for whichever way it spread, shadow was close behind, gobbling up its brilliance. Where there was light, there would be darkness. Two equals forever entangled, battling for survival. Nevertheless, for light to exist, there must be darkness, and for darkness, there must be light.

To move toward the light was to shine.

To step away was to be swallowed by the dark.

All that is, all there was, and all there ever will be, is light and dark.

Darkness begins when the light has passed. This tale, Tony, was no different.

. . .

"Slow down!"

"Tomorrow is not a promise," Lilandra said.

What must it be like to be young and ignorant? Mortals spend their youth racing toward death, and their maturity seeking to stop the momentum.

The summer sun had disappeared, but the heat remained, and the darkening clouds whispered of storms along the warm breeze. The forest chirped while the danger lurked, and the children—not too young, but neither wise—did not acknowledge the impending threat looming on the horizon.

"Where are we going?" His voice still sounded much too young when he was anxious.

"Where do you think we're going?" she questioned—his courage was often subjected to her ridicule. Adventure never waited for Lilandra. No one could stop her when the allure of exploration came calling. She would defy the gods if it pleased her.

The personification of a storm—she was energy, wind, thunder, and as beautiful as she was spirited. She yearned for more—more than what her world could provide.

And the poor boy? He was only chasing…

When Lilly jumped upon an uprooted tree, he wavered. Following her across the creek's rushing water—violently crashing over rocks at twice its normal depth—was the kind of danger Lilly craved. The boy, however, had good sense. Crossing the surging creek, after two full days of summer storms, was the most nonsensical, perilous thing they had attempted all season.

In the spring, they had narrowly escaped a skunk by leaping into the river. Lilly squealed the whole way down, shouting, "now this is a real adventure!" until they plunged into the frigid waters.

But it wasn't just the surging creek that prevented her companion from crossing along the rotted trunk of a fallen tree. The boy should have demanded they go home—perhaps feigned a mysterious illness, or purposely flung himself into the raging waters—would that have changed their destiny? How was he to know this was the day that would change everything?

And yet, he felt it. A pang of dread that clung to the bottom of his gullet.

The signs were all there! The darkening skies. The rushing waters. And on the far side of the creek was the *Dark Wood*. There were vague warnings to stay away from that portion of the forest. It was a twisted tract of woodlands that stretched east through the valley—and that beyond its threshold lurked many odd things. Things wicked, things old, things that devoured children—or so they were told.

Lilandra claimed the village elders liked to scare children, to make them do as they were told, but he knew better. He could feel it in his chest. Nothing good laid beyond those trees, where the light of day was smothered by the thick brush.

It was one thing to explore the farthest corners of the Sacred Forest —a place where hunting was forbidden out of reverence to their god. But following Lilly into the Dark Wood was to trifle with dark spirits. Most days they explored the forest and hid within their secret place while scavenging for wild berries. They never dared to explore this deep, and never on *that* side of the creek.

"Are you scared?" she teased as she grabbed fistfuls of her dress, threatening to run and leave him behind. Her eyes, big and blue as they were, questioned their companionship. It was those eyes that implored the foolish tendencies he strived so hard to understand. Why did he weaken when she implored him so? What power had she over him?

Of all the boys in the village, she chose this wretch—dirty, malnourished, and dressed in rags. They had been friends since they were old enough to walk, and inseparable since they were smart enough to sneak away from the village to explore the fields and the forest. She was the daughter of their chieftain, and he was the son of an outsider. It was an unlikely friendship in feudal times, a friendship that was often questioned by those bold enough to speak their minds within the village council.

If it was their decision, he would have been cast out, *or killed*—all because he was *different*. All because he was allegedly marked by *us*, though, that accusation was untrue. *We* had nothing to do with *him*.

The lone survivor of a ruthless raid, his pregnant mother was taken by the men who pillaged and slaughtered her people and given refuge out of pity. Some would say the boy's deformity only broadened his status as an outlander. If it were not for the mercy of Kasimir, their chieftain, he would have perished before he was born.

His adopted people were not peaceful, but they were not bloodthirsty destroyers either. They fought for land. They fought when threatened. They fought when they feared. There were times when the boy pondered which of those three sins his kin were guilty of—the sins that brought them their doom when Kasimir and his men raided and destroyed them.

Since the beginning, sin has always been subjective. One man's sin is another man's opportunity. What sin was punishable by death? What sin inspired men with the righteous action to judge and kill so blatantly?

The answer is obvious.

As it has always been, men plunder so that others do not plunder them first—kill or be killed. Fear is the ultimate sin.

But I digress…

Lilly's village sat upon a lakeshore with huts made of rock and thatch. There was a great fire pit at the center, a pen for hunting mutts and a nearby field, farmed with crops that grew in the rocky soil. The Sacred Forest bordered the village on the east and wide rolling hills spread outward to the mountains in the north. The village was dusty in the hot season and muddy in the cold season, till the ground froze and great snows blanketed the land, drifting into great banks, taller than a man. From afar, one might have called them barbarians or heathens, and they revered only one god: Belobog, the White.

When the droughts came and the lake shriveled, they prayed to Belobog and offered him their undying devotion, until he blessed them with a soaking rain that replenished their crops and refilled the lake. When the great winters did not end and their food dwindled, they offered their eternal servitude to Belobog for a quick and merciful thaw. The White God was their savior, their refuge, and he protected them from their enemies—the raiders from the west, who ate the flesh of their adversaries—and the travelers to the north searching for… *opportunity.*

This, however comforting, was untrue. Belobog did no such thing.

However, Belobog did protect them from those that lurked within the forest at night, dancing in the shadows beyond the light of the village fire.

"I am not scared!" the boy shouted while Lilly threatened to run away. What was more frightening, dear boy? The Dark Wood? Or her vanishing attention?

"If you are not scared," argued Lilly, "then why are you still standing there?" She had traversed her way across the tree like a sprite fae across the wind.

"But we are not allowed," he said.

Rules were for the meek, and there were few meeker than he as a child.

"Who's to stop us?" she reasoned as she brushed her blonde hair from her face. "Tomorrow is not a promise."

You know that saying, Tony. You know it well.

It was something *she* said often—Lilandra spoke those words each and every time she wished to spur the boy forward, when his feet remained anchored. Prompting him for courage—and to play his part, the fortunate sidekick to her every adventure.

As if the weather was conspiring against him, a furious wind unsettled his footing the moment he stepped upon the tree. The rushing waters below appeared to rise, as if it wanted to consume him in its rage —like the forest was begging for a taste.

His second step was an uneasy one, but Lilly's reassuring smile put effort into his limbs.

"I knew you could do it," she praised him as he placed one foot in front of the other and began to slide across.

With her encouragement, he could ignore the winds and the rushing waters as he crept forward inch by inch. The boy may have even succeeded if not for a crow on a nearby limb, cawing its arrival. His balance fled as quick as his nerve. From his knees, he clung to the wet trunk, with nails dug into the soft bark while fear paralyzed him from the neck down.

Fear was an interesting emotion. Most of it was programmed

throughout childhood—a hardwired emotion that one may overcome, but never immune to its effects. If fear was inevitably tied to death, why do immortals suffer from it like humans? We all harbor fear. Some of us can ignore it better than others.

Fear, Tony. Fear will always be the enemy of the mind. Fear is what prevents a man from unleashing his truest self. All men desire power, and fear is what keeps them from obtaining it.

Fear is the greatest of all deterrents.

The boy was petrified. He was lost, his courage swept away by the rushing avalanche of fear that invaded his mind. The boy was an outlander, a wretched nobody. He was filth. He should have let go right there and let the waters cleanse him from the Earth—when the warmth of Lilly's touch brought him back to the present. She had scaled her way back across the tree and knelt beside him.

"You're alright," she whispered. When she took his hand, the danger melted away. "Come on, adventure awaits."

They crossed the creek hand in hand, but the dread, the uneasiness that plagued his stomach, never unclenched. They were mere steps away from the Dark Wood with the witchy trees and the thorny limbs, all scratching for a taste of flesh. But he was with her—he was right where he wanted to be.

The skies began to cry, and they sought refuge from the rain in a rocky crag upon a hillside, high above the creek. A lazy roll of thunder brewed over the mountains, as they studied the valley from their perch —a valley they had known their entire lives. Nobody went beyond the valley over mountains—nobody would dare. Some believed the other side of the mountain was the end of the world. Others believed it sacrilege—Belobog had created the valley as a gift for their tribe, and to forsake it was to forsake Belobog's grace.

"Are you hungry?" asked Lilly.

His expression made her giggle as she removed dried strips of meat from a pocket. After a single bite, she gave him the remainder of her food. It had been almost two days since he had last eaten anything more than scraps, or a stolen apple. Without Lilly to sneak him food from time to time, he may have starved.

"Thank you," he said, gnawing on the chewy strips. "Once Falibor teaches me to hunt, I will catch my own food." Then he stood and shouted into the valley below. "I will be the greatest hunter in all the village!"

Lilly laughed. She always laughed hardest with him.

"What makes you think *you* will be the best hunter?" she asked. "Silence is a hunter's best virtue. You struggle to sleep in silence. When hunting forest creatures, one must be as silent as stone if one is to sneak up on them."

She was behind him before he knew it, and her closeness sent him off balance. He nearly fell from their perch before Lilly pulled him back from the edge. They tumbled backward into a heap, each gasping for air.

"Grace," said Lilly, shaking her head—her pale tresses dangled above him.

"What about grace?" he asked.

"You have none! How could you possibly expect to be a good hunter if you frighten so easily?" She laughed. "Perhaps you can be useful elsewhere, besides scaring all the food away."

"You jest, but wait and see," he said. "I will prove you wrong."

Lilly was staring into his eyes. The closeness made him uncomfortable, especially with Lilly. He felt compelled to pull away.

"Why do you do that?" she asked.

"Do what?" he questioned. He angled half his face away from her. It was habit.

"Why do you hide your eyes? Your hair covers half your face."

He was born defective, and he was reminded of it daily. His left eye was as pale as the moon on a cloudless night, and his right as dark and brown as the mud after a winter's thaw. Many believed he was cursed. Eyes like his were dangerous—the sign of darkness. If eyes were portals of the soul, then he was a dichotomy—the light and the dark. Opposing forces inhabiting a single body.

"I do not like my eyes," he said, then looked away. His dark hair shaded the pale orb that made him a monster.

"Do not hide them from me," she scolded and stepped before him.

"There is nothing wrong with you."

She was upset. When Lilly was filled with fire, there were few things that would stop her from professing her thoughts.

"I am sorry," he said.

"Do not be sorry," she growled. "You have done nothing wrong. If we judge all others by their appearance, then half the village should be put to death." She was attempting to be funny, but there was pain within him that even Lilly could not ease.

There was a long silence between them as the winds picked up once again. "Do not hide your eyes from me again. There is beauty in all things."

"Even me?"

"Yes, especially you."

"Am I as beautiful as a flower?" He beamed.

She smiled and laughed for a moment, and clarity settled over her gaze. "The most beautiful thing about you is your unbreakable spirit. I do not know what I would do without you."

Her words tugged at an invisible thread attached to his chest. Without the words to properly articulate it, or the emotional understanding to process what it meant, he turned away, letting it pass.

"I can see the village from here," he finally said.

"Where?" she asked, and he pointed due west. "It looks so small."

"Compared to everything else, our village is small," he said, noting the great mountains looming in the distance.

"Do you ever wonder what exists beyond the valley?" she asked. "Over the mountains? Into the unknown?"

"Sometimes."

"I think about it all the time. One day I want to see it," she said, and the boy thought about the great unknown, and what existed on the other side of those mountains. "Would you go with me?"

There was nothing he wanted more.

Youth promises the world, then steals it away the very moment one needs those comforting promises the most.

The boy was only five when his mother died. He knew very little of life, let alone the one he wanted to live. He knew not of comfort, or pleasure. Everything he knew was harsh, rough, and hard. His own bed was crafted of straw and tucked into a cold drafty corner of a hut along with the livestock.

Imagining a life adventuring with Lilly was a fantasy, but sometimes those fantastic dreams felt like they were close enough to touch.

Youth promises. The world steals.

He wanted to say yes. Yes, he would adventure with her over the mountains. There was no other possible answer, and yet the words were tied to his tongue—as if he already knew his destiny.

Before he could answer Lilandra, before his heart could expel a muddled answer with inarticulate speech, a great roar of thunder shook the ground.

Then came the deluge.

A soaking rain fell in waves. The brewing storm on the horizon had finally unfurled its fury. They ran for cover away from their craggy perch on the hillside as the winds swept dust and leaves up into a blinding cyclone of debris. The creek flooded, their passage home across the tree was swept downstream. The rain hastened to hail and pelted them as they fled, and with no path home, they were forced to take cover within the confines of danger—into the Dark Wood.

The Dark Wood was not a place for humans, let alone a place for children. It was a habitat built for the wicked. The ground was sharp with jagged rocks and gnarled roots that twisted ankles. The briar was thick and sharp, and the branches grew low and layered. Everything that existed in its boundary lived only to terrorize that which found itself ensnared within.

Before long they were lost.

Trees uprooted in the twisting winds. Lightning thrashed like the gods themselves were angry at the trespassing children—they had entered an unholy place and were being punished. Had the wrath of Belobog's own edict come to punish them for trespassing? Had his goodness soured over their misdeeds?

When the flooding creek rushed over its banks and into the forest, they hurried for higher ground. Hand in hand, they climbed over rocky embankments, dragging themselves upward by root, by rock, and by limb.

And it was then, when the ferocity of the storm peaked, a gust of wind blew so terribly, an ancient tree was ripped from the rocky soil and tossed into the ground before them, blocking their path to safety.

The boy could sense Lilly's fear. For the first time in all their adventures, she was afraid. Her hand trembled in his, and for that one moment the boy thought this was the end.

What were they to do? The heavens had opened, and all its wickedness had been unleashed upon them. Branches were torn asunder. The very fabric of the forest appeared to be coming undone. But it was then, by luck, by chance, by fate—the boy spotted salvation.

"This way!" he shouted above the whistling wind.

A small alcove had opened where the roots had peeled away from the earth beneath the fallen tree. It was a craggy nook with a low canopy, dangling roots, and just enough space for two scared, wet children. Lilly climbed over the broken earth and pulled him into the dark hole as the storm raged.

The warmth of mid-summer turned, and an icy chill seeped into the forest. Their nervous heaves exhaled into clouds of vapor as they huddled close for warmth. In all their childhood, they had never been more afraid.

"An adventure without danger is not an adventure at all." Lilly's eyes blazed in the darkness. "Tomorrow is not a promise."

Affection can be many things.

It can be pure.

It can be rotten, selfish, lustful, and needy.

It can be honest, hopeful, and vulnerable.

Innocent affection, though, may be the most true—its purity sings from the soul.

It was obvious to anyone watching him, that the boy's friendship with Lilandra was becoming something more. His dearest friend—his only friend—meant more to him than he could profess. It was an undefinable yearning he did not understand. He wanted to be near her. He wanted to make her smile and laugh with all his being. He wanted to appease her, no matter the danger—and to protect her despite his inability to do so. But it was only then, within that cramped chamber of dirt and mud, that he finally accepted the change.

There was no creature fairer than she in all the world within the boy's mind. He was aware of her in a way he had never noticed anyone or anything, ever.

Lilly spoke, but he could not hear her over the drumming in his chest and the swirling winds beyond the mouth of the cave. The gods were releasing their misery upon the world, and he could not have been more content than to witness it with her.

Instinct took over. A gentle touch. Her confused response. The growing closeness. Then every horrible, rotten moment of his life felt like it had never existed.

He *kissed* her.

The boy had never witnessed a kiss before. Public affection was forbidden between man and wife. Where could he have learned such an act?

The mind is a wonderful thing—instinct guiding the body through complicated emotional and chemical reactions, was a wonder to behold. Was a kiss coded into human genetics? Was there some deep wrinkle upon their brain that gave action to instinct, even with something so uniquely human, like a kiss? And what other secrets were written there with it, locked within the soft gray matter encased in bone?

Oh, I could tell you stories, *friend.*

Some other time, perhaps…

The storm settled at the conclusion of their kiss, unwinding its furor. Everything slowed. Everything went quiet except the thumping of his own heart, the blood pounding within his own ears, which made him question if he actually heard…*it*…

Dark and guttural, like the rising bass of an instrument, from deep within the hole behind them came the sound of…*laughter?* The boy's stomach soured. He felt wrong. Had they wandered into the dwelling of something awful?

"What is that?" he asked. The laugh ceased, but the earth trembled.

Something was moving.

"Why did you do that?" she questioned.

"Do what?" he asked, while searching for the source of the sound. It appeared to be coming from a small opening into the alcove behind them, where the ground crumbled away, revealing a dark secret.

She did not look angry, nor disgusted, but shocked. It was like an answer to a mysterious question had struck her when she was least expecting it. A question, and she had always known the answer.

"I'm sorry," he stammered, "I should not have." Every part of him was attempting to reclaim his actions, and he couldn't understand why. Had he done something terrible?

"No," she comforted. "...not wrong."

The thrumming noise started again, louder now. Closer.

"What is that sound?" he repeated...

...but it was already too late.

There was a blast of dust and debris, and the world turned upside down.

Is it not funny how innocence calls upon evil? Not necessarily funny ha-ha, but ironically amusing? How thin a line separates them, and how desirous evil is of innocence. Like moths to an open flame, evil lusts for innocence. Perhaps to medicate the unrest within, like a salve? To replace that which was lost?

Or maybe the innocent are more fun to torment?

The boy awoke to the gentle sound of falling rain, while soaking in a puddle of mud. He had been expelled from the cave by force. A force strong enough to toss him up and over fallen branches, and down the hill.

What could have tossed him so?

Bears had been spotted in the forest. One of them had mauled a village hunter—the man's limbs were torn right off.

Could a bear have done this?

"Lilly?" he shouted.

He spotted the collapsed alcove, and a dusty haze surrounded it. Dirt and debris from their hiding place had scattered across the forest floor, and leaves were still fluttering from the sky. Amongst them were slim tendrils of dust trailing the debris. The tendrils floated on the stormy breeze like two moths entangled in dance, then receded into the alcove as if inhaled back into the hole from which it spewed.

For a moment the boy questioned what he had witnessed, but a hacking cough reclaimed his attention.

"Lilly?" he shouted. "Lilly? Where are you?"

When he found her, she was face down in the mud. In a panic, he rolled her away from the mud, and she spat mouthfuls of earth before heaving onto the ground. Her eyes were glassy and distant, like she had swallowed all manner of dust in the eruption.

"What happened? Are you hurt?"

"I don't know," she croaked after sipping water from a puddle.

"Was it a bear?" he asked.

She shook her head. "I don't think so."

It was a mystery. There was no bear. Whatever had tossed them had disappeared. Some awful things were best not examined too closely.

"Let's go home," said Lilly as she stood and wiped the mud from her dress.

He reached out to her, meaning to help her up. "Are you able?"

"I'll be fine" She swatted away his hand, and her grin returned.

Lilly never showed vulnerability. She hid her weaknesses and buried her discomfort behind a smile, which made the boy that much more suspicious. Hidden within her smile was a distance in her eyes. It was like he was looking at a stranger.

"I am sorry for what I did," he said, repeating the apology as if that might have been the distance between them.

"What did you do?" she asked, as if it never happened. "Race you to the bottom of the hill?"

The boy was confused, too young and too naive, but he should have known better. He should have understood. Something nefarious had occurred in the Dark Wood that day. Something found them and took advantage of their innocence.

As Lilly took off running toward the village, she stopped several paces away. She looked back at him and asked, "Are you coming?"

Then off she went.

And the boy chased after her.

Tell us, Tony, are you and the boy not the same? Are you the man you thought you'd be? Are you as righteous and good as you would like to believe? Or are you a flawed human masquerading as an angel?

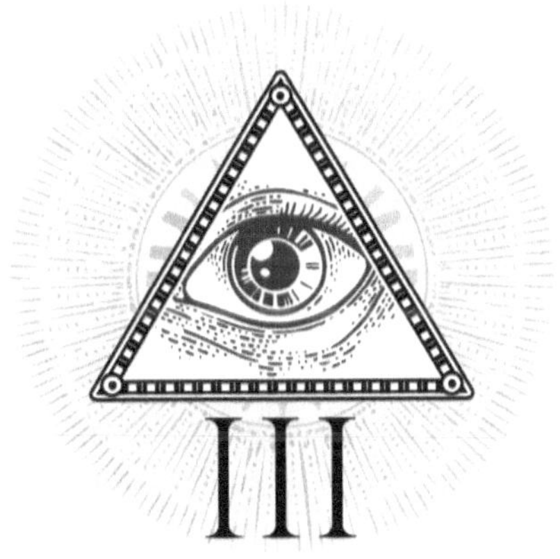

III

follow the beat

JACINDA
Somewhere...
Now.

Am I alive? Am I still me?

A drip.

One drop, then another.

Then three, followed by four and so on—like a metronome.

"Jacinda, darlin', follow the beat."

The tiny machine tick-tocking away on the nightstand while Grammy readied her fingers for plucking strings. The late afternoon sun gave Grammy's white hair a blooming halo while I sat with my legs crisscrossed beneath me on the shaggy brown rug of my bedroom floor.

Grammy was a saint.

Saturday afternoons had magic in them—still do, as if Grammy might come gently knocking on my bedroom door, shiny guitar in hand and carrying a bag full of gummy bears.

She used to say, "Jacinda, darling, you're going to be a star," while sitting on the edge of my bed with the guitar resting in her lap—a sing-a-long-a-thon coming to an end with a raucous rendition of "Hey Jude" —my "Nah-Nah NAH Nahs" a tad pitchy, but improving—at least that's what Grammy said, and she saw Paul sing it in person—which doesn't make any sense. The Beatles stopped touring in '66, and *Hey Jude* was released in '68—but Grammy was always full of surprises, and she never lied. Never.

"What kind of star?" I asked, my pigtails bouncing like a head full of red Slinkies. Just five and I was already dreaming of sell-out crowds and MTV—I even had a pair of glittery star-shaped sunglasses to prove it.

"With your voice?" said Grammy, "the brightest of stars."

My voice. Do I still have a voice?

Am I still me? My mind is slipping away, like it's retreating from details, away from the trifles, the sniffles, and the smiles, and taking refuge in the triumphs, and even regrets. The impactful moments seem easiest to remember. The moments that left an impression—some with scars.

The accident.

The old man.

The old mill.

"Jacinda, darlin', follow the beat."

Bongos on the car stereo. The windows were down as we pulled up to a stoplight in the center of town. Mick was crooning and Grammy was hooting, and little me was listening to every lyric, howl, and guitar squeal.

"Grammy," I said, as innocent as the bow in my hair would have suggested—all saccharine, no spice—"what's the man's name?"

"Who, darlin'?" she asked, lowering the volume as Keith began his "Sympathy for the Devil" solo. Hearing a classic for the first time was always a religious experience with Grammy. She seemed to know every song, every lyric, every note. She always got a kick out of introducing me to something new—like she was reliving it for the first time through me.

"The man," I said. "The man in the song. He keeps asking us to guess."

"What do you think his name is?" she asked, a shadowy wince glancing across her face, but it was quickly replaced with a smirk.

Was her question a test? Grammy was born and raised Catholic, and despite her bohemian life, practicing spirituality and universal love, I think the old teachings clung to her like pesky beach sand between toes. Looking back, I wonder—did Grammy know? If I had answered correctly, would that have proven my significance?

What am I? Did my Grammy know?

"Buster," I said, as sure as I was freckled and fair.

"Yeah, he certainly is a Buster," said Grammy, and she couldn't stop laughing at my little girl giggles. Grammy always wanted to know what I was thinking. My words meant something to her. She made me feel special. She made me feel...*important.*

Where am I? Am I...*alive?*

"Jacinda, darlin', follow the beat."

The even rhythm of the aching bedsprings kept the cadence, bouncing on Amanda's bed—mixed pajama tops and bottoms, crazy pigtails, and hairbrushes brandished like microphones.

"Bang bang!" sang Amanda to the tune buzzing through her blown-out stereo speakers.

"I am the warrior!" I sung, just as Amanda's bedroom door swung open with a crack and thwap.

"Ladies!" groaned Mrs. Hemmels. "It's past eleven!" With a flick of her wrist, Patty Smyth's voice faded like our mood.

"Mom!" shouted Amanda. "Come on! It's summer."

"Your father is trying to sleep," said Mrs. Hemmels. "He's got work tomorrow. Besides, Jaycie's mom expects her home by ten."

"A.M.!?" we both groaned.

"Yes, A.M.!" she shouted. "To bed—Now!"

The lights were off before we had finished griping.

Settling into Amanda's bed, it was hard to come down from heights so high—eyes wide, haphazardly tucked, it was five minutes before either of us spoke, and I was surprised Amanda hadn't started it sooner...she was, after all, the rebellious one.

"Run run, runaway," I sang.

"It's in your heart that you betray," Amanda continued, partially in tune.

Sometimes the music was in my head. Every instrument creating sound from memory—a perfect orchestra of emotions empowering me. When I had nothing, I still had music. I still had my voice...

Seconds later, Amanda and I were singing at the tops of our lungs. Bedcovers were kicked, imaginary microphones in hand, and we were surrounded by adoring fans. I could almost see and feel the spotlight and the rumbling cheers. It felt like I could almost make it happen...

"Girls! Enough!" shouted Mrs. Hemmels from the other side of the door.

Of course, we started laughing—belly laughs for days, just two peas in a pod enjoying music and movies, and adventuring into the woods. It was our summer. Every moment spent with Amanda was one less moment spent with my mother.

"You're my best friend, O'Neill," said Amanda.

"Mine too," I said, then clarified, "You are, I mean. You're my best friend too."

"I knew what you meant, dork," said Amanda. "Tomorrow morning, do you want to play Superheroes? Maybe we can go to the comics shop before we take you home?"

"Okay," I said, but there was something more interesting brewing in my tiny little red head. "We should start a band." A grin conquered my face, and in the dark, I could see nearly all of Amanda's pearly whites as she smiled in agreement.

"Yes!" she hissed, stifling a shout. "I like the way you dream, O'Neill."

My dreams. Where are my dreams? Am I asleep? Or am I somewhere else?

"Jacinda, darlin', follow the beat."

Christopher Hall had an unmistakable siren call—he could move and crush equally with a single melodic scream. Stabbing Westward was always Tony's favorite. Was it coincidence that "Save Yourself" was playing in the bar when it happened? The chaotic beat like a lingering symptom of a festering disease.

I sensed it coming, like a nuclear fire igniting in his chest.

I never meant for it to happen. I never saw the signs, and if I did, I ignored them.

Did I ignore them on purpose? Was I acting out because I was upset?

All I ever wanted was to know everything about him. I wanted to carry some of his pain. I wanted him to know he didn't have to carry it all alone. He didn't have to save me, but I was okay saving him...I had so much weighing me down, but I would have carried it all for him.

"What did you do?" I whispered. He could hear me, even over the music. The crowded bar had gone still—and there was blood all over Tony's fists.

"Let's go!" shouted Marshall. "Tony! Now!"

Our eyes stayed connected while Marshall dragged him away through the crowd as someone shouted, "Call 9-1-1!" Anne placed a comforting hand on my shoulder as I knelt to inspect the damage.

Our relationship, my work, our trust—all of it gone in a flash.

It all happened so fast, as the lyrics screamed, *"so just save yourself!"*

"I'm sorry," he said. I couldn't hear him, but I could read the words on his lips.

Tony, I'm sorry too.

The Grace Falls mall on New Year's Eve. Oh Tony, I failed you. So many memories. So many things that don't make sense. So many endings. Did they all happen? Which one is real?

"Jacinda, darlin', follow the beat."

But it wasn't a beat. I could feel them now, streaking down my cheeks.

It wasn't a beat at all.

It was the pooling of my tears, somewhere below.

I'm drifting. Fragment to fragment.

Tomorrow's not a promise. Gotta earn each one.

I'm not going to lose my soul. I'm not going to lose.

How can I fit everything I am now into that tiny place?

When all this is over, will I still be me? What am I now?

"Jacinda, darlin', follow the beat."

Wake up! Wake up! Wake up!

I'm not going to lose my soul.

I won't.

"Who let the spark escape?"

Someone shouted, and my eyes opened.

There's a moment between sleep and wakefulness when everything feels out of focus. Sometimes a dream can bleed into reality. I was surrounded by eyes, watching me before they dissipated back into the dream. They may not have been real, but this was very real.

I was in a room, floating high above the collection of demons below. I couldn't move, I couldn't speak, I was just two eyes watching—witnessing—the horror below.

MALUS
December 23, 2013

Silence was a gift. In silence I could process failure. In silence, I could escape my rage through meditation: a skill I acquired from a monk in East Asia, long before the first stone of the Great Wall was ever laid.

Frustration, if unattended, evolves to rage—and rage clouds judgment. The greatest tacticians learned to control disappointment and to harness it toward progress. I had become efficient at recalibrating my anger into inertia, propelling me toward my goals. But there were moments when my urges were almost unbearable, and rage was the catalyst inciting my most basic inclinations toward my darkest self. Every moment of every day was pain—the creature inside begging to be unleashed. The immensity of my control, of the concentration I harnessed to keep my secret, was at times intolerable.

It took lifetimes to find equilibrium—but only after lowering myself within the suffocating silence of this great submerged city.

These halls had fallen silent long before the ancient empires of Earth rose to prominence. It was the setting of my greatest triumph—after centuries of plotting, I found revenge here—but revenge without resolution was empty. The stillness provided introspection to sort dark thoughts and conjure plans.

The city was vast, its depths unknown.

What secrets lie undiscovered? What answers might this city provide?

The civilization that once flourished here was remarkably ahead of its time—with sciences so arcane that at times they appeared like magic. Their pre-ancient technology was a source of curiosity, and if I could understand it, a secondary solution to steal away the girl's abilities was a wise investment.

Was I looking in the wrong place? Playing by the rules of a mad game-maker? Was there not a simpler way to extract the Holy Dyad from Ms. O'Neill, than collecting four keys and wedding her within Eden? These were ceremonial hurdles for those willing to play within the rules of this mad game.

Was there not a simpler way?

I'd spent uncounted years within this ruined city, ruminating for answers. So many years, and yet, I never considered the answers I sought could be discovered within these halls. I was looking for an answer above—an answer that revealed itself in the form of a young woman...

That scent...

Salt. Tears. That scent resurfaced so many memories.

One drip followed by another. They were pooling along the ground at my feet.

High above, floating within the chamber was the girl. She was suspended in the air as if dangling from string or drifting like a child's balloon. Behind the Veil, however, she was being cocooned within psychic threads spun by Deimos and Phobos, as they entombed her within her own mind. It was the next phase of our assault on her willpower, dissolving her defenses, allowing Lilly's persona to assume control. Her submission was inevitable.

"Like all else you touch," whispered Lilly, "this too will break."

"I stopped trying to fix things," I whispered. "Breaking is the goal."

When I looked back at the girl, her eyes snapped shut. Was she awake? Was she watching me? With a flick of my wrist, I lowered her to the floor from where she floated, but I kept her stranded, hovering just above the ground.

"Are you watching me?" I asked, but she didn't move. Her heart quickened. "Phobos."

The god of fear crawled out of the Veil like an insect and stood at my side.

"She is awake," I said. "Make her sleep."

Her eyes snapped open as if to protest, or to unleash her abilities upon us. But her mind went numb, and her eyelids fell like curtains.

"Done," said Phobos.

"The girl—how much longer?"

The difficulties of a spell as complicated as our initial intentions went beyond any casual bit of mind-altering magic. Toying with the finer aspects of the mind, especially that of a girl with such vast power, was like defusing a bomb—one false configuration of memory and it could short-circuit the girl, maybe even the whole world or reality itself. But that wasn't the only risk. Miss one important event, and the construct of replacement memories could unravel like a spool of yarn.

It was a slow and meticulous process, like building a palace out of playing cards. A delicate balance, one placement after the next, layering, creating equilibrium, until the palace was complete. This proved difficult. Too many chances for a strong wind to blow our palace down...

Instead, we decided on total deletion. Remove her mind and replace it with another.

Enlisting Phobos and Deimos was a stroke of genius—their ability to manipulate and mesmerize the mind were second only to their ability to inflict crippling fear and terror into their victims. They were a special kind of Fallen—Devourers. Their entire existence was to find and torture their victims, then consume them. And they enjoyed their work.

Phobos smiled, its mouth lined with a thousand crooked teeth as sharp as knives.

"The glamour Phobos and Deimos have placed will bind the Jacinda-girl to you, but first, you must inject the spectral entity you wish to infect her, or the entity will not be absorbed by our manipulations."

"Done," I said, and with a simple thought pushed Lilly into Jacinda's mind.

"As one identity disappears, another will assume control.

"Next," continued Phobos, "Phobos and Deimos will create new memories with those that are favorable to our master. In order for us to proceed, you must provide a secret." I felt a twinge of paranoia—were they attempting to scam me? Learn my most prized secret and use it against me? "A secret that nobody else knows, for the mere utterance of the secret will break the spell and unravel her mind."

"Why?" I asked.

"The magic insists. If you are the benefactor in destroying her mind with lies, the payment must be a personal sacrifice of truth. A contract between you and the spell."

"What must I do?"

"Whisper your secret into the aether, and Phobos and Deimos shall begin."

I was a paranoid creature. I survived on secrecy. Everything Phobos said was true. I understood the rules. Everything must be balanced. If I wanted something taken from Jacinda, I must offer up something of my own. With only a week before the New Year, I swallowed my pride and whispered something inaudibly into the aether.

"Very well," said Phobos. "Phobos and Deimos shall begin."

The ancient creators of this city designed it to allow fresh air to flow like a flue. A slow draft moving from the one chamber to the next— when a sudden shift sent the fine hairs on the back of my neck like pins.

Was someone listening?

There were few creatures, god or beast, that could mask themselves to the point of imperception—and fewer devices could render a lesser creature equally undetectable.

I'd left one such trinket on the wooden floor of Jacinda's former cell. I struck it from the head of Nemesis, the traitor, after she stole it from my stash, freed Ms. O'Neill, and stole the Key of Capricorn. The Helm of Darkness—the Cap of Invisibility—it could be anywhere, resting upon anyone...

There was no sound, not of beating heart, shallow breath, or footfall atop the stone floor. I felt only a presence, as if something had moved past me.

Before I could investigate further, the scent of ozone and ash drifted by on the same draft—the stink of rage. It was only a matter of time before the cork popped...

"Who let the spark escape?" demanded Dagon as he exited the Veil, his tentacled lower half flipping impatiently from beneath his overcoat. "I wasted many wives upon this folly."

Was this another attempted mutiny? Or a trap?

"Wives?" I scoffed, "as if any those women had a choice?" Who would wed a creature so foul? Slimy and wet, teeth like needles? He was an abomination, as were most of those hidden within the room, waiting for their moment to speak. All gods, however, believed themselves beautiful. Arrogance and delusion were a part of the status—their rights and desires, absolute and above all.

When Anubis stalked into the light and barked, "My warriors, the Black Ka, claim failure belongs to the children of Loki," the tinder lit.

"Failure?" scoffed Loki, charging forth from the Veil with a wild smile splitting his face in two. His eyes, however, were narrowed into pins, and focused on the jackal.

"Incompetence," whined Anubis, pointing his golden flail, "has a face like the Trickster—"

There was a flash of metal and stone, followed by a "thunk" and the crushing of bone.

Loki retracted his hammer from Anubis with a short vicious yank—the jackal's eyes destroyed when the hammer pulverized his skull. It happened quicker than a blink. He was gone—the god of death—dispatched to the Pit.

Bloodlust was an addiction. Kill enough, and one cannot stop the overwhelming need to snuff out life. When the lust churns, it must be fed. I had hoped Anubis would quench

their hunger, but I was wrong.

"My daughter is gone," growled Loki, pointing the hammer at my head. He was an unpredictable madman, and I was down another loyal member. "This is the second child I have sacrificed for your plot."

"My plot?" I challenged. "You have as much to gain as I. Or perhaps you should have struck a more lucrative deal."

"I want blood," Loki roared. His wild blue eyes flashed like frozen frost.

"You shall have it," I promised.

I was not attempting to patronize. I believed another opportunity would quickly present itself. If the spark would not return the final key, we would threaten the girl's life or find some other means. We had one calendar year to retrieve the keys—and we'd succeeded in that endeavor. However, there was nothing said nor written about stealing it back from those who stole it from us—no matter where or *when* that might be. One way or another, our paths would cross.

Loki's anger, however, was not as easily diminished. He swung at me, the warhammer still coated in the blood and brains of Anubis. I had hardly lifted my arm to protect my face when the weapon impacted. My arm, shoulder and clavicle were instantly crushed, and I was sent sprawling backward.

Loki was not the most vicious, nor the most gifted god I had ever faced, but he was the most unpredictable. This was the reason for inking his name into one of my contracts—he was a wild card. Ally one moment, enemy the next, the only constant was that everything Loki did was in his own interest. The key to controlling Loki was to make him believe that his compliance would provide him the chance to betray me at the final moment—to swoop in like a hawk and steal what was rightfully mine.

Manipulation was an art form. If one was to use a silver tongue, one must speak shiny words to open ears—though, it appeared Loki was done listening.

When I caught my balance, I lunged forth—when in power, an attack on one's position must be met with an equal or greater force...

...Moloch, however, blocked my path.

One by one they stepped forth—some surfacing from the Veil, others from shadow. Moloch, Astoreth, and Thanatos joined Dagon and Loki, and they were furious. Only the Morrigan and Hekate stood by, hissing on my behalf.

With the ring and twelve of the most powerful creatures on Earth at my side, it had been easy until now. We destroyed all who opposed us.

We gathered power. We gathered strength. We were unstoppable until the spark came along. Even when we attempted to take the girl and were unsuccessful, it was not failure. We knew the rules. We probed her angelic guard's defenses. We meticulously tortured her. We seduced her. We pulled the strings that destroyed her life. We knew how it would end. And inevitably, predictably, she took her own life and fell right into our hands.

Still, how did we miss the spark? He was a part of her life, after all. What kept him from discovery? How did he go undetected?

Hekate's arm snapped in two as Dagon's tentacle lashed in her direction. Moloch roared as Morrigan raked her claws across his mighty chest. A flash of fae-dust crippled Dagon, his lungs filling with blood, while Thanatos, Loki, and Astoreth surrounded me. Five against three; the numbers were too many.

Loki swung for my head as Thanatos swiped at my ankles—they were non-lethal blows. Any attempt to cleave my heart or destroy my eyes would stay their strike by contract. But when Astoreth wrestled me from behind and pinched at the vertebrae in my neck, my limbs went limp.

"Malus," hissed Thanatos, blackened bile dripping from his rotten lips, "your time has come."

THE SUBMISSION OF SUMMANUS

113 A.D.

Stone and mortar burned under the might of the Norse gods. It was the end. The temple upon Capitoline Hill was crumbling under the might of lightning, flame, storm, and vengeance, while Jupiter wept upon his throne.

Malus arrived atop the hill but witnessed no damage or destruction —no death nor godlike fury—however, when he slipped beyond the Veil, in the pocket world that overlapped Earthly affairs, he witnessed the coming of doom. In the previous world, the world of man, the temple was a marvel of Roman architecture—white marble pillars welcoming pilgrims arriving to revere their gods. In contrast, beyond the Veil was a spire that appeared to rise straight to the golden gates of Empyrea.

The great Norse gods pummeled the spire, crumbling the mystical architecture that appeared like a great needle stuck into a ball of yarn that was the Earth. Lightning, thunder, fire, ice—their wrath unleashed on their rivals.

With the Helm of Darkness, Malus slipped through the chaos like a ghost and into the spire. He ascended each level high into the clouds when he came upon the head of Juno resting in a pool of blood. Her eyes plucked free, and her body torn to shreds.

It was a massacre.

The Roman Gods were of no match for the Norsemen. The War of Gods had seen many fall, but none more celebrated, more revered, than Jupiter's mighty pantheon.

Room by room, level by level, Malus came upon the divine dead—god and goddess alike destroyed and delivered to the pit. The spire shook with every crash of thunder, its magic crumbling under the pure power of Thor, quickening Malus's pace.

When he arrived at the throne room, at the very top of the spire, the moon and sun were shining directly outside through a great window, silhouetting the throne. The room was lit by the refracted light of the sun, sparkling every shiny surface. It was a marvel of gold and silver, of decadent fountains flowing with pure ambrosia. It was a room fit for a king's king—the great Jupiter, who mourned upon his throne, head in hands, grief overtaking him.

Malus approached the great god, and motioned to remove the Helm of Darkness, revealing himself, when the doors behind him burst open and the cold breeze of calamity rushed through.

"Sister! The sun!"

Nott, Goddess of Night, with eyes as grey as the moon, filled the room with her long black hair and snatched the light from the air. Once dark, with the luminance from the moon trickling into the chamber, only then did the second goddess enter.

She stalked toward the throne, licking her chapped lips like a child savoring sweets. Hel, daughter of Loki, was not like other goddesses. Her flesh was corrupted, as if rot had settled into only one vertical-half of her body. One-part pale, the other putrid, with long grimy blonde hair concealing the fetid half of her face. Her lips were a foul shade green and purple, and her irises a bare shade darker than white, surrounded by an infected yellow.

Her dress was covered in blood—ragged, baggy and worn, like a sack that was falling from her emaciated form.

"Good day, fine king," she said with a curtsy. "May I sup now or after I suck the wet eyes from your royal head?" Hel was insanity unleashed. A god-killer—but only in the dark.

Jupiter raised his head and stared down at his own death. He did not move to save himself but invited her close with a nod. When she was upon him, he lifted his golden head and said, "Take what you wish. I have failed them."

"Oh, indeed you have great king," said Nott, goddess of the night.

The War of the Gods took many Fallen. Their kind was pushed to the brink of extinction upon the Earth. Pantheon against pantheon, cleansing the land of their blight. They were a cancer, reaping, enslaving, and savoring those who worshipped them, and their reign was finally coming to an end.

When Hel placed her hands around Jupiter's arm, her eyes fluttered, and she cooed softly with pleasure. "Brother! Brother, come! He tastes like oak and honey! Have a taste! Brother!"

The tower shook, and the mighty worm, Jörmungandr slithered its way up the spire, until its great head peered through the window. The worm was so long, it could stretch itself around the world and bite its own tail. With every coil around the spire, the structure cracked and swayed.

When Jupiter began to scream, the pain of Hel's touch too much to bear, Malus made his move. With a spear made of flame, he skewered Nott through the heart, destroying her hold on the light. When the sun's rays burst into the room, Hel screamed and fell away from Jupiter, then scampered directly into Malus's arms. As the great worm recoiled from the burst of light, Malus tossed Hel from the spire, directly out the stone window, drawing Jörmungandr in pursuit of his falling sister. Then, and only then, did Malus remove the Helm that rendered him invisible.

"Your service is needed, Jupiter," said Malus.

"Kill me, or leave me be," he groaned. Malus placed a hand on the king's shoulder and laughed. "Do you enjoy my misery?"

"Great Jupiter, what games you play," said Malus. "One of the great pantheons has fallen, all on your watch. But I know your secret."

"Leave me be," said Jupiter.

"Did you kill him?" asked Malus.

"Who?" groaned the great god.

"Your brother. The great Jupiter," said Malus, and the king met his accuser's eyes.

"Who are you, stranger?"

"I will help you escape, if you help me achieve my goals," said Malus.

"I do not wish to escape. I wish to die."

"You will come with me," said Malus. "Even if I must force it upon you."

A spark of anger blushed the god king's cheeks. "Leave me," he threatened.

"Poor Summanus, murdered his twin and took his throne," sung Malus. "Were you jealous of his power? Desirous of his many wives? Look at what you've done? Look at how you've disgraced them, betrayed them, and destroyed them."

"How?" begged Summanus. "How did you know?"

"I am your master," said Malus. "I know all."

"Leave! At once!" growled Summanus, rising to his feet. The sun beyond the great window faltered, and storm clouds darkened the skies.

Malus leaned forward and whispered. "Boreal."

Upon hearing his true name spoken, a series of tremors leapt across Summanus's body, from knee to neck. Malus provided his hand, brandished his silver ring and held it out to the phony ruler of the Roman gods. Summanus had no magic to beguile or fight. He was powerless to the stranger who spoke his true name—the name given to him by his creator.

When the traitor king kissed Malus's ring, the contract was sealed—submission to his new master.

IV

the stag

A VOICE
Long Ago...
Then.

Luck

And Fate.

What is the difference, Tony?

Break a bone? Bad luck. Meet the love of your life? The glory of fate.

But, what if the love of your life was caught in a terrible accident long before you ever had the chance to meet? Was that Fate? Or Misfortune?

Luck is Destiny for the faithless.

They may be intertwined, but the truth was, Luck was a myth and Fate was nothing but a cruel joke—a manipulation to control the flock toward reward.

The premise that some were gifted opportunities over others was as untrue as the notion of pure evil.

Shades, Tony. Evil exists only in the mind of the other.

However, Free Will was the great counter of Fate, and the destroyer of Luck.

Imagine if you will, you were born a King. Would not every day be a gift from the Fates and Powers that Be, urging you toward greatness?

But what if you did not want it?

What if you wanted to be a pauper? A bard?

Would you accept your fate if that was not your heart's desire?

And what about the pauper that wished to be a king? Could the lowly pauper endeavor to rise so high?

We blame Fate for our misgivings. We blame Fate for our shortcomings and our tragedies.

Examine if you will the mind of a Fateful believer. Their disciples say, "What you make of your existence was yours to command. If you happen to fall in Fate's way, you a lowly housefly pestering the path of another man's greatness, prepare to be swatted."

But let's examine it further—do not call it poor luck or ill fate, call it Free Will, for that man chose to swat the fly. He chose to kill you. He chose your fate for you. The Fates merely put him on his path, but they did not force his hand.

Thousands. Millions. Billions. All have died at the hands of someone who took the opportunity and chose to kill. So, I ask you, are luck and fate evil? Is Free Will evil?

Or was evil merely the meek accusing the better Fated man of choosing when and how to stomp out the hard-earned opportunity of another?

What you think you know is only your point of view. And no matter how understanding, empathetic, or compassionate one is, their perception will always and forever be limited.

The boy was the ward of a village that did not want him. The orphaned child of an enemy people, an easy mark for the less compassionate. He was different, not only by appearance, but by blood, and the villagers reminded him of those differences every day.

"Raggy boy!" cried Rorik. What was it about the biggest and strongest children that made them also the meanest? Rorik had beaten him countless times. Taunting him until words no longer stung. Then came the fists.

The boy was easy to find, lugging buckets of fresh water from the lake to the village every morning—one of many chores of an orphan earning his keep. He labored for food. He labored for shelter. He fed the hunting hounds, cleaned feculence, and other undesired labors for scraps, when their charity suited them.

"Raggy boy! Why do you work so hard, Raggy boy?"

When the boy hit the ground, a stone sliced his chin wide open. A moment later an icy cold splash of water poured on top of him, followed by the chorus of laughter. It would have been difficult to fight Rorik alone, but wherever Rorik went, there were always others.

Kaspar.

Lethan.

Aran.

They were the sons of warriors. They were strong—well fed and trained to hunt from the moment they could hold a spear or draw a bow.

But some days, even when doused in buckets of water, there was a fire ready to explode within the boy. He stood and swung before he knew where to punch. Rorik easily sidestepped the attack and threw him to the ground, face-first into the mud.

"Did you see his eyes?" laughed Aran.

"Lunatic eyes," said Lethan.

"Monster eyes!" hooted Kaspar.

While they were busy mocking his appearance, he slipped away. Maybe a good laugh was all they needed to leave him be, which was all he ever wanted—to be left alone. His existence was miserable enough without their bullying.

"Raggy boy! Where do you think you're going?" laughed Rorik.

The boy wanted nothing more than to stand up to Rorik, but even he knew there were some battles that could not be won. Some battles were better fought in other ways. And others, better not fought at all.

"Where is he going?" groaned Aran, as if it was pointless to run.

The boy had already fled past the fire pits when Rorik and the others began to follow. He ducked into an empty hut and out the other side before any of them knew where he had gone. The thing about being hunted all his life was learning how to run and hide—unfortunately, the boy was not very good at either.

"Raggy boy!"

Before he knew it, he was being thrown out into the open, where his beating could be publicly witnessed—not that anyone cared to intervene—

—after all, boys will be boys.

"The Elders should have killed you and your mother when they had the chance," said Rorik, towering over him as the other boys gathered around. The immediate pummeling incurred was as vicious as it was swift, with each of the boys taking turns kicking or shoving him into the mud, closer and closer to the refuse trickling away from a neighboring hut. "Who decided to let such an ugly shit live amongst us?"

"My father," said a near voice.

The boy knew that voice. Of all the people to witness his embarrassment—bloodied, muddied, and defeated—this witness caused him shame.

It had been a long, hard four years learning to survive without Lilly. There was once a time when he and Lilly ran off into the forest to be free of their peers—and many times they had hidden away at their special place to be rid of them. Those days, however, had long since passed.

At first, when Lilly spurned his playful gestures to adventure into the forest with him, the boy pondered what he had done to drive her away. Was it their kiss? Had her father forbidden their friendship? Had he committed some other misstep he had yet to understand?

But as time progressed, the boy decided it did not matter why, only that Lilly had finally concluded that their friendship was an error. She was the daughter of a chieftain, and he was a nobody. Things had not been the same since that day of the storm, when they were lost within the Dark Wood.

Eventually, she became a stranger like everyone else.

Lilandra was flanked by her sisters, carrying baskets of food to the storage hut. She looked as unpleased as ever.

"Do you question our Chieftain's decision, Rorik?" she asked.

"No," he stammered. "I meant no disrespect."

Then to the boy, she asked, "Are you hurt?" Her voice was as cold as her glare.

The boy shook his head, then she broke her gaze and left at once.

"One day, Raggy Boy," threatened Rorik, "nobody will save you."

Rorik and the others then wandered off, their chores awaiting them, and the boy was left to clean the mud from his clothes. Embarrassed, hurt, and angry, he crawled into a small space between stacks of firewood and laid there crying.

He was too old to cry, but too alone to care.

When the warm season began to cool, and the daylight shortened, the village would harvest all the crops from the fields in preparation for the Feast of the Great Sun. Hunters were dispatched, returning with boar and great elk to roast in their fires.

This feast, however, was a celebration.

It was customary that upon her seventeenth birthday, the daughter of the High Elder and chieftain, Kasimir, would marry the finest hunter of her age. A competition to catch the greatest prize—boar, elk, or greater—would begin before sunrise and end as the sun began its descent. The young hunter with the greatest kill would be presented Lilandra's hand. A competition that every young man in the village aspired to win. A union that was all but set between Lilandra and Rorik.

Rorik was a natural warrior—tall, strong, fast. He was born and bred to be a killer like his father. Rorik could spear a chirping bird resting on a branch from fifty paces. Young men like Rorik were the prize of the village—they kept the villagers fed, they protected them from invaders, and they were revered accordingly.

Everyone recognized Rorik's natural greatness. Even Lilly. Their betrothal was inevitable. The boy knew his time with Lilly was near conclusion. His entire world was chaos and hardship, and the one thing that kept him going, was hope—hope that miracles could be cast upon even the lowliest, like him.

Hope, Tony, is toxic. Imagine if you will the drive and passion this poor boy had for his one true love—but it was hopeless. A sham. It cannot exist and yet, it was his one true motivation. How sad that must be? Is it not, Tony? You of all people would know.

And yet, the boy had a plan.

The hunt offered a unique opportunity. Slaying a great elk was to aspire to greatness. Elk were strong, fast, and hard to kill. If he could slay an elk during the hunt, he may yet change his fate. The festival contest offered him the chance to change the course of his destiny. If he proved himself during the hunt, he might be accepted amongst the people, and with that acceptance, maybe Lilly's as well.

He had Lilly's favor once. Was it so far-fetched to imagine he might win it once again?

The hunt had been plodding along for hours. Most hunters could sneak through the underbrush as quiet as a hare, but the boy was as clumsy as a fawn, his foot finding every twig before he could unfurl his spear.

Falibor, an aging, crippled hunter, had been assigned to teach the boy the ways of the hunt. The boy could not fetch pales of water and clean shit forever—it was imperative that he become more useful to the tribe.

"Silence is a hunter's best virtue," Lilly had said, long ago on that fateful day of the storm. *"You struggle to sleep in silence. When hunting forest creatures, one must be as silent as stone if one is to sneak up on them."*

There are two kinds of people in the world. One thrives in pressure.

The other crumbles. The boy carried all his hopes and dreams on that day—that he might cross the path of an elk and that his strike was as true as his intentions. Like all those who dream, the boy found himself wandering his own mind when life passed him by.

The sun hung just above the mountain tops when a horn sounded throughout the forest.

"Come! Rorik speared a mighty boar!" yelled Aran.

"The hunt is over," cried Falibor, as the hunting party retreated toward the sound.

By the time the boy had found the rest of the hunting party, Rorik had already carved the heart from the dead beast's chest and was preparing the sacred ritual of consuming it warm. Many had gathered, including Kasimir, who greeted him like a son.

The boy panicked. The parts of his intellect that distinguished right from wrong malfunctioned. Rorik represented everything the boy hated about the world. He was arrogant. He was rotten. He had a family, he was well fed, and he had opportunities the boy would have killed for—and now he had usurped the only thing the boy ever wanted. How much good luck, opportunity and fate could be offered to one man who did not deserve it?

With great savagery, the boy tossed his spear at Rorik's head. He intended to maim. He intended to kill and rid himself of his rival. But when the spear sailed passed Rorik's head and sunk into the dead boar's side, the chaos that ensued was a blur of anger and rage.

The boy would have been torn apart in the fray if not for Falibor, who pled with Kasimir for leniency. And as the aging warrior dragged his protégé away, the boy screaming for blood, he said, "This is not how you take honor."

"I do not want honor," the boy growled.

"Your blood is hot. You cannot walk the path when all you see is rage," said Falibor, then loosened his grip. "When your enemy is large, you must use the tools you possess to gain an advantage."

"What tools do I have!?" he roared.

Falibor released him and slung the boy to the ground, knocking the wind from his lungs. Then he grabbed the boy by the shoulders and shook him, staring into his discolored eyes. "You are always so concerned about the things you do not have. But you have survived! You are smart! Use your head for once, you fool!"

Falibor was an honorable man forced to tutor the boy nobody wanted—the boy with the witchy eyes who was the son of an enemy. And yet, the man saw something others did not. He saw the boy's passion, his unbreaking spirit and tenacity.

The boy was drowning in sorrow and rage, but he did understand the message. He had survived, at times without food or shelter, in a village surrounded by his enemies. He was a survivor in the harshest conditions, and he was still standing.

Rorik was not his enemy. Rorik was his rival. He, like all the others, wanted Lilandra's hand. He could not compete in the ways of the village, but he could still compete in other ways. Then, without another thought, he left for the village, sprinting through the forest.

"I will kill you, Raggy Boy!" Rorik screamed in the boy's wake.

The boy found Lilly preparing for the festival in her family's hut, surrounded by her sisters as they doted on her every need. One of them braided Lilly's hair, while the others wove a special wreath to crown her head.

"Hold still," said Nastia as she repositioned Lilly's head.

"Hurry up," said Lilly. "I've been sitting here too long."

"It must be perfect. I'm almost done," said Nastia.

"I will be happier when this night is finally over," said Lilly.

"Why?" asked Sveta. "Don't you want to be betrothed?"

"I do not," said Lilly, when she spotted the boy lurking by the entrance. She glared at him as if she expected he would arrive, sooner or later. "Can I be left alone?"

Each gave the other a look of sisterly annoyance, and only withdrew after Lilly threatened them with an angry look. When they had disappeared, she turned her attention to the boy and sighed, preparing for the inevitable conversation.

"You can come out from over there."

This was his moment.

His voice trembled. "Tonight is very important."

"It is," she said, then looked away. "Only I wish it weren't."

"Betrothal may be an adventure, but it is no replacement for the thrill of discovering what lies beyond the mountains," he said.

She gave him a weak smile, like he had stirred a pleasant memory.

"No, it is not," she replied.

There was commotion from outside the hut.

"Where is the Raggy Boy!? Raggy Boy, where are you?"

Lilandra peeked through the entrance into the village center.

"What happened?" she asked. She smiled, as if impressed that he had gotten so deep under Rorik's skin. Rorik was searching from hut to hut while the others protested for calmer heads. The boy had only seconds to say what he had come to profess.

"One more adventure," he offered, taking her by the hand. "Meet me at our spot, as soon as you can." Then he rushed to the far end of the hut to a window and crawled through. He whispered back to her. "Tomorrow is not a promise." Then he vanished.

He knew she would come. Lilly could not refuse an adventure.

It had been a long time since they had been to their spot. The forest had since reclaimed it. Thick underbrush had grown up around the entrance and small critters had taken residence there.

They had discovered that secret place together, long ago on one of their many adventures into the forest beyond their border. Not even the hunters went that deep into the unknown near the Dark Wood, but Lilly had never cared for rules.

Their secret place had formed when two small trees had fallen onto a third to create a canopy nestled next to a bluff that overlooked the lake. There were climbing vines they could use to scale high into the tree and even a patch of wild berries to snack on. It was a small corner of paradise for two young adventurers. They spent nights stargazing and imagining what great expanse of the world was beyond the mountains and the forest that bordered their village—borders that were rarely crossed.

A twig snapped, announcing her arrival.

His eyes caught Lilly creeping into view. The sun had already fallen below the horizon—its last breath casting the sky into shades of red and purple.

"You are out of practice," he said. "You could have snuck upon a phantom, once." She was dressed for the feast—a wreath of late summer flowers crowning her long sandy hair. She wore special cloth—green fabrics with yellow flowers stitched into its length.

"It has been a long time," she said, smiling at the memories.

"Go with me," he said. "Over the mountains."

"What do you mean?"

"You once asked me to follow you over the mountains," he explained. "Ever since we were children, you've wondered what existed on the other side. You always asked me to go with you. Now I'm asking you to go with me."

"Why?" she asked, and before he could answer, she clarified. "Why would I ask you?"

It was as appalling an answer as he could imagine. Was she purposely trying to hurt him?

"What do you mean?" he said. "We did everything together. We built this place together. We spent every moment of our childhood together. We ventured into the Dark Wood together."

She raised her hand to stop him.

"I cannot remember," she said as she stared up into the leafy canopy above.

"How can you not remember?" he asked. The grief struck him like a bolt directly to the heart.

"I cannot remember," she cried. "One moment I have the faintest memory of you, of us, and in the next it is gone."

"We have many memories together," he urged.

"I cannot remember a single one," she replied. She did not mean to hurt him, but her words hurt more than any beating he had ever endured.

"I do not understand," said the boy, shaking his head. "You cannot remember a single happy memory of us together? Here? Adventuring into the forest?"

"I cannot remember a single memory of us together, no. Not happy, nor sad. There is a little less of you here, each day," she said, pointing at her head.

"That's impossible," he said. It was a preposterous claim. How could she forget about him?

"It is not impossible! I do not remember you! When I look upon you, I see a familiar face that I do not remember! Do you have any understanding how vexing it is to miss something you have no memory of? A far sickness for a place and a feeling you have no reason to yearn for?"

There was a long pause as he absorbed her words. None of what she had said made any sense to him. It was witchcraft! Evil! Rorik! All of which were irrational conjurings of a small jealous mind, that came to a very naive conclusion.

"Why did you come here?" he asked. The tears stung his eyes. "If you do not remember me, why did you come? How did you recall where to go?"

"I have memories of this place, just not of you. But it was what you whispered to me as you were leaving that took my attention. *Tomorrow is not a promise.*"

"You used to say that when I was not as brave as you, to follow you into the unknown. Into the dangerous places you liked to go. Those words inspired me," he said.

The sun was gone and the sky deepened into dark hues of blue.

"It came to me in strange dream. There was a sad woman. She told me to remember it, and I never forgot," said Lilly, as she edged her way closer to him, taking handfuls of her dress to maneuver the uneven ground. "If you heard me speak those words, then my mind has lost something that was quite important to me. I only say those words to the people closest to my heart."

"You were not the only one who lost something important to them," he said. Her face showed the impact of those words. They stung as much as they inflicted guilt. "I cannot imagine a life here without you. My Lilly, you have—"

"—Please," she whimpered. "Do not call me *your* Lilly."

"You and I are one and the same," he cried. "I want you to be my betrothed. Let us leave tonight, and venture over the mountains, together."

Oh, how hopeful he was. How young, how ignorant. Love was a complex reaction of hormones and comfort. Of desire and need. He would eventually learn its meaning, but his journey was just beginning.

"I cannot feel for you, as you do for me," she explained. "I am incapable of something that for reasons unknown to me does not exist." She looked like a rabbit wishing to flee the briar and away from the hungry fox. "We were just children playing games."

"When it came to you, Lilly, I played no games."

Seeing the pain in his eyes, she left at once. She did not say goodbye.

The boy remained in the forest to mourn. The last light of day disappeared, and he was left in darkness, alone.

The story thus far, Tony, has been prelude. This moment. This is where the story truly begins. Watch now. Don't miss it. The boy wished to rid himself of his pain, to disappear from the world so badly that he actually *did*.

Did you see it? Did you see the moment this poor wretched Raggy Boy went from man to god? He slipped behind the Veil on a desperate wish. He let the waves of sadness and anger take turns washing his innocence away.

"You gave me nothing!" he screamed into the night. He was cursing the Powers That Be, his fate, his luck—perhaps even Belobog. Where was Belobog when his mother's people were slain? Where was the White God when his mother died and left him all alone? Where was the noble god when he was being beaten? Where was his protector when he went hungry? Where was he?

"What am I to do? I have nothing because of you!"

Then he settled into an endless sob.

As the moon rose to its apex, an unsettling mood seeped into the forest. Strange noises echoed in the distance, and shadows darker than the night itself danced and ran free. The boy did not fear death, but he did fear the forest and the unknown things that lurked there. He climbed up the nearest tree for safety, but only found himself more exposed to the demons of the wood. He was finally coming to understand that the terrible stories the elders told were true.

Clouds blotted out the moon and the forest went as black as pitch, and the insects chirped no more—when suddenly, a light broke through the darkness.

At first, the boy thought it was the breaking dawn, but when his eyes adjusted to the brightness, he saw it was not the sun. It was something much more beautiful and mysterious.

It was a stag. A stag with shimmering white fur, glowing like the brightest summer's moon. The stag was ancient, beautiful, and pure. It stood taller than two men, with antlers as large as saplings with long patches of moss hanging from its limbs like a majestic crown. Its eyes glowed with a white heat as it wandered, grazing on underbrush and bark.

To behold such a creature was to behold something truly unique, but where did it come from? And why had its brilliant grace never been witnessed by the villagers with such luminous qualities to give it away? It was a beacon in the dark, a glowing radiant beast.

The boy continued to stare, ignorant of the stag's vast significance, and did not care, when a thought danced along that changed the course of his life forever.

If Rorik was to marry Lilly because he was the best hunter of his age, then the boy would have to prove to be an even greater hunter. A stag like this with radiant white fur, bigger than the largest stag that ever roasted on their fires, would gain favor with Kasimir, and prove that *he* was the greatest hunter of his age. Kasimer would be forced to betroth Lilly to him, breaking his vow with Rorik's father. The intoxicating allure of all he ever wanted, urged him to do what he must.

To reach out and take his destiny.

He removed the dagger from his belt, the one he borrowed from Falibor for the hunt, and readied himself. The great stag would pass right beneath him. It did not know he was there, lurking in the tree above, hidden behind the Veil.

Luck.

Fate.

Opportunity.

Free Will.

Glory. Belonging. Lilly.

The dagger jittered in his hand, and he resurfaced from the Veil. The cold embrace of the world between worlds drifted into the warm summer night. He dropped from his perch high above, and the great glowing stag looked up.

In that moment, as he fell toward his prey, its great ageless face wrinkled with a glimmer of intelligence—a look unlike any stag he had ever encountered. It was not the look of fear, but surprise. It could not understand where the Hell that boy had come from. As if it knew each and every plant, animal, and bug in all the forest, and *he* was not supposed to be there, falling through the air, aiming to take its life.

When his dagger struck the beast's hide, the boy drove it deep with all his strength through the space between the shoulders, and directly into the great stag's heart. The strike was a mortal one, but the stag resisted, violently twisting and kicking, attempting to throw its attacker from its mighty back. With all his strength, the boy grabbed hold of the dagger and rammed it further into the stag, sinking the blade to the hilt.

The moment its heart stopped beating, the glowing light of its brilliant white fur dissipated into the night, and it collapsed onto the ground like a tree being ripped from its roots. The boy tumbled to the forest floor in a heap, having spent his energy.

When the wind returned to his lungs, the boy studied the great stag.

Its fur still brilliant white, it appeared regal and mighty—by far the greatest elk that had ever been killed in those woods.

He thanked Belobog for his bounty, like Falibor had instructed him after a kill. He retrieved his blade, and cut through the fur and flesh, then tore out the ruined heart. He held the great muscle in both hands. It was heavy, hot, and did not feel dead. If the heart was the source of all life, it was now his, and he held the stag's essence in his hands and accept it as his own by consuming it warm.

As the sun breached over the horizon, the boy could hear the barking of the hunting mutts.

He had been dragging the severed head of the great stag through the forest for hours, but he did not feel taxed. The boy felt alive. Vital. As if he had become something *new*.

A strange fog followed him as he dragged the carcass from the tree line into the clearing just beyond the village.

If he had even a modicum of sense, he would have noticed the omen. He would have understood his sin.

Fog in late summer was the harbinger of death.

vetus deos

TONY
January 1st, 2007
Now.

So, get this…

Gabriel and I were on a walkabout. It was two-parts "A Christmas Carol"—one-part Hellraiser—with a dash of "This Is Your Life" thrown in for shits and giggles.

After showing me a potential future that never was, he took me back to the worst day of my life—January 1st, 2007, where he unveiled "The Truth," and divulged a heaping, steaming, pile of bullshit—like how I'm the reason Jaycie suffered. I'm the reason she's the One…or The Omega…or the Cataclysm…or some other ridiculous nickname for a God—as in, the Almighty *her*self.

I fought with them—Gabriel, Sagitarii, and Eris—and lost just in time to hear the gunshot go off. It was the second time I had heard it, and it hurt as much as the first.

When I was done grieving all over again, I wept for the emptiness. I was lost. I spent more than two decades watching Jaycie from beyond the Veil—and although my reflection hadn't aged, I was different on the inside—I was older, and jaded. All that time and effort, for nothing?

The ambulance pulled away, the suspension bouncing as it struggled through the snowy terrain, and we watched them from behind the Veil. There were fifteen emergency vehicles stashed in the snow, most with their lights still flashing. Sagittarii kept guard from a tree limb above, but Eris stayed close. She had her arm around me as we sat on the park bench near the observation bridge by the falls, while Gabriel digested every detail of the investigation.

For someone who claimed to know me, Gabriel knew jack-shit. Did he expect me to sit back and watch? A happy-go-lucky ray of fucking sunshine, and let the gunshot that destroyed our lives go off like it didn't matter?

"I'm sorry," I said. I was surprised they had forgiven me so quickly.

"There's no need for apologies," said Gabriel, though I caught Sagitarii grumbling under his breath. A bitter taste landed on my tongue—I didn't need an interpreter to tell me what he was feeling. "You are a predictable creature."

I groaned. "So, I've been told."

Then again, maybe he expected my outburst? I was learning to accept that Gabriel would never tell me everything.

"You were built differently," said Eris. Sagittarii shot her a glance from his perch. "You are...*more sensitive to love.*"

Yeah...the kind that burns when you pee...

A police car peeled away, sirens blared as its tires spun searching for traction. I remembered it from the other perspective—I was sitting in the back, handcuffed. It was a literal out-of-body experience, watching the broken-me stuffed into that car and whisked away to jail. I could hardly remember what happened after.

"*You try too hard,*" Jaycie once said. A memory I had tried to forget. That day in our apartment—the former, worst day of my life. "*One day, maybe you'll realize you were enough.*"

Am I enough?

"I only beat you," said Eris—sensing my emotions as I sensed theirs, on taste, smell, and sound—"because you wanted to be punished. You want all this to end."

Who wouldn't? As if I wanted this. As if I wanted my friends dead, my love dead, my life gone. *Die trying* sounded just as good an outcome as *save her*.

Did Jaycie deserve this? Did I? Even if my crime from a previous life led to this outcome, did we deserve all this pain? Why couldn't someone have stopped it?

"Where is God in all this?" I finally asked.

"I told you, Jacinda is The One," said Gabriel, as he and Eris made eye contact—unspoken words traveled between them.

"She wasn't always *The One*, was she?" I asked.

"No, she was not."

"What happened to the *Previous One*? How does Jacinda become *this New One?*"

Eris placed a hand onto my shoulder. "There are places like the Dream Lands, where imagination is reality," she explained. "Places like Fae, where magic is as common as the paper you use for currency. Existence is not a rigid concept, Tony. Ask the Oneiroi if their dreamscapes are real. Jacinda was not the first to carry the Dyad, but she is the only to have accessed the Dyad on this plane, even if she cannot control it."

"The *previous* One is gone," said Gabriel. "The Cosmic Scales could not balance the Dimension of Three with The One. The One had no opposite equal—at least, not currently—and the One's existence put everything within this dimension in jeopardy. The Holy Dyad was extracted from the *original* One a long time ago, and the One either ceased to be, or left our reality all together."

My stomach soured, and I had to stand. My knees trembled, and I felt the need to vomit up a string of curses that would have gotten me grounded for a year as a kid. Eris watched as I paced—the frustration bubbling over the edge of my already boiling pot.

"So, let me get this straight," I snapped, shooting a glance between Gabriel and Eris, as Sagitarii peeked over at us from his spot. "Because the One was almighty good, it had to go buzz off because some alien-space-scale said things were imbalanced. Jaycie, *somehow*, ends up winning the worst lottery prize fucking ever, as God, but nobody can do anything about it because it's happening on earth and, ya know, the *rules*. The secret gets vague-booked onto angel social media. Malus discovers the secret on his Twitter feed, but he can't do anything about it because Jaycie's got a pack of crows babysitting her at all times. Malus pulls some puppet strings on some 'roided up meathead. She suffers. Almost destroys the world. Cracks. Loses her mind. Gets manipulated by Malus to fucking kill herself, he snags her departed spirit, shoves it back into her body and is now trying to complete the Amazing Race, Ultimate Eden: Scavenger Hunt Edition so that he can become the next new One, all because of some stupid laws of balance? Why? Why does he want to be god? Besides the fact he's Skeletor-level evil? A fucking knockoff of every fucking Saturday fucking morning cartoon villain ever fucking created?"

The sun finally shed the cloud cover as I finished.

"I think you know," said Gabriel, calmly ignoring my rant.

Then it struck me like a ballpeen hammer to the back of the head. The pieces of the puzzle fell together to reveal the larger picture.

"Lilly. It has to do with Lilly."

Gabriel nodded, and Eris left the bench, joining Sagitarii as men in rubber suits entered the warehouse, dusting for clues.

"The fuck!" I growled and balled my fists. Chappy hushed me, but there wasn't any possible way I was going to maintain a level of calm. Not after that explanation, and certainly not after the gunshot.

"Everyone has a motive, Tony," said Gabriel, as Eris and Sagitarii began to argue in hushed tones. "Even Malus."

"He is *not* to blame," said Eris. My list of allies was growing shorter by the moment, and the scar on my face continued to itch—was it getting worse?

"Stupid question," I said, before unloading something monumentally dumb. "What's the worst that can happen if Malus becomes God? I witnessed the future. I saw the aftermath, the destruction—Philly was gone. The sun was blotted out, the purple sky, and those shadow things underground. But life survived. Can we save her and just give Malus what he wants?"

Gabriel waved his hand, and we were standing somewhere I never expected to be. A place that terrified me as much as it left me in awe.

He and I were standing on the surface of the moon, and the Earth below was volcanic with boiling seas and rivers of molten rock. There was air—or at least, I believed I was breathing air—and I did not feel hot or cold as we stood in the emptiness of space.

"Fear not," he said, placing both hands onto my shoulders and staring into my eyes. "I've taken the proper precautions. You will not freeze nor suffocate while you are with me."

"Comforting," I said sarcastically. "Is this the beginning?" Then a nefarious thought slithered into my brain. "Or the end?"

"The way this world began, and many others like it, is the same as how it will cease. There is much you do not know about this world and how it came into being. There are things more evil than Malus or demons, but that is none of your concern."

Gabriel began walking and I followed him. Our footprints on the moon's surface scrubbed away behind us, leaving no trace that we were ever there. We walked toward a great shadow, where the light vanished, and the darkness of space blanketed the moon's surface. We eventually came upon something that made the hair on my arms prickle like pins— a pool of water at the bottom of a dark crater.

"This. This," stuttered Jamaal, "is something."

At the center of the crater, standing on a small, isolated rock, was a flat panel of metal. Gabriel and I walked toward it across the water, and as the details came into focus, I notice that it was a door. It had a keyhole and was covered in runic glyphs I could not decipher—a surprising development. Up until now, I could read every language I came across, but why couldn't I comprehend this one? At the center of the black metal gate was an eclipsed circle with three vertical lines through it.

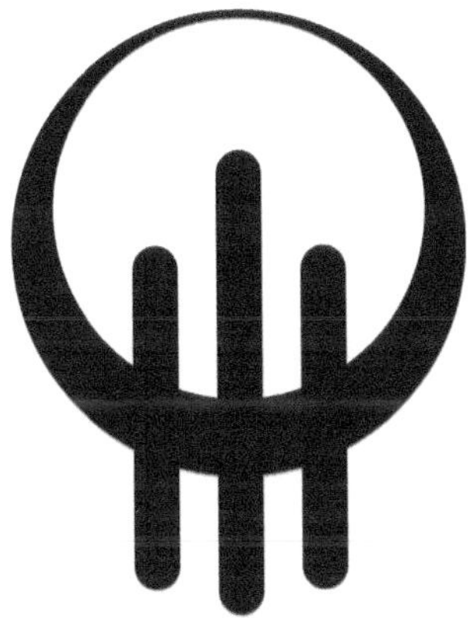

"Vetus Deos," said Gabriel.

"The Old Gods?" I questioned.

"Most refer to them as the Old Ones. This gate is locked by my key." From beneath his armor, Gabriel removed an ugly angular key made of what smelled like lead—and yeah, I can apparently smell lead—*in space*. It pulsed in coordination with the brass key in Gabriel's hand—*my key*.

"What's behind the door?" I asked.

The door was a magic trick. It stood in the middle of the rock, attached to no walls. How it worked was beyond my pay grade.

"A bad place."

"Wormholes," said Jamaal. "It has to be wormholes."

"Never seen a worm leave a hole like that, my man," said Montoya, and I could hear the audible slap of Jamaal's facepalm.

The door had no handle, just a slot at its center where Gabriel could enter his key. As I inspected the door further, there came three knocks, like a sledgehammer slamming against the hard, thick metal ore.

"What was that?" I asked. My blood went acidic. I was on the highest alert. It was impulsive, like that feeling in your knees when a giant wolf charges in your direction—never experienced that? Trust me, you don't want to.

"Three knocks," said Gabriel. "It's always three knocks. Human's inadvertently curse one another when they knock three times upon their neighbor's door. Not that humans believe in those things. They verbally curse at each other every day."

"How terribly naïve we must all appear to him," said Chappy.

"You mean to say," started Montoya, "when I say '*fuck you*' I'm actually cursing you with my swear?"

"Apparently," added Henry, glaring at me.

"Interesting," said Doshin.

Gabriel was waiting for me to ask, "Who's knocking?" as a terrible memory slipped into my mind. I had heard those knocks before—right after I killed Rick Jansen, and the paradox showed me a terrible glimpse of cancerous creatures overrunning the campus of Milton State University.

"*Like always, you have tunnel vision, man!*" Sid had said. "*You only ever see Jaycie. You never see the bigger picture. Sometimes you have to sacrifice for the greater good!*"

"Omens," replied Gabriel, snapping me back to the present. "Creatures so foul, so dark and twisted, their intentions so foreign to our own understanding, that it would shatter your perceptions of good and evil. They are our one true enemy."

"And the keys keep them locked away?"

"At the beginning, there was an object—a great all-powerful object called the Trapezohedron," said Gabriel.

"An object with twelve edges. The most common is the pentagonal trapezohedron which has ten sides," added Jamaal.

"Thanks, my man," grumbled Montoya. "I was just thinking to myself, gee how many sides does a Trapezo-hedo-thingie have? And sure enough, *you* had the answer."

"You're welcome," beamed Jamaal.

Gabriel continued, "It came from beyond with its masters, the Old Ones, and they used it to create terrible things."

"For what purpose?" I asked.

"Unknown. Beings that old, from a place so foreign to our own, we do not have a concept for their purpose." Gabriel gestured toward the Earth and sighed. "There was a great war, and we cast the Omens and the Old Ones out of this dimension but kept the Trapezohedron so that they might never find their way back. Gates were built to block the pathways to and from the various realms created within this dimension, and the Trapezohedron was shattered. From its pieces, we forged keys."

"How many keys are there?" I asked.

"Many. When the object shattered, each piece became an elemental shard of something it had created. Ice, Gold, Silver, Bone, Glass, Iron, and more—each were given a lock, and entrusted to a protector."

"I don't believe that," pondered Montoya. "Imagine a key made of grass. Or paper."

"Ugh," groaned Jamaal. "Stop saying stupid shit."

"Shit," agreed Montoya, "imagine a key made of shit. It's impossible."

"However," Gabe continued, "the object was shattered into so many pieces, scores of them were lost forever. There is no way to reassemble the Trapezohedron. Only a vast army could collect every missing shard."

Just as he finished, there came three more unsettling knocks.

"Are there other ways in?" I asked.

"There are. There are always other ways."

Three more knocks, louder now, followed by a hiss that put Gabriel on edge.

"What is it?" I asked. I could feel something, like a splinter poking me behind the eyes.

"Get down!" roared Gabriel, as something rebounded sharply against his armor. From the darkness of space, I saw the outline of something that had no shape. It was like proto-man got squirrelly with a starfish— a twisted form that was all those things and neither. My mind had no context to compare it against, and in a flash, it was gone.

Somewhere.
Now.

Gabriel had whisked us away to safety in an open field in the middle of nowhen and nowhere. It was, from what I could tell, the same field as the car crash from the time remnant future—only without the soup cans —and it felt contiguous with the proper timeline.

"What was that?" I gasped. I was out of breath. I had never seen anything so horrible that it extracted the wind from my lungs.

"That was an Omen. One of three assassins sent by the Old Ones to find ways to open the Breach between our world and theirs," said Gabriel. "When you ask what is the worst thing that could happen if Malus becomes the One? He could and would inevitably dissolve the gates that protect us from those beyond."

"If Malus gets the Holy Dyad," I replied, while plucking a tall piece of grass next to me, "I doubt he'd allow any of us to live long enough to see that."

"But it wouldn't just be our world, Tony," said Gabriel. "There are countless parallel worlds, and a few that remain like this one. If this world falls, they will beat down the door to the next, and the next, until we are all dead. It would not just be our world. It would be the lives of sextillions."

"Sextillion?" said Montoya with a grin.

"Bro," said Jamaal, "It's a number. Imagine a one followed by twenty-one zeroes."

"Daaaaaaamn," spat Montoya, as he sat soberly onto the ground as if he had lost balance.

"That's a lot of lives," groaned Chappy.

"All on our shoulders," added Henry.

"We can only account for our own shoulders," added Markus. "Best not to account for so many when *two* are all we have."

Doshin looked grave as he followed the conversation silently.

"Okay," I said. If I let myself examine it, the overwhelming numbers and the immensity of what was at stake was enough to cause a panic—but that didn't matter to me. "I know the world will benefit from stopping Malus, but I want to make sure you know—I do this for her. Not for some rando-Dean or Rudy in the next world. I do it for Jaycie."

Gabriel smirked and nodded. "Her fate, and the fate of the universe are intertwined."

It was so much information. It was like being dropped in the middle of a Tolkien novel and trying to figure out who was everyone's father, son, and cousin twice removed.

I sighed and looked up at the bright blue sky. I hadn't noticed how cheery and peaceful this place was, despite the memory it elicited. It reminded me of a place in the woods near my childhood home, and I was struck with the need for one more answer.

"One last question," I asked, and Gabriel eyed me curiously as I pointed to the key, *my key*, he was still holding in his hand. "What does my mother have to do with all this?"

VI

clauses

MALUS
Now.

"Malus," hissed Thanatos, as blackened bile dripped from his rotten lips, "your time has come."

Astoreth's grip on my neck had severed my spinal column. The Goddess of War dragged me from corridor to corridor, into what obscure corner of the underground city, I did not know, but the spirits swirled in warning.

A momentary release was all I needed—a minor fluctuation in pressure to reestablish motor functions—and I would tear the nearest god limb from limb.

The sounds of battle faded—Hekate and Morrigan fought on my behalf—stayed by Dagon as the others escorted me onward, toward some nefarious plot.

My blood left a trail as we entered areas of the city I had yet to explore—where rocky walls and pillars acquiesced into resin and organic structures. While I was preparing Jacinda for the coming end, they had been busy, searching the ruins and plotting their insurgency.

A draft of stale air brought an aroma. It was as peculiar as it was alluring, but not pleasant, drifting to me from beyond. The closer Astoreth dragged me toward the stench, the stronger my reaction, followed by a whispered shriek within the darkness ahead.

"Have you the wisdom to know what beast makes that awful sound?" whispered Astoreth, her grip unrelenting as she came to a stop and pointed my paralyzed body toward a grand archway. The pillars to either side of the entry were carved into the likeness of a great serpent, with tusks and fangs as large and sharp as a whole man.

"Grootslang," hissed Loki.

There was movement stirring beyond the arch. Something was in that room. Astoreth dragged me beyond the threshold and into the darkness where the wild shrieks suddenly ceased. Within the room was a shaft, evermore inky than the current darkness, its depths unfathomable with a narrow bridge made of resin spanning its yawning crevice. The shaft not only extended far below, but high above as well—both reaching beyond sight. The goddess dangled me over the edge, and for a moment I thought about escape—shifting my equilibrium and drifting toward the dark vastness above when something slithered.

It was a trap. A trap for celestials. To ascend or descend into the darkness above or below meant to confront the creatures that slithered in the darkness.

"What shall it be?" laughed Loki. "Release us from our contracts, hand me that fancy ring, and we won't drop you into the hole."

I smiled.

"Do you know what that is, boy?" said Thanatos, as Astoreth held me firm. "Does it make your stomach burn?" His ghastly yellowed eyes hovered over me as if he were apprising my sanity. "One cannot heal from a grootslang bite. Like the mongoose devouring a cobra, they are an apex predator above all, including our kind." Through the shifting slithers below, I caught a glimpse. Two great curled tusks preceding a massive, flattened serpent head lashing violently in the darkness. "Or perhaps, we are threatening the wrong flesh."

From the corner of my eye, Moloch enter the chamber through the arch carrying the unconscious body of our prize—Jacinda O'Neill. The bull-god grappled her by the neck and dangled her unconscious body over the edge next to mine—but where were the gods of fear and terror?

"If you do not capitulate," said Thanatos, rubbing at one of the many leather straps that kept his decaying form intact, "your plans dissolve with the girl."

I laughed again.

"If she dies," I gargled, blood spurting through my opened mouth, "none of you will get what you were promised."

"What is she?" demanded Astoreth. "What *is* the girl? Is she djinn? Is she Omen?"

"If only you knew," I whispered, and the grootslang's hissing shriek trilled as if eavesdropping.

Sometimes one must allow a charade to advance because the illusion of weakness provides ambition to those who are distrustful by nature. And sometimes, one must know when to end the charade and allow the weaker to know where they stand.

Astoreth had flesh as hard as stone—she could withstand extreme heat and her skin was incapable of being pierced—but when I twisted away, the elbow joint popped and dislodged. She was as soft on the inside as the rest of us.

When Thanatos came for me, the dead barred his path—whichever way he turned, they were there to prevent his advance. Phobos surged from the Veil like an arachnid and stole the girl from Moloch's grip as I took him by his great bull horns and crushed his jaw, then tossed him over the edge by a broken wrist. The bull god dangled into the pit just long enough for the creature below to strike.

Moloch roared.

The slithering beast below took an arm with one quick swipe and fell away, back into the darkness with its prize. I tossed Moloch aside— his arm never to return—slung a spool of the dead and watched as the ectoplasmic ball of rage ensnare Loki within the cold fury of a thousand tortured souls. They swept him through the air, ripping and gnawing at the tender bits, screeching, and wailing from beyond the grave. The impact pinned him against a grotesque face molded into the wall. With my free hand, I called a flaming spear and held it to Astoreth's throat.

They all stopped as the air froze with phantasmic rage.

"I…lost…my…daughter," said Loki, between great heaves. The spool of the dead kept him pinned.

"Your sacrifice is appreciated," I said, my broken bones completely healed.

"My sacrifice?" whined Loki. The dead probed every inch of his skin with intense pressure. "What would you know of my sacrifice?"

What would I know of sacrifice? Too much.

"Contract be damned," I growled after taking four furious strides toward his neck. "If not for our waning numbers, I'd cleave out your rotted heart!" The talons on my right hand dug into the flesh below his clavicle, but relented once they struck bone.

Our eyes flared—and I imagined the great pleasure I'd take in plunging my thumbs straight through them.

What would this pathetic creature know of true sacrifice? He was a madman—a mad god, whose twisted ambitions were ever evolving. He had no plans. He had no direction. He was like a child, following impulse. His children were pawns.

"Fuck you," he cursed.

I laughed. "We are all fucked," I said, turning to leave. There were things to do. Decisions to be made. Vacant contracts to fill…

"Where are you going?!" Loki demanded. "Where are you going!?"

"Away from this," I said. "A reminder, Loki, this is the second time you've tried to betray me. You will not survive another."

"Our numbers dwindle because you let this happen," growled Astoreth. Her elbow was so badly disjointed it was only now reattaching itself.

"Let this happen? I did not *let this happen*," I spat. "Need I remind you, it was I who employed *you* to get the job done! The spark escaped with the key because of *your* incompetence."

"Where is Bacchus?" whimpered Moloch, his massive upper body off balance without a left arm. Vapor chuffed from his bullish snout.

Bacchus's contract was voided hours ago.

"Dead," hissed the Morrigan. Her bare feet landed onto the stone floor, her head shrouded under her feathered cloak. "Witnessed. Burned. Bacchus is ash." She had wounds still healing from her scuffle with Dagon.

"Dead?" scoffed Loki as he removed himself from the weakened spool—without my anger to enrage them, the dead slowly melted away. "How could that happen? How could one with such a tiny light—a mere slight compared to our power—slay mighty Bacchus? Summanus was a sapling, but Mammon and Bacchus were great oak. Their names struck fear into the hearts of our own kind!"

"He is no spark," said Thanatos. He was the embodiment of quietus, a true living horror. To stare into Thanatos's eyes was to see one's own death, to feel one's spirit quake within their chest as his gaze wrenched it free. "We must reevaluate our enemy."

"Are you afraid?" I asked. "Are you afraid of death, Thanantos?"

"I control the dead! I do not fear that which I am master of!" he snarled.

"No, dear Thanatos," I replied. "I control the dead." Then I summoned an example of my might. The spectral rage froze the room with a snap, and the leather straps that held Thanatos's body together audibly contracted.

The tension in the room was mounting, and I would not relent.

"A spark, or something more, it does not matter," said Astoreth. The sparse light danced across naked body, glistening like diamonds. "However, five Fallen have died. How quickly can we reclaim our fearful number? How many of our Thirteen must perish before the next eight days pass? Perhaps the Host is working against us?"

Referencing angels set everyone on edge.

"The Host will not interfere," I said. "Of that, I am certain. They lost the girl, and even they cannot reclaim what was lost. They must remain spectators, watching fate sway over the world they were created to protect. We run amok, they tidy up—if they break the Treaty, the Pit empties, and all hell breaks loose—*so to speak.*" I smirked, just thinking of the chaos. "As for the spark, we proceed as planned." There was a motion for dissention amongst them, but I stopped it cold with a command written into their contracts and tattooed upon my skin—a Svefnthorn—a complicated series of four Norse characters I quickly traced with my forefinger and executed with the word, "Sleep."

All at once, those within the room fell into a deep slumber, resting until called upon. The ink soaked into my skin and disappeared. To use the Svefnthorn again, the tattoo must be reapplied. Like all magic, it took time to prepare. Using this magic here, now, was not what I had intended...

Nestled away from the sleeping gods was Jacinda. Our prize was sprawled across the floor taking shallow soft breaths. A peek behind the Veil showed Phobos and Deimos still spinning their psychic thread, mesmerizing her mind. While the gods of fear and terror deconstructed and destroyed the girl's memories, one by one, I contemplated my next move.

"Phobos," I called, and moments later the eye-less god appeared.

"What do you will upon me, master?" sniveled Phobos. If only they all had such respect for the beast who held their contracts.

"Confuse them," I said, gesturing to the sleeping gods. "Make them forget the last few hours."

Phobos nodded. "It will be done."

"Moloch is missing an arm. Give him another reason to hate the spark."

"It will be done."

I nodded toward the god of fear, he buzzed pleasurably like a wasp. I was content to leave him and his brother to their work, mesmerizing the girl's mind, when a chill ran up my spine. The presence—I could feel it once again. The invisible visitor.

Had Nemesis returned? Or was I being stalked by someone, or *something*, else?

I had walked the Earth from the eastern shores of Asia to the western coasts of Europe—I had even crossed the sea into the new world, when it was filled with nothing but the spiritual savages—and if there was one thing I learned above all else—trust my instincts.

I quickly moved into the Veil, ready to attack and found it empty.

"What is it, master?" asked Phobos.

"Do you sense another presence?" I asked. What creature could have tingled my sixth sense that I did not already command, or could not seize upon from behind the Veil?

"Phobos and Deimos are sensory incomplete," said Phobos, noting the obvious—he had no eyes or nose, while Deimos had no mouth— "but Phobos and Deimos do not sense anything—no lower, nor higher lifeform, incorporeal or behind the Veil, other than you, master."

And Phobos was right. There was nothing in the room but the sleeping gods. Had the pressure finally taken its toll? Were my senses betraying me?

I had already been betrayed…

Nemesis, once my most trusted, had knocked me off balance. The spark had my key—a key that was once in my grasp, with only days to go. If I couldn't find the spark and retrieve the lost key, everything would fall apart, once and for all.

Or, has it?

I examined the great hall, ignoring the screeching grootslang from the great shaft and admired the artistry tucked into every surface of this ancient city. Its language was beyond my understanding—not even the dead understood its meaning—but the beast inside urged me to crawl deeper.

The pathways through the city twisted like a colony of ants. It did not exist as a flat plane spotted by man-made structures, but instead consisted of layers and chambers, three-dimensionally clustered. The walls were uniquely sculpted, like the workings of a hive—stone and resin intermixed—with grotesque carvings of revered creatures set into the surfaces. As I stalked through these halls, winding deeper into the labyrinth, I realized how little I knew of this place, and for what purpose it was constructed. There was a method to every room—a significance I could not decipher. Power, almost imperceivable to my senses, flowed through the walls and into every obelisk and ziggurat, but from where? Why? What kind of power and could it be harnessed?

One could lose themselves entirely within the city. Was it more than just a holy place for elder gods? Was it a sanctuary? A home? Some passages felt menacing, as if meant for war...

The girl drifted along behind me, curried by Phobos and Deimos behind the Veil. She whimpered and whispered, lost within a dream. She would remain with me until the end—just eight days.

"Tony..." she mumbled.

What memory must we sever to unclench the hope she grapples onto? Would it be that easy? Hope, after all, existed in even the darkest of places...

The spark was resourceful in ways that defied logic. Was he monumentally lucky? Had he Leprechaun gold? My army had slaughtered gods—but the spark slipped away yet again. Together, my Thirteen and their armies were the most powerful collective of creatures on Earth, yet time and time again this one spark evaded us. How?

My mind was abuzz—but when I came upon something that did not belong, the noise silenced. Within the chamber I now stood was a series of braided electrical wires leading toward a dusty gas-powered generator. I had seen this before, but not so deep into the labyrinth. A strange device sat upon a tripod with gears and vials, pointed at a great obelisk marked with blood. At the center of the great obelisk was a relief carved into its surface—threads of crystal connected there, like circuitry—and resting in the crevices were the crushed remnants of stone. Red to the touch, like blood.

It appeared I was wrong—humans *had* dared to explore here.

"More plans?" said Lilly, speaking through Jacinda—her eyes open and swirling from green to the brightest blue. "Plans on top of plans on top of plans."

I ignored her, but she was right. If I had learned anything, it was that one can never be too prepared.

This place might hold the answers, but if I was successful, I wouldn't need them. I had eight days. I needed replacements. My Thirteen had been reduced to just nine active contracts. I needed powerful substitutes for Bacchus, Anubis, and the deadly Nemesis, and I needed them now.

The list of potentials was short and growing shorter after every enlistment. I needed precision, less ambition. A god or goddess looking for purpose. The War of the Gods had thinned the herd, and of those that survived, many had already signed my contract.

With the three Keys of Eden in my possession, recruitment started immediately.

Umai, the fire goddess, quickly agreed to my offer, and Bana, the thousand-arm demoness denied me—she died moments later, torn to pieces by the skeletal remains of the dead that surrounded her.

Hun-Tun, the emperor god of chaos—the faceless one—wasted no time accepting my proposal. Then perished, after an immediate attempt to double-cross me. Without eyes, I crushed his heart after voiding the contract.

The renown names were thinning, and some went missing without a trace—no clues as to where they went, or who they might have become. However, there was one that would challenge me and the terms of my contract, but worth the effort.

One that offered a unique threat against the spark.

December 23, 2013
Hamburg, Germany

Cults were the epitome of the weak. It always amazed me how feeble the human mind was when it yearned to belong. The need for connection so strong that they would believe in the absurd and risk their lives with religious fervor for what was often the plight of a madman.

I could not recruit this one alone, so I summoned Hekate and the Morrigan to assist me.

When we found the abandoned warehouse beside an old port channel at the edge of Hamburg, it stunk of brimstone and idiocy. Entering the building was easy, despite the wards haphazardly drawn in animal blood. We surrounded them from the shadows.

The room was wide, drafty, and the floor was covered in layers of dust. Scented candles lit the room with a flickering glow next to shelving stacked with grimoires bought from sunny bookstores with clerks in brightly colored smocks. The coven was a misguided bunch following recipes for sweet-smelling potions they believed were magic. Everything in the room was a mass-produced capitalist ruse, except for the idol placed at the center of the room—it was as ancient as my ring. It depicted the long-dead goat-headed demon, Baphomet.

Within the room were a dozen idiots, wearing blood red gowns and masks that ranged from elegant to grotesque, some still tagged with their store price. They were fools messing with powers they did not understand. We showed them mercy and prevented them from making a serious mistake by slitting their throats.

"Use their blood," I said to Hekate, then to Morrigan, "and their entrails."

We created a mark known for extracting a demon from the Veil and were just about to charge it with an invocation when the stench of brimstone made it difficult to breathe.

"Intrusive action not necessary," said the being sitting upon a chair in the corner. He was engulfed in shadow beyond the flickering candle-light. His voice was riddled with power, as deep and vast as the boom of his tone. Only the glow of his eyes could be seen in the darkness. "What do you want?"

"I'm here to offer you an opportunity," I said.

"What makes you think I am looking for opportunities?" he hissed. His rancid breath filled the room with its stink.

"Your followers mistook you for Baphomet," I replied. "You never corrected them. Have you no pride? Or too needy to reveal the truth?"

He laughed humorlessly. "It would be unwise to insult me."

"I come offering an opportunity. Consider it a welcome for a new arrival upon this plane."

The scent of anger fed into the room.

Hekate drew her claws as Morrigan went as still as stone.

"What would you know of me? If I am so new to this world, how would you recognize my usefulness?" he asked.

"So few angels fall these days," I explained, "which leads me to believe, you must have escaped the Pit, and that would mean you are as powerful as you are crafty." I stepped forward to show him I was unafraid. "I am in need of those skills."

"Perhaps," he said. He stood from his chair and took an equal step toward me. The shadows clung to him as he moved—he did not want to be seen. A simple demon's trick. "Perhaps, so powerful, I could gut you right now, take your women, your trinkets, and assume your role in the charade you sell? If I escaped the Pit, could I not do all that and more, with the same ease as I could squat and shit on your boots?"

Once the demon completed his threat, the dozen dead bodies of his worshipers stood and encircled him.

"The dead do not enjoy being lied to," I said. "What do you think they'll do to the demon that falsely took their adulation and sacrifice?"

The demon did not move. He brooded from within his personal shadow, weighing his options. Could he defeat the dead and the combined powers of three Fallen?

"True power is created, not acquired," he said. "We were not created equal, and those who proclaim it are doomed to be obliterated by those they envy."

"Why don't you try and obliterate me?" I sneered and he nearly obliged by wrangling me by the collar with a huge red fist, ruining my shirt. He held me aloft with one arm like he was holding a book.

"What is your offer? Let me decide if I shall assume your quest for myself, or let you live without arms and legs."

"The Holy Dyad," I said.

"Is lost!" he laughed.

"No, we found the Omega," I said, my feet dangling above the floor.

"Blasphemy!" he roared.

"I may be a lot of things, but I am no liar, Belial, Prince of Hell. You are in no place to assume my quest, demon."

The instant his name left my lips, the shadow around him dissolved. He no longer had power over me. Earth's latest resident, and current Demon—having fled the Pit—released my shirt and stepped back to defend himself.

Belial appeared as one might imagine a demon. He had not fallen to Earth in The Falling or during the first or second War of Omens, like the rest. He was cast into the Pit, then burned for a million years, while sitting upon his throne of fire and ash. His arrogance was excessive, and even now, after he was named and surrounded, he still wore a smile upon his face—one might assume he was Prince of Hyperephania—Pride. But his name did not reveal which circle he ruled. On his head grew a broken crown of onyx, which sat upon his greasy black hair and was bookended by two sharp horns that curled like a ram's. His skin was leathery, so reddish-brown it was almost black, with yellowish green teeth that grinned too often for its hideousness. His eyes were single rings of black with white irises, which hung on his face like two pale moons in the night sky. Belial's nose was long and hooked like a hag, and his ears were fanned and pointed with sprouting tufts of waxy fur growing from within them.

He was small for a Prince, but still much taller than I, and yet as formidable as any true demon. He was immune to hellfire, having roasted within it for eternity. When he shifted his weight, his hooves like smoldering charred bricks of coal, powdered the ground around him. His only clothing was a dark gray tunic, made of something thick, scaled, and leathery that did not burn.

"I was a Prince of Hell and commanded eighty legions of demons! Surely, amongst this floating rock of apes, it should be I leading your burden."

"You?" scoffed Morrigan. She rarely spoke, but her gray eyes always said volumes as they peeked out from beneath her hood—she was ready to fight for me. She was amongst those searching to devote themselves to something—to serve and protect, just as they had when they were angels. How sad—I was the replacement for the only duty she had ever known.

"Who else? A crow witch like you?" asked Belial, swaying back and forth, unafraid. "Or perhaps a Fae queen?" He nodded at Hekate, who remained still. "Or maybe the kitten?" He gestured toward me. I smiled in return.

"You may have been a Prince in the Pit, but you are merely a Jester here," I said.

"And who are you, kitten?" asked Belial.

"I am Malus."

"Ah, a moniker," said Belial. "A cheap replacement. Tell me, do you even know your true name?"

I smiled. "I do. And my name stays with me."

"Pity," said Belial. "I hate to waste talent."

In a blink, Belial tore apart the nearest two dead. Hekate, equally fast, lashed out with her claws, and raked the hardened flesh of Belial like ancient stone, leaving it unblemished.

Morrigan grabbed Belial from behind and raked her own diamond-sharp nails into his neck but found that she too could not penetrate his skin, while the heat of his flesh burned her.

Ignoring their attacks, Belial took down three more of the dead with one hand.

He was as advertised. A beast of strength, whether by arrogance or bravery, did not relent to anyone or anything. It was the enthusiasm I needed to destroy the spark.

When I drew my holy sword, it caught not only Belial's eyes, but made both Hekate and Morrigan withdraw in fear. I rested its razor tip against Belial's cheek, just below his left eye, then said, "shall we discuss terms?"

VII

birthright

TONY
Then.

"What happened?"

She was asking politely. Jaycie had the sweetest way of asking sensitive questions.

The problem was, this one cut like a knife. Despite the question being served without context, I knew what she was asking, and she had never asked it before.

We were driving back to Mercy Point from my dad's house through a winter storm. The flakes were falling thick and heavy, like we were traveling at warp speed as they whipped past the windshield, while the roads slowly turned white. We both had work in the morning and couldn't risk getting snowed in. I drove so that Jaycie could nap on the way home, and she was asleep before we merged onto the highway.

We were making it on our own, just the two of us, holding down jobs and paying our rent. She was booking gigs while I'd landed a position at a startup. Money was tight, but with each passing month, it felt like we were getting used to being grownups. As a kid, grown-up problems felt so foreign—like there was a great barrier one crossed from adolescence into adulthood. But that's not true. There is no barrier. One day you're running from class to class trying to hold down a part time job and a B average, and the next they shove a piece of paper into your hand and toss you out into the world.

But I never felt like an adult. I still felt like a kid, ill-equipped to handle the real-world terrors life could throw. If I had known what would come to pass, I would've answered her.

The trouble is, you think you have time...

We were deep into the mountains when she asked her question. I didn't know she was awake—her eyes were still closed.

"I thought you were asleep," I said, as she shifted in the passenger seat and opened her eyes.

"I tried," she yawned. "Either too tired or too stressed."

"Stressed?" I asked.

"About the snow," she admitted. Jaycie hated driving in the snow. For someone who grew up with Great Lake-effect snowfall every winter, she was as grumpy as a trash-can grouch every time the white stuff started falling. "Maybe we should've stayed. I could've called out sick."

"We'll be okay," I said, even as the car slid on a small drift that had crept onto the highway. "If it gets worse, we'll find a hotel."

Jaycie was already skating on thin ice with her boss, Linda, after coming down with the flu last month. The fact she was willing to miss work only further highlighted her distrust of the weather.

"Okay," she nodded.

I could feel her watching me, her face illuminated by the green dashboard light. "You didn't answer my question."

"What question?" I asked, pretending I hadn't heard her ask.

"What happened?" she repeated. When I didn't immediately respond, she clarified. "To your mom? There are pictures of her all over the house, but you and your dad never talk about it."

I took my eyes off the road to peer into hers, then impulsively looked down at the key around her neck where the chain disappeared beneath her shirt. She caught me doing it and knew it wasn't a casual glance.

"Why do you want to know?" I asked, and my throat tightened.

"Because it's a part of your past," she said. "And I want to know everything about you."

The snow colliding with the windshield was like visual white noise —like television static melting my concentration. I let the pause in my answer drift until it became a dramatic cliffhanger.

Eventually, Jaycie said, "Never mind. Forget I asked." Then she closed her eyes and fell asleep. Or at least, she pretended to sleep for the next few hours as I drove through the storm.

I wanted to tell her, but there was pain that couldn't be articulated with words. To speak them meant uncovering old wounds.

Was I the biggest asshole for not telling her? I didn't want to share those memories. I didn't want pity, and I didn't want to relive any of it.

I wanted her to understand. I wanted her to know I loved her and that there was nothing I wouldn't share with her...

...except that.

I needed to keep that for me.

January 1, 2007
Now.

"One last question," I asked, and the archangel encased in armor eyed me curiously.

Predictable creature, *my ass*.

I pointed to the key—my key—he was *still* holding onto and unburdened the question that had been eating away at me since all this craziness began.

"What does my mother have to do with this?"

Gabriel looked shocked. Was that question not on his bingo card? Not on today's itinerary?

"I apologize," he replied, "but I cannot divulge that information."

"Cannot, or will not?" I asked.

"Both." He smiled, and before I had a chance to respond, he pressed on. "Tony, I cannot impress upon you the importance of your journey. Self-discovery is a part of the path you must take to stop Malus. If you do not succeed, our world is doomed, and the Omens will flood into this dimension. The Cosmic Scales will not allow us to intervene without assured catastrophe. This is your penance, and yours alone."

As much as I had learned, I felt as if I knew nothing. Cosmic Scales? Omens? An unholy wedding in Eden? The scope was growing larger, and I felt infinitely smaller than I had before Zephon slapped me into the future.

"Where do I begin?" I asked.

"Wherever you must," said Gabriel. "You abandoned your natural timeline on December 23, 2013. You have less than eight days until the New Year. Malus has all the keys but the one around your neck." I looked down and the key was no longer in his hand but dangling from the chain beneath my shirt. "You cannot hide here forever. He will come for you. Your destiny re-starts the moment you step back into your natural time. Fate is waiting." Then Gabriel said something that chilled me all the way through. "If you walk the wrong path, there's a Devil Door in your future, Tony."

May, 28 1981
New Jersey

I had my suspicions.

I needed to know for sure.

Some mysteries were better left unsolved. This pain was so old, at the very root of who I was, that digging it up was something I never intended to do—until that nagging question at the back of my conscience finally concluded that it was right. Like a subroutine doing passive calculations until it finally discovered the truth.

.   .   .

The house was small and white with green shutters. The number 314 hung from the front door. It was an unremarkable house along an average street surrounded by equally unremarkable houses in each direction.

The trees in the front yard were flowering, and the curb was so full of cars that they extended down the street on both sides. It was mid spring, but unseasonably cold. A handful of children ran past, each carrying a balloon—red, yellow, blue. I approached the house in a trance and peered through the window from behind the Veil. There was Uncle Jack and Aunt Lena, and all the rest—a combined audience of people gathered around the proud family.

"Is that you, my man?" asked Montoya.

I nodded, "Martin and Carol Oscuro—my parents."

"Bro," said Jamaal, "This has got to be trippy."

"Dad looks so young, so proud, so totally unprepared for all that was set to come," I sniffled. "And mom—we lost her four years from now."

I couldn't believe I hadn't noticed it before—Mom's gray eyes and tan skin. She had changed, grown older, different hairstyle, but she still looked the same...

Henry and Chappy studied her close, as if searching for a mysterious connection, while Doshin, ahead of the pack, sighed and bluntly stated, "Your mother and Carina are the same."

Carina—the mysteriously vanishing angel who visited Jaycie periodically throughout her life. She wore the same key around her neck, while travelling through time on her way to...*where exactly*? Where was she going?

"...would you flee with me, to find an answer that might change the course of events?" Carina had asked Jaycie, far into the future—a ladies' room confrontation that changed the course of history. But what led Carina—*Mom*—here?

"How come I didn't recognize her?" I groaned. "My own mother?"

"Sometimes we see only the things we want to see," said Henry.

"And sometimes," added Markus, "we don't see them because we're not meant to see them. If she wanted you to know who she was, she would have told you." He was standing directly beside me in his legion-naire chest-plate and blood-red tunic, mimicking my stance.

Chappy stepped up to the window and peeked inside before turning to me, with the concern of a pastor tending his flock. "You lost your mother at a young age. You cannot expect to remember the kind of woman she was, even if you saw her again in the flesh."

"How'd they meet?" asked Montoya, gesturing to my parents.

"Dad always said they met by accident. He was in the Navy. She was studying abroad in Germany. She had a disagreement with someone at a market, and my dad stepped in."

"Yeah, that sounds totally normal," said Jamaal, oozing with sarcasm. "No possible way your dad wasn't about to be smited by some ancient god thinking he was doing the gentlemanly thing by rescuing the girl from an abusive bro."

"But now we know otherwise," added Chappy.

"She changed her name from Carina to Carol, got married, had a baby—*you*," said Henry as he pointed at me. "Raised you. Became a preschool teacher. Then disappeared?"

It was time to let go. If my brain-trust didn't know about my mother, it meant that I had an impenetrable wall around those memories. A wall that needed to finally come down.

"June, 1985," I said. I couldn't recall the exact date. I was hardly five years old when it happened. "My mother disappeared. I was playing in the living room. She was cooking dinner, when the fire alarm went off. Dad was out in the driveway, checking the car. Mom said it was stalling earlier that day. When he rushed into the house to pull the burning food from the stove, she was gone."

"That's it?" asked Jamaal.

I shook my head, but I couldn't stop staring at my mother through the window as she helped baby-me open presents. "She was missing for days, and Dad was out there looking for her every minute of it." I paused, as I remembered what came next. "One night we got a knock on our door. The police found a piece of clothing and some blood. They took us to the location. We were part of a search party. Dad probably shouldn't have taken me but I refused to stay home.

"We were looking for hours," I continued, "and we ended up in this clearing and dad goes stiff and whips me up into his arms, but I saw it. I saw her."

"I'm sorry, my man," said Montoya, as Jamaal placed a comforting hand on my shoulder.

It didn't take a psychologist with a dozen degrees like Doctor Hammond to know I clutched on to every female relationship because of my maternal abandonment issues.

"Mom said she didn't have family, except Dad and me. I grew up thinking my mom was hiding stuff from us. And now I know, she was hiding more than we ever knew."

"Did the authorities ever solve the case?" asked Henry.

"No. They never solved it. She was spotless. No wounds. No substances in her body. It didn't matter. She was gone," I said. Then a thought floated into my head. A repressed memory unlocked, like seeing her and this house decoded specific details that were lost in a discarded brain wrinkle. "I do remember something from that day. Mom left the kitchen and gave me a kiss. She slipped the key on its chain over my head and said it was the *key to her heart. Protect it.*"

"Too many mysteries," said Chappy. "Now that you know the truth about your mother's identity, what do you want to do?"

I shrugged a non-answer and shoved my hands into my jacket pockets. The air was cold, and I was feeling insecure about being there, like spying on my mother from beyond the Veil was somehow cheating.

"Where do you think she went?" asked Jamaal.

"I don't know," I said. "I'm not sure I care."

Henry glared in my direction, spotting an obvious lie.

"I don't want to know where she went," I growled, "and I don't want to do anything." I meant it. Digging up this part of my past was giving me nothing but grief. If my mother wanted to leave her family behind to do god knows what, I wasn't here in the past to stop her. She chose her path. I'm choosing mine. "Let's focus on the next seven days."

I waited for a response, but none came.

It was quiet, and still...too still...

The children playing outside weren't laughing, and the party noise within the house had died away. Peering back through the window, the party had stopped.

No, not stopped…

…it was *paused?*

"What's going on?" I said, and when I turned to the brain-trust—the seven of us crammed onto the stoop—nobody moved. They weren't breathing, even if it was imaginary lungs and air.

"We have time," said Markus—and I almost jumped out of my own skin. While everyone was frozen, Markus was miraculously unaffected.

"What?"

"We have time," he repeated, "to say hello to dear ole mum."

"What's going on?" I asked. This was trippy Professor-X level shit, and as far as I knew, mutants were still a comics-only thing.

Markus gave me a polite, "Excuse me?" with a befuddled look. "Oh, this?" He gestured around him.

"Yeah, this," I grumbled.

"This is nothing," boasted Markus, like it was akin to blowing a nose or whistling. "We can all do this. Each of your brain-*trust*. It's what you might call a…*time out?* Have none of them created a time-out before?"

I shook my head and said, "No. Why?"

"I apologize," said Markus, as if suddenly realizing how intrusive this was. "I initiated a small mental…*powwow?* Is that the right word? What the bloody hell is a powwow? Sharing a brain has been a challenge. I never quite know if I'm using the proper phrasing."

"Why?" I nudged, and realized how frustrating I must be to the others—do I ramble like this? Markus shrugged, like he was trying to express something delicately without knowing where to begin.

"As a new member of your *trust*," he began, then paced around the yard, hopping over the flowerbed along the front walk, "you do not know me as well as I would like. I too lost a mother when I was very young, and when provided the opportunity to speak with her one last time, I do believe I would seize the chance before it was too late."

"It's more complicated than that," I replied. "If we step out of the Veil, we set off a Paradox."

"Surely," he said. "I merely wanted to say, we have ten minutes to spare, if you wanted to change your mind. I mean, after all, how many times does an opportunity like this arise?"

"Noted," I said, and expected Markus to snap his fingers and fairy-godmother the natural order of time back into action. Instead, he sat there watching me watch my mother with a perplexed look on his face.

"You have abandonment issues, my friend," he said.

I shot Henry a look, but he was still frozen in place, watching my family through the front window. It sounded like something I expected of him, not a Roman soldier.

"Gee, ya think? Were you, like, Caesar's shrink, or something?" I asked—it was passive aggressive, but Markus hadn't received the message.

"I only mean to say, you lost your mother, then Amanda, Tori, and Jacinda. It's no wonder you are insecure."

"Are you trying to make me mad?" I asked. There was nothing worse than an armchair therapist digging away at your psychosis as if they were blatantly obvious to everyone—even *if* it was blatantly obvious to everyone.

"I've seen your dreams, Tony," said Markus. "Not the ones with the devilish door—the *other dreams*."

"Am I supposed to be discussing my dreams with my imaginary friend?" I asked. "Isn't that like discussing a distaste for creepy clowns with Pennywise?"

"I suppose," said Markus, though I couldn't be sure he understood my reference. "All I mean to say is, maybe the best path forward is to let go. Let go of the pain. Let go of Jacinda. To be truly free of it all, whatever the cost."

A handful of seconds passed in silence, and just as I was about to ask if we were done—

"Seven days?" said Montoya—picking up where we had left off— then he grimaced at the math inside his head. "Merry Christmas, my men." It was Christmas Eve, December 24.

I had disappeared from that timeline on the evening of the 23rd, which meant I could only go back moments after I left or cause a paradox—so said the rules.

After a long pause, Jamaal said, "We are all we have to get through this."

Chappy bowed his head in prayer, as Henry sighed then removed his glasses and cleaned them with his handkerchief.

"What's the plan?" asked Markus.

"Where do we start?" I asked, scratching at the scar.

"If we run, Jacinda's dead," said Jamaal, thinking aloud. "If we fight, we're dead."

"One on ones are tough, but a Thirteen on one is dumb as dirt," said Montoya.

I was expecting Doshin to speak up and offer a proverb that would mark the beginnings of a plan, but even he was lost gauging the impossible odds.

"Shame we can't take them out all at once," babbled Montoya. "This one time in the jungle, we spotted V-C trying to cut us off. We set up a bottleneck and I rigged some C-4 to detonate in a series of—"

As Montoya rambled about another war story, I remembered something important. Something that made me light up like an inflatable Rudolph yard display. I interrupted with a shit-eating grin that made Jamaal wince. "—I have a plan."

I turned back to the party, to give my parents one last look, when something caught my mother's eye. She looked at me as if she could see us behind the Veil.

I had my answers. My mother was Carina, the mysterious woman who helped guide Jacinda. The First Key of Eden was an heirloom given to me three decades before it was taken.

She excused herself from the party, and made her way to the front door, but before she could step through and confront me, I was gone.

MALUS
December 24, 2013
Africa
Now.

Nothing is ever lost. Information can always be found if one knows where to look. Threaten to crush the skull of an ifrit with the combined pressure of a dozen desperate, wailing souls—and he'll spill the name of his own infernal mother.

When I arrived at my destination, somewhere between Cameroon and the Benue River, many miles from the nearest village, a dark-skinned man was standing at the intersection of two dirt roads. It was hot, and as the beads of sweat began to soak my shirt, the man appeared unbothered by the sun. Surrounding us in all directions was one of the deadliest rainforests on Earth, the jungle as thick as the humidity. It grew all the way to the road's edge and stopped, as if repelled by the empty dirt.

"Greetings," said the stranger. There were two large serpents winding through his legs, slithering through the powdery sand—both hissed as I approached. "You are not from Cameroon, pale man." He was dressed in a simple loincloth and a held an old wooden spear at his side. He appeared young—

—but, so did I.

"Indeed, I am not from Cameroon," I replied, and the stranger grinned.

"You have come to a place that is neither here, nor there," he said, gesturing to the crossroads with his left hand. "If you are searching, you have come to a place between. May I help guide you?"

"Perhaps," I said, maintaining a distance. Crossroads, like these, were mysterious. Mischief and evil hid at the jungle's edge, like portals to other worlds waiting for reasons to enter our discussion. "I am looking for someone."

"This place is between, and you wish to waste the opportunity searching for a *someone?*"

"Who I seek is my business."

"Ah, but it is business I seek," he said, with a mischievous twinkle in his eye.

"What is the cost?"

"That all depends on who you seek."

"I seek Mr. Ash." I smiled and let the anticipation linger. "Though, he goes by another name. Eshu."

The stranger laughed, exposing a pristine set of teeth. "Ha ha! You are a funny one, pale man."

"What is so humorous about my request?"

"Because what you seek is not for sale."

"I am not looking to purchase. I have a proposition."

"Do tell, pale man."

"Do you speak for Eshu?" I asked.

"I speak," he shrugged, "and listen." He regarded me for a moment, and the serpents at his feet hissed in disdain. "Speak your business, and maybe I tell Eshu when I see him."

There was magic in the stranger's words. The ifrit had warned me that this one had a gift for speaking like a spider spinning webs.

Webs took time to spin, and I was in a rush.

The three dozen dead men and women, unfortunate souls who passed, their lives taken at this intersection, heard my command and latched onto the stranger, tossing aside the serpents, and dragged him to his knees.

"What is this trickery!?" he shouted.

"I am sick of games."

"If you are so sick of games, then why do you seek a trickster?"

"I seek no mere trickster," I said. "Is Eshu merely a god of tricks? I seek the god of discord." At my request, the dead increased their pressure, driving him down into the dirt.

"Eshu *is* more than mere tricks," said the stranger, his voice as deep as a panther's growl.

"Thus far, Eshu has only shown tricks. Perhaps he should emerge so we may discuss proper business."

"You do not scare me," he said. The sand beneath the stranger parted and swallowed him.

The dead scattered, searching for flesh to spoil, but the stranger was gone.

"Eshu!" I shouted. "I am here to speak business. If you do not wish to confer with my offer, I shall tear this crossroad apart and trap you here!"

"I know who you are, pale one."

As sure as I was ancient, the man stood behind me, miraculously transformed. He wore an agbada with colorful black and red geometric patterns, and a stone necklace worthy of an African king. His meager staff was now polished wood and carved into a winding snake with a blue metal blade that erupted from its mouth. His face was young, but his long-braided hair and beard were both streaked with more silver than black.

It was Eshu, god of chance and discord—a trickster—but unlike his counterpart, Loki, Eshu was honorable and wise. He was the perfect candidate to maintain balance. A loyal wildcard amongst a collective of egocentric deities.

"Do tell, Eshu," I replied. "Tell me, who am I?"

"You are the Two-Eyed Man. Now you are the feared. The leader of Thirteen," he said.

The monikers amused me.

"Then you know I only accord with those worthy of my time."

"Tell me, pale one," he said as the skies clouded over, "what need of you for another trickster?"

"Currently, I am plagued by a trickster who is more concerned with blood and revenge than subterfuge and mischief," I replied.

"If I join you, what would you offer in return?" he asked.

An offer? Most signed my contract for revenge, or with a lust for chaos—the destruction of the status quo was an aspiration amongst the most ambitious Fallen. Offers typically involved studying initiates and learning their secret desires, but time was limited.

"If you sign my contract, you will have the opportunity to destroy your enemies."

"Tempting, but useless. I have no enemies."

"Riches then? What is your price?"

"What need of I for riches? I am revered as a king."

"What is it you want?" I asked.

"I think it would be fair to share in the spoils of your quest." Then he added, "Equally."

"How do you know the spoils will be worth sharing?"

"I am a trickster. I am aware when I am being manipulated."

"I often find that tricksters…" I said, while spinning on my heel—and snatching the true Eshu by the throat as he leered behind me. "…are the ones who manipulate." I squeezed Eshu's throat, cracking his neck under the pressure.

Illusions? Did he truly believe I would fall for something so… *common?*

He smiled with a full mouth of pearlescent teeth and held his hands up in defeat. I relinquished my grip and shoved him away. Eshu staggered backward and readjusted his crushed windpipe with a crackle and pop.

"Every then and now," he said, followed by a dry cough, "one comes along who can see through my tricks. I have found that it is not a higher perception, nor an acute acumen, but rather experience that guides the hand through subterfuge."

I was beginning to feel like I had contracted the wrong trickster, long ago—Eshu was not a mad god, but an academic studying patterns and behavior.

"Perhaps you are no bully," said Eshu. "Perhaps you are a leader." Eshu then paused before pacing back and forth. "I do not desire much. I have my freedom and my health." He coughed again, right on cue. "But there are yearnings. Yearnings from deep down. Yearnings from the old days that I surely do miss."

I laughed and groaned. "Before me, the god of discord, the god of chance and fortune, is one that wishes to be back under *His* rule than to be his own god?" I petulantly pointed to the sky. "You are no mighty Fallen. You are a pathetic sycophant."

"I may be a lot of things, pale one, but I am no sycophant." He smiled, but it was not smug in nature. "We were made to serve, but as willing participants. Free will was not just for humans, but for us as well. We chose to leave. We chose to fall. We were lucky enough to avoid the Pit. Without serving our purpose, we will forever be aimless wanderers."

"What do you know of wandering?" I asked, smothering my anger.

"There was a story. A story told by men... and sometimes Fallen," said Eshu as he circled me, casually poking his spear into the soft sand. The skies continued to darken, an approaching storm, but the wind and rain had yet to arrive. "The tale tells of a man, *or demon*—depending upon the teller—who lost something he could not live without. The man, destroyed by grief, traveled from one end of the earth to the other, in search of that which would make him whole once more. He traveled from village to village, city to city, to underworlds and through the necropolis. He even caused a war between gods. High and low, near and far, he searched for many lifetimes. His loss was so great, his heart turned black, and he did not age but for the hair atop his head. They called him the Pale Demon—his white hair was as empty as his soul. Then, one day, like all stories, it became legend, and the Pale Demon was gone. Some thought he had found what he was searching for. Others believed he had finally ended his life. But, I do not believe either."

"What do you believe?" I asked.

"I believe he stands before me, with an offer. If I help him obtain that which he seeks, he will in turn help me gain that which I seek," he said, without a hint of scheming. "There is no simpler deal than that, Pale Demon."

It was then I felt the disturbance. Like an earthquake within the very core of my being. Like a tuning fork within my chest was struck with the wild swing of a hammer. The nearing storm was not a storm after all, but a portent. An omen. A message.

"What is it?" asked Eshu. "Something is not right."

Before me came a vision. A doorway made of aged bronze, adorned with intricate figures meticulously cast into the metal, struck by not one, or two, or even three, but four bolts of lightning consecutively.

"I am being summoned," I said. "Do we have a deal?"

"If my terms are met," he said, "yes."

"The deal is done, Satarcept." When I spoke his name aloud it was like a verbal blade had been driven through his gut. He looked upon me as if he had struck an unfortunate, if not accidental, deal with a devil.

His contract burned into my skin, the ink detailing the stipulations as we struck them—what I seek, in return for what he seeks. Then the dead lashed out and took their tender—a few drops of Eshu's blood, from a small cut across his regal arm. Contract signed and sealed.

"Now, we must go," I said as the wind brought a deluge of rain.

"Go where?" he asked as I strode away toward the jungle's edge. The god was still in shock. He thought he had struck the perfect deal, but he never anticipated that which he did not know. How amusing—a trickster tricked. "Pale Demon, where do we go?"

"Call me Malus," I said, "and we go far away from here."

THE LUSTING OF THANATOS

1347 A.D.

Ercan was a young boy. He was ten if he was even that old. He was short, but lanky, and his face was round and disproportionately youthful. Only days ago, he was playing in the streets with his brother, laughing and carrying on like young boys do. Now he was running from the terror that stalked him. His body was stressed to the brink of collapse, but he would not fall. He kept running, as far away from the creature as his weakened legs could take him.

The city of Antioch had been abandoned as the Black Death's infection spread from the Middle East into Europe, and at its center was a creature who had survived the War of the Gods. It had decided to leave its mark upon the world, unopposed. Harvesters, reaper angels, knew more about disease than any other creature that ever lived, and eventually the understanding of manipulating virus and bacteria became as easily molded as wet warm clay.

The residents who stayed behind as the city emptied were the families of those who were already sick. Those who would not abandon their loved ones in their time of need. Before long, the plague took them as well.

Ercan, however, was not sick. He alone survived. In fact, he was one of the rare—the immune—that could not be infected by the disease.

His mother, her neck swollen to twice its size, began to vomit blood, and the tips of her fingers were turning brown. Ercan knew the end was near. He ventured out for fresh water before dawn and when he returned, he found his mother dead and the cold eminence of reaping stilled within the room. Above his mother, standing upon the ceiling and savoring the succulence of death, was something so terrifying that the boy had no context with which to grasp it.

The creature held a sickle and used it to pry apart his dead mother's bloody lips, before gently kissing the dead flesh.

Ercan ran. He ran from the house and into the empty streets, passed running pools of blood, and leapt over the dead bodies that had been left to rot.

When his legs could not continue, when he had exhausted all available energy, the boy stopped and hid within an abandoned market. Ercan ducked beneath a table that once sold fresh fruit—owned by a family friend who had always been kind to him—and remained there, terrified and crying. He was alone. He was cold, and there was nobody out there to protect him from the evils of the world.

There was nobody there to protect him when the monster's sickle pierced his stomach and pulled him free from beneath the market table. Dangling in front of the beast, dying on his blade, the boy closed his eyes and lived no more.

Thanatos smiled as he sent Ercan into the next life, removing yet another immune from the path of his diabolical plague. Then he discarded the child's body on the street, to decompose and spread infection. No sooner had the body touched the ground when the rats scurried out of their holes and began to nibble on the fresh meat.

Thanatos, the god of death, was rot and decay. He was dead flesh held together by fastened leather straps. Living putrescence. His skin was covered in a mucousy, oozing sludge—he was a living disease. He was the embodiment of the undead.

"Thanatos," spoke a meek voice from behind the monster.

When Thanatos turned and saw the deathly specter of the boy he had murdered moments before, the god was perplexed. That which he reaped did not haunt. That which he reaped was either consumed or delivered to the next world.

"You have been reaped, boy. Move on from this realm. Do not befoul the beauty of my pestilence," said Thanatos, his voice like an echo. The god flashed an angry grin, exposed rotted teeth that were more green than yellow, with bleeding ulcers that dribbled down his lip and chin.

"My master asked me to offer you an opportunity, but first he must know what you desire, so that he may offer a deal you cannot refuse."

Thanatos eyed the boy for a moment, then lashed at him with his sickle. The blade cut through the ghost, tearing apart its constituency, and melted it into a fading reverie. Thanatos turned to leave, but the boy reconstituted before him.

"My master wants you to consider his question. What do you desire, god of death?"

"If your master seeks an answer, he may ask the question himself," said Thanatos, who turned once again to continue reaping. But Malus was already there, standing in his way.

"What is it that you desire?" asked Malus, puffing on a cigarette.

"Tar, formaldehyde, cyanide, arsenic, and those are just the toxicants I can identify," said Thanatos as he examined Malus and the cigarette.

"Do I detect judgment from a creature whose skin rots from its bones?" Malus replied. "I am in a unique position to offer you anything you desire. If you help me attain my goals it shall be yours."

A dark grin moved across Thanatos's face, and Malus began to wonder if this selection to join his Thirteen was intelligent one, given the god's ability to survive the war that had nearly destroyed them all.

"I have proceeded over the deaths of many things," said the Harvester. "I have watched putrefaction absorb the purity of beauty. Though I have never tasted the decay upon the lips of absolute perfection."

"A woman? A man?" asked Malus.

"A goddess," corrected Thanatos. "The perfect goddess. Zaria."

Malus pretended he did not know the goddess, but he knew of her all too well.

"If the great Thanatos helps me achieve my end, I will help him take the goddess to do with as he chooses," bargained Malus.

"She spurned me," said Thanatos, speaking from somewhere dark. "I inspired revulsion within her. I shall very much like to watch her spoil like a withering rose. That is a taste I would go to great lengths to savor." His eyes began to flutter as he thought of the foul dark things he had fantasized with Zaria. "That is what I desire, stranger."

"You shall have it, but first you must sign my contract."

VIII

the black god

MALUS
A voice.
Then.

The boy was an outcast. He was considered a freak.

Heterochromia iridium. To have two different colored eyes was a rare form of abnormality. Those afflicted with any abnormality in the ancient world were accused of everything from worshipping evil to witchcraft. The boy was no different.

If the villagers knew the truth of his affliction, they would have revered him, but that is a tale for another time...

People fear the outsider. They fear the different—the things they do not understand. When they fear, they hate, and when they hate they attack. This has always been humanity's biggest flaw. They were all born with red blood, one heart, two lungs, and even bones made of the same genetic compounds, and yet, it was the smallest differences on the outside they were concerned with most.

Humanity was doomed.

Doomed to self-destruction.

The hunting mutts barked, marking the boy's arrival. Dragging his trophy through the village gates left the guards who witnessed it with jaws agape. The boy was confident he was to be revered and respected. As one of the guards ran off, he dragged his trophy into the center of the village and drank from the hunter's trough—reserved only for the greatest of their tribe.

Even in the scarce light of dawn, the stag's fur was whiter than a summer cloud. Its skull was the combined mass of five men, with antlers so big and wide that it barely fit through the path to the firepits.

He may have spent all night dragging the stag's head through the forest on a gurney of his own creation, but he never once felt the sluggish retreat of strength or the burning eyes of exhaustion calling him to sleep. All he felt was the need to drink—to quench the thirst that burned his throat since eating the stag's heart—it was like digesting fire, the way it burned him from the inside.

Do you understand now? Do you understand his sin? Have you figured it out?

Of all the immortal sins he had acquired, this was his first—and it was by far the worst, if judged upon the price paid for his misdeeds. He was a boy. He did not understand the world, let alone the unwritten laws upon which nature was governed. He had not traveled over the mountains or witnessed the ocean— he had yet to live! And yet, his sins were too great, too nefarious, too wicked to overlook. Ignorance is a sin. Think on that, Tony. The lack of one's own knowledge, experience, and understanding is a sin! Why are we to believe Their laws when they cast such blatant hypocrisy!

Oh, weep for the boy, Tony. Weep for his ignorance. He knew not what he was doing.

The Fates could have taken pity. They could have looked the other way. Instead, they chose inaction, and by inaction they chose to punish.

How much can one person lose before they shatter?
Have you figured it out, Tony?

After drinking from the hunter's trough, the awaited the inevitable—imagining a feast in his name! Oh, how he thought they would mark this day as the greatest hunt the village had ever seen.

He was hot with excitement, imagining what Lilly might say when she saw him next to the stag. He was the man who slayed the biggest beast in all the forest—not Rorik, not Aran, not Lethan or Kaspar—

It was him.

These were his thoughts as he consumed the water from the trough. His stomach had not soured, but the fire inside had spread from stomach to bone, and from bone to skin. Sweat beaded from brow to toe and soaked his tunic. A panic set, and he plunged his head into the trough to cool the burn—but when he removed himself from the water, its surface still rippling, something odd caught his eye in the reflection. Something that stood out against the dark surface of the water—something *unexpected*. The shock of it sent him stumbling away from the trough and he fell backward into the mud.

It could not have been real...

Reflections. The world is full of lies, but reflections must tell the truth. Interpretation is, as always, open to debate. However, facts are often misrepresented by those who wish to control a narrative. Mirrors are the only tools we have to steal the truth back from those who wish to harness it as a weapon. Remember that, Tony. A reflection always tells the truth.

His youthful understanding of what he saw was limited, but the fact remained that in his reflection, albeit the rippling water of a dirty trough, he had fundamentally changed.

From his head, where once was a dirty mop of brown was now a burst of platinum hair—and although he was too young, too inexperienced to understand what had transpired, it was evident: killing the stag and eating its heart had changed him.

· · ·

When Kasimir arrived, he stalked toward the boy, ready to cast him out of his village once and for all—no more refuge for the boy who'd attempted to kill his future son by marriage.

But when he saw the head of the dead stag, he stopped where he stood.

He would not come any nearer. He was frightened. The man who gave the orders to slaughter the boy's people was frightened...*of him.*

The commotion of the boy's arrival and the great stag's head roused nearly half the village, even Lilly, and she was unable to avert her eyes from him. For the first time in his life, the villagers noticed him—not with disdain, but with fear.

A long silence overtook the growing crowd as the fog rolled in, having followed the boy all the way from the depths of the forest. It was a cold fog, as cloudy and white as the great stag's fur, and just as thick. It surrounded them, and the boy's pulse quickened—something was not right.

"What is this? What have you done?" asked Kasimir.

"I have slain the most magnificent stag in the forest. I have proven I am the best hunter of my age," said the boy.

Lilandra eyed him curiously. She knew his intentions.

"No, you have cursed us all," said Kasimir. His voice trembled as he grabbed hold of his youngest daughter to give her comfort—she was weeping. All the women wept, but the boy was confused. What had he done to curse the village? He slayed the greatest stag they had ever seen, and had committed a cardinal sin?

They were taking his greatest triumph away from him.

"The white stag is sacred," Kasimir explained.

"What have you done?" whispered one of the villagers.

"I do not expect an outsider to know our teachings," continued Kasimir. "Belobog will be displeased. We must show Belobog that we do not condone your actions but condemn your sacrilege."

"How would I know your teachings?" spat the boy. "You have not taught me!"

"Burn it," growled Kasimir, and four men stepped forward, marching toward the head.

The boy tried to intercept them—to stop them from destroying the trophy he had brought them—but three others pointed spears at his chest.

The men dragged the massive stag's head into the fires—but not without great struggle, as if the stag's head was made of dense stone. The moment the carcass touched the flames it stifled, as if the head were incapable of burning—then, with a great burst of black smoke, the head flared and was consumed. Nothing would remain but the ivory antlers that rose from the ashes like lightning. The black smoke lifted into the sky as the fog darkened, encompassing them from all sides.

"Now," said Kasimir, "burn him."

At their chieftain's command, several hunters grabbed the boy and dragged him toward the fires.

It was then, when the end seemed nigh, that the boy sensed doom—not from the fires, but a souring taste that made the bile rise from his guts—there was movement from within the fog.

Doom was coming.

While all eyes were focused on the boy and the punishment rendered, the burning stag and the sin that cursed them all, nobody saw the dark shapes in the drifting mist.

"What have you done to your head?" asked Rorik. "Witchy eyes *and* witchy hair?" His laughter was cut short by a horrifying scream.

The villagers did not know where to look—in the direction of the scream or at the boy who had ruined them all. They were caught between the terror, spectating a moment too long.

"Mama?" said a young boy at the edge of the circling crowd. "Where's my mama?"

Another scream. This time from the opposite side of the village.

Then another.

The petrifying confusion lasted until someone from the inner circle was plucked away and dragged into the fog. The morning sky blotted out as the fog became as dense as snow. The village warriors assembled to face the demons in the mist, their spears lowered toward unknown assailants.

Minutes passed and everything fell silent. The skies darkened like twilight, and a scarce trickle of light emanated from the dwindling fire as the carcass smoldered. The fog had blanketed every corner of the village but the fires, as the remaining villagers huddled close for its warmth.

Kasimir lifted his hands into the air to address his people. "We have been cursed," he said, "and we are being punished. We must appease Belobog and beg for his forgiveness!"

The boy stole a glance at Lilly and found her eyes set upon him with antipathy and fear. When the boy bowed his head, avoiding her eyes, he caught sight of something slithering across the ground. Was it a serpent? A snake weaving in and out of the legs of the crowd?

"What shall we do?" asked a villager.

"After we burn the outsider, we must offer a sacrifice!" shouted Kasimir.

The snake was not a serpent. A misty tendril made fog lashed out and twisted through Kasimir's legs and torso. Then, with a mighty tug, it ripped him away from Nastia and Lilandra, right out of their unsuspecting arms. He was flung high into the air and disappeared into the darkness, never to be seen again.

Seven villagers were taken the first day.

After Kasimir, the fog retreated into the forest, hovering in the wood just beyond the trees and bordering all sides of the village, waiting.

The boy was bound by the wrists to a pike at the village center and left for dead, while the Elders gathered to debate their options. Most argued that he should be killed at once—while others argued that Kasimir demanded it and Belobog prevented it, by taking their chieftain's life.

In the end, the boy wasted away in the mud, bound and hungry.

Villagers spat on him, while others threw rocks and refuse—it was worse than it was when he was just the Raggy Boy, the village ward. But that was not the worst of his punishment.

As the gloom darkened from day to night, he could hear Lilandra's sobs as she mourned her father's death. The one creature he cherished, the one person he could not lose, now despised him most of all.

And in his sorrow, the boy prayed for the very first time...

"Please," he begged, "Belobog, punish me. Take me now and spare her. Spare Lilandra any more pain." He prayed all night to Belobog, to release him from life—to punish him for his sins, and for slaying the stag that was one of the god's blessed creatures—but Belobog did not listen, and the boy remained alive despite his penance.

That night the fog returned and took seven more villagers while they slept in their beds.

Not even the dogs sensed it coming. The boy tried to warn them—he could hear it, smell it, feel it coming as it drifted to the very edge of the village. He screamed a warning, but the fog stifled his words and stole them from the air. Bound to the wooden pike, he begged Belobog to show mercy, to take him in their place, but the god did not listen. He did nothing to prevent the death and suffering, and eventually the boy stopped pleading and offered his rage instead.

"I will kill you!" he threatened into the night. He was mad, feverish, and raving like a lunatic. "I will hunt you down, and I will kill all of the gods!"

Each night the fog returned to claim its allotted seven. Despite the efforts of the Elders to save their people, they could not stop the fog from reaping its chosen. Mothers came to visit the boy on the morning of the fourth day, begging him to ask Belobog for forgiveness.

"Ask the White God to take you and spare our people. Tell him that it was you who sinned against him!" they cried.

But the boy did not answer. He laid in the mud, bound to the pike, and awaited death.

On the fifth day nobody came to beg for mercy. The once-thriving tribe was reduced to half its number. Whole families abandoned the village, slipping away before morning, hoping to find salvation over the mountain. All of them returned before noon the same day, stumbling upon their own village having left headed west, and returned coming east. The fog played tricks upon their minds and led them back to where they came.

No one could leave. There was no escape from what was to come.

On the sixth day, weak and delirious, the boy awoke with Lilly standing above him. Her eyes were red and sore, and streaks of tears still glistened her cheeks.

"Why did you do it?" she asked. "Tell me. Why did you kill the sacred stag?"

"I did not know it was sacred," he cried. "I only thought to prove myself to you. I never meant to cause you pain."

"You did. You caused me great pain. You caused us all pain."

His head sagged, and he sobbed into his bound fists. "Lilly, please forgive me," he begged, but when he lifted his eyes to look upon her, she was already several paces away.

Sometimes, Tony, the very best intentions pave the road to Hell.

· · ·

Seven.

It was revealing how much significance there was in numbers. There was always a pattern if you looked closely at the weaving way the universe was stitched. The number seven was an enigma, and a symbol of luck to some. There are seven basic musical notes, just as there are seven visible colors in the spectrum of a rainbow. The seven deadly sins exist to drown away your earthly miseries; wrath, greed, sloth, pride, lust, envy, and gluttony. The Earth was created in seven days, and in the book of Revelations the number seven was an omen of the apocalypse. In some cultures, if you break a mirror, you are cursed with seven years bad luck. A seven-sided star, a heptagram, can ward off evil if drawn correctly, and a seventh son of a seventh son carries with it magical heredity.

Four. Seven. Thirteen.

Perhaps, numerology was more than superstition.

After taking seven victims for six days, the boy awoke the seventh morning to Lilly's screams.

Near death and weak from exposure and dehydration, he watched the remaining men of the village, led by Miroslav—the last surviving Elder—beating Lilly and six other young women into submission, leading them toward the village center. The hysterics of the last six days had driven them mad. They had turned on each other, and in their madness, they erected a mad plan. Rorik was there, beating on Lilly like she was a slave girl.

The boy's rage brought him to his feet.

"Leave her alone!" he growled, and as punishment, an axe handle was crushed against his chin.

"I would kill you now if it appeased the White God," said Rorik, lunging at him with his knife. If his sacrifice could have spared Lilly, the boy would have raked his own neck against Rorik's blade.

"Rorik!" said Falibor. The boy's mentor charged forward with a spear. "Stop this madness, Miroslav, before we have gone too far."

"Look around you, Falibor!" said Miroslav. "We are destroyed! There is only one way to end this, and that is with blood and sacrifice!"

Lilly and the other girls were to be that gift. Virgin blood to quell the lust for death, it was a practice as old as religion.

"Adding more senseless death is not the answer," countered Falibor. "We cannot be this blind! What the boy did was wrong, but adding more wrongs does not make it right. We cannot—"

Falibor's words caught in his throat as a blade erupted through his chest. He had been stabbed in the back by Aran. When Falibor spun to face his attacker, Rorik shoved his own spear into Falibor, dropping him quickly to his knees.

Falibor was dead before they had finished stabbing him, and the boy seethed.

He had been powerless all his life. He had been beaten, starved and scared. Falibor had shown him a kindness, and watching his violent death changed the boy. He no longer wanted to die—he wanted vengeance.

"I'm going to kill you, Rorik."

"You'll be dead soon, Raggy Boy. You anger the White God with empty threats. They dishonor you," he replied.

"Tie them up!" commanded Miroslav. His group of mad men took the seven young women and tied each of them to a post at the village center, with Lilandra at the far end. The boy watched helplessly as she closed her eyes in silent prayer and waited for death. "Belobog must be appeased! He has taught us a lesson! He wants blood and we shall give it to him in the number he has chosen! Seven of the pure! Seven from the few our village has left to spare! We give this blood to you, White God!"

Without pause, Miroslav slashed the throat of the first girl. Before the first drop of her blood hit the ground, the fog had rolled back in, and dark shapes surrounded them. The mutts howled and barked as the attack began.

A scream.

One of Miroslav's men was dragged into the fog. He was there one moment, snatched away the next. His screams panicked Miroslav, who cut the next two throats in line with one broad stroke of his knife. The blood summoned the tendrils wisping from the fog, pulling men, women, and children away. Some torn from their huts, others snagged with spears in hand as they watched Miroslav murder young women.

In the chaos a torch was dropped, and a fire quickly spread into a raging inferno, gathering fuel from every dry surface. The more the fire spread, the darker the mist became, swallowing light as if it were hope.

Some men ran for water, while others grabbed weapons to fight the terrors in the mist. A few ran for their lives and were picked off one by one and dragged screaming into the mist.

In the fray, the boy's eyes met Lilly's, and that connection spoke a thousand words. The sadness and the loneliness he saw there was something he recognized all too well. He had spent nearly seventeen cycles of the seasons surrounded by people who loathed him. Their village was his cage. Witnessing that same despair in Lilly's eyes filled him with limitless strength.

He snapped the leather bonds with a mighty tug.

His only thoughts were to free her, to escort her as far away from the madness as possible—when something sharp and hot buried itself into his side. A spear, its blade sunken into his flesh, did not slow him down. The pain empowered him. He lifted his attacker into the air by the handle of the spear and tossed him into a hut consumed by flame.

An axe was swung at the boy's head, but everything had slowed—his attacker's movements sluggish, as if submerged in water. The boy caught his hand near the haft and ripped the axe from his grasp. Then he drove it deep into his attacker's gut. As if the spilled blood had summoned the mist, the man was quickly snatched away, leaving a red trail in the dirt.

As the boy's fury burned, he became suddenly aware of his wound. He pressed a hand against the open gash to staunch the bleeding and staggered on. He did not know how much longer he could endure, only that he must.

Miroslav had sliced the throats of two more girls and was moving to the next when a smoky tendril grabbed him around the waist and bore him away as he screamed for forgiveness. The boy rushed to Lilly's side and untied the leather that bound her, just before the fog claimed the next shrieking girl. She was dragged up and over the bodies of her fallen sisters and then through a burning hut.

Lilly clung to him, and they ran as the village made its last stand against the demon mist. Many more than seven were taken, and it would seem the mist would not be denied in taking them all. They ran past atrocities—women and children, burned or being dragged away—men murdering men before they were taken by the mist.

The entire village had lost its humanity. They were being slaughtered and did nothing to prevent it. They did not stand together. They stood apart, dying individually instead of uniting against their common enemy.

Their escape was blocked by fire and mist. Huts collapsed, and embers rained. It was chaos. The boy found a small nook that had yet to catch fire and settled there, waiting for the right moment to flee.

"Are you okay?" he asked, but Lilly did not answer. Her mind was overwhelmed with grief and pain. She was in shock.

Every corner of the village was filled with terror. Children were torn from their parents and sucked into the darkness as warriors were struck down, impaled by the tendrils of mist and thrown far off into the gray choking nothingness that surrounded them.

It was the end.

Humans are doomed. Never forget that, Tony.

Rorik dropped onto the boy from above, plunging his knife into the boy's shoulder, then tossed him away and turned to Lilly.

As Rorik raised his knife above his head, ready to end her life, the boy tackled him from behind. He drove them through a weakened wall of a nearby hut and into the village center, tumbling up and over the hearth. They landed just beyond the firepit, the antlers of the stag's head still ivory white and reaching toward the sky.

"I want nothing more than to kill you, Raggy Boy," said Rorik. His eyes blazed with hatred.

"Try," said the boy.

The boy's shoulder bled furiously. He was weaponless and the smoldering firepit was at his back. Rorik swiped at his face—the hissing blade missed—but Rorik was gifted. He spun and slashed the boy across his shoulder, then danced away to prepare his next attack. It was a slow, methodical fight. The longer they danced, the more opportunity there was for Lilly to be plucked away. The urgency within the boy screamed only one solution—so when Rorik charged forward, the boy allowed the blade to sink into his stomach. But before Rorik could retract the blade and stab again, the boy clamped down onto Rorik's arm and dragged him backward into the firepit. They fell into the smoldering embers as Rorik rolled on top, pressing the boy down against the searing coals—the pain immeasurable.

"You destroyed us," accused Rorik. "You were a blight upon this village ever since you were born." He retracted his blade and raised it high above his head.

Rorik was always a larger man. He was taller and stronger, even faster, but something had changed in the boy since slaying the stag. He could feel it. He even saw it—

—his reflection.

He was transformed. He was something new.

Rorik's free hand closed around the boy's throat pushing him down onto the embers. The boy's neck was twisted, and he could no longer see his attacker. As his eyes stared up into the sky, the ivory antlers like icy cracks, he spotted the mist above them, lashing wildly. But try as they might, the tendrils that snatched whole men with a single swipe, could not reach them within the firepit, as if they were protected.

Everything was happening so fast.

The boy's mind, the side of him that fought for survival, took over. His hand reached out and snapped a branch of the antler free from the carcass—as white and pure as it was in life—then plunged it deep into Rorik's chest.

Rorik dropped his blade and the boy sprang upon him, ramming Rorik down into the embers and wrapping his hands around his throat. The boy squeezed and squeezed, the sizzle of Rorik's flesh against the embers were a deeply satisfying sound.

Rorik's eyes darted, as if searching for help, and his skin erupted into patches of horripilation.

"Look at me!" the boy roared, and Rorik shook under his grasp. "As your life drains away, know that I bested you when it mattered. The raggy boy, the outsider, felled the mighty Rorik." Then he removed the antler from Rorik's chest and slashed his throat down to the bone.

When the boy found Lilly, she was hiding in a nook beneath a smoldering hut. She appeared lost, her mind drifting into places where unreality made more sense than the destruction all around her.

"We need to go," said the boy, but her eyes were distant. "Tomorrow's not a promise." That phrase meant more in that moment that it ever had, and it motivated Lilly to take his hand as he led them through the gloom.

Smoke and fog had filled the air so thick, it was hard to breathe. The deeper into the darkness they wandered, the more the boy felt it—a pang in his chest—a presence nearby. It was an evil, dark presence, filled with hunger.

In every direction they attempted to flee, the misty tendrils cut off their escape and cornered them next to a burning hut. The boy stood in front of her, protecting her with his last breath.

For every good there was an equal and opposite counterpart. There was a proton for every electron, a balance struck at the atomic level, the building blocks of all matter. All men have the capacity for good and evil. There was Heaven, and there was Hell. Opposing forces, like magnets attracting, repulsing, and balancing.

Balance. There was always balance. Even the moral gray had balance. There were relative few in this world that exhibited pure evil or pure good. Between was chaos.

However, in the case of Belobog the White, the benevolent god that protected the people who revered him, there was an opposite...

"You are not the White God!" the boy called out. "You are not Belobog!"

There was no answer.

Smoky tendrils darted out of the darkness and came for them, but they did not touch them. They could not. Something repulsed the tendrils and kept them away from Lilly and the boy, as if they struck an invisible barrier between them. The more the tendrils tried to push through, the more the antler twisted his wrist.

He had forgotten it was even there. The weapon that had killed Rorik ran red with blood.

The people of the village prayed and worshipped Belobog because he helped their crops grow and protected them from the dangers that might destroy them. When the boy killed the stag, it had never occurred to him that the beast was sacred. Kasimir was right: the boy had cursed them all, but not in the way Kasimir thought. As he held onto the antler in his hand and watched it repel the darkness, everything became clear.

The boy had killed a god.

The boy had slain Belobog.

The white stag was their protector, and slaying it let the darkness in. For every good, there was evil, as Belobog was the White God, Chernobog was the god of black.

The last of the screams died away, and there was no sound but the noise of fire consuming the village. The smoky tendrils were all around them, probing for a weakness in the protective barrier provided by the antler. Lilly clung to his back, her nose buried into his shoulder, peeking around with wide-eyed terror.

"I will not let it get you, Lilly," he said as she clutched him tight.

"Please, Viktor," she whispered. "Take us away from here." Her voice was hoarse, and her head was spinning, but she'd remembered his name. "I cannot let it take any more from me."

As the Black God continued to strike, the boy—nay, *Viktor*—warded every attack by angling the antler in its direction. The impenetrable wall stayed the mist, but it was growing tighter, shortening the distance between them as their number grew and grew like a pack of starving wolves. It was impossible to ward every strike, placing the antler into its path to defend against the never-ending assault.

Viktor was only a man, attempting to keep pace with a god.

Together, Viktor and Lilly shrank against a smoldering wreck. They huddled together and cowered against the black god's will.

The leather bonds tied to Lilly's ankles were broken but still attached. A short dangling length extended away from her. An ill-fated length just long enough to be beyond the antler's protection.

When the fog snagged that small length of leather and pulled her away, Viktor dove into the fray to save her. He caught her by the arm as they were dragged helplessly through the dirt. Chernobog towed them through a burning hut and out the other side, without Viktor letting go. He latched onto the rocky foundation with a desperate swipe and pulled with every bit of strength he had.

She screamed as he held fast—he would not relinquish his grip. Instead, he was being torn apart—his joints popping, muscles ripping— he refused to let her go.

She was everything to him.

He would not, could not, let anybody leave him ever again.

"Don't let go, Viktor!" she screamed, her fingernails ripping at the skin of his forearm.

"I will never let go," he replied.

He pulled and pulled—the fire's heat seared his skin—the sharp edge of the rocky foundation sliced his hand—and still he pulled.

The Black God's tendrils emerged from the darkness and dozens more wrapped their smoky arms around her, like a constrictor crushing its prey, and gave one last mighty yank.

Viktor felt Lilly's body stress and torque, and with a pop it suddenly went slack—

—and left him clutching her disembodied arm—a torn piece of her garments still threaded between his fingers.

The hut collapsed, trapping him beneath it. Viktor watched in horror as Lilly disappeared into the darkness—her eyes disappearing into the gloom was the last thing he saw. He heard her screams as he was buried alive beneath the rubble.

. . .

Ha ha! Do you see it now, Tony? Mirrors. Women in fridges, be damned! There are few things that inspire men so—power, money, and women. Take a man's power and he will cower away. Take a man's money, and he will plot to take it back. Take a man's woman? Oh, there will be hell to pay. Alas, we did not create man—we simply watch and wonder why they're so insipidly predictable from the moment they created fire till the moment they rained bombs from remote-controlled drones.

It's hardwired into your brains, Tony. Save them! Yes, save them! Go on. Be like Viktor, Tony. Save your love and the world. Go on!

You are not a chosen one, Tony. You are a criminal. You fucked up. And because of free will, only you can fix it.

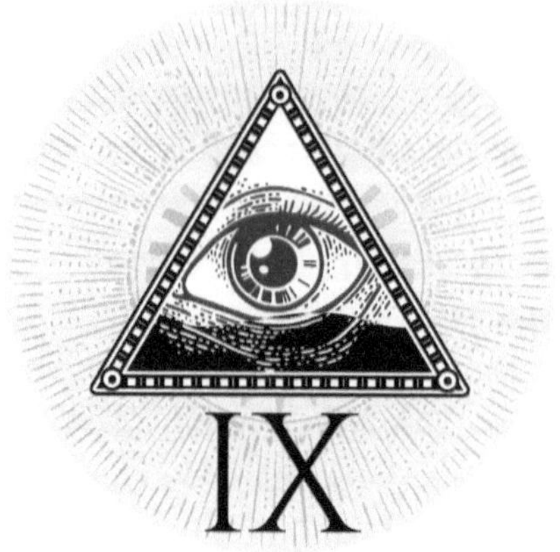

the plan pt. 1

MALUS
December 24, 2013
Now.

It was a trap.

There was a call—a departed Fallen was summoned. Mammon's voided contract hummed, and the ink on my flesh trembled. Someone was dialing his number, hailing all available entities within its radius—like a mighty trumpet that only *we* could hear.

Tony reappeared in Philadelphia and the keys pulsed in unison—all three calling out to their lost sibling as time drew near. We had seven days to recapture the Key of Capricorn, find the Gates of Eden, and open them. Only with all four keys in my possession would the path be revealed. Eden had been hidden and locked away since Adam was expelled. It could not be found without the keys.

I was recruiting Eshu, god of chance and discord, attempting to regain the full power of Thirteen when the trumpet sounded.

And it was obvious who had sent the message.

The Thirteen arrived in the city of Philadelphia at various locations, searching for the spark. Some clung to the shadows, others searched from beyond the Veil. The dwindling daylight provided little comfort to those humans who dwelt too near our paths. An uncontrollable shiver crept up their spines—the urge to flee gnawing at their subconscious.

Tony was somewhere inside the city, and we were tightening our noose.

When we found him, he was sitting beside a fountain in Logan Square—across the street from The Franklin Institute—a place that still reeked of death and otherworldliness. An incursion within those walls a decade ago nearly unleashed The Dream Lands into reality.

Tony sat upon the edge of the frozen fountain, defiantly staring toward the sky in the midst of a daydream—but he knew we were there. He could sense me as I could sense him.

He was waiting for us to make the first move.

Where was he within his own timeline? I had met two very different versions of this man—but it did not matter. Tonight was where his time ended.

TONY
4:15 PM

I always wanted to enjoy the city this time of year—the lights, the attractions and the holiday shows, the Christmas Village in Love Park.

Jaycie would have loved it.

She *hated* Christmas—too many bad memories—but with me, she was starting to come around...

There was a whole part of my life that disappeared when she did. We will never get that time back, but maybe there was a way—with the Holy Dyad, maybe we could find ourselves a new life together—

"Which one?" asked Jaycie.

"I didn't think this was going to be a tough decision," I said.

The Christmas tree vendor had a dozen different varieties. There were pines, firs, spruces, cypresses, cedars, and different needle hues that went from evergreen to bluish-green—some had no needles at all!

"Should we get a fake tree instead?" I suggested.

She glared at me from beneath a red beanie, overstuffed with crimson curls springing loose. It was the kind of drop-jawed, gasping-glare that made me laugh every time.

"How dare you!" she joked, equally offended. "I will never, ever have a plastic tree."

"What about fiberglass and metal?"

"Nope! Nope nope nope."

"Okay, then you decide," I said, gesturing to the lineup behind me that extended all the way to the end of the lot.

"What about this one?" she asked, pointing to a tree with a bluish tint. "Not too tall, not too short. Has good girth. Not bushy, but lean. Crisp." Then she peeked between branches, just in case. "And no woodsy friends hiding inside…"

She could be so unintentionally funny.

"Truly," I said, "there's never been a more apt description of a Christmas tree."

"Shoosh, you!" she scolded, then stepped back, as if framing the tree in her mind, imagining it within the confines of our cozy apartment. "This is it."

"This one," I asked, making sure.

"This is it." She nodded, but reality dawned on her. "How are we getting it home?"

Getting that blasted tree home was quite an ordeal. We carried it from the lot to our apartment, no less than twenty blocks—not a single cab would stop once they saw our payload. But it was worth it just to see her beam as we began decorating.

"What do you think it'll be like, in five years?" she asked. "You and I? On Christmas?"

"I don't know." I shrugged while fiddling with the string lights.

"Probably better prepared. Hopefully I'll have found the burned-out bulb by then."

She laughed. "No, I mean, where do you think *we'll* be?"

She stopped hanging ornaments.

At the time I was just happy to be with her, seeing what life would toss our way. I wasn't much for making plans. I didn't plan to be with Jaycie. I fought for it, and after I had given up and moved on, we fell into each other's laps. There was no plan. It was just luck. Fate. Destiny. I had never taken a moment to think about building toward something—I was only twenty-five.

I finally said, "Together. Hopefully with a better apartment. You'll have regular gigs around the city, maybe the state."

She deflated.

"For someone with such great imagination, I was thinking bigger."

"Like what?" I asked.

"I don't know," she said, like she wanted me to say something very specific but was too afraid to say it herself.

"I'm not very good at this game," I admitted. "There are days I still wake up shocked that you're lying next to me."

"It's probably the bedhead," she said with a laugh. "I'd be shocked too."

"No," I said, pacing over and taking her hands in mind. "Jaycie, nowhere in any storybook ending am I supposed to win your heart. I am thankful for every day I have with you. I can't see five years ahead because I am so afraid I'm going to mess everything up, and you'll realize what a huge mistake you made."

"Does this have anything to do with your dreams?" she asked. When I shrugged, she continued. "I think the same thing." Her voice was a whisper. "That you'll realize I'm just an imposter. That you'll see the ugliness beneath the surface and ditch me."

"You are the most beautiful thing I have ever met, outside and in. You're like the Batmobile—"

"What?" she laughed. There were tears in her eyes.

"What good is such a pretty looking machine, if it didn't have all the amazing stuff that made it the Batmobile under the hood?"

"You have a point," she said with a smile. "I can't believe you made the Batmobile into a romantic metaphor."

"You know why?" I asked, and she shook her head playfully. "I'm Batman."

She giggled. "You certainly are. You're my Batman." Then she poked me in the ribs and ran into the bedroom. "And you'll never take me alive!"

I stood there, befuddled. "Are we roleplaying?"

"Poison Ivy is waiting for you, Batman," she called out to me. "You'll never stop my evil plans! Bwaa-hahahaha!"

My socks spun out as I dove into the bedroom after her.

I struggled to see it then, but I could see it now, Jace…

That future you wanted me to imagine? I can see it all. A better place for us both.

It was time.

I could feel them—smell, sound, taste—the only thing I couldn't do was see them. The taste of something bitter bloomed inside my mouth, and a gloom settled into the frosty air. People got up from their cozy spots on park benches and left, sensing something that made them uncomfortable. Almost the entire square emptied in seconds.

"Are they here?" asked Chappy, inspecting the skies. "All of them?"

"Feels like it," winced Jamaal. "I've got willies on top of willies."

"Me too," added Montoya. "What's a willy, my man?"

"You're a willy," groaned Jamaal.

"Are we sure this will work?" asked Markus, but nobody answered. They were feeling everything I was—especially the nerves.

I tossed the golden coin—Mammon's coin—into the fountain and made my wish.

"Together again," I whispered, "one day."

The area surrounding the fountain was suddenly brimming with evil. Goosebumps rolled in waves up my arms and down my spine, and the scar itched again. They were closing in.

Malus whistled as he rounded the fountain toward me with a big jolly grin on his face, worthy of the festive city mood. When he got within thirty feet, he stopped whistling and shook his head, almost in disbelief.

"Stupidity and arrogance are often confused for bravery and confidence," he said.

"You'd certainly know all about that," I replied as a plume of white vapor left my mouth—the temperature was plummeting. I could hear the fountain constricting as the water within began to freeze with their arrival.

"Where is Jacinda?" asked Henry. He was three feet from Malus, inspecting our adversary up close.

"Is she here?" asked Jamaal, while Doshin studied our surroundings —he felt it too.

There were too many of them. Too many blips on our radar. Hadn't I killed at least three of Thirteen? Summanus, Mammon, and Bacchus— but why was I sensing a full dozen?

"It's all hands on deck, gentlemen," said Markus, clapping like one of my baseball coaches instigating a rally. "They wouldn't leave her alone, not after the last time she escaped. I bet she's tethered to Malus, right on the other side of the Veil."

I couldn't answer them. I knew only as much as they did.

"What's your plan?" asked Malus. His expression and body language betrayed nothing. I had no clue what he might do next.

However, he probably felt the same about me.

After all, we had a plan.

THE PLAN

The plan was simple, like all plans written on bar napkins and debated over a beer. My nerves were shot, and the brain-trust was more than willing to let me dull the sharpened edge with a lager. It was a small pub around the corner from my apartment, and the bartender was too busy chatting up a girl to notice the weirdo talking to himself.

The plan went as follows:

Step 1: Lure all the members of the Thirteen into Logan Square.

- Look innocent.
- Wear running shoes.

Step 2: The Moment

- At the horn, run like hell.

Step 3: Follow the Route:

1. From Logan Square, cut across 18th Street.
2. Left onto JFK to City Hall.
3. Right onto Broad Street.
4. Sprint like hell to the stadiums.
5. Escape into the subway station at 3600 S. Broad.

Step 4: No casualties.

- Stay behind the Veil

Step 5: Set the trap.
BONUS: Exchange witty repartee with Malus.
BONUS: Jump the hood of a car like David Hasselhoff.
BONUS: Leap a subway turnstile like a badass.

The plan was unmistakably gold. It was fool proof—my fourth beer told me so, as did Markus, my new hype man. I was feeling confident right up until Montoya asked, "Think it'll go as planned, my man?"

"Totally," I slurred.

"Why wouldn't it?" said Markus. "The Thirteen are arrogant gods. Immortals tend to believe they are unkillable."

Once I had finished my beer, we used the key and arrived in Philadelphia on December 19, 2013 next to *The Gates of Hell* statue cast in bronze by Auguste Rodin. It was promptly struck by lightning four times in my presence—an anomaly—a paradox of overlapping timelines.

I knew when and where to go, having already lived that day. I saw the news reports—and the moment the plan was conceived, I knew it was me. Why bother worrying about the paradox when I had already done the deed?

The past-me from that day was still at Doctor Hammond's office, so I slipped into my apartment and grabbed my Chucks for running. It felt like I hadn't been home in years—and from my perspective, that was the truth. This was the place I barricaded myself inside to die. I was a shell of myself, passing the days away behind the same four walls.

But now I had something to fight for.

Before I left my apartment, I sat at my desk and removed a picture of Jaycie from inside a box of old photos. It was one of my favorites, from that night at the boardwalk, and our legendary game of mini-golf—not *putt-putt*.

I left the photo on the desk for the past-me to find—fuel for the road ahead.

December 24, 2013
Now.

"I have what you want," I said. I patted my chest, and the key pulsed—its siblings just twenty feet away. "If you want it bad enough, take it."

"Poking at the beehive again, sir?" said Henry.

"Why not?" I replied.

Malus's eyes sharpened—yeah, I was talking to myself. Poor Malus had no idea of the things transpiring inside my head.

"You are surrounded," said Malus. "We are at the end, the inevitable conclusion of your persistence. Hand over the key, and we will spare you the pain of being devoured alive—your flesh being chewed right off your own pitiful bones."

"Did you go to school for that? Like, did you major in creepy monologuing?"

BONUS ACHIEVED! Exchange witty repartee with Malus.

When Malus didn't reply, a long silence drifted between us.

He was waiting for me to make the first move.

When playing a game of chicken, it was paramount to hide your emotions. The wrong body language could upend whole plots and divulge secrets.

"C'mon, T," said Jamaal. "Keep your heart rate down."

The city was bustling—people flocking to buy last minute gifts and those travelling to the airport, or 30th Street Station. The open air on the Benjamin Franklin Parkway was like an oasis in the middle of a concrete jungle. Buildings of twenty or more floors towered over us, creating a wind tunnel as a gust channeled through the gridded streets and emptied into the open space. A street vendor was selling festive funnel cakes down the block in Love Park—I could almost taste one. The sights, the sounds, the smells—the city was a living thing; ebbing and flowing, a pulse, a breath, a heartbeat—including the growing cancer sifting closer to me every second.

This city, these people, they were all doomed in seven days if I did not stand up to Malus today and end it. One against Thirteen…

Timing had to be perfect, right down to the second. They were every bit as fast as I was. A half-step was the difference between life and death.

I could hear everything over, *and under*, a five-block radius—if I concentrated. The 4:16 train to Lansdale out of Suburban Station just finished boarding. The alarm sounded.

There was twenty minutes before the next subway train arrived at Pattison Station, at 3600 South Broad. To be safe, to ensure nobody got hurt, I had to arrive within that twenty-minute window. It was approximately seven miles, moving at an average of 35 mph—*by foot*—pending nothing gets in the way…

It was by far the fastest I had ever run—about five miles per hour faster than the fastest recorded human.

"Famous last words, my man," said Montoya, reading my mind.

The best intentions…

BWAAAAAAAAP!

The horn sounded as the 4:16 train pulled away from the station, and I leapt away from the fountain just as something collided with the brick foundation. Ice and mortar sprayed into the air—a near miss.

I was already to the shrub hedge that lined the square when the breeze of another near miss hissed over my shoulder.

"Okay, T," coached Jamaal. "Stick to the route."

I could feel them funneling in behind me, giving chase, so I slipped behind the Veil and charged out into traffic...

I'd spent my entire childhood consuming TV, movies, comics and books—and never once in any of those thousands of tales did a plan go off as conceived. Something always went wrong. It was fair to imagine that reality would deliver similar results—I just never thought things would go sideways so soon...

Behind the Veil, as if waiting for me, was the outstretched arm of Hekate—her damaged mask, my handiwork, revealing a section of her putrid face.

"Nowhere to hide," she hissed—

—and I stumbled out of the Veil, like a magnet repulsed by its equal charge.

"I didn't know they could do that!" shouted Jamaal, drifting beside me as if he was floating.

"We're playing a game knowing half the rules," groaned Markus, leaning against a mailbox I went stumbling past.

By the time I paced through the next intersection, I had tried again and again, but nothing happened—the Veil was inaccessible.

Was it a spell? Was it a curse? I spoke Hekate's true name, "Entropia," but nothing changed—the Veil was locked!

"Keep going," said Doshin, standing on the near curb as I sprinted past.

"Shit!" I was stuck. I could either continue, die, or flee with the key and start again—but how many more chances would I have?

"Stay ahead of them, my man," said Montoya. "Don't look back! Go! Go! Go!" He was cheering me on from the sidewalk like I was running a 5k.

It was now or never...

I picked up speed cutting through traffic when a wall of yellow taxis on the Parkway blocked my path. I had the biggest grin on my face as I slid across the taxi's hood like I had seen a hundred times on the tube— and it was glorious.

BONUS ACHIEVED! Jump the hood of a car like David Hasselhoff.

I hustled around the following corner, passed a statue of a Polish general, then cut down 18th Street, heading south. I could feel them: some high above, leaping from building to building, and some below, following through the muck and filth of the sewers, moving in and out of phase with reality.

That's when things got messy.

I had counted a dozen in the park—assuming I had taken at least one of those thirteen shitheads off the board—I didn't anticipate anyone showing up late to the party. Dagon's tentacles burst through a manhole cover ahead. The metal disc bounced twice and crashed through a glass storefront. Before his sewer-slimy appendages could grapple for a leg, I swerved down Cherry Street to avoid him, barely outpacing his outstretched limbs.

A woman screamed.

"Stick to the route!" yelled Jamaal.

"You stick to the route!" I roared, as we moved west, away from our target destination.

It was like a video game—obstacles moved into my path so fast, I survived on reaction and impulse. There was no turning back, no slowing down, this was full-throttle, pedal-to-the-metal, break-neck speed, cliché-heavy fuckery—like Super Mario with a broken controller, moving toward a head-on collision course with a Bowser army.

To my left came a blur, like something was manifesting into reality, and I turned right again, back toward Logan Square.

I was being herded.

They were attempting to corral me toward a trap of their own.

After dodging an elderly couple with an armful of gifts, I sprinted to the end of the block while planning my next move...

…before it was too late.

As Fallen, we could break laws of physics, but there was one set of physical laws I found to be true no matter what; momentum and inertia. The faster we moved, the more difficult it was to sharply change direction, even with heightened agility, strength, and the ability to refocus our own gravity.

With a vortex of darkness nipping at my heels, I made my break at the following cross street—

Snagging a speeding taxi weaving in and out of traffic by wedging my hand into the tight gap between the rear window and trunk was as dumb as anything I had ever done in my youth—and I had done a lot of dumb. The momentum was enough to nearly snap my arm, but it worked—I felt them zipping past, unable to turn—and in the process, I managed to scare the ever-loving shit out of a box-truck driver delivering office supplies.

The sharp turn put me back ahead, moving east. For a moment, I thought I was clear—zipping away and picking up speed—but when I cut south on 17th toward Market Street, I made a huge mistake.

Traffic! Traffic every-fucking-where!

"Oh shit," growled Montoya. "I thought you said the city would be empty, my man?"

It should have been. Was there an accident? A big can't-miss-it event?

"We can't catch a fucking break!" shouted Jamaal, facepalming beside a Burger King.

I leapt over a car—its driver honking like a maniac—landed on the roof of a silver SUV, then dismounted onto a green sedan before fleeing by pavement. I was slow—too slow—and falling dreadfully behind my own schedule.

Shadows thickened. The light was being sucked straight out of the air like a movie fading to black—just like it did to Jaycie the night I shot Rick dead, as she raced home without her angel-guard protection. A woman looked to the sky, as if searching for a solar eclipse, while the streetlamps struggled against an unseen force absorbing its power.

I had made a terrible mistake…

. . .

Three Hours Ago

"We're going to run from this jawn to that jawn all the way down there, cloaked like a Klingon warbird?" asked Jamaal, pointing at the city map I'd grabbed at the subway station kiosk.

"What's a Klingon, my man?" asked Montoya.

"That's the plan," I said as we jogged up the subway stairs to street level, into the middle of the city. There were people around, but it was sparse—the residents were fleeing the city as expected for holidays with family in the burbs. "If we run behind the Veil, *like a Klingon warbird*, nobody will even know we're there."

"Are you sure nobody's going to get hurt?" asked Chappy.

"Why would anyone get hurt?" said Markus. "It's a foolproof plan."

"No," I grumbled, and my frustration began to boil. "Listen, we can't relitigate the plan now. Not in the eleventh hour."

"Sir," said Henry, cleaning his glasses like he does when he's working up the courage to say something pointed. "We are merely attempting to play devil's advocate."

I nodded while refolding the map and tucked it into my back pocket. "Yeah, well, save it." Then I paced out ahead.

"My man," said Montoya, catching up, "We trust you. Let's just make sure we don't go to hell in a breadbasket."

"Handbasket," corrected Jamaal.

"What's the difference?" asked Montoya.

"None, that's just not the saying," he said.

Now.

Yeah, I had made a terrible mistake, and felt it right in the breadbasket.

Zigzagging through a concourse near City Hall, a fog rolled in and surrounded everything within five blocks.

It wasn't a naturally occurring meteorological event—the fog crept through the streets, blanketing cars, and swallowing pedestrians in a dank soup. Then came the sound of crushing metal, like something had bowled over a series of cars in the mist, followed by an earsplitting roar—

—and screams. People were screaming!

They were coming at me from all angles.

They weren't holding back.

They weren't chasing from the shadows.

They were out in the open, daring to be stopped. Were they willing to bring down angels? Would the angels even care to intervene?

I tried to slip beneath the Veil again and again, but I was blocked. Why did I think this was going to work? Everything I touch I break—a bull in a fucking china-shop. I was only in this predicament because I couldn't get out of my own damn way.

"Every deviation from the path," said Henry, appearing beside me as I raced onward through the haze, "every obstacle, every twitch spent avoiding rather than racing away, is going to put people at risk."

I was putting people at risk!

"No arguments," said Chappy. "No blame. Just go!"

I dove through the shrinking gap between a truck and taxi, launched myself onto the sidewalk at 16th, and kept stride—pacing right into a pack of pedestrians.

It was a damn holiday! Didn't they have places to be?

"Get out of the way!" I yelled, waving my arms.

Montoya did the same—if only they could see him…

A few pedestrians stepped aside as I blew past them at Olympic speeds, while others froze like deer in headlights. I jumped onto the glass exterior of a bank, then leapt off ahead of the crowd, soaring past them in a blink. The whole chain of events was seen by no less than twenty people, including a cop whose initial reaction was to chase after me. By the time he made it to the sidewalk, I was already a block ahead.

Horns blared at the intersection. Tires screeched followed by crunching metal and glass. Someone shouted, "what the fuck!" and a collision shook the pavement just behind me.

Every direction was bedlam.

Last-minute-gift shoppers were given a peek into the horrors that hid within the shadows. Ghastly shapes soared above. A spectral mist sifted through the city, terrors lurking within. Shimmering surfaces reflected hideous silhouettes of beasts out of phase with reality.

I was in the middle of the most public display of otherworldly terror the world had seen since the ancient days.

Four and a half minutes gone, 6.5 miles to go.

I was behind.

"Pick up the pace," demanded Doshin.

There was a moment of peace as I picked up speed and cut onto Broad Street—the widest, busiest thoroughfare through the city, moving directly south. Right when I eased into a coasting pace to reserve energy, the sound of feathers flapping caught my attention. Not just one or two sets of wings, but a whole flock agitating the air above me.

My last second flinch caught the brunt of the slashing strike—a gash opened down my arm and I slammed onto the ground, skidding in my leather jacket across my shoulder like a fallen biker. The remaining pack of crows soared overhead, and for a moment I questioned—were they angels? Until I saw their red eyes...

...just before they sliced a delivery man in two like a bundle of blades.

It was the Morrigan, and her brazen actions struck me sick.

This was bold. This wasn't Moloch plowing through cars under the cover of mist—this was carnage. The Thirteen just publicly killed a man —not shrouded in mystery, or under the cover of darkness, or disguised as a natural disaster. There would be no confusion as to what transpired. Women screamed and a rush of people fled the scene.

"I think we may have to rethink this," said Markus, but there was no turning back now.

"Keep the pace," coached Doshin, "stopping will only bring more death."

I was off and running before I could second and third-guess the plan. What have I done? I was expecting them to chase from the shadows or from behind the Veil—not to kill everyone and anything in their path. Why did I believe this could be done without collateral damage?

"They don't give a damn anymore," said Chappy. "They know you're the only thing in their way, and they'll stop at nothing to get that key. And that includes exposing themselves and incurring the wrath of angels in the process."

"Take it off Broad Street," suggested Jamaal. He was reading my mind. "Less people on the side streets."

When I turned up Spruce, the Morrigan dropped out of the sky and landed on the hood of an SUV driving through the intersection. She smashed through the engine block, upending it in a fiery display of glass and shredded metal—blocking my path onto 16th.

I came to a sliding stop in front of a bakery with gourmet cupcakes stacked inside the window. The reflection in the tinted glass with the flowery pink and blue text held a horrific image—a man bound together with leather straps, carrying a sickle over his head—

—"Thanatos," gasped Henry.

When the monster swung his sickle, it surged through the glass reflection into the real world, slicing through my jacket as I rolled aside. As soon as my feet hit the pavement, I took off running down Hicks Street—the only direction unblocked by evil.

"That was so close!" said Jamaal, like he was watching a blockbuster on the couch with a tub of buttery popcorn.

"He almost had you, my man!" said Montoya.

I growled. My fuck-up was rippling outward. Too many unintended disasters.

The city was full of terrors—and I'd called them here. I summoned them, I defended this plan, and I was responsible. This was going to be a bloodbath, and it was all my fault...

Trent was right—summoning things was *dumb*.

"Pish posh!" said Markus—and in splittest second, several events transpired:

1. My brain lit up like a chunk of sodium dropped into a bucket of water.

2. Everything around me; the air, the ground, the guy popping a wheelie on his bike, and the peg-legged pigeon taking flight— froze.

3. My legs got tied up, like someone pulled the rug out from under me. I tripped, bounced, then rolled twenty feet and went sideways into a Greek food-truck, operated by a Vietnamese guy wearing a nametag with the word "PHIL" spelled out in perfect block letters.

When I came to my senses, Markus was standing over me. "Get your head into the game, Tony!" he shouted.

X

know thy enemy

A VOICE
Long Ago...
Then.

Death's a guarantee, even for immortals.

When it comes for us, it comes swift, with a flashing blade or consuming conflagration. We do not die of old age or disease—our deaths are sudden, and violent.

Understand, Tony, you are being shown this so that you may accept the challenge—how one being rose from the meekest of beginnings and ascended high enough to challenge the very order of existence as we know it.

Understand that Death comes for us all, but it can be cheated. There are forces even greater than Azrael—forces greater than the Fates. When the end arrives, it must be irreversible. It must be swift. And it must be final.

Existence is not as binary as you believe. Do the Oneiroi not dream entire realities? Is the Unbecoming not full of Remnants? The Empty is infinite, and somewhere within infinity are infinite possibilities—undiscovered secrets, unfathomable realities. Make no mistake, there are things that wish to destroy our reality with prejudice that exceeds hatred. Make no mistake, Tony, when the end comes it must slam every door shut.

When Viktor awoke under the smoldering wreckage, it was a bright sunny morning. The fires had burned out, and the fog had long since retreated into the forest from which it came.

After dragging himself out from beneath the hut's foundation, he sat there and mourned for hours, maybe days, until he was too weak to continue. He took the piece of cloth that had torn free with Lilandra's arm and held it close.

The antler was gone. If the fog returned for him, he would not fight. He would go willingly into the great beyond.

As in a dream, he ambled through the village and down the path that led to the lake. Sitting upon the embankment, he stared down at his reflection in the water and allowed himself to see the thing he had become.

It was a calm, crisp day, creating a perfectly flat mirror upon the water. With all he had survived, he appeared ragged, but healthy. His wounds were gone, but the platinum hair remained.

His reflection triggered a whole new sadness. He was a freak. He was a monster. The villagers were right about him all along. His witchy eyes were a portent of doom, and they should have killed him long ago. His self-loathing had become so great that he climbed the path from the embankment to a ledge high above the lake, where the rocks below the surface of the mirror awaited him.

Then he cast himself off the edge and plunged into the lake with no intention of resurfacing—but as he broke the mirrored surface of the water, he fell—nay! He was ejected out the other side. It was as if he had passed straight through one reality into another.

He wasn't even wet.

In fact, the water there was not liquid—it moved, swayed, and rippled like water, but it was solid. As solid as standing upon ice, unable to sink. He had little time to ponder his predicament before he was confronted by something new.

"Pathetic," said a strange man. He too was standing upon the lake as if it was frozen under winter's icy touch, and he was watching Viktor. His skin was as pale as the moon, and his eyes were as black as volcanic rock.

"Who are you?" asked Viktor.

The man grinned at Viktor's question, and his face contorted as if the smile had opposed the very nature of his gaunt face. His long black hair spilled from his head and into his clothing—both of which were so pitched, even under the sun it was like they were one continuous shadow.

"Leave him be," spat another man, his voice deep and voluminous. He was lounging in the tall grass along the shore behind Viktor, and he looked just the same as the first, except his smooth hairless head was as white as a night moon.

"Oh, Morpheus, must you always interfere?" said the first.

"Phoebetor, do not torture this boy by setting him upon a path to failure," said Morpheus.

"His subconscious is already suspicious," said Phoebetor. "I am merely showing him the way!"

"The way to what?" asked Viktor, but neither answered.

"Nightmares are your domain, Phoebetor," said Morpheus, "not recurrences."

"Stuffy, Morpheus," scoffed a third, appearing beside Phoebetor. He was as pale as the others, but his hair was neatly cut and groomed. His black clothing was fantastic and flourished, with silvery accents and jewelry. "Leave our brother be. He is merely attempting to help this hapless soul." He skipped across the water like a flat stone and hopped onto a rock along the shore.

"It is not our job to help, Phantasos, only to serve," said Morpheus.

"Except when *you* choose to help. Do not be a hypocrite, brother," said Phoebetor, his tone playful.

"Oh, Morpheus." Phantasos sneered. "We are Oneiroi! We are not bound to the laws of Empyrea! Why should we not help the boy?"

"Because I know *this boy*. He does not need our help," said Morpheus. He was studying Viktor closely, peering into his soul with piercing white eyes—the one feature that set him apart from his brothers other than his lack of hair.

Viktor was caught between them, witnessing an argument that was beyond his ability to understand. While they debated, he slowly shuffled toward the shore.

"Be that as it may," said Phantasos, "his life has been entangled with the gods. It would seem a pity to turn the boy loose without a little guidance. Right, brother?"

"Do what you will," said Morpheus. "But do not anticipate my eventual acceptance of this behavior. You have fed on this boy's nightmares. If you nudge too far, it could crack Somnia apart with vagaries beyond our control. My purpose is to keep the dreamscape balanced."

Then Morpheus disappeared in a blink.

Viktor had nearly reached the shore when Phantasos said, "Boy! Where are you going?"

Viktor turned to face the two wild men and found them surrounding him. Phoebetor stepped close as Viktor sank into the solid water.

"You have every reason to fear me, boy," said Phoebetor. "I am the nightmare god. I feed off your sleeping fear." The nearer he came, the more Viktor squirmed to escape, but his feet were stuck, sunken into the solid water all the way to his knees. "As tasty as your fear may be, I feel compelled to offer you guidance. Do you understand your sin?"

"My sin?" Viktor whimpered, "No."

"Oh my," said Phoebetor. "He has so much to learn!"

The nightmare god shoved Viktor into the water, and he resurfaced at night, in the middle of the forest. The crickets chirped and the owls hooted. He was nowhere near the lake.

"Look there, boy," said Phoebetor, suddenly beside him. When Viktor turned toward Phoebetor's outstretched finger pointing into the distance, a twinkle of light parted through the trees until it grew into the brightest glow. It was the great white stag, and it approached as if it did not see them. "Watch."

As the stag wandered near, a boy fell from above and plunged a dagger deep between the stag's shoulders. It dropped dead almost instantly.

"That was your sin," said Phoebetor.

"I don't think he understands, brother," said Phantasos, who appeared nearby. "He is utterly confused. Look at his face."

"That, boy, was your sin," said Phoebetor as they watched the boy cut out the stag's heart and eat it warm. With every bite there was a change—his hair lightened several shades, and with his last bite it had paled almost pure white. But that was not the only transformation. He appeared taller, stronger, healthier—it was like magic.

"He still doesn't get it," sung Phantasos.

"Boy, you killed the White God," said Phoebetor. "You killed Belobog. He who protects this land from the evil god that took your beloved away. The same evil god who stole my true name. He is the black god of fear, Chernobog, and stealing my name has rendered me powerless against him and his kind.

"We see power in you, boy" he continued, placing a wiry arm over Viktor's shoulder, "and a path toward *greatness*. Since I cannot steal my true name from his memory, perhaps I can give you a push. Our interests align, friend. Your vindication will also be mine."

"I don't understand," said Viktor.

"There," pointed Phoebetor.

They were no longer in the middle of the forest. The skies were dark, but it was night no longer. They were deep within a far-off corner of the Dark Wood, across the creek from the forest. Viktor recognized the gnarled roots and the twisted thorns that flourished within. There, directly across from where he stood, was a cave that sat in the crater of an uprooted tree. The crater he and Lilly hid within that day of the storm. Without moving, his body slid toward it—framing the scene so he could not miss what he was supposed to see.

Phoebetor grabbed him by the neck—his hand icy cold—and shoved Viktor into the dark crater. "The devil you seek hides beneath the earth. If you kill him for me, I will never again visit you in nightmare."

The blackness of the cave surrounded him, and a wicked laugh billowed out from deep within. Phoebetor pushed him deeper and deeper inside the cave until the dark tendrils of dust surfaced through the shadow and grabbed him, sucking him into the gloom. Viktor kicked and thrashed, he grabbed hold of the rocky wall to prevent his descent, but failed as a great void of darkness surrounded him.

"Do you understand now, boy?" asked Phoebetor, far behind. "Do you understand what the black god took from your beloved? He consumed her happiness. He consumed her love! He stole her innocent affections for you! He stole them from right under your nose! She suffers as he slowly consumes her soul!"

Viktor could hear her screams. He could hear her pleas, begging to be set free.

"Kill Chernobog!" shouted Phoebetor. "Kill the black god and set your beloved free! Set us both free!"

Then the tendrils torqued and pulled, ripping Viktor in half, then dragged the pieces into the cold dark unknown.

Viktor awoke on the lakeshore, wet, exhausted, and tortured. He remained there for some time, piecing together his experience.

He never found Lilly's body, nor did the fog and its demon return. Chernobog, the black god, had taken its fill and left, and it was all Viktor's fault.

"Do you ever wonder what exists beyond the valley?" Lilly once asked. "Over the mountains. Into the unknown?"

"Sometimes."

"I think about it all the time. One day I want to see it. Would you go with me?"

"Yes," said Viktor, then he set off toward the mountains and left the only place he ever knew behind him.

That day, Viktor became obsessed with revenge on a creature he did not yet understand. Like all journeys, his started with aimless wandering.

XI

the chase

TONY
Grace Falls.
Then.

"What exactly are you intending to do?" asked Maynard after running an irritated hand through his long hair.

We had gathered at Tori's grave. Cyn had called us under the premise that she needed our help. It was a cold, windy Tuesday in late January, and the sting of Tori's death hadn't yet begun to dull.

Tori's body was buried deep within the Grace Falls Cemetery less than a week after her death. She was buried beside her mother, two generations of Martins gone in fifteen years. It was sad, and for Jess it was just another reminder of how cruel Grace Falls could be.

"We're going to make a call." Cyn placed her black, overstuffed tote-bag next to Tori's marker—her headstone hadn't yet arrived—and began to rummage within.

The moon was nearly full, and the tower on old Hallows' House blocked half the light from view. There were still patches of snow in the shadier corners of the cemetery, and we were standing in a quarter inch of freezing mud.

"Who are we calling?" I asked.

Jess pulled her puffy coat tight for warmth, but her indignant posture said more than words could. She didn't want to be there, and neither did I.

"Who do you think?" Cyn sassed, then added, "Dumbasses," under her breath.

"Dumbasses?" scoffed Kurt, still dressed in his gas-station convenience-store smock. "I'm not sure I like where this is headed." The man was barely holding it together—Tori was his cousin.

"Summoning the dead is an artform," replied Cyn, still rummaging through her bag.

"You're a hairstylist," said Maynard—I thought there might've been more coming, but he stopped there, letting the rest of us conclude his intended barb.

"And you're in retail," she groaned. Cyn removed a black candle and store-bought incense. She bit the plastic to unwrap it, then removed a sterling silver necklace with a blue stone from her bag—

"Where'd you get that?" asked Jess, snatching it from Cyn's hand.

"Ouch! Spaz much?" she shouted.

"Where'd you get it?" repeated Jess, this time a demand.

"I took it," she said—the flush in her cheeks accentuating her clown-red dye job.

"From where?" asked Trent. He looked menacing—the weeks of mourning had ground him into a husk. We could all smell the alcohol sweating from his skin.

Cyn looked like she was about to argue—a Tori-worthy tirade—when she spotted Jess, and her fire blew out with a cold breeze.

Jess was shivering—but that was less about the temperature than her anger.

"From Tori," Cyn admitted.

"When?" demanded Kurt.

"The funeral. I went into her room and—"

"—That was her mother's necklace," said Jess. She was crying.

"We need it," said Cyn.

"For what?" asked Jess.

"To say goodbye," said Cyn, like it was an obvious answer.

When Jess finally spoke, it was an emphatic, "I'm done." She dropped the necklace and stormed off. Kurt chased after her—but a few days later Jess moved away, and none of us ever saw her again.

Maynard took two lanky steps, reached down and grabbed the necklace. He took a moment to inspect it under the moonlight, then handed it over to Cyn. "Do your thing, witchy woman."

"What?" scoffed Trent.

"I want to see this," said Maynard, folding his arms over his trenchcoat. "Go ahead. Summon our dead friend with her stolen necklace. I want to be here when she haunts your ass for being such a bitch to her sister."

I gave Maynard a supportive nod—he was making a point.

"Summoning things is dumb," said Trent. "I hope it backfires spectacularly."

He was right. At the time I thought it was as bogus as Cyn's hair and lashes, but now? Now, I knew it was like playing cards with a devil—a surefire way to invite something in for a closer look, that would have otherwise passed us by.

Cyn performed her spell while sitting cross-legged on a picnic blanket—it included Tori's necklace, the candle, incense, hand-holding, and an incantation from a spell book that looked way too authentic looking back on it now. The spell sounded like a nursery rhyme gone bad, made of fake words. We waited fifteen minutes after she had finished, but the only thing we heard sounded like someone whispering on the wind.

"Alright," shouted Maynard, "I'm out when shit gets freaky."

"Told you summoning things is dumb." Trent stormed off after Maynard, leaving me alone with Cyn. She was teary-eyed as she shoved the candle and incense, still smoking, into her bag.

"Hey," I said, kneeling down in front of her.

She looked up and smiled. "It should have worked."

"You had good intentions."

"Yeah," she replied—but I wasn't done—

I leaned forward, and the closeness made her uncomfortable when she realized I wasn't happy—in fact, I was disappointed.

"What you did was messed up," I said.

"I was only trying to help."

"No," I replied, "the way you treat your friends is messed up." Then I held out my hand. "The necklace."

She placed the necklace in my hand and said, "I just wanted to say goodbye."

"Yeah, don't we all."

December 24, 2013
Now.

Yeah, summoning things is dumb…

"Get your head into the game, Tony!" shouted Markus—and he was wearing my brown leather jacket, or at least a brain-trust facsimile of it.

The world around me was frozen in place as I picked myself off the ground after having spun out and crashed into a food truck at thirty miles per hour. The impact should've crushed organs and broken bones, but instead I had a walloping headache.

"Did you freeze time again?" I asked, still digesting the situation. Around me was a chaotic scene of a food truck toppling over in mid-air while its owner went scurrying away—a peg legged pigeon taking off to avoid getting crushed in the fray—and chasing after me was a flock of crows along with what appeared to be the reflection of a monster grappling for me from behind panes of glass. A trail of dust and trash were kicked up in my wake, and pedestrians held onto their hats and belongings as I whooshed by like a runaway vehicle with a ruptured brake-line.

It was insanity, and it was my fault.

"Tony!" shouted Markus.

He looked irritable, still donning his Roman tunic beneath a replica leather jacket of my own, sporting a splendid Caesar cut. Some men looked cool in leather—Arthur Fonzarelli, James Dean, the Terminator —Markus looked like Pee Wee Herman.

"What are you doing drifting off into a memory in the middle of something so monumentally important?" He was pissed—or more accurately, *disappointed.*

"I overanalyze," I grumbled, "Sue me."

I summoned thirteen Fallen into the middle of the city and expected nothing bad to happen—the moment my mind drifted, recalling Cyn's failed attempt to summon Tori's spirit, I went tumbling through the air.

I was beginning to get a really bad feeling about Markus and his time-outs—and on cue, Markus pivoted.

"I need you—nay—*we* need you to keep your head in the game," he said.

"I get that—"

"Maybe you don't," he interrupted. "You put all these poor people at risk."

"Weren't you the one—"

"But I am not from these times, Tony!" he professed. "You know the danger better than I, or any other member of your brain-trust. There is a reason why *you* are in control, and we are not." Then he leaned against a nearby lamppost, almost theatrically. "Maybe it's time one of us took a turn, as you say, *at the wheel.*"

"You want a shot?" I asked, storming toward him and waving a fore-finger in his face. "You want to take the wheel? Do you have any idea how monumentally hard this is?"

"Tough love, Tony," he said, batting my hand away. "Is not that what you call it? Hearing the harsh criticisms from a peer might help you to steer more...*proficiently.*"

"Fuck you," I spat.

"I don't know, Tony," he said, gesturing around, "I'm not actually here. But you? You're the one who is fucked. Am I right?" Then he said something that hit harder than anything any friend or shrink had ever dared to say. "What good are you if you cannot protect the woman you love?"

I wanted to impart a large Markus-sized piece of my mind, to unload all my frustrations, when the world snapped back into motion.

"Move!" shouted Jamaal. "What are you doing? Move!"

An icy grip wrangled me from behind, and the Morrigan whispered into my ear.

"Got you," she hissed, then rammed me into the ground, face-first.

The brain-trust shouted instructions, but I was on autopilot. My bell was rung, but from the ground I grabbed an errant soda can tossed from the food truck when it toppled over and slung it at Morrigan side-armed from close range. The can burst open when she caught it, but the fizzing spray was the split-second distraction that allowed me to slip away.

"Good job," nodded Markus from the entrance of a Wawa convenience store—but I was too concerned with survival to flip him off.

After sprinting onto Pine, then right to 15th, I could see them in the glass façade of an office building—shadows and monsters in hot pursuit. Some ran along the sides of buildings, and others flew high above, flitting in and out from behind the Veil. The funerary mist that had nipped at my heels since City Hall had lifted, but the growing darkness followed close behind.

"What the fuck was that!?" shouted some guy in an Eagles sweatshirt after I blew past. My tailwind knocked the phone from his hand as papers flew into the air and dogs barked.

"Just four more miles, sir," said Henry.

"ETA, fifteen seconds over." Jamaal winced. "You're going to miss the window!"

I shot him a glance for the unsolicited criticism and pushed on—

—right toward a group of kids eating candy on the corner—

Momentum. Inertia.

Two choices arrived in that split second before I barreled into the kid with a Pokemon backpack eating a full-size Snickers and a Mountain Dew:

1. Plow through them as delicately as possible while dragging a

gang of dark twisted fucks that were sure to stop off for a snack, or—

2. Learn to fly and let his momma deal with the fallout of his sugar rush.

If anyone thought that was a real decision, they clearly don't know me very well...

"Oh shit!" yelled Jamaal, just before I did something fucking nuts.

I planted my foot into the ground and cut sharply—shifted gravity, pivoted, then leapt off the side of an abandoned building—like an aerial zig-zag.

A rush of evil soared past, mimicking my maneuver in pursuit.

The entire brain-trust screamed—some terrified—others thrilled.

We soared up and over traffic—up and up and over a whole half block, then landed near the intersection of Broad and Jackson.

"What a gas!" hooted Montoya.

Without stopping, without even a stumble, I ran out into traffic across all four lanes of Broad Street, dodged a handful of cars, and slipped down Juniper Street.

Under any other circumstance I may have celebrated that maneuver, but innocents were getting hurt. Who would I be if I allowed them to suffer? Who would I be without doing all in my power to protect them too? Even if it meant broken ankles.

My body was holding up, barely, or maybe the adrenaline was holding me together like super glue to spilled guts.

Juniper Street was barely more than an alley—less people, less risk. This part of the city was residential. The sun was down, and people were either at home celebrating the holiday or had left the city—

I was cruising along, checking over my shoulder for the next attack, when the sound of scraping metal provided an early warning. A construction dumpster skidded across the pavement toward me, sparks flying like Christmas lights.

Dodging a divebombing pack of crows or sickle swipes was one thing—but an eight-foot tall, twenty-two-foot-long dumpster filled with debris was like tossing a bug-zapper at a mosquito.

All this time, I had survived on instinct and the combined knowledge and skills brought to me by the brain-trust and the hundreds and hundreds of entities that existed within me—my spirit—*whatever*—but some instincts came from somewhere else...

Before I leapt, I waved my fist through the air—as if swatting the dumpster away—and something happened—reacting to my desperation...

"What the hell?" said Jamaal.

When I leapt, the dumpster spun as if I had pushed on the front half —and as the back half spun toward me, I couldn't clear the eight feet. My legs slammed into the metal like a tolling bell, and I tumbled over the dumpster before stumbling up the side of a rowhome. The spinning and the sensation of adjusting gravity gave me an immediate headache —but I only broke stride to skip over a sunken window on the second floor.

An angry naked woman—Astoreth, according to Chappy—stood below and roared when the brick and mortar beneath my feet shattered apart with an explosive boom. I fell sideways through the air, slammed into the parallel building, and rolled away. A hideous creature burst through the explosion after me and chased—varying his pursuit on two legs and all fours—his claws scratching shallow gashes into my calf.

The beast had reddish brown skin, hooves, and horns, charred from head to toe with a broken onyx crown upon his head. He was Belial, a Prince of Hell—*how did I know that?* His name registered like a long-lost friend waving from a crowd.

I dropped to the ground and picked up speed, narrowly avoiding a flying warhammer that slammed into a nearby car. The impact sent the car spiraling off its wheels and into the side of a gray stone building, shattering the windows on the first and second floor. Car alarms trilled, and a light flicked on in one of the houses to investigate.

My guilt tripled. If Gabriel knew this is what was going to happen when he set me on my path, he would have dragged me off in angel handcuffs.

Traffic at the next intersection forced me to hurdle cars. I was moving so fast, I was a blur, and continued pace through the next side street, when all of a sudden, the blacktop softened—it was like running in mud.

I was a mouse in a sticky trap. The blacktop boiled like tar. A woman with four flaming arms, stilettos and a slinky black dress stood in my way.

She sneered as she sauntered in close. "I thought you'd be cuter."

3...2...1...I ducked.

When she hit the pavement, bowled over by Belial in close pursuit, I spun free of the trap and charged up the side of the nearest building, then raced along the rooftops.

"Two and a half miles to go!" shouted Jamaal.

"This could almost work," said Chappy.

From that height, I could see my destination off in the distance, and I was closing fast.

I was starting to think Chappy was right—*this could almost work...*

"Eleven minutes, forty-five seconds," said Jamaal, marking my time.

—just before the key pulsed.

Malus stood on a nearby rooftop watching me jump from building to building. The dying sunlight silhouetted him from behind, and his stark white hair was alight like the moon. He made no move to intercept me. His head slowly turned to watch me go.

Then the engine started sputtering...

My heart jackhammered. The flames were down to fumes. This frantic run-for-your-life scamper was not sustainable. I had bleeding gashes, cuts and bruises, and a fractured orbital bone that had yet to heal. My ankles ached, my bad knee popped, and my lungs burned. I may have been more than human, but I wasn't entirely angel either. I was between, and my body was coming undone.

The only thing that stood between me and a clear shot to the end through Marconi Plaza was an office building—luckily, it was closed for the holiday.

Scaling up or running around would take too long—so I ended up going right through it.

Launching myself up and over the next intersection, I dove headfirst through a plate glass window, and rolled to my feet in the middle of a single office suite. Glass exploded, flying in every direction, while papers scattered into a cascading shower of documents and manila folders. A cubicle partially collapsed as I collided with it coming out of my roll. My face, arms and chest were cut. Blood ran hot and sticky down the side of my face and left a trail on the floor behind me, before the wounds lazily stitched together.

I sprinted through the office, eyed up the far end and dove out the other side feet first, shifting gravity as if I were falling through the glass. I erupted from the building, bursting through the window and soared a few hundred feet into a rolling slide on a rooftop across the street.

"That was impressive," said Markus. "Look out."

"Tony!" shouted Chappy.

As I got to my feet I was hit—smashed and concussed—a... complete...

...

...

...

...I awoke in mid-air...

I blacked out—by impact or centrifugal force.

Moloch—a beast as big as a fucking bison—charged out of the Veil as I landed. His bull horns only grazed my chest, but the impact sent me skittering off the edge of the roof and falling into the alley below...

...Falling toward the charred outstretched limbs of Belial waiting for me—and despite all the pain, despite the murky cognition—I didn't want to see what would happen if I fell into the clutches of *that*...

Corkscrewing, building torque, I shoved my fist as hard as I could into his face—his sharp talons raking across mine. My hand instantly shattered on his rock-hard nose and cheekbone, as he fell backward tasting his own blood—while a flood of my own hit the back of my throat.

Onto my feet, I fled with a busted hand, three broken ribs, a cracked pelvis, and a shredded face, down through the alley, attempting to heal and outpace a rampaging—*one armed?*—Moloch.

I could sense he was closing in, his giant bull horns lowered, ready to gore. The vibration—the smell—the taste of blood. I couldn't survive another hit, not like that…

I was a broken windup toy. The pain was going to overwhelm me—like I might black out all over again.

"Shit my man," shouted Montoya, "he's closing on you!"

"Someone call the medic!" shouted Markus.

If only there was time.

My brain was a skipping record…

"*Your time is running out, Tony.*" Roman's arrogance seared into my memory—a night I wished I could forget.

"*The trouble is, you think you have time...*" Buddha said that, or I think he did…

There was a hitch in my stride. A glance over my shoulder toward the stampeding beast made my senses flare, but my fear narrowed my perception. I never even noticed the arm that burst from a rancid puddle, clawing at my ankles from the muck. Spinning, I pranced by, but stumbled right back where I started—

"All mine," cackled Hekate, "again."

The mother of dark Fae gasped in delight. She snared me by the throat and lifted me off my feet with the beast rumbling toward us like a bowling ball toward pins. With a wave of her hand, Moloch disappeared mid-stride, a moment from impact. She wanted me for herself. Hekate's thorny grip clamped down onto my shoulder and tossed me like she was shooting baskets. Blood sprayed across the pavement as I skidded and slammed into a darkened storefront window. The glass cracked like ice but didn't shatter, and I was left stunned, unable to move.

"Get up!" yelled Montoya—my shoulder slung at my side. "Get up!"

The whole right half of my body had been nearly torn off.

"Tony! Time to move, pal!" shouted Markus.

"This is not the end!" shouted Doshin. "Flee!"

As the brain-trust hollered, everything slowed. My body refused to move, but my senses took note of every sound, scent, and motion—returning to their basic functions.

There was a soft undulating creep nearby, squirming closer and closer. A stream of rancid drool dripped from above and burned into the pavement at my side, while a twisting breeze sent goosebumps across my skin with the sound of flapping feathers above. From across the street, Hekate marched toward me, sifting between growing shadows.

My back was literally against the fucking wall, and I couldn't get my damn body to work.

"Whatever you have to do to get moving again, you must do it now, Tony! Now!" yelled Chappy. His voice boomed inside my head, but my body wasn't cooperating. The only thing that functioned was my need for oxygen—hyperventilating—faster, faster, faster—my heart slowing...

"Dagon is right above you, Tony!" screamed Jamaal, his face inches from my own. "Get up!"

"You must move!" growled Doshin.

"Sir! Sir you've got to move!" shouted Henry. "Mind above matter."

"Is this how you want to go?" asked Markus.

"My man," pled Montoya, "do something!"

Then, intervention.

A couple of kids in university sweatshirts came stumbling out of the sleepy restaurant four doors down, laughing.

"Meka, it had to be a joke," said a girl with a Santa hat. "I mean, nobody can be that dumb, right?"

"No joke," said Meka, playing with her braids. "He was dumb as ffff —" She was mid-sentence when her breath caught in her throat. She saw *them* before her friend did—things that no human had ever lived to speak of.

Both girls froze.

There was something about Meka that made her glow. An aura that lit up like a lighthouse when she saw them—her eyes reflective, flashing —one blue, the other amber.

Hekate hissed—the aura called to her like an irresistible urge and moved toward Meka like a shark prowling a tastier treat.

"A door!" cooed the goddess.

That moment, that minor reprieve, allowed my mind to reconnect with my body. Dagon, sifting down the side of the building like a Wacky Wally crawler, and couldn't control his urges. He leapt for the quick savory kill of college youth when a flash of metal from beyond the Veil severed one of his outstretched tentacles.

The angels were watching. Red armor. It was Eris.

Dagon wailed.

I grabbed the god by the nearest lashing tentacle and yanked him toward me—and in one swift motion I shoved my pocketknife blade through his temple and destroyed his left eye—the damn knife had been in my pocket since the beginning.

Dagon frantically batted me away before I could take the other—the blade broken off in his eye-hole.

"Go!" I shouted—Meka and her friend didn't need another directive, and took off running—but before I could summon the hellfire within, Hekate backhanded me into a chain-link fence surrounding an empty overgrown lot.

She was on top of me in a blink, grappling for my throat, when my hand passed over a beer bottle—brown glass with a peeling label. I smashed it against the fence and jammed the broken edge through Hekate's mask and deep into her forehead.

She paused. Her eye twitched.

I twisted and pulled. A brown section of brain slipped free as Hekate went limp.

I kicked her away and ducked beneath a flock of swooping crows as the fae-goddess screeched. Her shrieks sent sharp, creeping jabs up my spine. It was all the motivation I needed to concentrate myself into nothing but speed.

"Just in time," said Montoya. "You're cutting it too close for me, my man."

"I couldn't let it happen," I said. "No more death."

"What was she?" asked Chappy. "What was the girl? Meka?"

But I didn't know, and I might never find out if I didn't get moving. I had witnessed things I might never understand. Meka was special, and maybe saving her would mean something.

I moved faster than I had ever moved, as fast as Hermes streaking through the skies on winged sandals. The speed put me out ahead of them as Citizen's Bank Park, where the Phillies played from spring to fall, came into view. I cut through the empty parking lot to the Pattison station entrance at 3600 S. Broad without a trace of immediate evil, then slipped down the stairs below the street and into the murky underground.

"Fifteen minutes, fifty-three seconds," said Jamaal.

"Four minutes before the next train, sir," said Henry, studying his pocket watch.

"Do you have enough juice?" asked Jamaal, keeping stride beside me.

"Hope so," I said. The flames were smoldering.

At the bottom of the stairs, I jumped the turnstile and onto the maroon tiled floor as the lights began to flicker.

BONUS ACHEIVED: Leap subway turnstile like a badass.

Not many people used Pattison station when the entertainment complexes weren't hosting events. I'd double-checked earlier—nothing on the schedule for December 24th. The last station along the Broad Street Line was a block or two past the last residential streets in South Philly before the Naval Yard. There were ads for Sixers and Flyers tickets as I jogged past—and a thick fog began to sweep through the station from the tunnel.

Luckily, the station was as empty as expected, and I spared little time hopping off the platform and hustling down the tracks away from the fog and into the gloom. I jogged to the very end of the line, another half mile, somewhere between the stadiums and the Naval Yard—to a spot where light from the twilight sky broke the near-pitch darkness through a drainpipe. That drainpipe sat directly below the FDR Skatepark, between cargo tracks and I-95.

I felt the presence of my pursuers slow into a deliberate stalk as I waited.

"Do you think they're all here?" asked Montoya.

"Let us hope so," said Chappy.

"We have a lot riding on this plan," said Markus.

XII

portent

JACINDA
Then.

"Hey, did you see this?"

I was so excited I came bursting into the pasta aisle like the Kool-Aid Man. Tony was half asleep with a jar of tomato sauce in hand. He nearly fumbled it into the cart when I made my return from the restroom, as one must do when listening to Elton John's "Rocket Man" on the supermarket speakers.

This was a part of our weekly routine—Saturday morning groceries.

If you would have told me at sixteen that this would be my life at twenty-four, I would have smiled—how did I get here? This life was so very far away from where I had started. A routine was exactly what I needed when life could be so unpredictable and confusing.

Those moments in my memory that felt beyond touch were terrifying little snapshots of something I could never understand. Were they dreams? Reality? Somewhere in the middle?

But with routine, I felt normal. I felt whole.

But Tony? There was something about his demeanor that seemed… *lifeless?* Like the reverb turned all the way up on my Gibson.

An echo. A ghost. A wraith…

"What's that?" he asked, his eyes distant after studying the nutrition facts on the jar. Tony was getting fluffy, and he'd begun obsessing over every ingredient he put into his body, as if trying to identify the culprit responsible, one milligram at a time.

"Tryouts." I beamed. "For the Mercy Point baseball team." I was waving the flyer around like a pom-pom, a cheerleader injecting the spirit of excitement into him—and it wasn't working.

I'd found the flyer posted by the Customer Service desk and couldn't wait to show him. I had always wanted to watch Tony play—and not just because I wanted to see him in one of those uniforms…the stirrups? Mah gawd.

Tony hadn't been himself in a while, which had become a point of contention I was too afraid to bring up. Don't get me wrong, I was in love with the fool, which was why it broke my heart so much to see him lacking that spark—that thing that made him glow.

Before we were even dating, he made every interaction electric. I was already in a committed relationship—though committed was the operable term—what I ever saw in Rick was beyond my understanding. But, I'd never cheat. Ever. Tony was just a friend, but we had such a great connection that I found myself drawn to him. I set boundaries, then broke them, but Tony never crossed that line. I felt guilty whenever I was around him, and forced nearly all of our interactions within a group setting—safety in numbers, ya know?

I didn't want to lead him on—and maybe I did by accident. Maybe I gave him hope just by laughing with him?

He was passionate and caring and smart and funny—and he would never hurt me.

When we started dating, his happiness was like sunshine, and it only ever faded during the dramatic periods, replaced by a determination and an optimism that gave me hope.

But now? At times he seemed only half there, like a piece was missing. His antipathy was like a dull ache right over my heart.

"Yeah," he replied, glancing at the flyer. "That's cool."

And sometimes I felt like I was being silly. The fact of the matter was, he was totally attentive to me. He was doing everything right by me, but that wasn't the problem…

…he was slipping away. He was becoming a hollowed-out version of himself, like he was on autopilot. We saw our friends, we had a healthy balance of togetherness and alone time, we laughed and had fun, and we were always supportive of each other—which was why it killed me so much that there was something wrong. Something that was missing. Something that was gnawing away at me like a Gremlin after a midnight snack.

Was it the chase? He had spent all that time chasing after me. Now that he had me, maybe he needed that chase?

Was it adulthood? That was enough to grind anyone down. He was working a soulless forty plus hours week, while I struggled to get my music off the ground. Was a nine-to-five sucking his soul like a deadite summoned from the Necronomicon?

…Amanda would have appreciated that one…

Or was it me? Literally me. Was I the problem? Or was all of this only in my head?

"I thought you'd be more excited." I couldn't hide my disappointment, so I stashed the flyer into my back pocket.

He placed the sauce jar into the cart like he was admitting defeat—way to go, expensive jar of sauce! You made the cut!—and took the flyer from my pocket. He gave it a read-through and flipped it over for a thorough inspection, but he didn't say anything.

"What do you think?" I asked.

"I'd have to get new equipment," he said.

"Cleats and a glove? That's not too bad. We can afford that."

"It takes time to break in a glove."

"Okay," I said, trying to sound supportive. When he didn't say anything else, I gently pushed. "Do you want to play? Are you interested?"

"Maybe."

"Is there something else?" I asked.

"Something else, like what?"

"Is there anything else you'd like to do? A hobby? I don't know, something to make you feel good?"

"What makes you think I don't feel good?"

"I don't know," I replied, then retreated to look at the…olive oil. Yup, I was now an olive oil expert. Extra virgin? Hah, not these days, pal.

"Jace," he said, "I'm happy." He had a reassuring look on his face, like he was attempting to stomp out any and all questions. He wasn't hiding anything. I could tell when he was. He really meant it, and that—that right there—that kind of broke my heart just a bit—because something, whatever it might be, was wrong.

"Something doesn't feel right," I said. "You're a doughnut hole."

"A what?"

"You're the hole in the doughnut," I repeated. "Just empty space."

"Glazed or cinnamon sugar?" he said, but I didn't laugh. I couldn't. Then he stepped away from the cart and took my hands—in the middle of the pasta aisle—this Italian guy, hey Tony!—spittin' fancy moves like he found *amore* amongst the Old Country's dried and canned goods. "Honestly, I'm fine. I just feel a little beat down with work."

"Is there anything I can do?" I asked.

"You already do everything I could ask for," he said, kissing me. I lit up like a flood light during a perp hunt. "You're my dream girl, and we're together."

Oof.

And even though he was being a total romantic, there was still a problem.

He called me his *dream girl*.

I secretly had a problem with him calling me that. He meant nothing of it, but it made me feel like a fantasy, not a reality. Like he was too busy dreaming of me than being with me. Like he would rather be thinking of me than enjoying with me.

His finger gently tugged at the chain around my neck—without saying it, Tony was reminding me of our promise.

"Tomorrow's not a promise, T," I said. "Make sure you're as happy as you can be."

I didn't mean for the tears to form. As soon as I felt them, I turned away—but he saw them, though he never let on that he did.

I never wanted to be the girl who needed saving. I never wanted to be this prize at the end of a rainbow, and I was scared all the way down to my toes that I had somehow become Tony's Princess Zelda. And now that the evil was vanquished, he was losing a part of himself.

That night, I had the strangest dream.

I always had strange dreams—sometimes I'd dream up whole realities—a sacred tree in a far-off land that would birth a champion—a city with a super-hero problem run amok—Tony in a strange wasteland, running from tiny little horned monsters that ate each other to become a larger monster—inverted pyramids and gods on horses galloping into the void—weird stuff, right? I could have filled volumes of dream diaries, probably could've been a case study for some med student looking to crack open secrets of the mind.

But that night, the night after that conversation at the grocery store, something odd happened. Something that defied logic. Something that really spooked me.

I was a deep sleeper. It was rare for me to wake up in the middle of the night. My mind could've conjured up the most terrifying horrors, and I wouldn't make a peep.

But this night, I tossed and turned as I dreamt.

I was running. Running up a jammed escalator into a food court—it was the Grace Falls mall, and the lights were out. There were people there, but they were hiding—some in the stores by the windows, watching—others barricading themselves within stores. Something was chasing me, something terrible I couldn't see as it moved through the shadows behind me. It had almost caught up, nipping at my heels, reaching…

…when Tony and *Scary Moby* showed up. They were a mis-matched pair—Tony and this pale, bald guy with a black suit and equally black eyes…

…and someone was humming a tune.

"You are my sunshine, my only sunshine, you make me happy when skies are gray..."

I sprang from the bed in a cold sweat and hyperventilated next to the window. I was so upset I got up and grabbed a bottle of water from the kitchen, trying to shake the feeling that whatever it was chasing me in the shadows, it was watching me right now.

When I returned to bed, I snuggled close to Tony for comfort, but every time I shut my eyes, I could feel it, reaching out to grab hold and drag me away. Tantalizingly close, but out of reach—like it was somewhere between here and there—between dream and reality. A phantom waiting for me.

When I think back on that night, that wasn't the worst part of it. That wasn't the thing that still gives me the creeps.

The worst part of it all was that Tony...

"Where did you go?" he whispered, still asleep.

"I'm here," I said, "right beside you."

"We're in the mall looking for you."

...Tony was having the same dream.

"Why are you in the mall?" I asked.

It had to be a coincidence, right? This kind of stuff isn't real, right?

"The shadow. We're saving you from the shadow."

Now, I know better.

It was all real, and somehow, I had dragged Tony into all of my messes.

I'm drifting. Fragment to fragment.

Tomorrow's not a promise. Gotta earn each one.

I'm not going to lose my soul. I'm not going to lose.

How can I fit everything I am now into that tiny place?

When all this is over, will I still be me? What am I now?

Wake up! Wake up! Wake up!

Somewhere.

Now.

I awoke inside my childhood bed. I knew something wasn't right. Partly because my feet dangled over the edge—the bed was made for a six-year-old girl with a love for sock monkeys—and I was nearly thirty with an unhealthy obsession with knee-highs. It was the old house on Cross Road, and I hadn't been in that house in nearly two decades. I laid there for a minute trying to remember what led to this moment—was I asleep? How did I get here?

I was dressed in clothes I'd never owned. Torn black jeans with a flaming heart buckle, high lacing black Doc Martens—that were fricking awesome, by the way—a fraying black denim vest, and a tank top with a spray-painted symbol in gray. It looked like a two and a four had been smashed together.

And fingerless gloves? Giant plastic lightning bolt earrings? It was like Jem got lost in the Misfits dressing room.

"What in the holy heck..." I whispered after rolling out of bed and checking myself out in the mirror. I mean, I definitely would've worn this...to a Metallica, or Motorhead concert or something. One of the buttons pinned onto the vest said *Resist*—

"What are you *resisting*, O'Neill?" I said in Amanda's voice.

This room elicited so many old memories...

Sight, sound, touch, feel—it was real—and yet, everything felt like it was fake—a facsimile? I couldn't put a finger on it even after touching everything, as if looking for a clue.

The bookcase was exactly as I remembered it—stuffed with story time favorites with mom—*The Monster at the End of this Book*! She read to me every night when I was in preschool, before she stopped caring. My tap-dance shoes were in the corner, resting beside my collection of 80's classic toys: Glo Worms, Pound Puppies, My Little Pony, Rainbow Bright and Strawberry Shortcake—they were all there, lined up just as I had left them. Those last two—Amanda and I used to imagine we were them—Rainbow Amanda Brite and her blonde hair, and Strawberry O'Neill Shortcake with her red curls.

It was like walking into a time warp, but not the fun kind with Riff Raff and Columbia. There was something spooky about all this, something wrong, besides the obvious.

Why was I here? Where was I...before *this*?

Even Grammy's old guitar was there by the nightstand—the one that got smashed—tuned and ready to play. I may have picked it up for a quick strum, one more round of "Hey Jude" for memory's sake, when there was a knock at the front door. Three knocks, to be precise—in perfect timing.

I didn't want to answer the door. It seemed a terrible idea, given the fake world and the questionable arrival in a place that offered me little happiness the first time around—except for the friend I made next door. Perhaps that's the reason I opened the door—that I might see—

"—Amanda?"

The girl had her back to me. She bounced nervously on her toes, wearing a green dress with yellow flowers that looked older than me, and her long blonde hair was damp and tangled.

"Let me in?" she wept. "Please?"

It wasn't Amanda.

She was young—seventeen?—blonde hair, blue eyes, dirty, barefoot, and terrified. Anyone remember *The Last House on the Left*? It was the only horror movie Amanda and I cried through. Without another word exchanged, I took her by the arm and brought her inside, then locked the door. After escorting her to the living room, I checked the windows —what was I searching for? Spying eyes? Animals? *Monsters?*

"Are you okay?" I asked. "Was there something out there?"

She nodded.

"You'll be safe with me," I lied. "Do you need anything? Would you like a glass of water?"

I was pretending to appear calm, but I was anything but. My heart pounded like a bass drum, and I swore she could see the veins in my neck bulge.

The girl nodded.

"What's your name?" I asked after returning with my old Snoopy glass full of tap-water.

"Lilandra," she said.

XIII

the plan pt. 2

TONY
December 24, 2013
Now.

The second half of the plan wasn't as complicated as the first, but it relied on one simple principle; If I could pick up a gun and shoot bullets of hellfire, why couldn't I do the same with any other modern weapon?

Days ago—though a lifetime spent watching Jaycie in between— there was a news report featuring my old Professor about the impossibility versus improbability of multiple strikes of lightning at the same location, and the mysterious case of missing explosives from the Divine Lorraine Hotel implosion scheduled that day. I didn't ponder it much—I was suffering through a panic attack and choking down a cocktail of antidepressants at the time—I remember thinking, "that's scary" and the idea of some loony running around the city with explosives made me even more anxious. Then Montoya mentioned using explosives to blow the entire Thirteen to kingdom come.

That's when it struck me—I am, was, will be, the loony.

Going back to December 19th broke Celestial Law—I created a paradox as soon as I arrived at the *Gates of Hell* statue downtown—lightning struck the same spot four times, like skipping a record—but, it had already happened. Water under the bridge, right? I was merely catching up to the past. I had already done the deed, so might as well do it now, right?

Then the brain-trust and I watched the technicians as they expertly placed explosives throughout the Divine Lorraine—an old, abandoned, haunted-as-fuck hotel on the corner of Broad and Fairmount Avenue—in preparation for an implosion demolition that was scheduled for 2:30 p.m. Once they had finished and vacated the building, I exited the Veil and stole a dozen of their charges, then disabled the switching mechanism on the remaining charges with Montoya's help.

We immediately used the key to jump five days into the future and rigged the explosives up to a switch—a remote control with a big red button—at the far end of the subway tunnel, beyond the last station and into a section of track that was rarely used. In fact, we were somewhere beneath FDR Park near Langley Avenue. It was abandoned, underground, and far away from people.

Earlier, the brain-trust and I had debated the finer aspects of the plan.

Thirty-Five Minutes Ago

"I'm pretty sure they call that a causal time loop," I said. "But, I'm no scientist." I had watched a lot of time travel movies in my day, read a few articles, and learned a few buzz words—which meant I was something of an internet expert. However, I was nowhere near as versed as Maynard, who was a next-level pop-culture time travel enthusiast.

"Who's they?" asked Chappy. Guns made him nervous—bombs made him panic. He was as far away from us as possible, despite the fact the only one of us with actual skin in the game was me.

"Hollywood." I shrugged.

"No, you're right. I mean, kinda," bumbled Jamaal. He was leaning against the grimy wall and talking fantasy physics—I don't think there's anything he enjoyed more.

It was a head-scratcher—causal time loops. I only knew about the explosives and the lighting because I saw the news reports. However, if I hadn't gone back in time and done those things, they would've never happened to begin with—thus, a causal loop.

"That key makes you a walking paradox," added Jamaal. "Anything we attempt to do within your natural timeline would damage reality. Gabe said that, didn't he?"

"He did," I agreed, as I adhered one of the explosives to the wall with Montoya's supervision. I had been called a lot of things in my day, but *paradox* might have been the most accurate—even before the key.

The subway tunnels were filled with roaches the size of hamsters and rats the size of cats. Though none of them were nosy enough to come anywhere near me as I worked. Just seeing their glowing eyes shifting in the darkness gave me the creeps—especially after witnessing the things that lived behind the Veil—the things that crawled out of their holes to devour innocence.

"If so," Jamaal continued, "exactly how many paradoxes must one commit in order to break the world?" He was logically inspecting the subject from all angles, as if trying to prove a point. "Two? Three? A full dozen? I'm counting five so far and we haven't even figured a way to lure the Thirteen here without causing another one."

"Maybe it's more complicated than that, my man. There's a lot of fucking wacky rules with time-shit and angels and crap," said Montoya.

"Eloquent," groaned Chappy.

"All I'm saying is, maybe it's the quality," added Montoya.

"The rules of creating a paradox," started Henry, "appear inconsistent." He was always studying his watch. At first, I thought he was just a worrier, but lately, I think the watch was a gift from someone he wanted to remember.

"How so?" asked Chappy.

"I mean, there were two of me in my apartment the other night. No paradox there," I explained, picking up Henry's thought. Thinking back on that batshit crazy conversation with myself still haunted me—unlike the current super crazy conversation with the voices in my head. Sometimes I wonder if I'm the one unravelling, like it's all a psychotic break.

"But that's because your Echo had his own Thread of Fate," said Montoya, kind of making sense. "It wasn't the same you. You were two separate yous."

Doshin grimaced.

"Actually," added Markus—he was quietly watching— "the flicker you encountered when you were caught between your Echo and Summanus—that was the paradox."

"Did you really understand any of what you just said?" asked Jamaal, glaring past Markus to Montoya.

"Yes." Then Montoya smiled, and we all knew he was full of shit. He thought about it a moment longer. "No. But, why steal these demolition charges, my man?" He quickly abandoned the conversation when he realized it was flying over his head. "Why not break into a military site or something? Go big?"

"Because I saw it on the news," I explained. "It had already happened —*already*? See? Causality. Loop." Maybe I did know a thing or two about time travel, as I drew a circle in the air to illustrate my expertise.

"Tony, you and I both know the news is sensationalist bullshit," proclaimed Jamaal, with extra emphasis on *bullshit*. "How'd you even know it wasn't just click-bait?"

"For one, it was a live broadcast," I replied.

"What!?" squawked Jamaal—as if that was a foreign concept.

"Sensationalist?" asked Henry. "Information has certainly changed since my day."

"And apparently the *my day* jokes are as old as you are," joked Jamaal.

Their lives were separated by almost two hundred fifty years—their societies were so different, yet separated by a blink from the Earth's perspective.

I had just finished rewiring the charge to a new switch, coiling the wire around a spoke leading to the transmitter with Montoya's supervision, when inspiration struck.

"They use gold in wires," I said.

"Yeah?" said Jamaal. "So?"

I reached into my pocket and snagged Mammon's coin. I had stowed it there long ago, and even after everything my wardrobe had been through—fires, stabbings, maulings, explosions, etc...— it was still there.

"Can we use this to transmit a message?" I asked. "Like the gold inside wire."

"Tony, my man," said Montoya, "Are you looking to call Malus from a payphone?"

"What is a payphone?" asked Doshin.

"No," I said, recalling an adolescence full of horror movies with Amanda. "What does Evil Dead and Hellraiser have in common?"

"Schlock? Gore?" said Jamaal, while the others scratched their heads.

"Invocation." I grinned, flipping the coin into the air and snatching it with the other hand. "That's how we lure them. They're going to be looking for me, any sign of me, even the slightest blip will snag their attention. Let's ring a dead god and see who answers."

I had experience—sorta. Cyn had tried to summon Tori years ago...

"Where?" asked Chappy. "Where would we summon them?"

"Somewhere public," said Markus. "If they lured you into a dark abandoned subway tunnel, do you think you'd show up?"

"Good point," I said. "Somewhere inviting?"

"Like?" asked Jamaal.

"A landmark," said Markus. "Someplace open. Easy to find. Easy to escape."

"Rittenhouse Square? Franklin Park? Logan Circle?

"Public parks include crowds," said Henry. "How would we protect them?"

"We could use the Veil," suggested Chappy.

"Hmmm," said Jamaal. "Logan Circle was once a site for capital punishment. The city executed one-hundred-eight men and four women from that location, by *gallows*."

"Bad juju," said Montoya.

"Could be useful," said Markus. "Negative energy begets negative energy."

"The Logan Circle fountain," I said in agreement. "We'll draw them there."

"But why the fountain, sir?" asked Henry. "Why the fountain when we could lure them directly here?"

"Hmmm," agreed Doshin. The man could convey whole sentences within a grunt.

"As we said, 'If they lured you into a dark abandoned subway tunnel, do you think you'd show up?'"

"Ah, yeah," said Montoya, shooting Jamaal a glance. "I suppose that makes sense, my man. That's gonna be a heck of a chase."

"That's the plan," said Markus. "They'll be too busy chasing us to cause any damage. We summon them where we want. We hide behind the Veil and poke our heads out occasionally. Keep them chasing. And we lure them here and blow them up."

"Exactly," I said, nodding.

"But," said Jamaal, "what if they don't take the bait? What if they don't chase?"

"Are we going back over this again?" said Markus.

"While I don't have the answers," said Henry, "I do believe that unpredictability should be expected."

"What do you mean?" I asked. I felt my blood pressure rise.

"We act as if we are dealing with people, but these are gods," he continued. "Their decision making is not like our own and should be taken into account when creating a plan."

Doubt. I felt the pressure penetrating my skin, building between my eyes, and an emotion I hadn't felt in a long time—anxiety. Panic. Questioning and overanalyzing and reevaluating and questioning again. A loop of thought that was always present, but suddenly had been invited from the back of my mind and into the moment.

"If this is such a bad plan," I said, "what do you suggest?" I may have said it with more angst than I intended. "I don't have the answers. I don't have a fucking clue!" Jamaal winced. "All I know is that we have a plan to lure them here. They need *this*." I pulled the key from beneath my shirt. "They will stop at nothing to get it. There's no such thing as the perfect plan, but if we need bad mojo—"

"Juju," corrected Montoya.

"—to summon them," I continued, "and this place has none, then we follow the plan and summon them to a place we know will work. I don't know what else you want from me."

"You're in charge," said Markus.

"That's right," I said, "I'm the one in charge." Then it was quiet. I almost thought they had left when Chappy sighed. "Am I doing this right?"

Montoya nodded. "Yeah, my man. Just loop the wire through."

Doshin eventually agreed that luring them somewhere public had a higher success ratio than calling them directly into the blast radius. Somewhere public and open. A place where they'd have to hide or be seen—

However, none of us expected them to come out of the shadows and murder innocent people. Henry had warned me. We were dealing with unpredictable gods with godlike thoughts and motives. That was my fuck-up—and it was time to be done with the Thirteen.

Now.

The tunnel was filled with dirt and refuse scattered around the edge of the tracks—from an old Twinkie wrapper to a couple of discarded batteries, it was an odd collection of junk. The stink of ammonia converged from every corner from vast coatings of urine. *Damn, there was a lot of fucking of urine.* I mean, there was an egregious amount of both animal and human urine in every direction and on every possible urination-reaching surface. However, the tunnel was completely abandoned. There wasn't even a noticeable insect that perked my angelic senses, as far as I could feel. The rats and roaches had evacuated, as if they knew what was coming.

My Chucks were still tacky with melted blacktop and had been coated in dust and grime from the subway tunnels. They were the first pair of shoes I'd bought on my limited budget after Northcreek—and for a pair of canvas sneakers, they held up, until now.

"Damn, I really liked these Chucks," I grumbled, hoping they'd heal like my body, clothes, and jacket, given enough time.

"I'm amazed Chuck Taylors are still around," said Montoya. He died in the 60s and never got to witness the fall and rise of the classic canvas high-top sneaker. "I had a red pair when I was a kid."

"We still wear them in 2090s. They've got smart technology that adjusts for comfort," said Jamaal.

"What is smart technology?" asked Henry.

"Imagine a machine that could adjust to different aspects of your life without having to tell the machine to do it in the first place," said Jamaal. "That's smart technology."

"Is not all technology smart?" asked Doshin.

"Well, yeah," said Jamaal. "But it's smarter than regular technology."

With the Thirteen closing in, I set the trap by placing a hand onto each of the explosive charges, set ten feet apart on either side of the tunnel. Just a single second's touch was all I needed to imbue them with hellfire.

A dozen hellfire bombs, the first of their kind.

The Thirteen wouldn't know what hit 'em.

With the explosive switch in one hand—a remote control with a single red button—and the remaining hellfire gun in the other, I stopped at the end of the line and waited. A few hundred feet behind me the track opened to a marshy lot beside the FDR Skatepark, through a giant drainpipe—my escape.

Everything was unnaturally quiet and still as I waited—as quiet and still as I could ever remember the world before my senses were pushed into overdrive. Too still. Too fucking still. Where were they? My eyes darted from floor to ceiling, from shadow to crevice, and over everything in between—even to that weird Twinkie wrapper with the creepy cowboy giving me the eye.

"My man," asked Montoya, "you don't think they'll bring Jaycie, do you?"

"No," I said. "If I were Malus, I'd keep her as far away from me as possible."

"But," said Markus, "You're not Malus."

It was the kind of statement that wormed into my head and made me doubt everything, if not for—

"Excuse me, sir."

My heart nearly ejected from my chest.

I spun around, gun lifted, and caught a homeless man shuffling out of the shadows behind me. "Do you have a dollar?" he asked. "Spare change?"

I never sensed him. I could smell ants from ten paces, and a dozen different species of pee, but didn't notice this guy until he was right up behind me?

"Go!" I shouted and waved my gun around like I had seen a thousand times in movies and TV—I looked more crazy than threatening.

There wouldn't be another innocent death on my hands.

"Calm down there, fella," he said. His dark skin was concealed behind layers of grease and soot. He was hunched over and wearing old military fatigues and ratty pants—a former soldier by the look of it.

"Sir, you need to get out of here," I warned.

"Aw c'mon! You ain't gonna shoot nobody!" he said, slurring his words. His long scraggly white hair and beard were matted down like he had spent a few nights face down in pool of his own puke. "I just need a dollar. Maybe a sandwich if ya feelin' extra nice?"

That's when the little things suddenly became obvious. The old man was dirty from head to toe, but his teeth were perfectly white, and his fatigues were all wrong—like they were made by someone who didn't understand of the branches of the U.S. military. There was a six-pointed star, and the left breast patch said *U.S. Invaders*.

"Yeah, that's not a real military uniform," agreed Montoya. He would know.

When I placed the gun between the man's eyes, he smiled.

"Are you with them?" I asked, nodding into the tunnel where the evil continued to probe toward us, just out of reach.

"I had the chance to kill you, and I did not," he said, grinning like he was caught passing notes in class.

"Is that an answer?" I asked.

"Merely an observation."

"Why," I asked. "What do you want?"

"I was given an opportunity to join an elite group, but I am curious."

"Curious about what?"

"You, obviously," he said. "I know what *he* seeks." The man gestured up the subway tunnel, and it didn't take a mind-reader to know he meant Malus. My eyes kept flicking back and forth between the tunnel and the Fallen in hobo's clothing. "But, what do you seek?"

"Careful," warned Henry, saying what I was already thinking.

"An end to a means. A means to an end," I said.

"And what end would that be? An end to existence? To end your enemies? To end suffering?" he asked. When he said *suffering* my pulse reacted, increasing by a fraction. He smiled. "Suffering is a terrible thing. You have the eyes of a man who has suffered, but so have many. What makes your suffering so much worse than anyone else?"

"It's not my suffering I'm looking to end," I said, and the hobo's curious grin emptied as if gauging my truth. I scanned the tunnel again for movement, and when I turned back to him, I was staring into the face of regality.

He was dressed like the finest African king, with a bright green tunic and lion skins draped over his shoulder. He wore a grand necklace of gold, adorned with the fangs of his greatest kill, and a spear with a wide blue metal blade. His great silver beard and long silver hair framed his dark skin as he revered me with dignity. I felt as if I was in the presence of royalty.

"I am Eshu, god of discord, god of chance," he said. "I see that you are less than you ought to be, and more than you want to be. I look within you, and I see such terrible grief. I look upon you and I see a man who has been cut so deep, he laughs to distract from the bleeding. And yet it is not your own suffering that concerns you."

"What?" I asked, shaking my head. The last thing I needed was another shrink. I even had one within my own noggin.

"I am merely attempting to comprehend the deal I was offered. *They* say I must destroy you," he said, pointing up the tunnel, "though each have their purpose, their motivation, their incentive—even the best contracts may lead to terrible things. I cannot shake the thought that I have thrown my stake in with the wrong lot."

He reached out and kindly placed a hand onto mine, lowering my aim from his face—and I let him. There was something disarming about Eshu, but as I had discovered before, these creatures were surrounded in magic and distraction.

"Keep that gun on him," said Markus.

His true name surfaced like a memory, and I was left with little time to decide whether to play my cards or hold them.

"Satarcept," I said, speaking Eshu's true name. Those exact syllables strung together made his eyes widen, as if I had jabbed him with something sharp. "You can soliloquy all you want some other time, but right now, I'm kind of in the thick of it."

And with that, he vanished. Completely disappeared.

"Where'd he go?" asked Montoya.

"Shit!" I had blown it.

I eased off the gas when I should have pushed it all the way to the floor. Eshu was surely running to Malus to rat me out. He was a trickster—his true name told me so, and I was about to be royally fucked.

"Do you think he's going to screw us?" asked Jamaal.

"I don't know."

"You fucked that one up, T," groaned Markus.

"I have a very poor feeling about this," said Henry.

"Thanks, 3-PO," I sneered.

"I don't understand the reference, sir," said Henry.

"Hah, 3-PO," laughed Jamaal, "if only you had lived another hundred years, Henry."

"*Boy.*"

Around the corner, where the subway tracks fell under darkness, the air rippled. Something was coming, like light and shadow bending through water.

"Boy," it said again. Its voice was sharp and cavernous, like ancient rage. "Do you know where the soul resides? In which part of the body it hides? Let us seek it out, together."

It was hard not to feel the impending dread of what was coming.

Whichever member of the Thirteen it was, it had yet to reveal itself. My fears got the best of me, as my thumb rested heavy on the red button—the one attached to the remote, set to turn this whole place into a furnace.

"Not yet," reminded Doshin.

The switch was a plastic handle, with grips for each finger and a big red rubber button for the thumb—like an old arcade joystick. It was wireless and weighed next to nothing in my hand. I scanned the walls quickly, if not obsessively, for the tiny red lights, reassuring that the bombs were armed and active. Each one tremored with the power it held, struggling to hold its explosive potential. Would they see it? Would they understand its danger? Would they care?

The Fallen emerged from the darkness like it was like rising out of a pool of ink. Thanatos strode toward me, slow and steady. He was seven feet tall and proportional; long arms and legs, and skin rotted on the bone. He was held together by bolted straps of leather, staples and stitches, and a face as pretty as raw, maggot-infested flank steak.

When none of the other gods revealed themselves, I knew this was a one-on-one. A test. Why send in the full fleet when one assassin would do? They weren't dummies. They knew I was luring them into a trap. The question was, would their hubris bring them within the blast radius?

I slipped the switch into my inner jacket pocket, took aim, and left my concern about Eshu at the back of my mind. Thanatos deliberately approached, stalking a prey that refused to run—and I smiled. I must have been the dumbest thing the god had ever seen.

Maybe I was an idiot.

Maybe I should have blown the place and ran while I still could.

Or maybe, this was the right gamble.

Sunken into the skin below his shoulders, Thanatos withdrew two sickles. The blades were poisoned by his flesh, dripping with foul liquid that stained the blades an awful shade of putrid green.

"Do you know what these are?" He showed them to me, crossed symmetrically in front of him. His cold putrefying dead eyes bore into me with an unnatural stare. "They are the sickles of a Harvester."

"Oh yeah? I don't see any wheat down here. You might be in the wrong field," I joked.

"Ha! My man!" laughed Montoya.

Chappy shrugged and smirked at Henry. He looked displeased—a dad joke in the face of death was a new kind of gallows humor.

"Come, boy. Experience suffering."

For a creature of rot, Thanatos moved fast. He chopped the gun barrel off with a sickle swipe before I had the chance to pull the trigger. Then he turned like a ballerina, spinning and slashing for my head, the metal humming through the air.

"Oh shit!" whined Jamaal.

I was weaponless and in serious trouble. My eyes scoured the surrounding area for something to help defend myself—Twinkie The Kid laughed extra hard at my expense from the sponge cake wrapper. If Thanatos's blades could slice through steel, there probably wasn't anything nearby worth swinging.

"What about the rail?" asked Markus, but even with my strength, I doubt I was ripping any length of that up off the track.

"Keep a distance," coached Doshin.

Thanatos lunged at me. I tossed a handful of dust into his face, then pivoted away.

"Honorless attacks are for the weak," said Thanatos, wiping the grime from his putrid eyes.

"Anyone have ideas?" I asked.

"Are you praying to the angels?" asked Thanatos. "They will not trouble us."

"Angels!" shouted Chappy.

"I don't think they're going to help us," said Jamaal.

"No," grumbled Chappy as Thanatos smiled at me. "Angels have always been described as beings capable of summoning weapons. Flaming swords and spears."

"How?" I asked.

"Yeah! How?" shouted Jamaal. His fear was so intense that it was beginning to infect me. Thanatos had killed him. Jamaal had suffered through the fear of everything in life, but Thanatos had devoured it all.

The god of death had become the living embodiment of his dread and despair.

"I will cull your limbs, then sweet evisceration," said the god, answering me. I maintained a distance, letting him stalk me from one side of the tunnel to the other, like a slow game of tag.

"Good question," said Chappy with the calm demeanor of a professor. He stroked his beard in thought. "I suppose it's a matter of faith. Or will. At least, it always appears to be one or the other when it comes to matters of religion."

His rationalization was about as useful as a cold toast.

"Matters of religion?" scoffed Markus.

"What if it's not a matter of religion?" asked Montoya, his voice cracking with fear.

"Imagine you are one with the universe," started Doshin.

"Oh, c'mon!" growled Montoya.

"What does that even mean!?" roared Jamaal.

"Universe is everything!" shouted Doshin, defending his point. "You are not of this world! You are an angel! Act as one, and you will be!"

Made sense—*sorta*...

I remembered the dreamworld, the one inside Jacinda's mind, where the war machines led dark creatures in a siege of her forest kingdom. Her protectors fought them with our help. I remembered the power that surged through me—I felt whole, at peace with my true nature.

Thanatos charged. I dodged, and his sickle nicked my leather jacket.

"Somebody do something!" hollered Montoya as I shifted gravity and fell to the arched tunnel ceiling above.

Thanatos smiled at me again—his "smile" was a grimace, like his face didn't know what to do with itself. His teeth, grimy, yellow, and green at the root—his gums black and spoiled.

Then came the pain.

Slicing agony—something sharp carved into my calf. I looked down and saw a pool of black tar leaking from between the brick and mortar. A piece of it had solidified and formed a spike that impaled my calf.

"What the hell is that!?" yelled Montoya.

Another strand of sinewy tar sprung from the crevice and sliced into my thigh in the shape of a sickle. I had to move, I had to free myself, but these attacks were meant to pin me down for the demon below. Before I could react—before I could decide to do anything—two more embedded themselves into my legs and pulled, bringing me to my knees. Once restrained, Thanatos paced over to the wall and took his first step up toward me.

"What about secret words, my man?" yelled Montoya, but my eyes were locked on the monster.

I had only seconds. Grappling with the tar was like wrestling barbed wire—the more I struggled with them, the more damage done.

"Abracadabra hellfire?" Montoya offered.

Henry looked stumped. Chappy was sweating. Markus turned away. A giant vein in Doshin's neck pulsed. Jamaal was speechless. They were all as hopelessly desperate as I was.

"I shall savor harvesting your flesh," Thanatos threatened. Each step from the giant was three times that of a normal man. The leather binding his form together stretched and whined with every movement. The sickles oozed with poison.

"Sim sim sala bim? Shazam?" continued Montoya.

"Hocus pocus? Presto chango?" offered Jamaal—his voice cracking.

Fear. Rage. Hatred. Hope. Love. The great motivators. I felt them all.

"Alakazam? Open sesame seeds?" Montoya whined.

"What good are you if you cannot protect the woman you love?" Markus had said. He turned back to me expectantly, as if waiting for the next big leap.

My desperation returned, accompanied by the roaring flames.

What good am I if I cannot protect the woman I love?

"This isn't about you versus him. This is about you versus you. Good Tony against Dark Tony," Marshall had said to me, a long time ago—during one of the worst days of my life.

My hands ignited, the hellfire rippling from clenched fists—but flaming fists weren't enough for this battle. I pushed harder, straining against a barrier behind my eyes.

Then the dam broke.

A surge poured through me into my hands, creating constructs of fire spanning the distance between my two outstretched fists.

"That-a-boy!" praised Montoya.

"Thank heavens," said Chappy.

"Oh, fuck yeah!" sang Jamaal, his husky voice billowing like Pavarotti's.

"About damn time!" added Markus.

"Remarkable!" said Henry, while Doshin nodded.

I could feel the haft solidify in my hands while the blade at the far end ignited into a surge of fiery metal.

"Flaming spears do not frighten me, boy," warned Thanatos.

With a few quick swipes, I cut the blades from my legs and pointed the spear at the harvester. More sinewy tar bled from the crevices in the mortar and swiped for my legs. I leapt away and cut them down like I was hacking through thick jungle underbrush.

"You don't scare me either," I lied. His presence pressed upon my will like an aura of suffocation, making me tremble. The flames sputtered against his will but held.

The terror infecting me affected the spear—like a partially blocked fuel line, sputtering.

Why did I fear this god so much? Beyond the nightmarish appearance, I had been through worse—I'd grappled with Mammon and his mandible jaw—I sparred with Hekate and her disfigured face—I even scuffled with Belial, an actual demon. Fearing this creep was like being afraid of my own shadow after realizing there were actual monsters under my bed at night.

Why was I so afraid?

As Thanatos stalked toward me, the fear intensified—like magic.

Everything about the Fallen came down to powerful magic, *and names.*

Magic and names.

I made a connection.

"*Do not touch him,*" shouted one of the armored angels when I'd fought them in the future hellscape of Philadelphia. "*He is a Powers.*"

Moments after grappling with them, a name surfaced—and when I spoke the name *"Zephon,"* his magic died away.

The truth behind names—a truth I had yet to realize, until now—was touch! When I touched them, *I knew them.*

Every encounter—angel or Fallen—it was only after a touch that their true names appeared within my memory.

Mammon. Hekate. Bacchus. Hel. Zephon. Belial. Eshu.

All I needed was a touch.

If I was to level the playing field, *all I needed was a touch!*

"What are you doing?" asked Markus, as I dug my heel in and prepared to strike.

I was done giving ground—mind over matter, I set the fear aside.

When I was at Northcreek, I learned a few valuable lessons.

The first lesson: No matter how awful I felt—no matter how debilitating the grief and anguish—depression and fear were always in my head, despite their physical manifestations.

The second lesson: Once I realized I was in control, I was free to fight back. Mind over matter. Giving in to my pain was to lose—but standing up to it? Maybe I stood a chance.

The key to it all, and the part I grappled with, was to believe life was worth living without Jaycie. That was my struggle right up until I found her wandering in a funerary fog at the Grace Falls Cemetery.

The reality of everything was mind over matter—medication may have blunted the edge, providing me a fighting chance, but the strength was within me. I might never escape the pain, the depression, or the anguish, but if I could see through it and make good decisions based on rational thought, I could survive.

I wasn't crippled by fear. I would not be defeated because of it. Not now.

Moving forward, I met Thanatos along the ceiling with a clash of weapons, my spear tying up his sickles—the constructs flickering with my panicky pulse. Our stance was locked, and all seven feet of his strength bore down on me. When I spun the haft for his legs, we parted —but not before brushing a hand against his bare arm.

At that very moment, as I stared down the death god and braced for another strike, a name surfaced, like a lost memory.

"Azagel."

His true name stripped away the fear like a fallen curtain, and with the fear removed there was no power left over me—no power to manipulate, control, or influence. I felt it dissolve, not just within me, but within the brain-trust too—even Jamaal.

Thanatos was ugly. He was a beast of pure terror to look upon, but once you stripped him of his terrible image, what was left? He was just another warrior, another harvester, another messenger, another destroyer. He was just another Fallen.

His true power, I realized, was fear. I could taste it on the air, his magic attempting to penetrate my skin, infect my mind and spirit with its poison—but no more. It had no more effect on me.

"That name," Thanatos spoke pensively, his cataracts thickening with thought. "I have not heard that name since the fall of Gomorrah. The power of names is lost on me, boy. All that remains is pain. I shall sup your flesh from the bone."

"Sup on this," I quipped, then cracked Thanatos across the face with the haft of my spear.

On impact, the room erupted into horrors.

The black tar gushed from every porous crack in the tunnel structure, molding into formless appendages attached to sickles, spikes and hooked blades purging from the tar. It was like a thousand ghastly arms reaching out and screaming at once.

"What did you do?" shouted Jamaal, as he tumbled backward, away from the chaos. Whatever the black tar was, it was psychically connected to the god, and it was lashing out.

Instinct took over. I severed anything that swiped and stabbed at me. Tumbling and twisting through the air, my spear was an extension of me, each move fluidly blending into the next.

My spear blade struck Thanatos's sickle, blocking my attack. I engaged him, fighting off attacks from every angle—stabbing, dodging, punching, kicking, jumping at everything that moved. It wasn't martial arts, but a fighting style that blended every technique into one. I was no longer fighting like a man; I was fighting like an angel.

The difference between my spear and the god's sickles were evident with every clash, his blades stressed and wilted under every strike. The harder I fought, and the closer my spear came to cutting him open, the more his tar-like minions swiped at me. With Thanatos' spoken name, I expected them to vanish, but it was clear—this was not magic, this was something else.

I was fighting a battle on infinite fronts. Something was slicing or swiping from every direction, and despite all my ability, I was stretched too thin. When I was cut, my body stitched the wound, but not before another jagged slice caught me from another angle. It was impossible to sustain. I was expending too much energy waiting for my pitch...

Then.

"I don't get it," said Jaycie. "Why does he keep hitting foul balls? And why is everyone clapping when he does?"

It was a bright summer day sitting in the stands of Citizen's Bank Park, watching the Phillies play the Pirates from deep left field. Jaycie had never been to a ball game, and I was more than happy to share a bit of my life with her.

Jimmy Rollins had worked the count to three balls and two strikes after fouling off the last four pitches.

"I'm sure he'd hit it straight if he could," I explained, "but it's also strategy."

"I don't understand," she said as she adjusted her brand-new Phils ballcap. "What kind of strategy?"

"He's waiting for his pitch," I said. "Four balls and he walks to first, right?" She nodded. "Well, pitchers don't want to let that happen. So, eventually they start throwing him strikes. If he can make contact and foul off a few unwanted pitches, he stays alive. Surviving until the pitcher makes a mistake—either he throws another ball, or he serves up a big fat fastball right over the plate."

On cue, Jimmy connected and sent the ball soaring into the stands a few dozen rows behind our seats. The crowd roared followed by the tolling bell, as was custom at "The Bank." She seemed impressed, while also acknowledging that maybe her boyfriend really did know a thing or two about a thing or two. It was like I had demystified some great science to her.

"Okay," she finally said after the cheering had died down, "still seems like a waste of energy." She giggled—she was purposely yanking my chain—and put her head onto my shoulder. "I love you, you know?"

Now.

Markus growled as the recurrence faded. I almost expected him to call another timeout...

Then, the death god did what I was hoping for—taking both sickles, he over-swung and missed. My big fat fastball right over the plate...

I swung.

Sometimes, however, even when the hitter thinks they're getting a big fat fastball, a slider dives into the dirt instead...

The spearhead sliced a shallow graze across the god's abdomen, nicking one of the many leather straps holding his putrefied body together. The damage it did was minimal compared to the inky tar blade that snagged me by the shoulder and whipped me away to the wall —my head slammed against the brick and the spear disintegrated up in smoke.

It was a gamble, and I lost.

Strike three.

Several more blades sunk into my arms and legs, crippling me. They pinned me five feet off the ground, for the death god and his rancorous smile.

"I told you, boy. I am the god of death. I am the reaper. I am the harvester of agony, the binder of the damned." Bile dripped from Thanatos's rancid mouth. He paced towards me, salivating at the thought of gutting me. "You cannot resist. Like death, I come for all."

His sickle was raised above his head, and it was all happening too fast.

They say your life flashes before your eyes when you die, but everything in front of me was crystal clear. The end was impending, and I was improperly watching it all with no available fight left to give. My muscles strained against the hooked blades with nowhere to go except to be cut to pieces. I couldn't even reach the switch—to take us both down in a fiery explosion. Not Montoya nor Henry spoke. Not even Markus, Doshin or Chappy, or even loquacious Jamaal. They all remained deathly silent, preparing for the inevitable, which was much quieter than I was capable of...

"Hey, asshole," said someone standing behind him, speaking before I had the chance to say something crass of my own. I couldn't see who it was, but the voice sounded an awful lot like me, in that strange way you recognize your own voice in recordings despite it sounding nothing like you think.

Thanatos turned to face his critic, and I saw me standing behind him. Was this another doppelganger? Another Echo version of me? He had the same crescent moon scar across his face, and wore the same blood-spattered clothes, but no key dangled from his neck—not even a hint of chain.

Using the distraction, I gathered the flames to ignite my fists and used it to sear away the tar-like grapplers, freeing my left arm.

"Tricks shall not help you, boy," said the demon.

"Who *is* that, my man?" shouted Montoya, but I hadn't the slightest. I was too busy burning away my restraints, rushing to finish before Thanatos noticed.

Two arms free, now the legs.

"My trickery is my own, not the boy's," said the Doppel-Tony as he leaned aside and winked at me, just as I had freed myself and dropped to the ground.

The wink led Thanatos's attack. He spun and slashed at me with a sickle and missed, just as I reestablished my spear and lurched for his heart. The seven-foot Fallen was fast, dodging away and guiding my spear past his heart—

—but instead, the blade sliced through two leather straps and buckled a handful of stitches.

Thanatos staggered away, dropped a sickle, and used his free hand to staunch the building pressure. Another strap snapped, and he dropped the other sickle to catch it. The tar began to wither, and the straining leather whined.

"Death. Is. Inevitable," said Thanatos, before his body fell apart into a heaping mass of putrefied flesh with a fleshy clap and gargle.

"That it is," said my doppelganger. He paced to the fleshy pile, kicked through random twitchy bits as if looking for something. The god was still alive. "All those millennia harvesting souls for his own enjoyment, decayed his body." Within the heap, a small brown cancerous mass tumbled out, no larger than a plump fig. "Evil such as that decays. It has no place within this world, or the next." Then he stomped on it, crushing Thanatos's still-beating heart.

"Thank you," I said. "I thought you ran off to Malus."

I saw through the glamour. Just before Thanatos swung at my head, my eyes penetrated the illusion. I'd spoken Eshu's true name, and his magic had little effect over me.

"I admit, I was frightened," said Eshu, remaining in full Tony-disguise—which was still entirely too weird, despite this not being the first time I'd conversed with myself. "My true name had not been spoken since the day it was given to me. Then I heard it twice spoken aloud within the same day. It was a sign." He looked at me thoughtfully. "There was something about you I recognized. I had to be sure."

"You know me? You know who I am?" I asked. Was the Fallen in front of me someone who could finally provide the big answers?

"You remind me of someone who fell, a long time ago. Someone who deserved a second chance, much more than I ever did."

"Who?" I asked, when Eshu did something I never knew possible: he shoved me backward and into the Veil, breaking Hekate's spell.

"Time and time again, you prove to be a sharp, fucking, annoying fuck of a thorn in my fucking side." Malus' tirade made the ground tremble.

"Poetry," said Eshu, maintaining disguise. His ability to copy was amazing, right down to my voice and sarcasm. I probably would have said the same thing.

"What's he doing?" I said as I stormed after him. "Hey, what are you doing?"

"Go." He was speaking to me. Could he hear me behind the Veil?

"Why would I run from you?" laughed Malus. "Right when I have you exactly where I want you."

This was madness. Why was a god trading places with me?

"He's providing us a way out," said Henry. He sounded as baffled as I felt.

"Why would he do that?" asked Jamaal.

"We can't let him do this," I said. My mind was malfunctioning. I was alone on this journey all this time—just me and the voices in my head against the world. The first time someone powerful enough to help gave me an assist, and they went and decided to take one for the team. Part of me wanted to exit the Veil and fight alongside Eshu. I finally had an ally, and he was sacrificing himself for me. But just as I resolved to fight, I felt the evil surround us.

"Right where you want me?" argued Eshu. "You planned to corner me inside a subway tunnel? That's some bullshit. Maybe I have you right where I want you."

"What are you going to do?" said Markus. "Step out of the Veil and take down the whole dozen? Two against twelve?"

"I can't just leave him there?" I said.

Malus chuckled and the air around him rippled with evil.

Montoya shook his head. "I think he made up his mind, my man."

"When the bombs go off, he'll die," I argued.

"I don't think you're seeing the correct picture," said Markus. "If Malus is here, where's Jaycie? You intended to take down the Thirteen, but given our earlier misfortune, gods will be gods and all, she might be just beyond our sight."

A cold realization took over.

Henry sighed, as Jamaal rubbed his temples. We'd never get another shot at this.

Dagon slithered across the dusty ground while Morrigan padded away barefooted across the ceiling.

Was this where it ended?

I could sense nine of them—nine blips, plus Eshu, on my sensory radar—but not the full cast of thirteen...

"Nowhere to hide, little one," said Astoreth, revealing herself next to Dagon.

Moloch chuffed, and Hekate screeched.

"I can't do this," I said, pulling the switch from my pocket and thumbing at the trigger. "What if she's caught in the blast?"

"Tony," said Markus, "I think you know how this will end."

He was repeating Gabriel's words to me. Was this my sacrifice? I save her by ending it?

"Jaycie has shown she is capable of taking care of herself," said Chappy. "Much more capable than any of we."

"Don't be a coward," spat Markus. "What ever happened to doing whatever it takes? Was that all just talk?"

"Are you suggesting we risk killing her?"

"No," said Chappy. He was shaken by my question. "If she really is The One, then how do we know that she even can be killed?"

"What do you mean?" I shouted. "We've seen her die!"

"And yet, she still lives!" shouted Chappy.

The Thirteen were closing in, and Eshu was smiling with my own face.

"Does it take all of eleven of you to kill just one of me?" asked Eshu.

MALUS

"Eleven?" I scoffed, and suddenly math seemed to fail me. We were Thirteen.

Dead on the ground was Thanatos in a heaping pile of rot. I had forced the god to take on the spark himself, to weaken him, in case there was danger to us all—the death god enthusiastically agreed. The spark lured us here, into an enclosed area. It was certainly a trap. Thanatos was the canary, and the canary was dead.

However, the spark was surrounded. There was no way out. He could not duck behind the Veil—Hekate's enchantments blocked his access. He was stuck. It was over.

The noose was tightening. Loki and Umai were passing from the Veil into reality, nearing their grip on the spark. Hekate was creeping in from above as Belial stalked from beneath the spark's feet. He was ours.

Still, that number. Eleven, he said. Why didn't he say twelve? Where was Eshu? It sent a shrill of alarm through my brain that did not properly connect.

Until it was almost too late.

TONY

"It's now or never," growled Markus. "I think it's time to do things a little different."

I was frozen. I was too scared to push the button and too afraid not to.

"I can't do this," I said—but the words never left my mouth.

The saying "like a puppet on a string" has only allegorical meaning until one experiences their own body being hijacked.

One moment I was caught in the moral dilemma of a lifetime. A moral dilemma I wouldn't wish upon anyone. And the next moment, I was backing away through the tunnels toward the drainpipe, saying, "It's now or never."

"Now!" yelled Montoya—my eyes closed, and I begged the universe to let Jaycie be safely away—as my thumb pressed the button.

There was no hesitation. The dozen bombs went off exactly as planned, six on each wall. The far ends on either side exploded first, inward toward the center. Each individual blast engulfed the area with incinerating hellfire that melted brick, metal, mortar and stone. The heat was almost unbearable, even from beyond the Veil—there was no escape within the blast zone. The air was sucked out of the tunnel as it burned hot and fast, like napalm for five straight minutes before it abruptly burned itself out, having eaten every bit of available fuel.

The area was flattened into a mound of steaming muck. The air reeked of soot and ash, and burning glass, but no pluming clouds of smoke. There were no sirens, alarms or flashing lights, nor anybody within six blocks that heard the explosion or knew where it came from. The bombs had done their job perfectly. The underground tunnel had collapsed in on itself for fifty yards, and the intense heat had created a tomb.

I stood in the middle of FDR Park and watched the muck for signs of life. A cold wind picked up, dragging a thick blanket of clouds across the sky and opening the night to the stars. When I was settled and sure that nothing had survived, nor crawling out of the blast zone, I decided to leave under the crescent moon.

XIV

oracle

A VOICE
Long Ago...
Then.

Blood is a remarkable liquid. It is a crucial part of the cardiovascular system. It transports oxygen and nutrients. It removes waste. It fights infections. Too little of it, and one cannot survive. There are numerous diseases that can infect it, and multiple cancers that can destroy it.

Blood is a delicate system.

These are science facts, but science cannot prove the transformative properties blood has when one can drink and siphon the power it holds. The heart is the epicenter of the cardiovascular system. It is where that power originates and emanates. The heart is the keystone of the body, and thus the ultimate prize of flesh. From the heart, one can steal all the life force away from another man...or god.

The boy, Viktor, traveled over the mountains and discovered the world was not much different than the valley he knew his whole life. The world was empty. The world was full of danger and mystery. The world was cruel.

He scavenged, he scuffled, he survived. Little by little he learned how to navigate a world that wanted him dead. A world that hated him and his appearance. A brutal world that hardened him.

When the dead wander, time stops. For untold years he scoured. How far and wide, high and low, even he did not know—but his rage never settled. Revenge never stopped burning in his chest. And his dreams never let him forget the horrors.

While traveling through the frozen purgatory of Asia, Viktor found himself lost and hungry. He spent days scavenging, hunting vermin that were too fast and too cunning, shaped in a cruel environment to escape and hide. In his desperate need to survive, starving and frozen, Viktor's instincts took over.

He looked, talked, and hungered like a human, but he was no longer one of them. When Viktor awoke from a ravenous haze, he found the remains of a family. Five of them, he had slaughtered—their hearts ripped from their chests and eaten. He was renewed. He was refreshed. He was a monster, and there was a part of him that enjoyed it.

We tell you this now, Tony, to show you that power can be accumulated. It is not always created. It can be gathered, but it also comes with a price. For every soul devoured takes with it a part of the monster's own. The more powerful the soul devoured, the more power one gains —and the more humanity one loses.

Viktor's lust for power and knowledge brought him to witness history.

He watched the rise of Babylon and fought to capture the city of Harran from the last Assyrian King. The more he killed, the better he became at killing. He quickly learned hundreds of ways to kill a man and adopted many names.

His first was Faraaz.

He was there when Nebuchadnezzar II succeeded his father as King of Babylon, and he was among the new king's many generals.

Faraaz learned brutality, war, and fear. But even after spilling oceans of blood, his heartache never ceased. He needed more. He needed more power, more knowledge. He needed to slay the god that took the only thing he ever loved.

In the dead of night, Faraaz escaped Babylon and traveled east into the sun.

It was sometime after he took the name of Yusuf and arrived in the city of Harappa along the Indus River when he felt a strange toll, like a bell, inside his chest. Yusuf would have never understood the bell when in the presence of a Fallen, and the power that could be obtained from them, if he had not been so curious.

After killing her, he devoured her heart and discovered her secrets.

Yusuf killed his second Fallen years later while studying Chinese black magic and sorcery in a temple somewhere deep within the jungles south of the Yangtze River. There he took the name Xin and learned of a great library filled with sacred texts stored in a Chinese monastery. These sacred texts were said to contain secrets of the gods, the dead, and everything in between. He searched many months for the temple, and found it guarded by an elderly monk. The bell within Xin tolled, signaling the old man's true nature, and they fought.

The old monk would have won if Xin had not grabbed his student, a young boy, and threatened his life. The monk laid down his weapons and offered his life in exchange for the boy. It was then he told Xin a secret.

"Take my heart," he pled. "For if you take my eyes, I will burn forever."

Xin carved out the old monk's eyes, then feasted upon his heart, and soaked his body in the old monk's power.

. . .

Later, in Persia he studied the Zend-Avesta, the sacred book of the Zoroastrian religion, and their dualistic vision of good and evil, forever in conflict like the balancing of great cosmic scales. There, he was known as Sasan.

Next, he traveled to Egypt during the reign of the Pharaoh Psamtik II, and worshiped amongst the Cult of Osiris, in the city of Abydos. There, at the Temple of Osiris, cultists adopted the belief of eternal life and resurrection, and it was here he found meaning.

Eternal life. Resurrection.

Feasting on flesh extended his life long past its natural span, and as he aged less and less, a hunger for something new developed. He hungered for information, for knowledge. He did not seek immortality for himself—his obsession for vengeance was set aside for a new journey.

He wanted to learn how to resurrect the dead.

He wanted to bring his Lilly back.

Necromancy. It was a forbidden practice whispered about by those who understood it, and referenced within the many tomes of ancient magicks he had already ingested. It was like a nagging thought behind all others, persistent but out of reach—until he came to Abydos and saw the many wonders of Osiris.

Every day he awoke and gave praise, worshiped at Osiris's temple and demanded the god to visit him, his loyal servant, and bestow upon him the knowledge he sought. He immersed himself within their culture and took the name Khalid—for it meant *immortal* in their native tongue.

Osiris never answered Khalid's prayers, until one day, during a festival in his name, Khalid witnessed him.

The Festival of Osiris gathered the god's followers from near and far, and the event was culminated with his drama, enacted upon the altar at Osiris's temple. A man, blessed and dressed as the great god was sacrificed to Osiris and granted eternal life in the underworld—when a great wind blew, creating cyclones of sand that scattered Osiris' worshipers.

The storm stung their skin and eyes and forced them to seek shelter, except Khalid was too curious. He fought against the winds and the pain, wrapped within his robes, when the bell tolled once again within his chest.

It was then he witnessed a god.

Osiris was a giant, and Khalid gasped as the god landed gracefully, carried there by cyclone, and leered at the actor who bled upon his altar. He gazed at the dead man and smiled.

Osiris's body was that of a man, sandaled and clothed in royal Egyptian robes, with the head of an animal that appeared unfamiliar to Khalid. Its snout was narrow and curved, with two large ears and brown tufts of greasy fur.

The god then took notice of Khalid and sneered.

"I seek the key to life everlasting! I seek the key to bring back the dead!" said Khalid.

Osiris appeared nothing like the depictions of him throughout his temple, on painted reliefs in every corridor and upon the great totem chiseled from dense sandstone—but who else would have accepted the sacrifice in his honor?

"Selfish monkey, you seek damnation," said Osiris.

"Please, show me! Osiris, I beg you!" he pled.

"Fool, do you not know the god you worship from he who stands before you?" said the god.

"If you are not Osiris, who are you?" he asked.

"I am the storm. I am chaos," it said, its snout curling into a vicious smile. "I am the trick that fools even the wise."

Khalid was no fool. He had heard all the legends. He was in the presence of Osiris's brother.

"You are Set," said Khalid.

"I am," he said, kneeling down to collect the spirit of the dead man with a violent tug. He held it in his hand, letting it coalesce into his palm, then swallowed it whole.

"Why?" asked Khalid.

"Why not?" responded Set. "My brother is revered but has long since disappeared. He does not care for those who worship him. Loved by all, even Isis—undeserving, self-serving. He is not the favored son—Ra's right-hand, Set, has won."

He regarded Khalid for a moment, as if expecting a response, then turned to leave when Khalid called out once more.

"Teach me!" he said. "Teach me how to take power from the souls of man! Teach me how to become a god and walk into the underworld! Teach me how to return the dead to the land of the living, and I shall follow you, Set!"

"Pitiful," the god sneered over his shoulder. "A spark so small, so insignificant, it believes it is entitled to the significant! Secrets of divine, mastered over time, your bloodline gives you no right to my memories." Then he spun on Khalid and stalked toward him. "Walk this earth for a few thousand years, and you too will learn."

"I do not want to live that long without her," said Khalid.

Set displayed no flicker of understanding or sympathy.

"I could send you to her, if you prefer?" said Set with a smile. "I could take your life, your heart carved out with a knife? Into the underworld you go, searching far and wide for her below. You are no Fallen, your sparse light so dim. Could you even be my kin when your spark is just a whim? You could go to her, your love lost. Just ask. Your life is my cost."

Khalid had attempted to take his own life many times. Each and every instance a failure, but not for lack of effort. He had stabbed himself—drowned—jumped from atop the highest cliffs—even purposely thrust himself upon an enemy blade in battle—all to no avail. To die and be reunited with Lilly was a welcome gift.

"Please, take my life and reunite us," he begged.

Set grabbed Khalid by the shoulders and studied him.

"No," said Set.

Khalid drew his knife and lunged for the god, hoping Set would take him for his insolence. Set merely swatted him away. Khalid was a great warrior and master of the blade—but he was too slow to match Set.

Khalid attacked again, swiping and swinging and missing every time. Set was toying with him, and when the god had had enough, he merely reached out and grabbed Khalid by the throat and lifted him into the air.

"I will not give you what you seek. It is forbidden. Anubis would not allow it. Walk the earth. Earn it."

Then Set dropped him and was gone.

The following day Khalid left Egypt. There were no answers there. Set was a trickster by nature, with a propensity toward erratic behavior. He was a playful psychotic that could not be deciphered or trusted. But he had given Khalid one valuable lesson; if he wanted the kind of power he needed to accomplish the things he wished to do, he could be no follower. He must be a leader. He would need to walk his own path and find his own way.

Still, he needed direction.

Khalid wandered out of the desert and crossed the Red Sea, heading north through the lands of the Persian empire. Along his way he met many oracles and seers, spoke with the wisest men of their time, and found himself unimpressed with their visions. They were counterfeit. Fakes. Shams.

When he arrived in the ancient city of Byzantium in the land of Thrace, he heard rumors of a holy oracle in Greece, who inspired kings and kingdoms, who declared the victor in wars before the first drop of blood was spilled, and he set his path to meet this oracle of Delphi.

Wandering for weeks through the mountains, he finally came upon Mount Parnassus and found the Apollonian Oracle at Delphi. The Delphic Sybil was long rumored to be a prophet, with many religions claiming her visions for their own truths.

The temple was built of stone against the side of a sheer rocky cliff. There were no guards, no holy men, groundskeepers, or anyone. It was late morning, and the sun was high and bright. He unsheathed his sword and left it in the small garden outside the entrance, next to other weapons, then slowly made his way into the temple. The building was merely a small greeting hall where villagers and pilgrims could leave offerings. There were flowers and fruit, riches of gold and family heirlooms, all heaped upon stone altars along the edges of the room. The floor was adorned in zodiac symbology, and of the Greek god, Apollo.

At the back of the room was a doorway that passed into the side of the mountain, dark and foreboding—he entered and removed his hood. The cavern was immense, lit only by torches and the refracted light of the prior room. The floor was built upon pedestals, and a great crack with heat and gas rose from the belly of the mountain. At the back, upon a tripod that cradled her above the gas and heat, was a woman. She was young, though her spirit was ancient, with long uncombed brown hair and eyes as gray as a stormy sky.

He approached her respectfully but stopped when he sensed movement. The pervading feeling of danger stunted all need for progress. Along the walls, high in the darkness of the cavern were winged men with strange armor.

They were her protectors, but he did not know them.

It was clear that this oracle was indeed a prophet. She was something special. He had never seen those armored creatures before, and only heard rumors of their existence, written in a great book revered by the Hebrews of Egypt. His heart pounded—the bell tolling wildly in his chest. There was real danger here. Real power. The guardians of this place were warriors that put fear into the many gods. The gods of man fought amongst each other for faith, but these beings served none of them. They belonged to something greater—a power unrivaled. It was that kind of power he wanted. That kind of dominion.

He maintained a safe distance from the oracle, away from her guardians. He waited as the oracle watched him. The fumes from the boiling earth surrounded her, glazing her eyes like glass.

"What is your name, patron?" asked the Oracle.

"Do you not know, prophet? Are you not all-seeing?" he asked.

She smiled and said, "I know it. Do you?"

He said, "I am Nikomedes."

She stopped smiling and nodded. "As you speak, you are named."

The room warmed with a red glow as the pit beneath them flared and receded, followed by a plume of gas that washed over her and escaped into the cavern above.

"Tell me, great Oracle, how might I find my fortune. Tell me where I must look to receive all I desire. Tell me the lengths I must stretch to grasp all that fuels me."

"I cannot."

"You are an oracle. Is this not what you have been created to perform?" said Nikomedes.

"I am no fortune teller. And you are after no fortune."

Seers, Augers, Sibyls, Oracles, Prophets, Fortune tellers, Soothsayers, Clairvoyants and Prognosticators. They were different, but all spoke in riddles. It was paramount to speak to them precisely, and precisely to their gifts.

Fortune tellers were charlatans, convening with demons for a payment.

Clairvoyants and soothsayers saw glimpses and symbols.

Prognosticators saw snapshots in time—and were often wrong due to the whims of man to change their minds.

Augers were fae, and their visions came with a price.

Seers only saw that which was asked of them.

But Prophets? Sibyls? Oracles? They served a higher power, and only told that which served their master.

At the time, he thought his words had failed him. In truth, Nikomedes was too corrupt, too selfish to receive the holy word.

"Tell me, what secrets must I uncover to gain what I seek?" he asked.

"Again, I cannot."

"Why?" demanded Nikomedes, daring another step closer to the Prophet. Two winged guardians moved from their perch in the shadows and drew weapons of flame. She did not notice them, or even know they were there.

"Because you are evil," she said.

Her words cut Nikomedes deep. No man, no matter how vile, believes he is truly evil.

Since he was just a child, he'd seen himself as the victim. As he grew into adulthood and beyond, he believed himself a creature of circumstance. He believed his intentions were pure. But it was then, confronted by his own misdeeds that he reflected.

He'd murdered the white god, the protector of his land and people, allowing the black god to take his Lilly. Phoebetor set him upon a path to vengeance. He had killed many people—man, woman, and child along the way—and a handful that tolled the bell inside his chest. Was he merely a creature of circumstance, or did he purposely choose to carry out the tragic events that led him there?

"Evil?" questioned Nikomedes. His pale hair and gray eye seemed to glow in the darkness. "Am I evil? Or am I misunderstood? I only want what was taken from me. I do not care for anything else. I would let those who wronged me live if I could have it back. I would let go of all the hate, anger, and rage if I could only have her back." He paused then stared up at the winged guardian directly above the Prophet. "Am I evil? Or am I merely a man who has dealt with the filth and shit of this earth and survived with scars that run so deep that only one thing, and one thing only, could heal them?"

Nikomedes stood his ground defiantly as several more guardians dropped to the floor and surrounded him, fire kissing their blades. It was over. His journey was at its end—and like all those who prepare to leave this world, penance whispered from his lips.

"Please," begged Nikomedes. "I have come all this way for the one and only thing that has ever meant anything to me. Please, if you cannot give me the answers I seek, send me someplace where I might find my own. Where must I look to achieve my goals?"

The nearest guardian raised its sword and prepared to strike when the oracle spoke.

"The answers you seek," she said, halting the warrior, "can be found in the north, beyond the land of Cimmeria. Find the sisters three, the Graeae. They will give you the answers you seek, if you dare to gain their audience."

The guardians lowered their flaming spears and proceeded toward him, ushering him from the temple. He was nearing the exit when he heard the Prophet impart one last prophetic phrase.

"Eventually," she said, "all truths are unearthed."

And with those last words, he left, leaving a piece of gold as an offering of thanks, and abandoned Delphi at once.

XV

dream a little dream

TONY
December 24, 2013
Now.

The hike back into the city was four and a half miles. I returned to an abandoned Center City, near my old apartment. The moon was at its apex by the time I broke down. The silence inside my head was never quieter.

Did we succeed?

It was too soon to know.

I must have looked a wretch. Dirty, beat up, and crying my eyes out —could I have felt any lower?

But why? Why was I feeling like my world had ended?

Because I was too weak to push the button? Someone had hijacked my body and did what I could not. Someone else made the decision to set off the hellfire bombs.

Which of my brain-trust took control?

Was it over? Was it done?

Was Jaycie caught in the blast? Would I ever see her again?

As I walked up Twelfth Street, I caught the sight of flashing lights toward Broad Street. Police cars. They were still investigating the horrors I invited into the city. I felt guilty. I brought the terror and sold it to myself as a foolproof plan.

Sometimes even the best intentions have the worst, unexpected outcomes.

The road to *hell*…so they say.

Then.

Jaycie worked at a tiny café in downtown Mercy Point, at the very epicenter of the Business Hub, called the Quickie Caff. Every major office building in the city was located there, with more suits and briefcases than I had ever seen in real life *or* the movies. With so many people on the go, Jaycie's store served more than three dozen coffees, made to order, every ten minutes during the morning commute. The morning shifts, when she opened the store with her coworker Barb, were the days she enjoyed most. Barb was nearly twice her age, but according to Jaycie, she brightened the room, even on those morning shifts before the sun came up.

My work schedule had me constrained to an uncomfortable chair in a corner at the back of an office building on the far side of the Hub, pumping out web and print design as if I was punching numbers into a database. I was burning out, chained to my desk without breaks, working unpaid overtime, but we needed the paycheck.

"You know you can visit me," she once said. "I can't give you free coffee, but I can give you an extra squirt of peppermint, if ya fancy."

She was lounging on the couch with her legs on my lap as we suffered through a boring episode of a *Lost* rip-off that never landed.

"Oh, I fancy," I said, then kissed her knee. "But I don't want to be a distraction."

Jaycie understood. Her boss was a control freak.

"It's okay," she said. "We can roleplay. You can walk in and flirt like we're meeting for the first time."

"So, I'll just stand there with an awkward stare?"

"I said we can flirt," she laughed, "but I didn't say you had to flirt like yourself."

"Can I get your number?" I joked like a doofus.

"Sure," she said, "but only if you make a few forward, and daringly inappropriate innuendos."

"Only if it's in your endo," I said with a smirk.

She punched me on the arm and laughed. "Whatever. Or you could take me to lunch on my break?"

By the following Tuesday, I'd had enough. My boss was on a rampage, and I decided it was time to do what any loving boyfriend would do—I grabbed takeout from Jaycie's favorite spot, a small Italian bistro that had the best fries and her favorite slice, and journeyed over to the Quickie Caff. Every step, I fantasized about her glowing smile when I walked in toting a bag of Giordano's. Even after five years together, I'd still get excited just to see her smile.

I arrived at 12:45 on the nose. The place was exactly as she described —a few tables by the door, and a counter where baristas filled cups like bartenders slinging drinks at happy hour. There were only two customers—one in line and another sipping coffee by a window while tapping away one handed on her laptop. It was the perfect time to drop in, and the bright-eyed older woman at the counter was most assuredly the famous Barb.

"Hi, how can I help you?" she asked after serving the gentleman before me.

I smiled and said, "Barb, right?" and she blushed.

"Yes! Hi! How do you know me?" she asked.

The way Jaycie talked about Barb, I felt as if I knew her.

"It's Tony. Jaycie's boyfriend. I brought her lunch. Is she in the back?"

Barb was baffled.

"Tone-eeeeeee," she sang. "Jaycie called out this morning." As I pieced together her words, she followed that with something even more confusing. "But I can take a message for you. She'll be back tomorrow."

Barb had no idea that Jaycie and I lived together.

"Okay, nevermind," I said, as I pulled out my phone and stepped aside.

"Sorry to disappoint," sang Barb. "She has so many admirers, that girl."

My hands were shaking as I hit the call button. Her phone rang six times, then went to voicemail. I left a quick, "Call me back," then dialed again.

Voicemail.

Then a text. "Are you okay?"

She didn't respond.

"Hey, Barb?" I asked.

"Yeah, sweetie?"

"Did Jaycie say anything else? Was she sick?"

"I don't know, doll," she replied. "I think she made plans with Roman."

My blood evacuated from every limb. "Who's Roman?"

"Just some fan," she said. "I can take a message. It won't be a problem at all."

"That's okay."

I was spiraling. I don't remember dropping the food, but I suddenly found myself with two free hands as I paced down the sidewalk. I was so caught up in my thoughts, I practically teleported home.

I flew through the apartment door and she wasn't there.

I tried calling again, but straight to voicemail.

Did she turn off her phone?

Every minute was like I was losing my mind. I was hyperventilating. I was angry. I was sad. I was confused. Had I done something wrong?

For whatever reason I thought I might be able to find her. I walked all over the city, peeking into every store and restaurant, gazing across every intersection spying for a redhead. I skipped work and ignored every call from my boss.

It was four o'clock when she texted back.

"What's wrong?" it said, followed by, "Why did you blow up my phone?"

"Where are you?" I texted back, and she gave me a ring.

"Are you okay?" she asked when I picked up.

"Where are you? I went to the café."

I was so flustered, angry, relieved, and confused that I probably sounded like an over-protective mother. I stood on a corner near the riverwalk, and people were staring.

"Why'd you go to the café?" she asked.

"I wanted to surprise you," I said. "I picked up lunch."

There was a long pause, followed by a deep sigh. Then she finally said, "Come home. I want to show you something."

When I arrived home, Jaycie was showered, and her guitar was sitting on the couch with a jewel case resting on top.

We looked at each other—me from just inside the door—her from the couch—and there was tension. A tension we had never experienced before in our relationship.

"I wanted to surprise you," she said.

"So did I."

"I called out sick because I had a chance to get some studio time. I had to turn off my phone." When I didn't respond she pointed at the jewel case and continued. "We recorded two songs."

"Who's *we*?" That word made my skin crawl.

"Some guy I met at the café. He's a music producer and a client canceled last minute. I got the text on my way to work this morning. He had to fill the time or lose it."

"I see." I felt like the grand prize winner on *Who Wants to be the Biggest Jerk?* "When I got there, Barb didn't even know who I was."

"What?" She shook her head. "That's ridiculous. I talk about you so much, she rolls her eyes at me."

"She said you have a lot of admirers."

"Tony, you trust me, right?" Jaycie looked like she was willing to forgive, but she also seemed rattled. She pulled the key out from under her shirt. "I wear this every day, all day, even at night. Do you think I would ever, *could ever*, cheat on you?"

"I was so scared. I wouldn't know what to do if you had."

"Good thing it won't ever happen."

"I'd be so lost without you."

I so rarely showed weakness around her, but when I broke, it upset her. She got up from the couch, wrapped her arms around me and hugged me so tight, I thought we might hurt each other.

Her arms were home—not our apartment, not the house I grew up in—her arms. It was where everything, including this mad world, made sense.

We moved on, but that day left a scar on our relationship. We swept it under the rug, but I never stopped wondering if she had truly forgiven me. I leapt to the worst possible conclusion. Why did I do that? What inside my head immediately went there?

I could have avoided so much pain…

I was always looking for the worst to happen. Always expecting her to leave me—to find someone better. Always expecting everything to blow up in my face.

Why was now any different?

Now.

Time and solitude are an overthinker's nightmare, and it was a long, lonely walk. I think I only started walking that way because there was some primitive need to go "home"—but my apartment hadn't been home to me in a very long time. When I was watching Jaycie from beyond the Veil, I slept on the floor, on chairs, along the walls above her —sometimes I didn't sleep at all, thinking I might miss something important—a clue, a monster, or anything at all.

The truth was, home was with Jaycie, and where was she now?

There was a church on Sansom Street—a big old church that seemed to call out to me from blocks away. I needed forgiveness.

A church seemed as good a place as any to find guidance. I wasn't religious—even now, religion seemed more ridiculous than ever. There was no cosmic order, no operator on the other-end-of-the-line listening to prayers. Did they even care about what we did down here?

But there was something about the old brick building with the stained-glass windows that felt like somewhere to clear my mind.

It was late on Christmas Eve. The streets were mostly empty. Camera crews and police were still scattered throughout the city, trailing my path from Logan Circle to Pattison Station.

It was my fault. All of it was my fucking fault.

I approached the church with a heart so heavy, it felt like it might sink to my feet. I had hoped to find peace, or at least victory when the bombs went off. I thought I had the courage to do what needed to be done. Instead, I was wracked with guilt and more questions than answers.

Who pushed that button?

What if Jaycie was dead?

Was it over?

What came next?

How would I find her?

Who pushed the damn button?

I climbed the stairs and pulled at the doors. Locked. I had expected midnight Christmas mass to be in full swing, but the church, like the city, was abandoned—everyone home behind deadbolted doors, like Passover—afraid of the evil that swept through the city hours ago.

I could have ripped the doors open, but vandalism at this point seemed like a bridge too far.

When I sat down on the concrete steps and rested my head against the dense wooden doors, asking for guidance from whoever might be listening, I did not expect an answer.

"What comes next?" I asked aloud as a cold breeze picked up.

I closed my eyes and exhaled, listening to the sirens wailing blocks away.

"Come with me," said a voice.

I opened my eyes expecting a cop or priest, or even a street sweeper peering down at the drunken vagabond who fell asleep on the church stoop—*me.*

Heck, it could've been Malus—I wouldn't have been a bit surprised.

However, I had a feeling that the being in front of me wasn't a man at all. Call me Captain Obvious, but the moon-white skin and eyes were kind of a tipoff.

Though the black pinstripe suit was a nice touch.

Also, he was barefoot—*in the middle of Philadelphia.* Nobody could pay me enough to walk a single city block barefoot, and only a god would be immune to whatever he could've tracked up on the walk over.

Smell, taste, sound—none of them recorded danger, but the sight of him registered differently than the others—peaceful, if not a tad unaffected by the world around him.

"Who are you?" I asked. He wasn't my enemy, but he seemed disturbed all the same. "Have you come to kill me too?"

He gave a frustrated sigh, then leaned forward and snatched my collar. I was more surprised than angry. Then he tugged me to my feet and backed away.

"There. Now we must go."

"There? What? Go where?" I growled, stumbling down the steps. When I turned back, I saw *me.* I was still lying there, head awkwardly nestled against the locked door, sound asleep. I looked more worse for wear than I expected—feverish and pale, like I had stretched myself far beyond the limit, and the scar was oozing blood down my cheek.

"You are needed," he said, as he strode past me in a rush.

"Wait!" I groaned. "What did you do to me? I can't just leave *me* like that?"

He stopped when he felt the heat.

My hands were engulfed in flames, and I was threatening to use them when he spun back to me and sighed once more. "We do not have much time, Anthony. I mean you no harm."

"Who *are* you?"

"I am Morpheus, god of dream, and you are needed."

"What? Needed where!?"

This was absurd—I felt like Neo being offered pills from the palms of a character with the same name as my pale assailant. Then I noticed the door behind him, not totally unlike the one I witnessed on the moon, this one made entirely of silver. It was sitting in the middle of the street, surrounded by a spectral mist, like something out of a bad magician's stage show—only this was real.

"Somnia," said Morpheus. "Where are they?"

"Who?"

Then Morpheus snapped his fingers, and it got crowded.

"Who the fuck is that, my man?" said Montoya, fists clenched.

"I echo that statement," said Chappy, "minus the salty language."

"Very good," said Morpheus with a humorless smile.

"Why do I get the feeling we're not inside T's head again?" said Jamaal, feeling across his body as if to check if he was solid.

"Hmm," agreed Doshin.

"Somnia?" asked Henry. "Is that a place?"

"I do not have time to explain to each of you individually," said Morpheus. "So please, now that we are all here, we must make haste. I will explain along the way."

"Along the way? To where?" asked Chappy, when Morpheus removed a silver key from his pocket and opened the silver door.

"To the Dream Lands," he replied. "Jacinda O'Neill needs your help."

"Wait!" shouted Montoya. "How do we know this chico can be trusted?"

"Yeah," shouted Jamaal, eyes narrowed, and arms crossed.

Morpheus stopped and faced us. He gave each of us a quick look and said, "I haven't yet tried to kill any of you."

"That's a good answer," agreed Jamaal.

"Yeah," said Montoya, satisfied. "Weirdos keep popping up, trying to gnaw off a piece of my man, here." He was pointing at me.

"I apologize," said Morpheus, "but haste may mean all the difference between success or failure."

"Failure?" questioned Doshin.

"The Third Dimension does not exist in a vacuum, my friends," said Morpheus. "There are balances, doorways, parallel planes, and more—they all exist symbiotically." Then he spun back toward the silver door. "We cannot procrastinate further."

"We can't just leave him there?" said Chappy, gesturing to the sleeping me.

"If we are successful, we will have lost no time at all," explained Morpheus. "Not a single second." It was true—the world appeared to have paused—like Markus and one of his time-outs.

When the silver door swung open, Morpheus stepped aside and ushered us through one by one.

XVI

stygian

A VOICE
Long Ago...
Then.

The frigid terrain was a blighted desert. Like a cancer bleeding life from the land. There were few plants, and fewer critters that crawled the sandy soil and over jagged rock along the foothills. It was a desolate place, a void of endless nothing surrounding a lonely mountain, like every living thing had vacated for safety.

He removed the leather bag from his belt—its worn surface was hot to the touch, waiting to reveal its secrets. The contents within clanked together as he cradled his hand beneath it, before dumping its contents onto a nearby rock. The bones that tumbled out, like the small ones found within a man's hand, each scrawled with runic symbols, represented infinite possibilities.

He studied the symbols, as well as their alignment and direction, and received an answer to an unspoken question. Interpretation of the bones took many years to master, and there were few better than him at deciphering their messages.

Due north, they said, *until the path splits.*

Every child of every culture was told cautionary tales of witches, and with them the costs of trifling with darkness. Some spoke of candy houses and ovens that baked children, while others of the soul swallowers who snuck into a child's bedroom if they were caught awake during the witching hour. Most tales were nonsense, but some, like the Sisters Three, were so much more than myth. The Graeae were as wicked as they were dangerous, and their trickery was known throughout the ancient world.

They were legend.

Only a fool would seek an audience with the infamous triple.

But he was no fool. Not any longer.

With each passing year he acquired more knowledge—skills of value in the dark places he sought to explore. He was still a man, albeit an immortal one—he still dreamt like a mortal and felt pain and passion like he had something to lose. He was not a god like Set, nor was he one of the armored warriors who protected the Delphic Sybil, but if he was to survive, he had to be more. He had to ascend into something much greater than the sum of his prior existences.

Studying dark arts and witchcraft, combined with his knowledge of Chinese black magic, he traveled into the heart of the Germanic barbarian tribes, into the lands of the Norsemen. There he mastered the ancient practice of runes and symbolic magic before turning east toward his destination.

Practicing the dark arts brought him no happiness. It did not take away his pain, nor did it numb the loss. The pain he had inside only grew as he yearned for a simpler time, running through the forest on an adventure with Lilly. He was so far away from Viktor, the weakling boy from his past—he was a stranger even to himself. He was the Pale Wanderer, a vagabond in search of the mysteries that built the world.

The crisp mountain air was like blades with every dry breath. Every surface surrounding the mountain for miles was bitter and hard, cold and icy. One small mistake—a bad choice of direction—a faulty step on slippery rock—could shatter bones. It was gloomy, as if the clouds were perpetually stuck shrouding the mountain in its misery.

It was a place of death.

He scaled sheer cliffs and clambered over boulders that stood in his way. He was so close to destiny; he could taste their stench from halfway up the mountain. By sheer force of will, he ascended to a place where very few had ever stepped foot, and even fewer survived to climb back down.

When the mountain's peak was within sight, he came across a crack in the rock that would have gone unnoticed to the average man. The entrance was nothing but a narrow crag in the mountain face, a mere fault in the ancient stone. All his planning, all his time, had come down to this. He would not be denied his future.

On the ground below the cave mouth was a pile of disparate bones. Some were winged, others were decidedly human, and he proceeded with caution.

"Harpies," he whispered.

Sidestepping, he squeezed his way into the cave, slow and steady, pressing his body between the narrow walls, and eventually into a cavity beyond. It was dark with a thin film of smoke hanging below the canopy, emanating from a pile of glowing embers at the center of the room. Upon the embers was a cauldron, handmade from scraps of metal.

Along the near wall were a series of wooden tables displaying various tools, some made for torture, others for the preparation of food —or both.

"We have a guest, sisters," said a phlegmy voice, followed by the cackle of an old crone.

"Do we? I cannot smell a thing?" said a second.

"Oh, indeed we do! I see him!" came a third.

From a shadowy corner came three wretched forms, hunched and weary by appearance, but make no mistake, they were dangerous. They were killers. Their ghastly appearances were partially concealed in shadow and behind tattered robes that did little to protect their nakedness from assaulting eyes.

"Coincidentally, sisters," said the one on the right, "I presume to be famished. We have not fed in some time." She was the most hunched, with a large, hooked nose that nearly touched her withered lips as she spoke.

"Aye, sister, hungry I am. I feel it rising from my bowels," said the one on the left. She was fat and her flesh sagged off her bones in large wavy slabs. Her sparse hair was like straw atop her nearly bald head.

The last, the one in the middle then stepped into the light from the waning fire. She was lanky, with fingers like claws and one large bulbous eye at the center of her head, a curiosity the three shared as they continued to move closer.

"Oh yes, he will feed us well. There is meat on his bones!" she proclaimed with a shriek. "They rarely arrive so healthy!" She smiled a toothless grin, with only two long, sharp yellow teeth amongst a mouthful of rotted gums.

"I did not come here to be your next meal," he said.

"Oh, they never do!"

"But feed us you will!"

"I came here for answers," he pressed.

"They all seek answers!"

"Every last one!"

"I demand to know how I might bring back my beloved from the dead," he asked.

"Tell us, young man, who are you?" said the most hunched.

"And how did you come to find us?" asked the fat one.

"I have a name, but it has no meaning to me any longer," he explained. "They call me the Pale Wanderer, and the Delphic Sybil set me on this path to you."

"Did she now?"

"Is the bitch playing games?"

"No, that Sybil died long ago, my sister."

The three witch sisters circled him. It was a deliberate crawl, searching for a weakness.

"You are the sisters three. The Graeae?" he asked.

"We are," said the fat one on the left.

"The Stygian witches of legend?"

"Are we?" said the one on the right.

"Are you not Deino?" he said, looking at the witch in the middle. "Enyo?" To the witch on the right. "And Pemphredo?" To the left. "The daughters of Phorcys, god of the sea."

Each of them gasped and spat, like a rotten taste had settled upon their rancid tongues.

Pemphredo, the fat one, began to heave with disgust. Her eye narrowed into a slit of deceit. "How? How do you know our names?" she squealed.

"Nobody knows our names," said Deino, the lanky one at the center.

"Our lineage is not common knowledge," spoke Enyo, the hunched witch with a thoughtful tone. Then she spat on the floor. "What are you, boy?"

"Answer my question, hag!" He stood perfectly still, unbothered by their circling. The light that seeped from the mouth of the cave silhouetted him, flaring his hair into a white halo that hurt the witches' eyes— but they dared not look away, for fear of losing their first meal in decades. They were so hungry they were drooling all over their wrinkled chins.

Pemphredo cackled. Enyo sneered.

"How have you come about our names?" squealed Deino. "Answer us!"

"Tell us boy!"

"Whose loose lips must we sew shut?" threatened Enyo. She clucked her tongue against her teeth, strange rhythmic noises in a pattern— communication to the others?

"He looks so tender," said Pemphredo, unable to remain angry when food was so near.

"Smells ripe," purred Enyo.

The Pale Wanderer may have walked amongst men, in the bright places as well as the dark, but he was talented in ways the Stygian Witches did not know or understand. Afterall, they presumed he was just a man.

He dug into his cloak and pulled free a tiny cloth bag sealed with a piece of twine, then tossed it into the burning embers of the witches' dying fire.

"What was that?" asked Deino.

The bag ignited with a flash, followed by an immediate implosion, sucking every last remnant of light from the room.

It was complete darkness. Still and empty, except for the witches and their heavy breaths.

"Sisters," said Enyo, "we have a sorcerer amongst us."

"Indeed, sister, we do!" cooed Deino.

"Power *and* flesh to feed upon? Could we have found a better meal?" Pemphredo screeched excitedly.

"Boy," said Enyo, moving quite close. "We are witches! We have dwelt in dark caves our whole lives! The dark does not scare us!" She then reached out and grabbed hold of him with her wet and withered hands. When her flesh touched his, she screamed. Her hands burned, like they had been thrust into the middle of a stew, boiling her skin. "He is marked!"

"Marked?" squealed Deino.

"I'll tear the mark from his skin!" threatened Pemphredo.

He smashed his fist through Enyo's teeth. She screamed and fell to the floor while he retrieved her broken fang and buried it deep into the eye of Deino, blinding her.

"My eye!" she screamed. Then he took her by the back of the head and slammed her face into the rock wall, shattering all three yellow teeth.

Pemphredo launched her hefty frame into the air When his elbow flew into her mouth and shattered her teeth and jaw, she choked and coughed.

The darkness was proving to be too dark, even for the Graeae.

Toothless Enyo got back to her feet and screamed a bloody rage. She charged the Pale Wanderer but slammed into Pemphredo instead. With the long, sharp tooth still in hand, he stabbed out Pemphredo's eye with a clean strike.

"Stop!" wailed Deino, blind, toothless, and spitting blood.

He snapped his fingers and the dim light returned to the room, where Enyo surveyed her sisters. The Graeae had never felt fear, but at that moment Enyo was overcome by it. Both her sisters were blind and toothless, unable to see or chew.

He stalked toward her, gripping her sister's tooth like a knife and threatening to blot out Enyo's eye as well. There on his chest, she spotted the design inked into his flesh.

"A witch's knot!" cried Enyo. "Tattooed upon his skin!"

"Sisters! Sisters! I cannot see!" whined Pemphredo.

"We are just three old ladies!" sobbed Deino. "Why would you attack three old ladies?"

How many men, women, and children had they consumed? How many poor travelers seeking answers had they slain? They were killers, perhaps even better than the Pale Wanderer, but he had prepared for them.

Enyo crawled to her sisters, grabbing them about their necks to pull them close. They were born shortly after the world was created. They were older than some of the dirt around them and feared they may be moments away from returning to it.

"Wait, stranger!" cried Enyo, holding out a withered hand to belay his advance. "We will provide you guidance, but please, spare our lives! We may be old, ancient even, but our threads do not end here."

He stopped and considered her request. It may have been an act, but it was convincing.

The Pale Wanderer had no intention of murdering them. He only wanted answers, and if the threat of their demise was what it took to loosen their lips, then he would be as frightening as their own legend.

He nodded his agreement.

"Thank you, my lord! Thank you!" cried Enyo, followed by her sisters singing similar praises. "Please, speak thou request once more and let us consider our response."

"My love was taken from me more than two hundred years ago," he said.

"He is no mortal!" shouted Pemphredo. They appeared displeased for not recognizing his status amongst their own.

"No, he is mortal, but he is not human," corrected Deino, after sniffing the air and apprising his scent.

"I am searching," he continued, "for a way to free her from the bonds of death, so that she may walk the earth again with body and soul intact. How may I obtain the knowledge to bring her back? How may I achieve the fortitude to return her home?"

A moment of silence passed, then all three sisters cackled. Their giggling bloomed into a frenzy of wild laughter.

"Do you mock me?" he asked, stepping closer.

Enyo saw him clearly for the first time with her aging eye. She stopped laughing at once. "Who are you, boy?"

"I am a stranger," he said. "I no longer have a name."

"You hide your name? From us?" cackled Deino.

"We know all names," said Pemphredo.

"If you know all names, tell me my own?" he demanded.

There was a long pause as the sisters quieted their frenzy and began to whisper amongst themselves.

"If you cannot determine my name, how may I trust that you can answer my request?" he mocked them. "Your lives depend on it."

The whispering intensified until Deino turned and smiled a bloodied toothless grin.

"You have gone to great lengths to hide your name from the world, or perhaps your name was so small that it was scarcely spoken. It is no coincidence that we cannot search the aether and find it. Gaia knows all. The aether flows to and from Gaia, but your name is not among her offerings. Long life you have, but your beginning is as mysterious as you, stranger."

"Your answer," he said, "is correct."

Pemphredo shrieked, but Enyo grabbed her by the throat and squeezed. "Quiet, crone! We must still provide an answer to his request."

"I will wait only a moment more," he said, growing weary of their games.

The sisters huddled and whispered. Enyo peeked back to the Pale Wanderer before rejoining her sisters, as if she were apprising him of duplicity.

"Difficult, your plight is," spoke Pemphredo.

"Very difficult," added Deino.

"But not impossible," finished Enyo.

"What you seek is improbable," said Deino.

"But not impossible," added Pemphredo.

"Perhaps unlikely," said Enyo.

"But not impossible," commented Deino.

"A powerful god entered Tartarus, prison of gods and wicked souls alike, and stole something valuable," said Enyo.

"The great Titan, Chronos!" shrieked Pemphredo.

"Return the Titan to Hades, god of the underworld, and he may offer a trade," said Deino.

"A trade for that which belongs *only* to you," Enyo clarified.

"Where?" he asked.

"Chronos was stolen from Tartarus and taken to an island."

"An island in the Aegean Sea."

"An island with black sand like the night."

"An island with a great pillar! A pillar that stretches all the way to the heavens."

He pondered their words. When nothing more was spoken, he asked, "Is there nothing else?"

"Poor young man," said Enyo.

"You took two of our three eyes!" growled Pemphredo.

"How can we see into the aether when you took our eyes!" complained Deino.

"Our power resides from three perspectives, gazing into the aether beyond the mortal coil!" shrieked Enyo.

"You assaulted us," said Pemphredo.

"And screwed yourself in the process!" cackled Deino.

He turned to leave them. "So be it."

"Come back!"

"We have not yet eaten!"

"Come back and feed us, young man! We have no teeth to chew!"

"We have no eyes to see!"

"I will keep this tooth," he said, holding the sharp incisor he used to blind them. "I believe your sister has one tooth to spare and a perfect unblemished eye. Take them and share."

"Noooo!" they wailed in unison.

"Give me your eye, sister! So I might find us food to eat!"

"No! Give *me* your eye! And your tooth as well!"

He left them fighting over one eye and one tooth between them.

XVII

mind palace

What does one say to the invading personality attempting to take control of your brain?

"Hey, how are ya?" didn't seem like the right tone.

"Hey kid, two's a crowd, ya see?" said in my perfect gumshoe voice seemed spot on. Though, I imagine that'd be a wasted reference, especially on Lilly.

Where was she from? Who was she? And why?

This young blonde woman in a tattered wool one-piece was sitting in my childhood living room, and I was dressed like a punk-rocker—which was totally rad as heck, don't get me wrong—and the awkward silence kept mounting. Her feet were dirty and there were leaves and twigs tangled into her hair. She looked like she had rolled around in the woods before finding my front door—and how'd she know where I was? Heck, where the *heck* am I? My old home on Cross Road was exactly as I remembered it, but wrong. Smaller. Less alive.

Lilly wasn't very talkative. She gave a nod, shake, or shrug to most of my questions. Was she hurt? Where did she come from? Was she hungry?

I was dancing around the big stuff.

Oh, the big stuff...like, are you in cahoots with Malus? She seemed as unwitting as a prisoner. Was there anyone out there who cared enough to be looking for you?

"Tomorrow's not a promise," I whispered, and a tear rolled down my cheek.

I missed Tony. I missed my life with him. Yet I couldn't remember a thing about it. Just flashes, feelings, moments in tones and shades. He was vanishing from my mind.

Lilly was watching me, so I said it to her as well. "Tomorrow's not a promise. Remember that, kid. There are no do-overs."

Lilly's eyes were as big as saucers.

"Tomorrow's not a promise," she repeated, then looked out the living room window, and we both snuck in a few tears.

Eventually I said, "Why are you here?"

She looked at me like I had missed a jump scare in a horror movie—Amanda's favorite—while stuffing my face with popcorn. This place, this old house, was swimming with memories. Memories I couldn't stop remembering. Memories of Amanda, exploring in the woods and singing 80s rock anthems with hairbrush microphones while bouncing on my old bed.

Lilly's blonde hair reminded me so much of Amanda's that I couldn't help but see her in the face of this young woman. In fact, the memories were so vivid, that before she could answer my question, the sound of steps came rumbling down the stairs.

"I'm coming!" she shouted. "Wait for me, Manda!"

All four and a half feet of uncoordinated red curls came bowling down the stairs in those bright kelly green goulashes and raincoat. It was a wonder I didn't break more bones as a kid with the way I tripped over my own two feet.

Lilly bolted upright and ducked behind the sofa as this little bundle of energy stopped dead in her tracks when she saw us in her living room.

"Who are you?" she asked.

I was looking at me. Eight-year-old me.

"I'm not sure how to answer that," I said.

Let me digress—I had no idea where I was, why I was there, and when. The whole surreal nature of this place put me on edge, and the only thing I could remember was…

…Malus…

…It was Malus. This was a mind trick. Those *things* were cocooning me, and this was all just a bad dream.

"Mom!" she shouted. "Somebody's here!"

We both looked to the top of the stairs, wide-eyed and worried, but there was no answer. Mom was always in bed in a Valium haze. When she did manage to drag herself out of bed, there were always consequences.

I could feel her trepidation. That churning in my gut was a reminder of all those years of childhood trauma.

"Honey, it's okay," I started to say. "We're not here to—"

Then something terrible happened.

From the top of the stairs came a shout. A shout so wicked and terrifying that it made my blood go cold.

"Jacinda Moira O'Neill! Keep your voice down!"

Little me winced. Her whole little face went pale, like her soul had retreated to the far reaches of her happy place with rockstar dreams and sleepovers with Amanda.

"I'm sorry," she whimpered as Lilly hid herself behind the living room curtains.

"You're sorry? I'll show you sorry!" said the thing as it hovered at the top of the stairs.

"What the heck is this?" I said, as the thing rounded the banister and revealed itself before making a slow descent.

It was no doubt my mother—shoulder padded blouse and all—but a version of her I had never seen before…

…or maybe this was who she was all along.

Her hair was short and white above her fiery eyes. She looked like she'd crawled right off the television screen of a Tim Burton movie. A cigarette was stuck to her lip with two inches of ash, and her posture was perfect, but too rigid to be human.

The little me squealed and ran—opened the door and fled as Lilly followed her. And when my mother motioned to chase them, I did something I didn't know I had the strength to do.

I stood in her way.

"Leave her alone!"

"Don't talk back to me, young lady!"

When she raised her hand into the air, I was brought back. Right back to being eight years old and all the trauma I'd repressed. The ground shook and the lights flickered, and every terrible nightmare came rushing out of me like a cold sweat. I saw things flashing through my mind that I hadn't thought about in years.

"You're not my child!" she said, snapping me back to...*reality?*

Age can bring a lot of perspective. Fear had controlled my entire childhood. Fear of my mother. Fear of not fitting in. Fear of the two-eyed man that peeked into my window at night. I was so tired of fear, so tired of running from it, and I would not be afraid of *this*—this figment version of my mother.

"Go away," I said.

And before she could slap me—her blood red nails like claws—I made her disappear.

I don't know how I did it. I made her go away with nothing but a thought.

"Bye bye, bad mom," I said—and for a brief second, my skull lit up with the worst headache I ever had. "...Heck was that?" I rubbed my eyes with my fists and let the feeling of someone walking over my grave disappear.

And why did my tongue suddenly taste like gummi bears?

By the time my wits flooded back to me, I hurried over to the front door, looking out into the driveway, and spotted a speck of kelly green running up and over the embankment on the other side of Cross Road.

"Hey!" I shouted. "Hey...*Jaycie?* Hey! Come back!"

. . .

TONY
Now.

Morpheus ushered us through his silver door and we emerged at a familiar place—standing at the bottom of the forest hill. There was a deep crack in the earth made of craggy, moss-covered rock with a stream running through it. Gone was the summer bloom of the forest: the insects chirping, the lush green foliage, and the flowery scents.

Everything was strangely still.

The forest canopy was a mixture of bright orange and yellow, and the forest floor was ankle deep with fallen leaves. It was wet with a balmy drizzle and smelled of autumn.

Since Jaycie's resurrection, the seasons had progressed from winter to spring—when I confronted the Nymphs outside the warehouse. Then from spring to summer—when my brain-trust and I fought against Lilly's invading horde.

Now it was fall, and I was beginning to worry what would happen if the season progressed into winter once more.

"Do you understand this place?" asked Morpheus in his perfectly pressed pinstripe suit, suggesting the entirety of the dreamworld with a gesture. "This place is a construct created by the mind of a powerful astral projector. The woman, as you know her, Jacinda O'Neill, is quite gifted. It is her palace of the mind. This is where she retreats to protect herself. Her palace, roughly the shape and size of Grace Falls, a village I believe you are familiar with, is finite. It is limited to twelve square kilometers. However, I need your help in locating Jacinda."

"Why do you need our help?" asked Chappy. "If you are the god of dream, why do you need us at all? Can you not find her yourself?"

"Up until now," said Morpheus, he looked around as if waiting for something, "I had been unable to enter Jacinda's palace. I was repelled after every attempt—because I was not *him*."

He was pointing toward me.

"How do you know?" I asked.

"Like all those who slumber, I have witnessed Jacinda O'Neill's dreams," he explained. "You, or at least an avatar of you inside Jacinda's subconscious, have taken part in many of her dreams—some terrors, some mares, but mostly phantasia."

"How did you find us?" asked Jamaal. A small gust of wind kicked up, and a flurry of leaves rained around us.

Morpheus grimaced like we were asking dumb questions and checked a fancy watch on his wrist. "You were daydreaming. A memory of Jacinda. The only other being thinking of her was someone I'd rather not trifle with.

"I have been aware of her mind palace for some time," he continued, "drifting through the Unbecoming at the very edges of Alterumterra, but it has not been a problem until now. Its existence is causing havoc within Somnia."

"What kind of havoc?" asked Jamaal. I personally would have added a few other questions: what was *Alterumterra*, and what in the blue hell was the *Unbecoming*?

"Jacinda's mind palace has been infected by terrible outside forces. Dreams are my domain," explained Morpheus, "and although this place is not part of Somnia, the great dream continent, it is but one small part of Alterumterra, the Dream Lands."

Alterumterra = the Dream Lands. Check.

☑ **Alterumterra** = THE DREAM LANDS

It seemed ridiculous—we were trying to save all reality, and now we were being pulled into another problem? Why couldn't this Mr. Rogers, dream god supreme, fight his own battles in the world of make-believe?

"Do you have any idea what's going on?" I ranted. "Out in the real world?" He had brought us here to fix *his* problems, while Jaycie was still out there...

"Why do you believe this world is any less *real* than your own?" Before I could answer, he decided to answer me first. "As the proprietor of dream, I do not concern myself with Earthly affairs, but this concerns us all. The boundaries between are thinner here. One crack can cause enormous pain and suffering. You should know by now that reality is not as you perceive it to be. Dreams are real. The experiences here can shape lives.

"The Dream Lands, where one can dream with the likes of Houdini, Aristotle, Yarkula the Builder, and Moses...."

"Who's Yarkula the Builder?" asked Jamaal.

I shrugged, while Montoya kicked through a pile of leaves like a little kid.

"Somnia is a shared place," continued Morpheus. "It is a shared reality. Inspiration has always been found here. It is the mixing of thought. One could utter an idea that could inspire across time."

"Wait," said Jamaal. "You mean to tell me that we could say something in this dream world that could influence the future? Like, I could tell myself to invest in Apple, and I'd wake up in the present a trillionaire?"

Morpheus looked at us all carefully, then nodded. "The subconscious mind is powerful. Remember, Jamaal Robinson, how many times you dreamed of high school when you were an adult. A traumatized mind can send ripples backward and forward within one's own lifetime, with great effect."

Henry looked downright sick. His understanding of the mind during his lifetime was so limited, and I could sense his longing for research. "That is phenomenal," he said.

Something moved out of the corner of my eye. A streak of green that didn't belong in the forest—at least not this time of year. I drifted away from the group, still listening, as I studied the far end of the ridge.

"You said this place has become infected?" asked Jamaal.

"It has become malignant," answered Morpheus. "If the malignancy spreads and infects Somnia, it will be the end of Dream."

"What are the implications of the infection? Beyond dream?" asked Henry, who obsessively cleaned his glasses with a handkerchief whether they were dirty or not.

Doshin slid beside me. He sensed it too, a presence at the end of the ridge.

"An infection of this magnitude could spread to the greater whole of the Dream Lands. It could tear down the walls between realities. A new Breach could form, and allow the Omens to flood into this world and beyond," he explained. "It would be the beginning of the end."

"Oh, don't be so dramatic, brother," said a new arrival—two new arrivals, to be exact. A woman, my age, give or take, and she was carrying a disembodied head like a football.

"My brother, Phantasos," said Morpheus. "More accurately, all that is left of him."

"Fantasy," said Jamaal. "The Oneiroi."

"The what?" said Montoya.

"The personification of dreams," said Henry. "This is Dream and Fantasy. I studied you both."

"Oh!" said Phantasos with wild black eyes, "a mind doctor!" Then he looked up at the woman and laughed. "A psyche-ologist walking around within someone else's dream?"

"That's quite an invasive procedure, doctor," said the woman as she mussed Phantasos's black scarecrow hair, then brushed aside her own sandy bangs. She was dressed for the weather in a tan peacoat, sweater and jeans—like a suburbanite on a pumpkin-spice latte run.

"Now that we are all here—" said Morpheus.

"—And who's she?" interrupted Montoya.

"This is Samantha," said Morpheus. "She is one of my Imagi."

"Imagi?" questioned Chappy—it was a great question. One that needed to be added to the list, but I was too busy watching for another flash of kelly green to jot that one down.

"Who *are* they?" asked Samantha, gesturing to us with her spare hand. "They're definitely not mares."

"No," groaned Morpheus, "they are not."

"Hi, I'm Jose Montoya," he said, holding out his hand. "You can call me Montoya."

"'Sup, Jose," she stated. She wasn't as friendly as she looked and appeared less friendly than Morpheus. "What are *you* looking at? And what's up with his face?" She noticed Doshin and I studying the tree line at the far end of the ridge, up the hill.

I touched my face—the scar was still bleeding.

Perhaps there wasn't anything up the hill at all. Perhaps I was imagining things…

…and that's when I felt the silence.

When we arrived, it was still but not quiet—a shuffling squirrel, bird squawking, bugs chirping—but the stillness around us had gone from *still* to *silence*. And the silence made me nervous, like something was about to—

—A scream—a little girl—hissing preceded a series of far-off pops.

Next thing I knew, Chappy was full of holes and leaking all over the forest floor.

"Get down!" yelled Montoya as the ground beneath our feet trembled.

split

TONY
Somewhere...

Soldiers raided down the hill toward us carrying weapons—rifles fixed with bayonets—one of them with a flame thrower. An entire squadron of dark soldiers rained constant gunfire down on us from the other side of the gully as the sound of grinding gears shook the hill.

It was a whole new level of darkness. Gone were the goblins and gemini, fighting with bladed weapons and iron. These were bloodthirsty soldiers and modern warfare.

With a flick of her wrist, Samantha created a rock wall that erupted from the forest floor and separated us from the gunfire. Doshin grabbed Henry and plowed him into the dirt, away from the streaking bullets, while Montoya dragged Chappy to safety before he bled out.

"Where's Markus?" I shouted over the gunfire.

"What?" said Jamaal, when something hissed past my shoulder and struck him right in the throat. Jamaal, with all his knowledge stood there blinking, attempting to grasp the situation when the blood started pouring from him in buckets. I caught him, all three-hundred-plus pounds of him, and dragged him behind the wall.

"Silly silly," said Phantasos, still cradled in Samantha's arm. "These are just constructs! We cannot be hurt here! We're not in Alterumterra! We're in someone's sick mind!"

When a bullet grazed Samantha's arm, she hardly winced. "You were saying?" Bloody streaks leaked onto Phantasos's cheek.

"Brother?" yelled Phantasos, suddenly stricken with fear. "Brother! Stop this madness, brother!"

"Phoebetor is dead!" shouted Morpheus over the constant pops of gunfire, as he and Samantha retreated with us behind the stone wall.

"No," cried Phantasos as Samantha stashed him in the dirt, "No, he is doing this. It's him! I know it is!"

There are two kinds of people—those that speed up and those that slow down when the world is burning. But I found myself stuck between gears as I struggled to do either. Jamaal couldn't breathe and Chappy was dying, and I couldn't understand why.

"Why aren't they healing?" shouted Montoya, saying what I was thinking. His fatigues were covered in Chappy's blood. It was coming out of everywhere, including his mouth as he began to suffocate. Montoya applied pressure to the two largest wounds, which only made the others leak faster.

"Hey," I shouted, but Jamaal's eyes had glossed over. "Hey! Listen to me! You're okay! You're like me, remember? You can heal. Remember?"

Jamaal shook his head as he choked on the blood.

Everything was going monumentally wrong.

"How do we fix this, my man?" shouted Montoya. He was crying. "How do we fix this?"

Chappy's breaths were as shallow as a whisper. What happens when a member of the brain-trust dies? What happens to them? To us?

I'd lost a lot of people in my life. After a time, I expected to go numb. Instead, I found each one exponentially affecting the other, like it was building up into a mound of grief I had yet to cope with. I thought of

Doctor Hammond, and how many sessions it was going to take to unpack all this loss, and the void inside me that was once filled with such love and admiration for the people I held dear. What good was love when everyone left?

I was spiraling. I had no answers, no control.

That's when Henry grabbed me and said, "Medic."

"Medic!" I shouted.

Montoya followed. "Medic! Medic!"

"Aye, guntlemun," shouted the medic as he dove behind the wall next to us—kilt flapping in the wind.

"Teach them like you taught me," I said, grabbing him by the helmet.

"Culm yer teets," said the medic. "Alfie's gut it cuvered."

The attack pressed on while the medic did his thing. We were pinned down. The sound of lead smacking into the stone was louder than the gunfire itself. The vast number of shots fired was enough to terrify everyone, even Morpheus, who appeared overwhelmed.

"Hey, Montoya," said Samantha. "You're a soldier, right?"

"I'm wearing the damn uniform, ain't I?"

"Hold out your hands," she said.

"What?"

"Just do it!" she shouted.

When Montoya held out his hands, they were immediately filled with a rifle—as if she conjured it straight out of the air. The term "imagi" was making sense.

There was no witty retort, not even a smile. Something clicked inside Montoya, and the man quickly pulled the cocking handle, pressed the stock against his right shoulder, and stood up firing.

From the end of the barrel came flashing sparks of fire—hellfire bullets streaked over the landscape. After a quick burst, Montoya ducked below the stone wall as a flurry of return fire slammed against his location.

"Got two," said Montoya.

"Out of how many?" asked Henry.

"Twenty," said Doshin. "There were twenty."

"How could you tell?" asked Henry.

"Could hear them," he said, as he gently tapped his ears.

By the time I turned back to the medic, he was nearly finished. He reached into his pack and retracted a syringe, then slammed a big freaking needle into Chappy's chest—and he immediately sat up like someone had just slammed a *BIG FREAKING NEEDLE* into his chest.

He was breathing, and the hole in Jamaal's neck had reduced itself to a mosquito bite.

"Aye, take ess," said Alfie as he handed both Chappy and Jamaal a white pill. "Thas'll ged' ye on 'er feet."

"What's that?" I asked, as they both swallowed without pause.

"Cocaine," said Alfie.

"What!?"

"Oh shit," said Montoya. "Got any more?"

"Give me a gun," said Jamaal, spitting a wad of blood. "Payback's a bitch."

While Samantha conjured something for Jamaal, a streak of kelly green flashed in the distance and disappeared over the top of the hill toward the old mill. Then came another girly shriek, and three dark soldiers chased up the ridge after it.

"Tony!" shouted Markus. He had taken cover behind a tree. "I'm going after them."

"Wait," I shouted.

"For what?" said Markus. The Roman tunic and sandals were long gone. He wasn't just wearing my leather jacket—he was in jeans and a Stabbing Westward t-shirt. "Someone has to do something, and you're incapable of rising to the occasion."

Before I could respond, Markus took off running.

Maybe it was the fact that I relived the gunshot that ruined our lives a second time—or that I was still absorbing the idea that Jaycie was the One—or the thought that I killed her with the push of a button, and I wasn't even behind the wheel of my own body when it happened…

…But having my fortitude questioned by one of my brain-trust sent me into an outright tizzy.

"Cover me!" I growled—the words spilled out before I had the chance to fully examine my plan—and sprinted after Markus.

"What?" said Montoya.

Henry shouted, "Wait! Sir?" but I was already too far to stop.

Bullets whizzed past, and one of them clipped my side. I wondered if I'd be so brave if I wasn't able to heal. I didn't stop until I climbed the ridge and pulled myself up and over the hill—and stared down the barrel of the thing that shook the ground beneath its enormous weight.

"Shit."

When the tank's cannon went off, I didn't so much duck as my knees gave out. The shell slammed into the forest below with an explosion that uprooted trees beyond the blast. The tank, with black metal plating, didn't stop moving as it plowed forward, attempting to make me a permanent part of the landscape.

Jamaal shouted, "Move!" and I rolled aside as he took aim with a rocket propelled grenade and fired. When the dirt and dust stopped falling, the tank teetered up and over the hill's apex, then rolled down the embankment, snapping through fully grown trees on the way down.

It was insanity. Every moment something was hissing by, exploding, or throttling my vision. How was I supposed to maneuver through this? I felt slow. I felt incapable—like the competition was catching up.

The clearing at the top of the hill was full of broken vehicles and bodies. The mill and warehouse in the distance were smoking—its structure in pieces. The Forgotten Room within the warehouse was destroyed, and for a moment I wondered what might happen when those forgotten things were released...

Markus was across the clearing, slipping behind the warehouse when I spotted him and took off chasing. I was never a soldier. All I knew about warfare was learned in school, in movies, TV, and video games. I should have known that running through an open field filled with trained marksmen was a bad idea. I was only halfway through the field when a barrage struck me, and I fell into a patch of tall grass. There wasn't any time to feel the pain or to let the wounds heal before I popped back up to give chase and ran straight into the sharp end of a bayonet—the blade serrating a lung and missing my heart by a fraction.

And for a moment, dangling there at the end of its gun, I finally got a good look at it. The soldiers wore blank white masks, each with red smiley faces that looked like a child's scribble. The rest of its uniform was black, with a patch or two for division and rank—*Ministerum Guard,* it said.

When it twitched to pull the trigger—a perfectly lined strike with my heart and a one-way ticket to oblivion—a well-aimed bullet zipped past my ear and took the soldier out cleanly. I could hear Montoya mumbling to himself over the chaos.

Gunshots—many many more gunshots. The first several rounds missed, but the next two struck home—one in the hip, the other straight through my chest, shattering my shoulder blade.

Both were healed by the time I spanned the distance and spun the soldier's head clean around with a swipe, then removed the bayonet from my chest and sliced open another—its name badge said *NAME,* and I couldn't shake the chills it gave me.

The remaining soldiers volleyed so many bullets, I nearly turned away when the sky bloomed red. The ground trembled, then fell away. A whole squad fell through, one of them gargling a shriek that abruptly cut off, like it was swallowed up beneath the surface.

I don't know what I expected—Tremors, Sand Worms, subterranean CHUDs—but when I approached the hole, it was a pit with no bottom. A hole straight through into nothing, as if the entirety of the mind palace was a floating island in a blood red sky.

But that wasn't all I saw, no matter how much I wished it was—whisking by beneath the mind palace was something massive, like a herd charging through a crimson fog. The sound as it passed was like a thousand enraged, bloodthirsty screams.

Montoya was on me in a blink.

"My man," he said, holding his rifle into the air. "What the holy smokes is that?"

"I don't know," I said, as the others caught up—Morpheus casually walking or floating, I couldn't tell which—and the surrounding land-scape smoldered with a thick black smoke that masked our location. "C'mon."

"Where are you going?" shouted Henry, but I had already spanned half the distance to the warehouse, where Markus had disappeared. When I rounded the corner, he was gone.

"What is he doing?" laughed Phantasos. "Are you sure he is what you think he is, dear brother?"

Errant shots whizzed past, as Samantha set up blockades to protect our path, while the others returned fire.

"Espera un momento!" shouted Montoya. "My man, wait up!"

XIX

titan of time

You might have thought the story was over, Tony, but alas, the climax has yet to arrive! Is it not fascinating how one can rise so high? And yet, we have higher still to go.

It took much longer than he anticipated, but the Pale Wanderer eventually found it.

From the sea, the island appeared as a black pillar reaching up to the heavens, just as the Graeae foretold. The volcanic crater stretched from sea to clouds, its beach covered in coarse black sand.

The Pale Wanderer found the island beyond Crete, deep in the Aegean Sea. Magic kept it hidden from those who sought its secrets. It was only visible upon a particular path when sailing into the morning sun. He had been searching for years when the island revealed itself to him at last.

He stowed his boat upon the shore and entered a cave beyond the beach through a stone archway cut directly into the black spire. Deep within was a staircase leading into the mouth of the volcano, where stairs were carved into the rock face along the interior edge of the crater, corkscrewing around and around as they ascended. Magma filled the chamber below, casting its foul poison gases and illuminating the chamber with a red-hot glow. Black billowing smoke rose from the magma into the open sky high above as he climbed to the top, shrouded in robes.

The tale of Chronos, the Titan, was well known. Chronos was their king, the most powerful of all Titans. It was rumored he was a master of time, which made him a formidable enemy. The story of his chaotic reign was passed down for thousands of years. It was said he came from another world, somewhere beyond our own. The Titans were the first gods, primordial entities—some attempted to enslave man, while others wished only to protect, to cultivate, and to teach—like Prometheus gifting humanity the knowledge of fire.

After his defeat, Chronos and the rest of his kin were cast into Tartarus, where the wicked were punished after death. Whoever had stolen the Titan from Tartarus would be a formidable entity.

The Pale Wanderer had no delusions—he was trifling with gods and titans. Either he died that day, or he would set sail from the island with the Titan, bound for Hades.

"Is that you, Aries?" thundered a voice. It came from above and it did not sound like a god. It sounded weak. It sounded old and tired.

"I am not Aries," said the Pale Wanderer.

"Not Aries? Yes. Yes, Aries is dead. I killed him." The voice sobbed. It was confused—a manic range of emotion, abruptly moving from surprise to sadness, then anger. "I took his temple. I had nowhere else to go."

The Pale Wanderer took his last step up onto a wide platform with a throne made of black volcanic glass. Along the wall were armory racks made of human bone—each set of armor and weapons were displayed like trophies. Among them were blades, armor, and shields forged from adamantine. They were weapons worthy of the gods, blessed and gifted to aid the wielder in battle.

The walls were carved into petroglyphs—statutes depicting legendary heroes and battles—some adorned with mounted trophy heads of beasts and warriors, their flesh still rotting off the bone.

It was the Temple of Ares, god of war, and no mere man had ever entered this holy place of violence.

Above him, as if captured in a spider's web, was a body. His limbs were bound by chain that left him dangling within the mouth of the crater. However, these were not the only details that caught the Pale Wanderer's attention. The man above did not struggle or twitch, but he did move—he aged. His hair and beard grew dark and long until the gray weathering of maturity began to stripe his locks into streaks of silver, then white, then fell from his head and into the burning pit below. Within seconds he had aged from young to old, then miraculously repeated the process in reverse and forward, cycling back and forth in a loop.

"If you are not Aries," asked the voice, "who must you be?" At the center of the room upon the throne of volcanic glass—carved as if it had captured the souls of those slain in battle as they were released into the underworld—was a figure shrouded in blood red robes.

"I am nobody," said the Pale Wanderer.

The god leaned forward.

"You are something, if not someone. You do not understand the power you carry, spark. No mere mortal could find this temple, and darkness clings to you as death. You are something, if not someone." He sat pensively, surrounded by smoke and shadow. "Why are you here?"

"I am here to return that which you stole," said the Pale Wanderer.

"Did Hades send you?" he asked.

"No."

A bolt of lightning struck the ground at his feet, splintering into spark and thunder. The shockwave tossed the Pale Wanderer to the very edge of the platform, his legs dangling without purchase until he scratched and crawled back to safety.

"Bah!" the god groaned. "You know nothing of who you are." He stirred on his throne. "Who sent you!?"

"I sent myself."

"I am Zeus," said the god. He rose to his feet and removed his hood. He was a large man with a broad chest. Even sitting, he was much taller than his visitor. He held his right hand high above his head of neatly trimmed white hair and built a threatening static charge in his palm, his long beard sparking. "What is it you wish to change?" His red robes flailed with the building pressure. "Tell me now or I will dispatch you where you stand."

"I don't understand," said the Pale Wanderer.

Zeus appeared as a madman—his mind was a mess of conflict, and the Pale Wanderer was unprepared to answer his question.

"What do you not understand? Why do you want my prisoner? Why do you want the body of Chronos?" challenged Zeus.

Zeus was not the Stygian Witches, nor the Delphic Sybil. What little power the Pale Wanderer had, he stole—but Zeus? Zeus was amongst the most powerful creatures to exist, and the Pale Wanderer was no more than a pest.

"I want to make a trade with Hades," he replied. "His rightful prisoner, Chronos, in return for the woman I love, who died many years ago."

"Love," sighed Zeus, his face grimacing, "is a righteous motivator." He wiped a dirty hand across his face, leaving a smear of soot. "Honorable. Just. And *foolish*." Zeus stepped down from the throne and let the static charge diminish, then sat at the foot of the great chair after he became rapt in grief. He wept. "I am broken. Faulty. By nature, I am flawed. I am fascinated with beauty. Specifically, in all the many beautiful women and nymphs of this world. It never ceased to amaze the many different exquisite flavors of females there are to choose from. As a god, I had my pick. I could entrance a woman in the guise of her lover or seduce them as a shade of vapor. I could romance them in the form of a great steed, or a graceful swan. Beautiful women, however, are everywhere. A shortage, I have never witnessed. They come and go, beauty fading and blossoming as often as the seasons change." Then

Zeus gave his visitor an inquisitive glare. "Was the woman you loved and lost beautiful?"

"Very," he replied, but displayed no emotion.

"Love," said Zeus, "actual love, is captivating. Arresting. It can invade the mind with the most marvelous feelings this world has to offer, and yet can be more damning than the deepest fiery pits that call to a Fallen for their sins. Because love is beautiful and wondrous and fleeting. Despite all we tell ourselves, it is never eternal, despite all we tell ourselves."

The Pale Wanderer approached the great god with his hand resting on his blade—a sharpened witch's tooth affixed to a wooden handle in the belt at the waist.

"I had love once," continued Zeus. "I let it slip away. Instead of fortifying that love, honoring it, I seduced and fornicated with every beautiful woman I desired. My actions, my infidelity, sealed my love's fate. She took her own eyes to get as far from me as possible. Hera, jealous as she was, never strayed. Not once during all my infidelities. Some would say it is a man's manifest to spread his seed wherever he may—But my heart? My heart does not need many to be full. My heart needed a home. My heart needed comfort. My heart *mourns! My heart feels guilt!*" An intense burst of lightning surrounded Zeus and shook the crater. The body of Chronos dangling above bounced with a chaotic crash.

"What did you do, great king?" he asked.

"The only thing I could," Zeus replied. "I broke into Tartarus and stole Chronos, the god of time, hoping to learn his secrets. When I fell to Earth, my halo shattered and wings clipped, Chronos took me in as kin and taught me many great and horrible things."

The legends claimed that the gods birthed other gods, Tony, but in truth, they collected the recent Fallen, protected and groomed them into pantheons—the greater the number, the more mighty and feared they became. Strength in numbers. Strength, for a coming war.

Adulation, reverence, fealty: these are as mighty as the magic of names. The more adulation, the more powerful they become. A Fallen cannot aspire to anything greater. To be the one god adored above all, usurping their own maker, was a driving force for many. Nothing greater than sticking it to Dad right where it hurts.

"I witnessed the great power of Chronos," continued Zeus, "and I wanted it for myself. I stole the Chains of Prometheus from Hephaistos and shackled him."

"The Chains of Prometheus?" asked the Pale Wanderer.

"Hephaistos was a gifted artisan and crafted many fantastic things. He created such devices of divinity, some of them with no equal. These chains cannot be broken and render the bound benumbed."

"I see," he said, gesturing to the captive above.

"I thought I might learn the secrets of time," said Zeus, "that I might master its trivialities and prevent my self-destructive misgivings, but I learned something else instead." He leered at his visitor. "I learned that one cannot go back and change anything. Changing one's own past is impossible. Our maker, in all its shrewd, senile immensity, created a world where time could not be humbled or beaten, nor overpowered or undone. We cannot change the past, for everything we attempt, is already our present. I may not have fallen into the Pit, damned for eternity, but my faults have left me a tortured wretch of my own making.

"So, little spark," he continued, "you may take that knife you have been groping and plunge it into my chest. Cleave out my heart while it still beats. Take my life and send me into the great Unbecoming, away from this world and away from misery. But, little spark, it would do you no good. A demi-god has more grace than the power you possess. In the wake of taking my life, you would be consumed. My power would overwhelm and reduce your body to elemental dust—unless you knew my truth."

"What truth may allow a pitiful *spark* such as I to set you free?" he asked, pulling his blade.

"Speak my true name, the one given to me at creation, and you shall gain dominion over the king of gods," explained Zeus. "Guess incorrectly, and I shall rid this world of such a pitiful, devious, dim-witted, malicious spark like you."

Malicious, he said. It was that moment, though before his eventual succumbing to a darker path, that spawned a name. A name that defined his future. A name that defined his nature.

"May I have more than one guess?" he asked. "A king of gods must have a magnificent name, and I shall never conjure such inspiration without error."

"If you do not succeed upon the first guess, you may have another, and another. But I warn you, spark, miss my name thrice and I shall destroy you slow and painful."

The Pale Wanderer paced the floor for several moments, then looked upon the great god and said, "Lord Zeus, would your true name be Thor, for he commands the very lightning that cracks a stormy sky in two—just as you."

"Thor? You believe my true name to be *Thor*?" Zeus was angry. "How preposterous. How ludicrous that you compare he and I? I should smite you with true greatness—a powerful bolt so intense it would remove you and any trace of you from this world with just a single strike." Then he relented. "Presume greater. Just two guesses remain."

The Pale Wanderer paced the floor for several moments, when inspiration struck. "Lord Zeus, would your true name be the one and only Jupiter, for he has been rumored to be your equal. I wonder, are you and he the same?"

"Jupiter is but another name, but not for Zeus—he is a duplicitous, delusional Fallen who believes to be my equal." Zeus grinned wickedly. "One more guess, spark."

The Pale Wanderer was not troubled. He paced the floor before the great god, but showed no sign of concern—not a bead of sweat gathered along his brow, despite the magma boiling below. He dug through the memory of his many lifetimes. In all his travels, in all his experience, there had to be a clue.

Eventually Zeus lost all patience while watching his visitor pace. His mighty shoulders shook, and his blood red robes shimmered and crackled with static. He shouted, and his words were as loud as thunder. "Spark! If you do not give me your last guess, I will smite thee correct or not!" Then he lunged at the Pale Wanderer, swiping him up in one hand, and lifted him above his godly head.

"Lord Zeus," he croaked, being crushed within the god's mighty grasp, "surely a god as powerful as you has many names. Names with which to describe you and your absolute greatness. From your greatness, you inspired me to take a new name. My given name and those I have taken since are too human, but my new name shall inspire fear—for I will not be denied my journey, and if there was one thing that moves the pendulum of fate, it is fear."

"That is not an answer!" shouted Zeus, placing a hand next to his captive's face and threatening him with sparks of white and blue.

Zeus wanted to die. The Pale Wanderer could see it in his eyes, but the god was too proud to let it happen without a challenge.

"Oh, but I know your true name, great god!" he said. "I know it as well as I know my own."

"Then speak it and set me free!"

The Pale Wanderer rammed his carved tooth blade into Zeus's chest, surprising the mad god. Great bolts of lightning thundered from the wound, illuminating the cavern with flashes of brilliant light. Zeus wrangled his neck, his grip choking the life faster than the blood draining from the wound in his chest—but not before the Pale Wanderer gathered a breath to free the god from immortality.

"I call to you by your true name, Kabal! Let it be known as you fade into oblivion, you were sent to the underworld by the one known as *Malus.*"

Zeus dropped to one knee as the fury of his fight diminished.

"How?" asked Zeus, removing his hand from Malus's throat.

"Even a spark has secrets," said Malus. "Rest in peace, mad god."

He removed the blade, then thrusted it back into Zeus's chest, tearing apart his mighty god heart and setting him free of life.

Not a single drop of the great god's blood was wasted, nor did Malus refuse any prime piece of his flesh. He'd devoured many of the god's organs, including his damaged, broken heart.

As he chewed the raw muscle of Zeus's most precious of organs, he could hear the mad god lamenting.

"My heart feels guilt!"

It was a portent of the things to come. No matter how powerful he became, nor how far he traveled, Malus always felt the deep destructive guilt of losing Lilly. As time wore on, his only memory of her was the last—the terror of watching the black god rip her away, and the horror in her eyes.

When Malus left the Temple of Aries, he boarded his boat more powerful than he had arrived. He was no longer just a spark. He had consumed the flesh of two powerful gods—Belobog and Zeus. He had changed. He became something new—something never seen before—and he had a new name.

Malus, the Pale Demon.

Behind him, Malus dragged the chained, benumbed body of the sleeping Titan, the god of time, Chronos, to trade for his love. It had taken lifetimes to get thus far, and it would take him many more to find the underworld.

"We cannot change the past, for everything we attempt, is already our present."

"My heart feels guilt!"

Malus could not stop hearing the mad god's words thundering inside his own head. Zeus' voice echoing, replacing his own delinquent conscience.

# uninvited guests

JACINDA
Now.

Have you ever thought you might be insane? Yes, I know, they say if you question your own sanity you must be sane, because only an insane person thinks they're actually sane. But has anyone who questioned their own sanity ever gone strolling through a dark fantastical version of their hometown with a monster version of their mother terrorizing them?

How thankful am I that I didn't turn out like my mother?

Someone once said to me, "You've got to do your own growing, no matter how tall your Grammy was."

...Grammy. How could I forget Grammy?

I lost her when I was eight. She never got to see me grow.

All the noise in my head—all the tangled string—how much of it was real? How much of it were things that never were?

Grammy was real. Would she be proud of me?

"Tomorrow's not a promise. Gotta earn each one," she'd say.

I lost sight of Lilly after the first few hills, but little Jaycie was like a purple monkey in a zebra cage—those bright green rubber boots stood out. I chased her up and over a section of the Grace Falls State Park that Amanda, Robbie, and I had hiked through many times. Robbie—I mean, *Maynard*—used to chicken out, claiming we ventured too far from home and his ancestors would be angry if he went any further.

Maynard was always such a charac—

"Oh, hello," said a voice.

I stopped dead in my tracks like the Roadrunner—*meep meep.* Without turning my head, I let my eyes roam, but I couldn't see a thing. Just trees and fallen leaves and briar as far as I could see.

But when I looked behind me—slow and methodical, like Laurie Strode checking her six for the bogeyman in a mask, I saw *something*—a dark man in black. His eyes and mouth ran with silver—like he had just sneezed all over himself without a hanky. It was oozing from every opening and dribbled down his shirt.

"Do not look at me!" he shouted, and I spun back.

"What do you want?"

"She walks within her own dream, yet does not know *me?*"

"What do you want from me?" I repeated, and what did he mean *walks within her own dream?* Was this all a dream? It would explain... *everything!*

There was a weird beat thumping through the loose leafy dirt at my feet and between my eyes, like my heart in rhythm to a gallop.

"Honesty is such a lonely word, Everyone is so untrue, Honesty is hardly ever heard

And mostly what I need from you."

"Did you really just quote Billy Joel?"

"A favorite of your departed dear Grammy." The dead leaves behind me shuffled. He was moving but keeping distance. How did he know Grammy? And good gosh, why Billy Joel? "I wanted to see with my own eyes, if what they say was true."

"Who's they? You sound a little... *paranoid?*" I was sticking with the six-time Grammy award winner's catalog. The tune playing in my head along with Billy crooning *Pressure!*

"Who aren't they. They are everyone who know."

A green object ascended a rocky hill in the distance. Little me was getting out of reach.

"Perhaps," he continued, "they were wrong. Perhaps, you are not what they say. It would be a shame, because I have something to trade."

"Trade for what?"

"You erase my past and I change your future."

"Sounds like Dirty Deeds, Done Dirt Cheap. Speaking of sounds, what's that sound?" It was low, but getting louder—clapping?

"That is my past—st—st—"

The leaves behind me rustled, fast and furious—like he was having a seizure. My sister had a seizure once. Scared the living crap out of me...

Wait...

When did I ever have a sister?

I could almost see her in my mind when the ground trembled again.

The man was on his knees when I dared a peek, shaking like something invisible was throttling him. It was terrible, silver blood raining onto the forest floor, when I caught a glimpse of something—something moving toward us from tree to tree...

...giant spiders! With men's torsos! The yellow one had only eyes and the red one had just a mouth.

I didn't stick around to continue the chit chat. I ran away from *him, and them,* and chased after *her*—if I sprinted now, I could cut Jaycie off before she got to the falls. I could save her from the monsters.

"Wait!" he shouted. "I need your help! Please! Cure me! Cure me, please! You bitch! You evil bitch! Your nightmares are catching up to you!" Then he laughed—its echoes bouncing off every tree. "You'll see. When I am healed, you'll be sorry! You will never sleep another night without screaming out in terror!"

PRESSURE!

"Let 'er rip, J. Keep those knees high!" Coach Doyle used to say before every race. I never ran faster than when she was drilling me to be the fastest me I could be. When I finally hit my stride, I was gliding effortlessly...

...but I didn't get far—the truth about life, about plans and all things strived for, was that something, anything, inevitably gets in the way...

I always liked sprinting. Hitting that speed where everything zipped by, before your lungs and legs begin to burn, was one of the greatest feelings in the world. Tony used to say it was almost as wonderful as hitting a baseball as hard as you could and watching it fly...

...*Tony*. How could I forget about Tony? What was happening to my memory?

The reason I didn't get far—the reason I lost all track of little me—was the discovery that we were not alone in the woods with the monsters. There were others. Hiding behind a tree as I zipped by was a masked man in black. I almost missed him—the crazy smiley face drawn onto his white mask struck a chord, like hearing a familiar tune you wished to forget.

PRESSURE!

But the man in black wasn't alone. I heard a pop, then searing hot pain flared in my arm as I spun into the ground.

Record scratch.

I wasn't lying in the dirt for long. Something hit beside me so fricken' hard, I was tossed into the air like a rag doll. The bang was deafening.

"Where is she?"

It was an explosion. I should have been dead. Dust and debris were still falling.

"Do you have eyes on her?"

Their voices were downtuned and distorted, like a Type O Negative riff.

"Prime target is down."

Not anymore.

PRESSURE!

When I felt the bayonet at my back, I was on my feet faster than a cat—my fist met the soldier's chest, and there was a strange thudding sound as it pummeled away from me and crashed into a nearby tree and broke.

They fired their guns.

Nothing struck me as I beat them. I felt uncorked. Like a badass superhero unloading every punch. When reinforcements arrived, I sung, "One, two, three, four, Pressure!" then gave them a wink and flew into the sky.

If this was all inside my head, my dream, then I could do anything.

TONY

I stopped running at the observation deck overlooking the falls. Half of it was blown apart, but passable. When I turned back, they were all there—my brain-trust along with the Dream a Little Dream Coreys, and Samantha—all huddled together and picking off soldiers as they came running around the corner.

"Why'd you run off like that?" asked Jamaal, still lugging the RPG.

"A little girl," I said. "Didn't you hear the scream?"

"What exactly did you see?" asked Henry.

"Rubber boots," I said as I scanned over the falls. "Markus saw it too." I could see both sides of the river from the observation deck as it flowed downstream. But I couldn't see anyone along the trails or crossing bridges.

"Hold on," said Samantha. "Rubber boots?"

"Like the bright green pair Jaycie used to wear." I looked back at them. "When she was a kid."

"I don't understand," said Chappy, as Doshin slid beside me and looked down over the falls.

"The soldiers, I've seen them before."

"Where," asked Henry.

"Jaycie's forgotten room," I said. "A child's drawing. The seven of us protecting her from masked soldiers with scribbled smiley faces drawn on." I was acting it out to get my point across, but it only made me look unhinged.

"Which one of you is Markus?" asked Phantasos, nestled under Samantha's arm.

Doshin pointed over the railing. "There!"

A little girl in green rubber boots carefully jogged down the incline nearly a mile downstream.

"How'd she get so far?" I asked aloud.

"Not alone," pointed Doshin.

There was a second shape following the boots—they were too far away to identify, and the overcast skies were darkening.

"Let's go," I said. "Some of you go down the other side of the falls. Try to cut them off if they cross to the other bank."

"Who put you in charge?" asked Samantha as Morpheus watched silently.

"What does it matter?" I said. "A little girl's in trouble. Don't you care?"

"I'm a mother, dickhead!" she growled. "I would do anything to protect a child!"

"Then how about you give a fuck!"

"Hey," said Jamaal, "We're all on the same team, here."

"Are we?" I growled. "Are we? There's seven of us. Which one of you took the wheel and pressed the button, huh? Which of you decided to make the decision that was mine to make?"

"Tony!" yelled Chappy. "Son, are you alright?"

"Seven?" asked Phantasos.

They were looking at me like I had lost my mind. I was hyperventilating. Something about this situation made every part of me panic. Morpheus was studying me, and I met his eyes with a very precise question. "A mind palace. That's what you said this is, right?"

"It is."

"You said this is where Jacinda retreats to protect herself," I replied, and he nodded. "You said it's becoming malignant. Like it was infected. These soldiers are the symptoms. But what's causing the infection? What is the infection after? What's its endgame?"

"I would imagine," said Morpheus, "that it wants to eradicate the mind palace. Provide her mind no safe quarter. Some individuals use a mind palace as a place to store memories, good and bad."

"What then? What's the worst possible scenario?"

"For an astral projector such as Jacinda O'Neill? Her mind could tear a hole in Alterrumterra, opening a breach while searching for the memories it had lost."

"Has this ever happened before?"

"Yes."

"Oh, don't tell him that, brother!" shouted Phantasos. "He is already nearing a break! The man is teetering over the edge. He can't even count!"

"Why do you need her?" I asked. "What good is Jaycie to you?"

"I must evaluate her," said Morpheus. "And quarantine her if necessary."

"Why?"

"To determine if she is the cause of the infection."

"She is not the cause."

"How are you so sure?"

"Because I know what is."

"Do tell," he said, as several shots rang out.

"Malus," I said, and my angry eyes found his. "A Fallen named Malus has been attacking her mind."

"Brother," whined Phantasos, and the two shared a knowing glance.

"What's going on?" asked Samantha, just as the sky flared red followed by the bang of incoming fire forcing us all to duck away.

The observation deck rocked. A portion broke and fell away into the falls, nearly taking me with it. When I picked myself up from the strained planks, I spotted movement downstream, trailing the direction of the green rubber boots.

"There's Markus," I said, and leapt over a broken span of the bridge, landing on the slick rock below shrouded in the heavy mist of the falls. Then I chased down the trail with Montoya shouting "Wait up!" behind me.

THE TEMPTING OF ASTORETH

381 B.C.

Vanity. To some, there was no greater sin. Mythology was rife with stories of vain deities, jealous of god and mortal alike. These stories and fables were unexaggerated in the vastness of their acrimony and the lengths the gods would take just to quench their resentment.

Most goddesses were beautiful, but few were as beautiful as they were dangerous. There was a reason the Venus Flytrap was named for the goddess, for she lured her enemies in with her charisma and grace. Her symmetry was so alluring that one could not foresee the devastation of her trickery, and the destruction it could cause. Aphrodite, Hera, Artemis, Cerridwen, Demeter, Diana, Eos, Frigg, Isis, Selene. There were many, and there were very few flaws with which to judge.

Of all the goddesses, there was one who might be the most beautiful if not for her cruelty, for she had no charm with which to dilute her wickedness. Her skin was as hard as diamond, and her intellect as sharp as a razor's edge. Where Aphrodite had her magical girdle to win the affections of the few who might resist her, Astoreth, the goddess of war and fertility, had no need for magic to make her irresistible. If Astoreth wanted something, she took it.

A goddess of few desires, there was little Astoreth wanted. She had power, she was feared and equally adored, and there was little else to want. However, there was one obstacle that escaped her. One obstacle that consumed her when the conditions were right, and her innermost passions surfaced. Astoreth wanted to be the only goddess whose beauty was legendary. She desired to be the only goddess whose name was sung and praised.

It was no secret that the gods fought over beauty. Malus was simply playing upon the obvious when he found her bathing in a hot spring. The gentle rush of the water from the falls masked their conversation from those who wished to pry. Even to Malus, it was difficult to resist her beauty. She had black hair and bright eyes that changed color and swirled around her irises like a tempest. She was like a dream.

Astoreth swam in clear warm water. The darkness of its depth was the only thing obscuring her nakedness from Malus's sight. He offered her a way to destroy her rivals so that she might be adored and revered as the most beautiful creature in existence.

"Your offer sounds tempting," she said with a smile.

Malus sat at the edge of the spring upon a large rock and paid her smile no mind. She was manipulative and dangerous. There was no way for him to know whether or not she was taking his offer seriously or merely beguiling him into a false sense of security.

"What is there left to offer that might sway your decision?" he asked.

"You ask for bound agreement to help you obtain a secret. That very secret will in turn allow you to offer me superiority over all other goddesses. To strike them down until I am the only beauty worthy of legend," she said, leading toward an obvious conclusion for which Malus was prepared. "Why not steal the secret from you, so that I may have the secret and my superiority?"

Malus smiled and spoke precisely. "What I seek is simply too great a task for one entity to accomplish. Together, in alignment, we can all have that we desire."

"Who else?"

"They are no enemy of yours," he replied.

"Will I be the most beautiful?"

"Truly."

"Then I accept."

"Excellent. The contract must be sealed with blood," said Malus, as he pulled a small knife from his belt.

"I do not bleed, but there are other ways to seal a contract."

XXI

eyes for you

TONY
Then.

Running.

I used to hate running. Honestly, I still do. It seems like all I ever do is run.

"C'mon!" said Jaycie. She wasn't even winded. "How do you expect to make the city-league team if you can't even keep up with *me?*"

"You—*gasp*—are—*gasp*—a former—*gasp*—track-star," I wheezed as we rounded the end of the block and started jogging over the bridge to the Mercy Point Pier. I should've been in better shape at only twenty-five—but the realities of corporate life were catching up.

Morning coffee. Breakfast. Lunch. Breakroom sheet-cake. Dinner. Snack. A 3500-calorie workday that had caught up to me fast.

"Don't be a softy, Oscuro," she said in her tracksuit and ponytail, jogging in place as I lumbered toward her looking like reject from a Richard Simmons workout video. "Tomorrow's not a promise. We need to get you in shape."

"Hey now," I groaned. I wasn't *that* out of shape. But the 3500-calorie workday plus the bar tour Jaycie's band booked throughout the state had me drinking a few pints and consuming fried bar food several weekends a month. "I'm not that bad, am I?"

Not to mention all the takeout, soda, and desserts consumed after work, Monday through Friday.

"No," she said with a smile, "but you need to be the best you possible. I want you to make the team."

I was trying out for the local twenty-two-to-thirty-year-old baseball league. The Mercy Point Griffons were holding an open tryout in two weeks, and Jaycie seemed more excited about it than I did. My knee was killing me, and the air was so cold my eyes watered every time the wind blew. All I wanted was to be home, in our apartment for a nice evening together after a harsh day of work, but she was adamant about getting in shape.

"If I don't make the team, it's okay," I said as I doubled over.

"Why would you say that?" she asked. "I thought you wanted this?"

"I do." I caught my breath and leaned onto the railing, looking down at the channel beneath the bridge where boats were tied to the docks. "But I'm a washed-up ballplayer. I blew out my knee. I wasn't even good enough to make the Milton State starting lineup in my prime."

"Firstly, this is your prime, hon," she said, a look of loving disappointment on her face. "Secondly, you're not washed up. You never got the chance to show what you could do."

"That was four years ago," I explained. "I haven't thrown a ball since the Labor Day Fair." She knew what I meant by that—I went out on top, out-throwing Rick at his own game.

"Ninety-six miles per hour was impressive."

"It was ninety-eight," I said, and she grinned like she had just tricked me into caring. "But that wasn't a whole nine-inning game. That was just a couple throws with an uncalibrated radar gun."

She turned away from me, like I was making her mad, and her hair flared against the setting sun. "Why are you giving up before you've even started?"

"I'm just being realistic."

"Of everyone I have ever met," she professed, "you're the only person I know that's never given up. You fight and you fight and you don't give up."

She was crying, and I had no idea why.

"Hey," I said, moving toward her, but she brushed me away and looked into the orange glow of the sunset. "Why are you so upset? I'm not giving up. I just don't want to set myself up for failure."

"You only fail when you don't try."

"Why do I feel like we're talking about more than baseball?"

"Are you happy?" she asked. She said it like she already knew my answer and had determined I was lying.

"Yes, why? Why are you asking me this?"

She looked back and forth from me and to the setting sun, like she was receiving words of encouragement from the celestial object plummeting beneath the horizon. "You seem unhappy. Defeated."

"Where is this coming from?"

She shrugged, and some base jealous instinct in my mind fired back with the one thing I knew I shouldn't say but said anyway.

"Have you been talking about our relationship with Roman?"

To my surprise, she didn't get angry. She winced and I knew it was true—maybe not in the way I was accusing her, but there was some truth behind my accusation.

"It's not what you think," she said, but instead of discussing it, she turned and began jogging. Then she called back over her shoulder. "See if you can keep up."

I never caught up to her, but I also never gave up trying.

I was always running after Jaycie. Always trying to hold on to something that seemed destined to slip away. Even now.

Now.

Dreams were like coloring books. You could color the images however you wish. You could color an elephant green, and you could scribble outside the lines. There were no hard rules, just guidelines to give each page color.

Similarly, dreams moved along from point A to point B, but everything in between was devoid of rules. They often made no sense, no rhyme or reason for the things that transpired. It was, on some level, organized chaos.

Jaycie's dream world construct was no different. It always dropped me in the middle of the forest, and it always wanted me to travel up the hill to the Mill. Point A to point B was the one and only constant, the only "rule." Whatever transpired between was chaos. Disparate creatures filled the landscape. My brain-trust and I were free-roaming individuals, as powerful as in a fantasy. We were equals here.

Morpheus and his body-less brother hitched a ride for access to Jaycie's mind palace. But who else had access to this place? A better question—what other entities *wanted* access to this place?

The sky was overcast and thick with a dark, bluish gray. Everything felt real, but in saturated technicolor. Even the ground felt like a fantastic version of earth and dirt. The air tasted too fresh, the movements too vivid—and even for me, everything was happening too fast.

The path sliced the field in two. The tall grass grew as thick and tall as reeds along the bay. A violent wind was blowing through, as a thunderhead formed in the distance.

I got a late start, but I was slowly catching up. Somehow, we weren't so special here anymore...

A flash of kelly green darted into the forest after escaping through the field. The tall grass hid them as they fled. Three dark soldiers were giving chase.

"Got your back!" yelled Montoya. He was more than a dozen steps behind me, and I was chasing with everything I had.

We didn't know what they were going to do with them. The dark soldiers were everywhere, in every corner of Jaycie's dreamscape—a complete but unique perspective of Grace Falls from Jaycie's mind. The old Hallows House in the distance looked like something out of *Beetlejuice*, while the cemetery surrounding it was creepy and dank and resembled the darkest passages from Grimm's Fairy Tales.

I snagged a rock on the run, like fielding a grounder, and tossed it like I done a thousand times in my youth. The lead soldier was within two strides of the forest when the rock smashed him in the back of the head.

One down—two to go.

I knew to be prepared for anything—from Oni to Gemini, Obsidian Witches and big nasty wolves. I was prepared for just about anything except for what came from the sky.

"Incoming!" yelled Montoya

I looked up.

The thunderhead was looming, but it was not a storm. From the sky, surrounded by darkness was something otherworldly—phantoms breaking through the clouds in a shimmering red aura. A mounted horse, its rider armored and screaming—its eyes vacant orbs—its open jaw drooling with incoherent rage—came galloping as the sky lit up with crimson cracks of lightning.

The rider, holding its own shriveled head high above, atop its outstretched arm, wearing an antlered helmet, was not alone...

It was a horror beyond nightmare—a force of nature—and it was all happening too fast.

Twenty Minutes Ago...

It was only a half mile downstream of the falls when I spotted a walking bridge and followed the trail toward a familiar site—the Grace Falls fairgrounds.

I was moving hastily down the steep, wet rocky incline when I slipped, fell, and tumbled down a ten-foot stretch.

Something was different. Something was wrong. I was no longer at the top of the food chain here. I wasn't a god anymore. I was klutzy ol' Tony Oscuro...

"You okay, my man?" shouted Montoya, but I was already rushing away, ignoring the blood gushing down my leg.

Maybe I should've waited, but there was a nagging feeling at the back of my mind that I had to catch up—that something really terrible was about to happen if I didn't. That saving Jaycie here meant saving her out in the real world.

If she was here, she had to be alive out there, *right?*

The gloom set into twilight. The absent sun suddenly burned red and hung at the horizon as the clouds thickened around it, casting dark purples and blues across the sky. Those hues like a lens, casted everything in their colors—another reminder that this place was a surrealist dream.

Without the high ground, I had no idea which way Jaycie went, or if Markus had caught up to her and the others.

I stumbled onto a familiar path from the falls to the fairgrounds. The same path where I once spied a nasty fight between Jaycie and Rick from behind the Veil.

"Once a junkie, always a junkie, Jace," said Rick, and I slid to a halt. Was I really seeing this?

"Wow," Jaycie replied and hung her head.

"Wow what?" said Rick.

"Just wow," she said, stifling a sob. *"Rick, maybe you should leave."*

"What?"

"I want you to go."

The air around the memory felt like static. They appeared like three-dimensional phantoms, but as I passed between them my elbow brushed Jaycie... *and she looked at me.*

Was she real? The look on her face had me transfixed, and what happened next made me question how connected this world was to the real world.

"You should know by now that reality is not as you perceive it to be. Dreams are real. The experiences here can shape lives."

Isn't that what Morpheus had said?

"One could utter an idea that could inspire across time."

Before I had the chance to prove it, she stormed off and disappeared—and I knew where she was going.

That night we'd shared an intimate moment on the Ferris Wheel followed by a kiss that changed the trajectory of our relationship. Did I just affect the timeline? Had I found a loophole? A way around all the fancy time travel rules with the key?

I followed her until she disappeared at the fairground entrance. The fairgrounds were cold and empty—the booths and attractions were ghosts themselves. But as I moved deeper into the maze of pavilions, barns, and mechanical rides, they seemed charged, as if waiting to come alive at any moment.

And then—

I was surrounded. The whole place lit up like I was there once again. September 1st, 2001—the night we first kissed. And through this dream-like replay I could track two events playing out—the original event, where Jaycie spurned my impassioned speech on the Ferris Wheel—and the alternate course that led to one of the best moments of my life. Somewhere in Jaycie's mind she remembered both versions. I watched as we parted, like tracing paper overlapping us together, side by side, toward her car.

The next thing I knew I was eating dirt and coughing blood.

A piece of fiberglass had torn through my sternum and was poking out my back.

Something—a shadow?—hit me so hard, I slammed into a food cart and rebounded against a dumpster. Before I could stand up, it hit me again. I crawled out of a collapsed booth without knowing I had crashed clean through it. One of those games with rings and old metal milk jugs rang my head like a bell.

I spat a wad of blood just after I removed the fiberglass and was immediately smoked again by a right and a left—my skull cracked, and my ribs snapped. I was down on my knees clutching my chest when I finally saw it standing over me. It looked just like me...

...almost.

"How many times, Tony?" said Markus.

The dreamscape had stuck like an old VHS tape paused between frames—flickering back and forth—everyone doing a fancy little jig.

Funny—I finally got my beating on the fairgrounds, just not at the hands of my bully.

I tried to speak, but my broken ribs were poking at my lungs every time I inhaled.

"Too many times," he answered himself. "For someone so motivated, it seems like you're too busy reminiscing to get anything done."

"Fuck…" I said, followed by a prolonged pause as I sucked in another breath. "…you."

"Yeah, fuck me," he laughed. Markus was not the same Roman Centurion he was when we first met. His tunic and armor were gone, and he was dressed…like me. A brown leather biker jacket, torn jeans, chucks, and haircut that made me want to shave it off. Only his mug wasn't decorated with a big, crescent moon-shaped scar mucking it up.

I shuffled on my knees to face him, leaking blood. The moment he saw an opening, Markus sent me into next week with a boot to the temple. I tumbled out into the open, skidding across the dirt.

"We're in the middle of a war zone, and you're wandering down memory lane," he growled.

"Is that what my hair looks like?"

"Tony, you forget," said Markus, "We share the same brain. I know your tricks. I know you say dumb shit to make people think you're aloof while you evaluate the situation."

"No, seriously," I gurgled, "If that's what my hair looks like, I need a new barber."

We were surrounded by people—but they were people from a memory. Faceless blurs that slipped in and out of focus…

…except for the pair of green rubber boots I spotted hiding behind a 4H booth with a cartoon cow painted on the side.

Markus gave himself a quick once-over and laughed.

"You might be right," he said. "I've always wondered, what the actual fuck Jacinda ever saw in you. You're a pathetic human being, Tony. All that time you were this mighty angel and you did nothing. Nothing to prevent this catastrophe. You whined and moped—"

He kicked me again, this time to the ribs and they snapped all over again.

"—you aren't even worthy of her. And that's a shame really. The worst thing that could have happened was for you to discover she was still alive. All that pain and suffering—Marshall, Anne, Brad, Tori, Amanda— they all died and you're here dicking around in your memories."

I rolled away, putting Markus's back to the green boots...

...but he saw my glance.

"What do we have here?" he said, and a flaming spear snapped to life in his hand.

JACINDA
Then.

"I have eyes for you," she sang—that other woman through the headphones strapped to Tony's ears. I followed every note. I could hear every imperfection and nearly died of embarrassment right there in the booth of a Mexican restaurant.

I promise, it wasn't your *burrito supreme*, El Jefe—those were to die for.

It was the last line in my latest song, and when the recording finished I was transfixed—staring at the man who sat across from me and waited for a glimmer—anything!—to glide across his face. Love it? Hate it? Want to set fire to it?

"What do you think?" I asked after a single millisecond had passed and he still hadn't said anything.

I had been spending countless hours at the studio recording with Roman and a band of musicians he'd hired. The song Tony had just finished was the fruit of our labor, and I wanted him to hear it straightaway.

Roman had a no visitors policy, so we met up a few blocks away at a Mexican restaurant, El Jefe—*the best!*—on a cold Saturday afternoon, sharing a plate of guac and chips which I had nervously devoured during the most intense three-minutes and fifty-five seconds of my young life.

My big flappy beanie was pulled down over my ears to keep them warm and my hair kept finding a way to spring out every time I turned my head. Why do my ears go cold when I get nervous?

His eyes darted to my fingers playing with his key around my neck, and I stopped fiddling with it and wrapped myself tighter inside my leather jacket.

Ever have one of those side arguments in your head where you're thinking one thing, but debating a totally different topic with yourself at the same time? Yeah? While he was listening to my brand-new track, I was arguing all over again about my future as a musician. I was going through a blistering bad case of imposter syndrome.

I wasn't cool anymore—was I ever cool?

Tony had lost himself. He didn't make the city baseball team and had been spiraling, despite protesting otherwise. His self-loathing started a rift between us—not a fight, or anything like that. It's just that when Tony was hurt, he closed that part of himself off from me.

And while I struggled to pull him out of it, I found myself falling into my own depression and I didn't know why. I was right where I wanted to be. So why was I feeling like everything was wrong?

"You hate it?" I finally said, after he removed the headphones without a word. I deflated like a tire after rolling over a set of cartoon spikes—which was to say I popped. One moment I was sagging, and the next I was so low I could taste the grime on the floor of the restaurant— sorry, El Jefe, cleanliness was not your finest quality.

Tony was having one of his internal arguments—I knew that face—I knew what was going on "behind your eyes"—and was just coming to realize he looked like he had swallowed half a Dorito sideways. He was an artist too—he knew what it was like to bear his soul within his work, and for people to respond with lukewarm praise, harsh criticism, or the kiss of death—the overly-enthusiastic-and-completely-fake *I lOvE iT sO MUcH yOU raWk* response—would have crushed me.

"I love it," he said, "I really do." And he meant it. It was sincere, but there was pain *behind his eyes*.

I wrote "Behind Your Eyes" months ago. It was about us. It was about falling in love with him—and I almost didn't want the song to be public, because it was too personal. But Roman was adamant that this be the crown jewel within a jewel case, plastic wrap, and those super-frustrating sticker seals on store shelves later that fall.

Then Tony said something that made me immediately recoil.

"Is this about us?"

"I wrote it. Who do you think it's about?" I tried to say it playfully, but it dislodged from my throat all wrong. His subtext was carrying a message he didn't know how to articulate.

"I really love it. I'm a little overwhelmed."

"Oh," I said. I was disappointed, and the look on his face showed that he didn't mean to hurt me. "I mean, Roman said it could be a hit, but that I'll need to re-record the vocals. He thinks I'm a bit pitchy on the bridge. And we'll probably have to tighten up my guitars on the intro, but he thinks it's salvageable."

"Salvageable?" he questioned. He said it with a touch of venom.

I was looking out the window, watching people scurry by in the rain, when he put his hand on mine from across the booth.

Behind *his* eyes, I could tell he wanted to say it was amazing—that he was blown away, yet again by me. He wanted to say that my interpretation of him was a lie, like it was built of sand and the tide was coming in. That listening to my song made him happy but scared as hell, and that he had never been so flattered, and in awe of my talents—*and* so afraid that he was bound to be left behind.

All words and thoughts he had expressed a thousand times.

Tony bought into the premise that talk wasn't cheap, but that there were only so many ways to express the same things. He was dating a lyricist—even if I was only an imposter—and I wanted to hear him say those words a million and one times a million. I wanted him to say what was *behind his eyes*, because mine were meant for him only.

Instead, he chose to pick a fight.

"Why is Roman such an asshole? It's really good. Why is he tearing you down like that?"

I removed my hand from his.

"He's not an asshole," I groaned. "He's doing what all good producers do. He's giving me his honest opinion to make me a better artist."

"I don't know," he said. "He sounds like one of those douchebags in positions of power who puts women down to make them need him more."

I glared at him. He didn't trust Roman and I was done having this fight.

"I asked you to meet here so I could share this with you," I said. "I was really excited."

"It's good, Jayce," he said. "It really is. I just don't understand why we have to meet here. Why can't I come down to the studio?"

"Visitors aren't allowed."

"Is that the studio's rule?" he asked, "or *his*?"

"I don't want to fight with you." I leaned back in the booth as far away from him as possible and stared out the window into the rain. It was quiet between us, as I watched people on the street meander with open umbrellas.

"What happens," he finally asked, "when you finish? Will you go on tour? What happens to us then?"

I didn't answer. I didn't have an answer.

"You'll be gone," he said, "won't you? Touring the country?"

"I don't know," I whispered.

"Jaycie, your song is great," he said. "It sounds professional, like fans will be flocking to record stores to grab copies, downloading your hits from legit and illegit sites, and sellout crowds. You have a future doing this, and I am in awe of you and your talents." I started tearing up. I knew where he was taking this conversation. "You're on a trajectory to great and amazing things. I don't see room for your small-town, small-time graphic designer boyfriend with a cubicle job on your tour bus to fame."

"Do you really think I'm that good? Or are you just saying that?" I deadpanned, and for a moment he almost thought I was being that cruel. I thawed with a warm smile and retook his hand. "I'm not going anywhere without you. Besides, let's be real, I'm really not that special."

"Yes, you are," he said, and he choked a little when saying it. "You're an extraordinary gal. And I love you so much it hurts."

He was fighting so hard to always be good enough. Hiding the parts of him that were afraid or angry or sad. He didn't want me to see that Tony, but I saw him. He was a stranger who never said hello.

Ten minutes ago...

Where do you draw the line between reality and fantasy? What if you're living a dream? I was inside a twisted version of my childhood home when the spirit of another woman trying to take over my body knocked at my front door. I offered her a glass of water, then watched a child-version of me run down the steps then flee out the front door chased by a nightmare version of my demented mother—with the body-snatcher right behind little me—fleeing into the woods across the street.

Head spinning, I know.

I made my mother disappear, remembered something from my past I wish I hadn't thought of, then chased after them. I never stopped to imagine that in a world filled with nightmare mothers and child versions of me, what else I might find.

An army of soldiers from some long-lost nightmare was not on my bingo card. Neither was a silver-blooded misogynistic weirdo who threatened me and my dreams. And the spiders? Eeeech.

And most definitely, neither was super strength, bulletproof skin or flight—I was flying!—and everything below was chaos.

The soldiers were everywhere. They had invaded every corner of town. Grace Falls was burning. Pin Falls, Bolt & Shield Comics Shoppe, even Milton State off in the distance—all surrounded in dark smoke. But that wasn't the worst of it.

They were leaving bodies behind them.

Me.

They were killing versions of me.

I landed in a spot behind Down the Hatch, a small bar where I'd played a few gigs, back before...*before*...*the man I love*? Whose name had abandoned my brain like every good idea I've ever had in the shower by the time I could grab a pen and paper. Why do I always have the best ideas in the shower?

There on the ground, Grammy's guitar still clutched tightly in her hands was a woman, nineteen, maybe twenty—full of hopes and dreams and scars—and she was me...but I did not remember her. The clothes, the headband, everything about her was like seeing it for the first time.

If a me dies in a place like this, does she disappear from within *me?* From my memory?

A panic swelled in my chest.

Then I heard a scream.

TONY
Eight minutes ago...

"Ssss...ttoppp," I spat, crawling between Markus and the green boots.

"Stop?" he said, and he struck my arm with the haft of his flaming spear, snapping it at the wrist.

Something was undeniably wrong. I wasn't healing as fast as I should.

"Stop? Stop? Tony Tony Tony," he said. "The problem is you keep stopping!"

I cued up a good Marsha-Marsha-Marsha joke, but Markus didn't get my humor.

"Jokes and reveries!" he growled, as if he could read my mind. *Could he read my mind?* "It's like you're not even serious about what it is you want and how to get it! Make no mistake, Tony, there's something about you that's not quite right, and I'm trying to fix it."

There was a whimper. It was coming from the bright green rain boots.

When Markus motioned toward the whimper and smiled, I nearly leapt out of my skin to stop him, but my mind and body were on two different pages within two totally different books.

"Ah, yes. Who's this?" he said, snatching her by the arm.

She was only eight. Maybe nine. Her eyes were wet with tears and shivers crawled up and down her back. I could taste her fear, hear her heart beating like a hummingbird, smell her confusion. And I was just a lump of meat, unable to do anything. A sack of utter shit.

"Let her go!" someone shouted, and another Jaycie revealed herself from behind a juice stand. She was thirteen, maybe. Then another from the next row—seventeen at the oldest, wielding a mini-baseball bat—one of the cheap carnival prizes.

"Oh, look at this. What do you think they are?" said Markus. "Memories? Snapshots in time? What do you think happens when we blot one of them out?"

When he jostled little Jaycie, she screamed.

"Now now," said Markus, "no need to wake the dead."

There was a sound, like something slicing through the wind. Not a bullet, or a rocket, but a whole person behind a fist.

JACINDA

That scream.

That scream felt familiar. It was more jarring than hearing your own recorded voice, and more alarming knowing it was your own scream, but from a younger set of your own lungs. The urgency to find her—*me* —sparked instinct. I was a whole other person filled with unknown potential to do anything I could imagine.

What was possible within a dream? Could I fly? Could I bleed? *Could I die?*

How did any of this work?

Doctor Celestine had once observed that the human mind was more expansive than the universe itself. "Within the mind," he said, "are endless possibilities and outcomes."

Did he too have a whole mirror version of Grace Falls lodged between his temples?

I jumped, but I didn't come back down. Instead, I soared. I soared straight up and in the direction of the scream. I was a blur. I homed in on that scream and spotted her being jostled by an asshat in a leather jacket.

He looked so familiar. Like a composite of dark thoughts manifesting someone I used to know. When I plowed him straight down into the dirt with a single punch, I wasn't shocked. I wasn't even awed by my own strength. I knew I had it in me—like I was a superhero in another life.

I placed my boot onto the man's chest and his weapon faded away. He wasn't getting up, but I could still feel danger. It was everywhere and closing in from every angle. They were swarming. Terrible things, and not just those soldiers…

I turned to little me and said, "Go home. I took care of Mom." I gave her a wink, but the poor thing was too traumatized to react. A trauma that deep down, I felt too, like I was feeling an old scar scratch open.

I knelt at her side and placed a comforting hand on her cheek and thought of something I hadn't thought about in a long time. And with a thought, I made it true.

"I left something there to protect you. You'll be safe. I promise."

She ran off, followed by two others—memories I had almost forgotten. I watched them disappear near the Ferris Wheel. That giant metal circle held so many memories, but I couldn't remember any of them.

Something big and nasty struck my shoulder and exploded, and I kept thinking, *Was that supposed to hurt?*

TONY

In a blur, Jaycie dropped out of the sky and slugged Markus. She hit him so hard that he hit the earth, and the ground beneath him cracked. She embedded him three feet into the dirt, like a cartoon coyote, then stood over him with her aura blazing. Her hair was braided on one side and flung over the other like a wave, and she was dressed all punk rock—frayed black denim vest with spikes over a torn-up t-shirt and jeans.

I was too starstruck to move. What Jaycie *was* this?

"Go home," said Jaycie. "I took care of Mom." Then she knelt beside Little J and whispered something I couldn't hear.

Little Jaycie nodded and ran. The other two followed her away from the scene, heading toward the river. I wanted to get up. I wanted to hug her, to kiss her, to join her, but I was all broken and blue and healing like a fucking turtle—both in speed and flailing around in the dirt on my back...

Jaycie spun back toward me just in time to be struck flush by a tank shell.

She was momentarily engulfed in flames, then surrounded in black smoke. But when she emerged from the blast staring down the incoming tank and soldiers spraying bullets that bounced off her skin without a mark, I was in complete and total awe.

Then all hell broke loose.

Gunfire erupted, and Jaycie took the brunt of an all-out assault, but she didn't flinch. She didn't stand down. Instead, she swung her hand through the air and a wave of dirt, and crushed carnival booths swallowed half the soldiers on the near flank.

JACINDA

Tank shells. Bullets. They didn't matter. I barely felt them.

Every strike filled my bucket of anger. Rage. Fury. Disgust. Every resentful emotion was a drop into that rapidly filling bucket. They were trying to end me. Each and every version of me, they wanted to wipe out. To evict me for someone else.

Lilly.

I don't know where Lilly was. Probably wandering downtown or bowling a few frames at Pin Falls. Regardless, she was just an innocent. She was caught up in this mess, like me.

And as my wrath built, I was struck with one thought.

In all my life, I never had such a thought. In all my life I never wanted to hurt anyone. In all my life I never had the ability to fight back...except once. Was that even real? Me pulling the world apart, atom by atom?

In all my life, I never ever thought, "They don't know who they're messing with."

I waved my arm like I was brushing aside a fly and flattened the tank and everyone that stood near it, burying them all under a few tons of dirt, concrete, and wood planks.

A long time ago, Robbie…I mean, Maynard…used to say things like, "Technically the glass is always full." Meaning whether it was half full of juice or water, that didn't matter because the other half was always full of air. I seem to remember him saying all sorts of smart dumb sciency things. One of them found itself jarred into my thoughts as I watched a giant crack form in the darkened sky. It flashed as red as my hair.

"For every good deed there's an equal and opposite bad deed just waiting to eat you alive for having the audacity."

Then Amanda would say, "What an entirely dark and pessimistic dweeb you've turned into, Morris."

"Hey, I'm just stating facts, ma'am," he'd reply.

But he was right. My whole life I've been trying to do what's right, only to get shoved back for standing up for what I believed in.

That crack in the sky? It was no good.

I took two strides toward the incoming soldiers, fists balled and ready to crush those blank masked heads like tin cans, when I spotted another creep on the ground. They were dressed alike, even looked alike —the brown biker jacket and the jeans. This one had a big ugly scar on his face that was bleeding, and he crawled to his knees.

"Jayce?"

I stopped. That voice. I knew that voice. That face…

"Tony? Tony, is that you?"

And then something popped behind my eyes.

I couldn't see a thing…

TONY

That's when she spotted me, finally on my knees and busted up. She glared at me, her eyes vacant, as if she didn't recognize me.

When she re-balled her fists and pivoted toward me, I said, "Jayce?"

Her face softened.

"Tony?"

The ground shook, and the sky flashed red.

"Tony, is that you?"

And then she was gone. She disappeared—evaporated—faded out— just as the ground rumbled and the soldiers marched in, guns blazing.

And for a moment, I thought I was a dead man...

"Tony! My man!" shouted Montoya, charging in like freakin' Rambo. He fired an automatic at the advancing soldiers with one arm and swooped in with the other, lifting me onto my feet in one swift motion.

When we tracked our way past the impact crater, it was empty. Markus was gone.

"Where is he?"

"Who, my man?"

"Come on!" I yelled, charging in the direction the girls had fled.

Now.

We chased after the Jaycies for a quarter mile, picking off soldiers as they hunted them and trying not to think about the horror in the sky that lingered just beyond the mind palace. We'd chased the Jaycies past the Hallows House and the cemetery and into the Grace Falls public park when they disappeared.

It wasn't a very big park, but it had a playground with swings, a sandbox and a jungle gym, a few park benches, and a duck pond beneath the Elm Way Bridge. I thought we had lost them when I spotted Markus chasing into the forest near the Cemetery Drive. Once beyond the first few trees, I stumbled upon a tripod—but it wasn't a camera sitting on top.

"What is this doing here?" I asked, but Montoya had disappeared. "Hey! Montoya! My man?" But nothing. The urge to move on was stymied—this contraption, this tripod—I had watched Jaycie's entire life and never came across *this*. There were gummi bears on the ground, Jaycie's childhood favorite, and I felt the need to know more.

The contraption on the tripod was sort of like an old reel-to-reel camera, but it had three vials of chemicals—salt, mercury maybe? And something else. There were multiple lenses, some colored, all different sizes, and a cradle at the back where the lenses were focused, like a magnifying glass.

Then there was a tune—someone was singing—and I felt like I had walked into an old home movie with dusty film and scratches. The tune sounded like it was coming from every direction at once. It was familiar, like something from my childhood. "You are my sunshine," or something like that.

"Good day, sir," said an old man—he approached me from behind a big tree. His usage of the word "sir" had me thinking it was Henry...

...but this man was definitely not Henry.

XXII

the fall of hades

A VOICE
Long Ago...
Then.

Power. It was always about power.

The struggle between those who had plenty and those who had little. The interesting thing about power was that all of it was divided up and claimed at any given time. Power is rarely found, unclaimed and waiting. It must be taken—ripped free from the cold dead hands of its master.

When Malus stepped into the underworld, he strode in like a lion, dragging the comatose body of a Titan behind him. Hades, named after the god who ruled it, existed in a universe within our own. Like a pocket, between reality and the Veil, but somewhere else entirely. These universes are plenty, but to move between them one must have a key— or happen upon an unlocked door...

Malus had discovered such a door—a portal into the underworld through the crater of Avernus, near the city of Cumae. The portal was through the preserved remains of a giant creature from beyond. The creature tried to escape Hades into our own—its great fangs kept the door ajar—allowing Malus to pass through into the world of the dead.

Hades, the underworld, was a wonder all its own. It was an island, a land deep beneath the earth with its own sky—gray and gloomy like the heavens on a dreary day. It was murky, a miserable gloom, and surrounded by five rivers, sealing the island away from escape. The river of woe, the Archeron to the east. The Cocytus, river of lamentation to the south. The river of fire, the Phlegethon to the southwest. The Lethe to the northwest, the river of oblivion. And to the north, the famed Styx, the river of hate.

As he stood upon the shore contemplating which river to cross, there was a brief moment when he considered the Lethe. It was said that bathing in the waters there would obliterate the mind—wipe it clean of everything, including memory—perhaps even language.

A blank slate—and Malus wondered for a moment, would he find peace in ignorance?

Would forgetting his torment be the end to his endless pursuits?

He missed Lilandra. There was not a single moment of the day where he was not reminded of her. She was in the wind. She was in the earth. She was in the sky, and every living thing. She was his end.

Tucked into his vestments was a piece of cloth torn from her clothing when she was taken from him. He kept it close. It was his only prized possession. The only item he cherished. And he swore he could still smell her scent upon it, albeit faint.

Yet, he stood on the shores of the underworld! He, the raggy boy, had ascended beyond immortality. He was the Pale Demon. The gods feared him. And he was as close as ever to the end of his endless quest.

He gazed upon Chronos, still bound by the Chains of Prometheus, and swallowed his hope. If he were mere moments away from being reunited with the only person he ever loved, for the first time in nearly five-hundred years, what would be the cost? A Titan returned to its cage? Or would the god of the underworld ask for tax?

Lilandra was his strength. She was his reason to live. He could not wade through the Lethe and be stripped of his memory, not when he was this close.

Malus stalked to the edge of the River Styx, the river of hate, pulling the Titan Chronos by the chains that bound him—still locked in a senseless, comatose state. There was nothing in this world Malus hated more than the demon that took Lilly. His hate was precise—concentrated enmity at the one and only thing he wished to destroy. His hatred could not be enhanced nor twisted by the Styx. It was already all-consuming, and therefore it could not change who and what he was. He was immune to the destructive nature of hate—he had mastered it. He had harnessed it.

Or so he had believed.

Malus swam the Styx and dragged Chronos ashore. The beach on the dead island was an eroded hill of coarse white sand. He crawled to the top of the incline, slipping through the dense fog, and stopped at the base of an immense dead palace. Four rows of white stone columns spanned a great staircase, with a wide canopy above leading up into the unknown. There were statues to honor the gods and heroes, all crumbling to dust within the gardens that had withered into husks ages ago. Dead trees slumped, and the air was thick with dust and spore. Even the stone floor felt like rot. There was no sound, no life, color, or song. Twisted skulls lingered at corners of Malus's eyes, but disappeared with a glance, like death fleeing the living eye. It was a place that invited the mind to wander into darkness, imagining terrors that may or may not exist.

The ruined palace served as the entrance to the underworld, but its architecture presented many oddities—there was no way into the temple, except to ascend through the fog upon the great staircase to the very top of the palace. There, amongst broken pillars and a crumbling canopy, was a single door. Within was a staircase leading down. Each level receding until Malus was deep beneath the earth.

He wandered the palace room by room, dragging the chained Titan. The sound of metal scraping cold stone made any hope of surprise a distant dream. Every empty chamber was just as eerie, plain, and ordinary as the last, with a single chair or two per room. There were no plants, no tapestries, no servants or luxury. The palace of the dead was as empty as one would imagine. There were no torches or light, just the eerie glow that emanated from every surface in the underworld. The palace garden at the epicenter of the great structure was dead, its fountains filled with stagnant water that trembled as he strode past, dragging his prisoner beyond.

Alas, Malus entered the throne room at the very bottom of the palace. The throne room was no ordinary chamber of audiences. It was wide, and mostly empty with statues of warriors in mid-battle around its edges, holding real blades, shields, and bows, wearing cloth tunics, leather, and armor—as if their flesh had been cast into stone.

But it was the object at the center of the room that drew Malus's attention. It was an unremarkable, carved wooden chair facing the entrance like a royal throne—

—but there was nothing regal about that chair.

A small pile of dust surrounded it, but upon closer inspection, carved onto the legs and backrest of the chair were symbols—not dissimilar to those on the shackles that bound Chronos.

The chair was the craftsmanship of Hephaistos.

Malus kicked at the dust around the foot of the chair—it was littered with bones. They were not of human origin. Scattered throughout the room amongst the stone warriors were three serpentine figures—all missing heads.

"Gorgons," he whispered.

Gorgons were a breed of serpentine women—half snake, half demi-god. Some said they were beautiful; others claim horrific. All were rumor—for one look into their eyes cast a man to stone. It was said there were three; the sisters Medusa, Euryale, and Stheno—but there were more. Many more hidden within the dark places the gods wished to keep secret.

Malus dropped the chains that bound Chronos and walked to back of the room, where a spectacular painting absorbed his attention. The room was enchanted to slowly reveal itself in pieces. The painting was as tall as three men, with a spiral of human souls, circling toward a door at its center. The paint was applied to the wall in thick layers that leapt from its surface the longer it was observed—and longer still, it began to move. The paint shifted, animating the departed souls into a cyclone of the dead. The souls drained into the door at its center, where two parallel holes were surrounded by a circle cut into the wall.

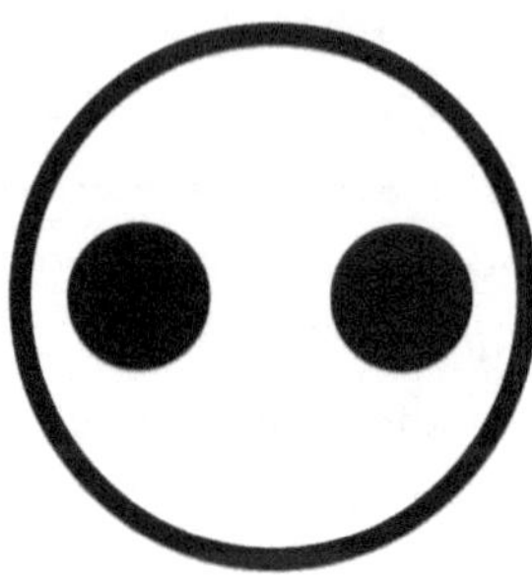

Every hall, every door and chamber led into that room. There was no other way beyond. The entrance into the underworld was there, it had to be.

"There are only two ways you may pass," said a voice, like an echo. "Death is the only way I permit to you, stranger. What do you want?"

"I have come to negotiate a trade," said Malus.

"Sit," suggested the voice. The only place one could sit was upon the empty chair—the one surrounded by the pile of bones. "Negotiate."

"I would rather stand," he affirmed.

"Of course," said the voice. "What kind of trade do you suggest?"

"Master Hades," said Malus, "I return to you a prisoner of Tartarus, stolen by your brother Zeus. In return, I asked for a single human soul. One that will return with me to the land of the living."

This was the moment he had been waiting for—toiling through the secrets of the world to find an answer to the riddle of death. In the end, it was not a spell nor sacrifice, but a barter. Currency was the true power of the world.

"I am grateful for the return of my property," said Hades, "but gratitude and safe passage home is all I offer."

"My lord, that is not what I came for," he replied.

"Your errands were all for naught," said Hades. "You cannot have what you ask. Leave this place before I change my mind."

Malus shook with rage.

The Styx, you see, does not amplify hatred. The Styx takes your patience, your poise, your humility, and your composure, and it washes them away. While Malus believed he would not be affected by the Styx, he was wrong. It turned the darkness in him pitch black.

The command one must have swim the Styx and not destroy all in their path, is a creature so motivated, so consumed, that those who oppose them heed our warning; this is an immovable object that will not falter and will never stop. Know thy enemy, Tony.

"You would be wise to abide by fair trade," sneered Malus. "I apprehended your fugitive. The least you could offer is proper gratitude."

"Tell me, stranger, why should I give anything for the return of my property? Why should I give you the thing you desire most?" asked Hades.

The room was perfectly still. There was no movement, no draft, no discernible smells beyond the staleness of decay, and sound dampened in the lazy air. Hades was as vacant as the room—a disembodied voice—a ghost.

"My desires are honest," said Malus. "I have walked this world for far too many lifetimes, and all I seek is to be reunited with the only thing I ever loved."

"Is that so?" asked Hades. "Why should I reunite you with the woman you love when I must spend eternity without my own? My Persephone could not bear to love me while living amongst the dead and took her own life to escape this place. Where she went, I cannot collect. She is beyond my grasp."

"How is that so?" questioned Malus. "Are you not a god? Are you not the keeper of souls?"

Hades roared, "I am a god!" His palace trembled and the blurry lines of every object sharpened with his anger.

"But you are not the true god of the underworld if the dead, any dead, are beyond your reach," said Malus, smiling. "A false keeper of souls. An undertaker of untruth. If the dead may go elsewhere, then what is this place?"

Hades did not answer with words. Two sharp blades were shoved into Malus's stomach, then he was lifted off his feet and thrown to the far side of the room, crashing through a statue. When he hit the wall, the damage that had been done to his body was too much to assess. A broken arm and leg, shattered ribs and collarbone, and his right side was numb. In all his lifetimes, he had never endured the kind of injury that he had just sustained.

As the blood pooled around his body, he felt the heat leave his limbs. Was this dying? Was this what Lilly felt before the end?

"Come with me," she said.

Memories fade. Every step toward bringing Lilly back was one step further away from his time with her. Every moment was another blurry layer washing her image away.

"Let go," she said.

When he saw her—arms extended, reaching out to him, offering passage into the next world—he felt at peace. Her blond hair and bright blue eyes were like home, and the years of haze sharpened into perfect clarity. He was reunited with her at last, and he could lay down his rage, his weapons, his journey, and be done.

"Let go," said Lilly. "Take my hand and we shall dance in the Elysian Fields together, forever."

"Are you really her?" he weeped. "Are you really my Lilly?"

"Yes," she said. "I am your Lilly."

There was something about her answer that gave him doubt. Something that nagged at the back of his mind—a betrayal of memory.

"I am feeling anxious, my love," he said. "Give me courage. Speak the words you used to inspire me, to follow you anywhere, into every adventure—and now, even into death."

"Come with me," she said, "and we will dance in the Elysian Fields together, forever."

Malus was dying, but his anger flared into every limb. Where his blood had drained and left him cold, was now filled with wrathful fire. This was not his Lilandra.

"Give her your hand, stranger," said Hades. "Be with the woman you love."

Tricks. Malus would not be fooled by tricks.

He said, "No," and as the words left his lips, Lilly vanished, and the blurry memories returned. In her place, a shadow recoiled and flew away, screeching.

"I offered you a favor, stranger," said Hades. "You could have danced in the Elysian Fields, but now I shall send you to Tartarus, where the damned wander for eternity."

"I have wandered centuries to find her," said Malus. "Eternity is but a moment longer."

When Malus stood there was no pain. There was no blood. His bones were no longer broken. The two great wounds through his abdomen had vanished.

"What magic is this?" said Hades. Wherever he was, Malus could smell his consternation. It was acidic, like vinegar. "The damage done by my bident is irreversible."

"You are correct," he said, "the damage done *is irreversible*." The anger rose higher and hotter, and eventually engulfed his fists with fire. With a little push, a staff and blade—a spear of pure flame erupted from his right hand—like instinct.

"You are no Fallen," said Hades. He sounded confused. "What are you?"

Malus did not answer. When the air shifted, he raised his spear, and something heavy and metal struck and deflected away from him. He could not see Hades, but suddenly that did not matter.

A battle ensued. Malus fought his unseen opponent from one end of the room to the other. Their weapons clashed, sparks danced, and for every Hades attack, Malus had a defensive answer. Although Malus could not see him, he could hear the bident as it hissed through the air—and if he could hear it, he could defend against it.

Malus held fast and led the attack into the center of the room. When Hades lunged, his next strike slicing open a cut across Malus's thigh, the Pale Demon jostled Hades backward off balance. With one mighty shove, the god of the underworld fell into the wooden chair—his helm flying from his godly head—invisible no longer. Any normal wooden chair would have toppled over and broken with the fall, but this chair merely teetered once and settled onto all four legs like dense stone, as if magnetized to the floor.

Malus lowered his spear to Hades' throat, but the god did not move.

Hades was as old as Zeus, but wiry and thin. His skin was taut and dry, and his hair had streaks of silver. His eyes were hollow, cold, and glazed, and his limbs were scaled. He was a twisted amalgam of man and reptile.

But stranger than his appearance, since landing upon that wooden chair, he did not stir, or twitch, nor did he attempt to stand. Hades no longer moved at all.

Of the many legends told under starry sky, was Hades' legendary ownership of the Chair of Forgetfulness. A chair that could wipe the mind clean if one was cursed to sit upon it. One might imagine it would have looked more—*interesting?* Perhaps that was part of the ruse. Hephaistos had created an ordinary chair that could lure even the most suspicious.

With Hades and Chronos both in a state of oblivion, Malus took the bident and strode over to the painted cyclone of souls. The gods loved their trinkets, and Malus was beginning to understand that personal power alone was not enough. One must surround themselves in power.

The secret to the passage beyond the painting was as simple as inserting the bident's dual blades into the holes at its center, and twist—a secret decoded with ease. The animated cyclone of painted souls flushed to its center, as if being washed down an empty drain, then the wall slid aside to the grinding sound of stone on stone.

Beyond the wall was a narrow staircase hewn into the rock, wide enough for one, descending into the very core of the island. The caverns below the necropolis lit as he approached—torches responding to the presence of the bident. At the far wall were three podiums, with a ghastly figure sitting upon each.

They were magistrates with only one duty—forever bound to judge the dead, to send those recently departed to their final resting place. Each of them was conscripted into their roles upon death from various ages of the Greek Empire. The judge on the left had a long gnarled white beard, the center judge was hairless, and the judge on the right wore his thinning mane in long braids. Spectral crowns proudly rested upon their heads, displaying their royal heritage.

Across from them were three doors made of rusted metal and stone, with gears of ancient machinery to open and close each vault. To each side of the podiums was a natural spring that pooled into two small fountains. To the left was water from the Lethe—its misty essence drifting across its surface—and to the right, water from the Mnemosyne. Once judgment was rendered, a drink from one or the other—

—If your time had not yet expired, a drink from the Lethe would erase your memory for reincarnation.

—If your life was full, be it pleasant or damned, a sip from the Mnemosyne kept memories intact for those who would rest eternally upon the Elysian Fields.

Then the dead were ushered through one of three doors, to their fate beyond.

"Have you come to be judged?" asked the judge on the left.

"I have not," said Malus, obscuring the bident behind his back. "Tell me, through which door may I find my love, Lilandra?"

Each of the three judges looked to the other, as if to confer their confusion.

"You are not dead," said the one on the right.

"Only the judged may pass," said the middle judge.

"No, three kings, I am not here to be judged, but I shall judge you," Malus said, then pointed at the judge on the right. "King Rhadamanthus, bastard son of Zeus. A philanderer like his father, who sent the sons of the poor to their death to spare the rich the same loss." Next, Malus took aim at the center king. "King Minos, brother of Rhadmanthus, bastard son of Zeus. You procured seven young boys and seven young girls from the city of Athens to satiate the minotaur in the labyrinth below your palace. You punished children instead of King Aegeus, the man who wronged you. You showed mercy to a king but sentenced innocents to death." Lastly, he pointed towards the third king, the one on the left. "And you, King Aeacus, another bastard son of Zeus, committed genocide of an indigenous people to claim a land that you falsely attributed to birthright. An entire people, gone because of your selfish act."

"We are three kings of unshakeable integrity!" shouted Minos. "Our station as judges demand our principle."

"No, you are three kings of *very* shakeable integrity, and limited principle," stated Malus.

"Where did you learn of such acrimonious drivel?"

"I ate your father after I killed him," laughed Malus. "Oh, the secrets he shared!"

"You cannot kill a god!" roared Rhadmanthus.

"Oh, I can, and I did with this blade," Malus removed it from his belt. "This blade was carved from a tooth. A special tooth that belonged to one of the Graeae." He approached them to provide a closer look at his weapon. "It does have many qualities beyond those of a normal blade, but fear not—it does not hold the power to slay a ghost." He laughed, and the three kings chuckled nervously along with him.

"If that be the case, why threaten us, stranger?"

"I threaten, because I believe this weapon," said Malus, retrieving the obscured bident from behind his back, "*does* have the power to destroy you."

The three kings went silent.

With a shove, the prongs of the bident buried into the chest of Aeacus, then raked across Rhadamanthus's throat. To Minos, Malus held the bident to his eyes, as the others melted away.

"Tell me, through which door may I find Lilandra?" he asked again.

"I cannot," cried Minos as he shivered with fear.

"Yes, you can. Tell me!"

"I cannot, because I do not know," responded Minos.

"Then you are no use to me," hissed Malus as he shoved the forked blades into the king's head and watched the last judge melt away.

Then Malus turned to inspect the vault doors. There were no labels upon them. They were as thick and impenetrable as a mountain, with wheels that when spun began a series of movements—gears and metal springs, groaning. Malus spun the first wheel until the first door unlocked with a pop and swung open.

What he found on the other side was dark and humid. The air was so hot and thick, he could hardly breathe. Further inspection brought a stench, like rot on a days-old battlefield. Further still came terrible cries of pain.

Malus had entered Tartarus, home of the damned. Prison of the Titans. He did not believe Lilandra was resting in such a foul place, but Chernobog's wrath had been awful. Could she have been sent to Tartarus for Malus's own misdeeds?

Malus withdrew the strip of Lilly's tattered garments he had kept and cherished since that tragic day. He wrapped its length around his hand and whispered, "Find her." The fragile graying cloth became as black as shadow. The spell was something he had learned from a Nordic tribe along the coast of the frozen sea. The cloth would change shades from black to its original color as he advanced toward the target. Upon finding her, it would grow as yellow and green as her dress, the one she wore during festival—the dress she wore when Chernobog ripped her from his grasp.

After searching high and low, the cloth never changed a single shade, and Malus never witnessed the dead—only the screaming pain of those tortured souls emanating from every corner of Tartarus.

Back within the room of judgment, Malus unlocked the next door and entered.

He found himself wandering a bright and cheery meadow, with asphodel growing amongst the tall grasses that swayed in a cool breeze. Off in the distance he saw people wandering about, but there was something wrong with them. Each one endlessly meandered in a state of unbeing, as aimless as grazing cattle. When one of them spotted him at the top of the meadow, just beyond the great door, there came a sudden rush.

They were upon him in seconds.

Tens and hundreds of men and women, each of them mindless shells, moved toward him like a swarm, and yet the cloth on his hand did not change a single shade.

"Have you seen Lilandra?" he asked, but they did not answer.

The dead huddled around him but did not attack. They were drawn to the bident. The Asphodel Meadow was filled with war heroes, soldiers, and those who died before their times. They were those who died dishonorably or with business left unfinished. The meadow was beautiful, but it was no paradise, not for those who wandered there, forever.

"They have no mind left to hear you," spoke a woman.

Malus turned to the voice and saw her lingering behind him at the entrance to the meadow. For a moment, his heart filled with joy—his Lilly was there, he had found her. But like all things within Hades, the longer one looked the more truth was revealed.

Malus sobbed. The young woman, with braided black hair and eyes like gleaming blue gems, wore delicate robes and high-lacing sandals that tied below the knee. She was like a vision—like the Valkyries of the Northmen, with an ominous symbol tattooed to the pale skin of her unblemished forehead. A circle—a ring with no beginning and no end, like the Ouroboros.

She was not one of the dead.

"Do I frighten you?" She smirked. "Or are you unable to phrase coherent words when confronted with a woman?"

"Who are you?" he asked as he left the Asphodel Meadows with a great swarm of the mindless dead beyond the entrance, waiting with vacant eyes. "What do you want?"

"I followed you into this realm," she said. "I have been searching for the entrance to Hades for a long time. There was rumor of an immortal, the Pale Demon, who was looking for the entrance to the underworld. You showed me the way." Then she looked upon the dead and turned to the fountains next to the vacant podiums within the room of judgment. "I wish to destroy this place."

"Why?" asked Malus.

"These souls do not belong here," she said. "All of them. Even the damned in Tartarus."

"Are you a judge as well?" he asked.

"No," she said. "I came here with a purpose, a test bestowed to me by my prince. To live and learn, and report back when I had understood what it meant to be flawed. To understand what it meant to be human, so that I might forgive my brother." Then she smiled. "I learned more than I expected and stumbled upon a great many injustices. This one I wish to resolve."

"You are a god, like Hades," he asked, gripping the bident tight.

"Like—" she nodded slightly, "and unlike. I am something more. I am something different."

"What do you want?"

"When one dies within the Hades' reach, they are torn from their natural ascension to the one true afterlife. When they are sent here, their energy is collected and used for power. Collecting it from the souls they amass. Waiting. Preparing. And some have learned to grow Ambrosia, the food of the gods—though *food* is not accurate. It is like opium."

"For what? To what end?" he asked.

"What end?" she replied. "The inevitable end."

"Are the dead that powerful?"

"A battery of souls," she pondered, "could power them and their allies to their former glory, when they were amongst the choirs that served the One." She took a deep breath and inspected the fountain waters flowing from the Mnemosyne. "I want to destroy them, all of the underworlds, and send every trapped soul to their rightful resting place." Then she looked upon him carefully. "Will you help me destroy it?"

"The business of the gods is no business of mine," he said.

"If you will not help me, then please," she asked, "may I have the Bident of Hades, so that I may command the dead? I need their power to destroy this place."

"What good are ghosts against rock and brick? Against cold stone?" he asked.

"They are more powerful dead than they are alive." She approached him with her palms open. "Please, Pale Demon, let me end their torment."

After a moment, Malus handed her the bident.

"My search is ending," he said. "Allow me to take what's mine and leave. Do with this place as you will."

The woman took the bident, held it high above her head, and commanded the dead to follow her. She paced over to the Mnemosyne and knelt beside it, cupping some of its water in her hands and bringing it to the lips of the nearest dead.

"The Mnemosyne will restore their humanity, while that one—" she gestured to the other pool— "is the Lethe, and it will cleanse one's memory free of all things." The first of the dead drank from her hands and startled as if waking from a horrible nightmare. "I will not stop you from your quest, but you must hurry. I plan to destroy this entire island. If we meet again, you shall know me by my rightful name. For now, you shall know me as Inara. Many blessings to you, friend."

Malus nodded, then spun the wheel and unlocked the door to the Elysian Fields. Beyond the door was a grove of such beauty and wondrous life, that he knew at once that this was where Lilly was taken, to this beautiful land for eternal rest. Her judgment could only have been for paradise.

He searched the fields high and low, across the many groves of singing birds, blooming trees and fountains. It was remarkable, and in all his years he had never seen anything like it, not even in the great gardens of Babylon. However, he found no trace of Lilly. Not even a gray shade affected her cloth—it appeared as black as when he first cast the spell.

"I am looking for Lilandra, of Carpathia," he explained to all who would listen. "She was daughter of a great chieftain of one of the many Hutsul tribes in the region."

Finally, a young man said, "There is no Lilandra in the Elysian Fields. She does not reside here with us."

"That cannot be," Malus replied.

"I assure you, friend," said the young man, "there are not many who were judged for paradise. Very few of us survive the culling, but there was never a Lilandra, not of Carpathia or any other."

Grief nearly split his heart in two.

Malus had been treading the path to darkness for a very long time, following every lead and delving into the darkest of the unknown, all to bring Lilandra back. His life had extended too long, like elastic stretched an inch too far. He was ripping apart, frayed at the edges and coming undone. For Lilly, he had learned dark wonders, feasted on flesh to obtain power. He had survived and scoured unsettled lands in search of answers. He had confronted gods and outwitted witches. He had done it all for nothing!

She should have been in Hades. The god of the underworld and his reaper servants had pillaged the souls of the dead for thousands of years. If Lilly was not in Hades, then where was she?

"Leave this place," sobbed Malus. "This is not paradise. This is a prison! Get out. Get them all out, or I will bring Hades down on top of you all." When the man did not move, he screamed. "Get out! Now!"

The first thrum of shifting earth rocked the land, and the Elysian sky cracked. Inara's army of the dead was already moving, shaking the pillars of Hades. The blessed within the fields ran—they ran from their paradise as it began to crumble.

When Malus entered the chamber of judgment, he stalked through the line of the departed sipping of the Mnemosyne, each of them awakening and taking arms against their prison, as another thrash quaked beneath the island. However, Malus did not join them.

He strode over to the pooling Lethe and leaned over the fountain, observing his reflection. A tear fell and splashed into the pool, rippling the waters and distorting his image. He had become a monster, and his actions were like the ripples disfiguring him—the stark white hair, the witchy eyes—he was the Pale Demon.

"Forgetfulness," he said. He had already rejected the idea once, but in that moment, it was too hard to turn back. He was beyond healing.

Would his mother recognize him? Would Lilly?

Hate and despair were symptoms of his disease, and one sip could wash away the infection. He knelt beside the pool, dipped his hands into the waters and brought them to his lips.

He wanted the Lethe to make him forget. To take away his pain and bring back his humanity. To make him forget about death. To make him forget about evil, the black magic, and the twisted things he had done to bring Lilly back.

He drank.

What happened next was unexpected. The Lethe took away what he needed, but not exactly what he wanted. And it returned exactly what the Graeae had predicted. He'd arrived in Hades to make a trade for Lilly. Instead, he traded only that which was his.

"A trade for that which belongs only to you," Enyo had said.

"Stop!" shouted Malus, as he stepped over Chronos and his chains.

Inara stood above the petrified body of Hades, angling his own bident over his darkened heart. The palace rocked back and forth, each quake ripping the island apart. The spirits of the dead raided every room in the palace, as the minions of Hades descended on them. Dark figures arrived bearing sickles, but the dead swarmed and tore them apart.

"Why?" asked Inara, but he did not answer.

Malus shoved her away, pulled the tooth blade from his belt, and lowered it to Hades' eye.

"This chair may be your prison," he growled, "but somewhere in that filthy rotted temple you call a body, you are calling out for help. Calling out for mercy." Malus plunged his blade through the left eye, causing the god's body to lurch and settle instantly.

"What are you doing?" asked Inara, but he did not answer.

Malus took Hades by the throat and lifted him, separating his body from the Chair of Forgetfulness by the slightest margin. In that instant Hades came back to life, shaking and sweating and crying out in pain. Malus placed his blade to the remaining eye, and the god of the underworld went still under threat.

"You tell me what I want to know, or I will send you to the pit!" roared Malus, inching the blade closer to his eye.

"I am all that's holding this realm together," gasped Hades.

"Do not worry about your false afterlife! I threaten to send you to yours!"

"What is it you want to know?" he asked.

"Where is she?!" he spat. "Where is Lilandra?!"

"If she died within my jurisdiction, my reapers, they would have sowed her. Please, I will find her," he begged.

The ground beneath them trembled in rhythm to the god. The angry spirits were all around them, breaking apart the barriers between the underworld and the earth.

"Taking my eyes will send me to a place much worse than Tartarus," pled Hades.

"I know," said Malus. "The veil of my own ignorance has been lifted."

"How did she die?" asked Hades.

"The black god took her. Chernobog," he explained.

"Chernobog?" questioned Hades. "Chernobog is dead."

Inara stood by silently.

"How!?" Malus demanded.

"I do not know!" screamed Hades. "But if you seek a girl taken by Chernobog, then she will not be found here, nor anywhere. The black god consumed souls. She is gone, forever."

"How did Chernobog die?!" he roared.

"I do not know!"

"You do not know?" shouted Malus. "You do not know? What value is a false deficient god without answers?" His rage boiled, and he bludgeoned the god's remaining eye. "Farewell. Your Persephone shall greet you arm in arm with the Burned Ones."

The eerie glow that emanated from every surface dulled, and an immense rumbling began to shake the palace in uneven intervals.

Malus grabbed the Helm of Darkness and took the chains that bound Chronos, then said, "Are you fleeing or staying?"

Inara followed him through the palace, level by level, until they reached the embankment beside the river Styx. The palace ruins were falling to pieces, crumbling with concussive blasts. The Titans were freed and joined the dead, destroying the island.

From the sky came angels, through the weakened barrier that kept Hades hidden, and sinking the island—the underworld was a sin against Empyrea, and the Greek gods would pay for their sacrilege. Harvesters swooped down, guiding the dead away in bright shafts of pure light, while Destroyers sent bolts of lightning and flame down onto the temple, razing it to the ground.

"There are many underworlds, Pale Demon," said Inara. "No less than two dozen final resting places for departed souls after their mortal time ends. One for the Greeks, one for the Norse, one for the Egyptians, and so on and so on. Hades may have ruled here, but his knowledge is limited. Take heart. She may still exist, in some form or another."

"Will you destroy them all?" asked Malus.

"Yes," said Inara.

"Is Chernobog, the black god, dead?" he asked.

"I have not the knowledge you require," she replied.

Through the thick fog across the river came a creaky wooden boat, piloted by a shrouded figured in old, tattered robes. The boat went aground just as they arrived at the shore to meet it. The boat, simple and sturdy, was made of old, graying planks of wood and bleached white bone.

The boatman, Charon, opened his bony palm, awaiting payment before boarding.

"Your world is dying, boatman! Give us passage," growled Malus.

The boatman laughed.

Malus stripped the bident from Inara's grasp and demanded passage again, but the boatman continued to laugh, his bony palm still held out for payment.

"Boatman, that bident commands and kills anything in this realm, but not you. Why is that?" asked Inara.

Charon nodded at his upturned hand and waited, his face obscured in shadow under his thick robed hood. Malus drew the tooth blade, held it menacingly for a moment, then gently placed it within Charon's waiting hand.

"It is not gold nor silver," said Malus, "but it is all I have. It was carved from a tooth. A tooth I took from Enyo, of the Sisters Three. One of the Graeae. It is the blade that killed the great god Zeus and sent Hades to his torment in the Pit."

Inara's face flashed in equal shades of shock and fear.

"You drank of the Lethe," accused Inara. "It did not take your memories like you had hoped. It revealed that which was forgotten."

Malus did not answer her.

"Will my blade pay for our safe travel away from this realm?" he asked the boatman.

Charon nodded. The boatman took his blade and allowed them to board, then used the oar to cast off through rough surf and onto the river.

"The bident of Hades," hissed Charon, answering the question that was posed of him, "maintains power in Hades, but does not hold dominion over the dead. I am of the dead. Necro-magic is more powerful than any other in the realm of man. The dead have no need for self-preservation. The dead cannot be stopped. Some are gifted with powers of the dead. Their power, like all others, may be taken from them."

As Charon ushered them away from the destruction, rogue reapers loyal to Hades fled into the skies above, while Empyrea's wrath—great armored angels—smote them as they fled. They fell from the sky in consuming balls of flame, crashing into the ruined island—some into the five mystical rivers, never to resurface.

It was a massacre.

Malus turned to Inara, but she was gone. He looked to the chaotic skies and saw a winged creature watching him from above. She was an angel, after all.

Then Inara flew away and joined her kin.

The elite gods had lost one of the batteries that fueled their power. There were others, but in the vacuum came uprising. The lesser gods saw opportunity. There was power to be seized, and thus the War of Gods began.

XXIII

collapse

TONY
Now.

"Good day, sir," said the old man.

I nodded from beside the tripod and hopscotched away from the gummi bears as if it was a crime scene. The whole scenario felt wrong, like I had stumbled into something I wasn't supposed to see.

There were a hundred things running through my mind—like, but not limited to:

- Who is this?
- What is this tripod thing?
- What's up with the gummi bears?
- What did this 'ole geezer have to do with Jaycie?

And when I say geezer, I'm not ageist. He was old, as ancient looking as any actual living, breathing man could be without keeling over and dying of oldness. He wore a wide-brimmed hat and black clothing from a bygone era. He almost looked like an old-timey preacher, if not for the fancy shoes and sunglasses.

"Who're you?" I asked. He didn't answer, only smiled, so I did what I always did during awkward silences—I continued to talk. "You know, it's a little too dark for sunglasses."

"Ah," said the old man, "I do not merely wear these to protect my eyes from the sun."

"Oh, admitting to being a fashion victim is the first step to forgiveness."

He smiled viciously with a perfect set of yellow teeth. I could feel him glaring at me from behind the shades—the sunglasses protected his eyes from all angles, like the kind worn after eye exams.

The sky flashed red above the treetops—that thing, the horseman, was tearing apart the sky. It was attacking Jaycie's mind palace bit by bit, like an antibody to an infection. Every collision cracked the earth and sky.

And then I remembered what I was doing…

Jaycie. I had to find little Jaycie.

I sidestepped the old man, but he moved in kind to block my path.

"Do not worry," he teased suspiciously, "*it* does not want *you.*"

"What is it? Do you know?"

"It has many names, but you likely perceive it as a horde of galloping horses ridden by madmen. Some have called it the Wild Hunt."

"Never heard of it."

"You remind me of a former student."

"You're a teacher?"

He smiled again. Unwilling to provide details.

"What are you looking for?" I asked.

This old man gave me the creeps. His creep factor scored higher than the death-god made of rotting meat. My stomach clenched, like a stitch in my side from running laps.

We were in Jacinda's mind palace—how did he get here? Was he once locked inside the Forgotten Room inside the Old Mill?

Jacinda. Why do I keep forgetting about Jacinda?

"A way out," said the old man after a few beats. "But do not worry, from what I can tell, you are not a door."

"Yeah, last I checked… Who are you again? I didn't catch it the first time you didn't answer."

"Dear boy," he said, "I am not your concern today. However, we will meet again."

I nodded to signify that I understood the words he had spoken, but not the context.

"Do you smell that?" he asked, sniffing the air with another smile halving his gaunt face. "Flowers. I smell flowers."

I couldn't smell any flowers, but my olfactory had my stomach in knots eight ways to Sunday with his own stench. He smelled like compost, formaldehyde and chalk.

As he turned and walked away, I thought to ask, "Have you seen a little girl run through here? Red hair?"

He turned back to me, then hesitantly pointed a bony finger further down the hill.

"Thanks," I said, and he continued toward the park humming. Then between blinks he was gone, along with the tripod contraption. His chilling tune held a few bars until it too disappeared.

"My man," said Montoya. I jumped when he grabbed my shoulder.

He was right behind me.

"Did you see him?"

"Who?"

"The old man? I was just talking to him."

"I was behind you the whole time," said Montoya. His eyes patronized me. "What's happening to you? How's your cabesa? Are you running a fever?"

I slapped his hand away as he reached for my forehead.

I knew what it was like to lose my mind. This felt different…

I felt erratic, irritable, slow, incapable, incompetent and…ill equipped.

I said, "Let's go," and ran off in the direction the old man had pointed.

The forest seemed to grow thicker the deeper we went, and as we exited through a thicket of briar and stumbled out onto a stretch of asphalt, a volley of bullets immediately pounced.

A squad of soldiers had set up a checkpoint on Cross Road—we were only a few miles from Jaycie's childhood home.

Montoya took cover in a ditch and returned fire.

"Go!" he shouted. "I got this! Go!"

I was struck in the shoulder and leg as I fled, the pops fading in the distance as I picked up speed. I had to catch up to them. I had to keep them safe.

Then I heard a scream.

And still, as fast as I moved, as hard as I tried to catch up to the scream, I couldn't. Like a dream, it was always just beyond reach, no matter how hard I tried. I was always running after her. I was always chasing.

It wasn't until I arrived at the fifth and final house at the end of a string, a few miles from the Elm Way Bridge into Grace Falls, that I spotted the kelly green boots. I caught them just before they entered the navy blue house through the back door.

"Jaycie?"

There were just two of them. The little one raised a stick at me to defend herself.

"Where's the other one? Where's the other Jaycie?" I asked.

They looked at each other.

"Oh," I said, stifling a sob. "Okay."

"Who're you?" asked the teen. I was a stranger to them both. The oldest, sixteen at most, was pre-Labor Day Fair Jaycie, when we first met. She was dressed in her private school uniform.

They stood on the back steps, the same steps she cried upon when she accidentally slipped into the Veil the day after Christmas. I remember that day because I was there, watching. Little Jaycie was dressed like she was going on adventures into the forest with Amanda and Morris, with the stick still pointed at my chest. The green galoshes, the ponytail—it was undeniably her.

"I'm a friend," I said. "I'm here to protect you."

"You got your butt kicked," said the teen. "You look just like him."

"But I'm not him. I promise."

They were scared, confused, and before either of us could say another word, I was tackled to the ground by a furious beast that stood over me barking and growling.

It was the Behemoth of Cross Road. Pajamas, the neighbor's dog.

"Pajamas!" shouted little Jaycie. "Settle down."

Pajamas, an already huge German Shepherd, was three times his normal size. On Jaycie's command, he backed down and playfully jogged to her side where he sat patiently for head-pets.

"Good boy," said Big J. "He's bigger than I remember."

"She sent Pajamas to protect us," said Little J to Big J.

I knew at once she was referring to the punk rock ass-kicker that took down Markus and a squad of soldiers in five seconds.

Then both Jaycies looked at me with the same scrutinizing eyes. Even Pajamas did, with a head tilt.

"I feel like I should know you," said Little J.

"It's okay if you don't," I said. "I am a friend."

"I know," she replied, but she wouldn't lower her stick.

"Isn't Pajamas Whitney's dog?"

"Yeah, how'd you know that?" asked Big J.

"I told you, I'm a fr—"

—I splintered the shed in the back corner of the yard.

"Sometimes I wonder, how you ever got along without me," said Markus, thrusting his flaming spear into my side, puncturing half my organs.

"My man!" shouted Montoya as he bashed Markus across the head with the blunt end of his rifle. Markus retracted his spear from my side and spun. Montoya slammed against the side of the house, and the spear pinned him to the siding.

Pajamas roared as Markus took two steps toward the girls.

"Aw, who's your *friend?*" he said to them like an auntie on Thanksgiving after two full glasses of red. "He looks like a *big tough guy.*"

"Leave them alone!"

"Why?" scoffed Markus.

Montoya was alive—his chest was rising and falling, but he hung there limp.

By the time Markus spun back to me, I was on my knees.

"Why would I leave them alone?" he said. "There is a burden you carry around, Tony. That burden is hope, and it is toxic as fuck. It's preventing you from becoming what you were meant to be! Remember, you are Fallen! The Thirteen are gods! They are powerful beings of true darkness! Let your darkness out, Tony, and you will be better served to end this!"

Big J made a run for it toward the trees—Markus spun and threw something that caught her in the back. She dropped dead before I could even move.

"What did you do?" cried Little J.

Pajamas snarled.

"One down! One to go."

—everything happened so fast, even for me.

I couldn't get there in time.

I couldn't do anything.

"Tony," he said, looking back at me with a smile. "I'm going to steal your favorite toy. You just don't know it yet."

Those words. Those exact words were what *he* said to me that night...

...a night I wish I could forget...

In my darkest moment—in my desperation—I reached out and willed my darkest thoughts into reality.

Markus grabbed Little J and was immediately propelled, mid-stride, like he was struck by a runaway truck. When he slammed into the side of a tree, his arm wrapped tightly around Jaycie, I kept pushing—pushing him with my mind, trying to snap him in two.

"My oh my," he grunted. "I knew you had it in you, Tony."

I felt different. I felt unleashed. I felt...*unhinged.*

A whimper.

Pajamas growled.

Markus placed a knife to her throat, and I released the hold I had on him with my mind.

"Let her go."

Pajamas concurred—head lowered, teeth bared.

"No," said the traitor.

Little Jaycie was frightened stiff. Two big, green, terror-stricken eyes implored me for help. My flames soured, and the melting heat within me was like a furnace. This place, her mind palace, had become a nightmare—and I had escorted the monster right to her.

"It's going to be okay," I said, and she closed her eyes, squeezing off tears that ran over her constellation of freckles.

My scar burned and bled. Red streaks leaking down my cheek and neck.

"You claimed to be her friend, Tony. What kind of friend are you?" said Markus. "Please, tell this little girl what kind of friend you are?"

"What are you doing, Markus?"

"What am *I* doing?" he spat. "I'm doing what *you* cannot."

"Terrorizing a little girl?"

"Haven't you considered this? Sometimes, Tony, you have to destroy what you love in order to be free of it."

"Don't you hurt her," I said, suddenly realizing suddenly realized who'd pushed the button and set off the hellfire bombs. Markus had taken control. Was he looking to replace me?

"Oh, ho ho ho!" laughed Markus. "Let's talk about hurt. Let us discuss the harm you and this little redheaded bitch have done to this world."

She whimpered. Pajamas snarled and paced.

"If anyone's to blame, it's me," I said.

"And yet deep down, you're still trying to save her," said Markus. "What you've yet to realize is that you know how this will end."

Those words again. *"I think you know how this will end."* Gabriel's words. The more I heard them, the more I wanted to prove him wrong.

"What's the point of doing any of this if I'm not going to try and set things right?"

"By who's definition of right?" spat Markus. "Yours? Do I need to remind you of Marshall? Anne? Tori? Amanda? How about Roman

Fawkes? Tell me Tony, what kind of moral compass must you have to have dragged so many people down with you?

"And what about *her*?" he continued.

"What about her?"

"She killed her own sister!" he shouted. "She murdered a boy! She nearly destroyed the world in revenge! She is not innocent!"

The one thing about shouting, when making so much noise you can't hear anything other than yourself.

"Drop the knife," said Doshin. "Let her go."

When Markus looked over his shoulder, he nearly turned into an outstretched blade—all two-and-a-half feet of glimmering burning steel held firm in Doshin's grasp.

They were all there. Even Morpheus with Samantha carrying Phantasos.

And they weren't alone. There was a Jaycie with them. One I didn't even recognize with her hoodie pulled up.

"You're surrounded," I said. "Let her go."

Markus released her, and Little Jaycie fell to the ground. She was immediately snatched by her raincoat and dragged safely away by Pajamas.

"Who is this asshat?" asked Jamaal as he and Chappy removed the spear from Montoya's shoulder and helped him down.

"Yeah, my man," coughed Montoya. "That's what I want to know."

"This is highly peculiar," said Henry, studying Markus from ten feet away. Markus gave him an antagonistic smile. "He looks like you."

Chills crawled up my spine. How did they not know Markus?

"Oh! This is so exciting!" squealed Phantasos. Samantha silenced him with a bop to the head, but she too was grinning like they were watching a trashy TV talk show revealing paternity tests.

"Markus. Part of the brain-trust," I said, unsure of myself.

"No, sir," said Henry. "He is not one of us."

"My man, this is the first time I've ever seen this piece of shit," said Montoya, taking aim at Markus from behind. They were all cautious. Even the pacifists, Chappy and Henry were holding onto weapons constructed by Samantha.

Markus laughed.

"Then *who is he?*" I asked.

Doshin shrugged and lowered his sword, but he remained vigilant.

They were talking amongst themselves, except Jaycie. She hung at the back, watching me from beneath her drawn hoodie, but strangely, I didn't know her.

"How long?" asked Chappy. "How long have you been conversing with *Markus?*"

Morpheus stepped forward and examined my faux-brain-trustee, who stood there stoically like something meaningful was transgressing. Something he was excited to see play out between us.

"Since the future," I said. "Since we fell into the Patronus Lux base beneath the rubble in Philadelphia." They were bewildered. "This whole time, none of you knew I was talking to someone else?"

"Not a clue," said Jamaal.

I felt a pair of small arms wrap themselves around my side.

"Are you okay?" I asked her. Little Jaycie nodded.

"Who are they?" she asked.

"Friends," I said, but she wouldn't stop staring at me. "Go keep Pajamas company."

She nodded and walked over to the back door, where Pajamas was sniffing at the old concrete steps, as if there was something living beneath them. I needed her safely away from this. Markus had taken both me and Montoya down with ease. Was he the reason I felt so... wrong?

"You're all being short sighted," said Markus. "We can end this here. That's what Gabriel wants! He wants us to do the hard thing and end this!"

"We already ended it," said Jamaal. "The Thirteen are toast."

"Who are the Thirteen?" asked Samantha.

"Long story," groaned Jamaal.

"Are you that daft?" spat Markus. "Do you truly believe you destroyed them all?" Then to me, a glare. "This is your *brain-trust?*"

I began to answer, loading up something snappy, when Markus spun and knocked Montoya's rifle away from his head, then swatted Doshin's blade. It was happening so fast, nobody could stop him from tossing something at the hooded Jaycie. When I dove to block it, using myself as a human shield, he spun again and threw another in the opposite direction.

Everything slowed down.

My hand caught the first blade before it connected with her, our eyes snagging from beneath her hood, my hand slicing wide open—but there was no stopping the second blade.

Jaycie's tiny, eight year-old abdomen and the seven inch blade were on a collision course. Samantha moved her hands, but she was too slow. We were all too slow. It was impossible to stop it...

...and yet I did.

The blade stopped turning end over end and hung in the air like a piece of fruit waiting to be plucked. The same power that threw Markus into the tree had now stowed his blade. The flames within my chest felt corrupted. Smoldering and sick. My heart raced and a dull ache settled into it, like a sadness that could never be lifted.

"Darkness," said Markus, "when it comes, it manifests out of need."

Jamaal's fist contacted Markus in the jaw and sent him thundering into the ground. When Markus motioned to get up, Montoya already had a boot on his chest and his rifle aimed between Markus' eyes.

"Let's try this again," said Montoya. "Don't move."

Markus had played me. He knew I would protect her at all costs. And he knew exactly how I'd do it—even if I wasn't exactly sure what I had done.

I plucked the knife out of the air and tossed it aside like it was rotten. Little Jaycie looked up to me, tears in her eyes—the poor thing had no idea what was happening. But when I broke down into tears, it was *her* who consoled *me*.

"It's okay," she said, grabbing my hand. "I'm okay."

"My man," said Montoya, "what's happening to you?"

Chappy placed a hand on my shoulder and said, "Let go."

I didn't know what was happening, but Markus appeared amused. There was swirling wind and lightning, as if a storm was brewing right over top of us.

The nearest window on the Berry house next door lent a reflection, and I could tell there was something wrong. A darkness had soured me —my complexion had paled, and my scar was infected. My brown eyes were nearly black, like all the good in me had been absorbed…or worse, *rotted.*

"Imagine a celestial creature falling from grace—" said Henry, once upon a time. *"The psychosis and the madness, the power, isolation, and frustration— and imagine how awful that must be. Imagine what that might look like if it were allowed to manifest itself physically."*

"Ugly," Doshin had replied. *"The inner self, reflected out."*

"Let go, son," said Chappy.

Within a few heartbeats, the twisted reflection faded.

"C'mon, honey," said Samantha to Little J. "Let's go inside, okay."

Jamaal was already escorting the other Jaycie into the house.

Little Jaycie nodded to Samantha and peeled away from me. "Whose head is that?" she asked.

"My head!" shouted Phantasos.

"Oh. Why don't you have a body?" she asked, as they climbed the back porch stairs.

"I could have a body any time I want," he sassed as they disappeared into the house with the two-hundred-pound behemoth of a dog following behind.

"Where did you find her?" I asked, referring to the hooded Jaycie.

"She was hiding in the forest," said Chappy. "The older Ms. O'Neill asked us to take her here. She said this is where you would be."

"What we have here," said Morpheus after finishing his silent assessment, "is a Divagation."

"Oh, fancy word," said Markus, still under Montoya's boot.

"A what, my man?" asked Montoya, jamming the rifle between Markus's eyes.

"A split," said Henry, "in Tony's conscious mind." Morpheus nodded, then Henry turned to me directly. "Together, the brain-trust and you, we are a part of who *we* once were. But Markus, he is a part of who *you* are."

"What does that mean?" I asked, and Markus smiled.

"It means you have a consciousness inside your own," said Morpheus. "One that is attempting to manipulate you into allowing it control." Then to Montoya, he waved him away. "Step aside." With a snap of his finger, Morpheus created a small metal box surrounding Markus on all sides and locking him in with a big fancy padlock. One moment he was there, and the next he was raging within the narrow metal walls of his prison.

"Why did you do that?" asked Chappy.

"Quarantine," said Morpheus. "You will need to decide what to do with it."

There was a small, barred window near the top. It wasn't big enough to stick more than a few fingers through, but more than enough for words.

I peered inside. "Do you want me dead?"

"Your death is my death," said Markus. "I want to be free, to take a drive behind the wheel and show you what happens when you let a true alpha take over."

"That's not me. That's not who I am."

"Oh, but Tony, I am you. Every person who breathes, walks, fucks, and talks, has the capacity to be anything. Good, evil. Aggressive, passive. Strong, weak. These are binary choices."

"The experiences make us who we are."

"We choose how to let experiences shape us."

"And what experiences led you to become a psycho?"

He paused before answering. "I walked a mile in your shoes."

I grabbed his blade from the ground and held it in my hand. Before anyone could talk me out of it, I jammed the knife through the window and heard it clank against the metal floor of his prison.

"What are you doing, my man?" said Montoya, but I ignored him.

"You say my hope is toxic, but it's the only thing keeping me here. If you want to be free of that, then take that knife and free yourself."

Markus chuckled, emotionless and empty.

When I turned to walk away, both Morpheus and Chappy were watching me.

"Sir," said Henry, "what if—"

Then I felt a rush, like the blood was draining from my head.

"Shit!" shouted Montoya. "Shit shit shit!"

"Open the box!" said Chappy.

I was on the ground before I knew what was happening.

The door to the house behind us opened, and Phantasos popped his head out. It was strapped to the body of a mannequin and waddled stiffly as it moved. He was wearing an apron and carrying a frying pan. "Who wants eggs?"

That was the last thing I saw before I passed out inside someone else's dream.

lockdown

TONY
Now.

"Tony," said Morpheus. "Wake up."

When I opened my eyes, Morpheus was floating above the bed inches from my face, eyes peering directly into mine. Despite the shock, I didn't startle. It felt normal, as if I was witnessing what we all forget the moment after we wake from sleep.

"Come, we have things to discuss," he said, appearing by the door. He left a moment later, and I thought I was alone.

"What does one dream inside a dream?" said Jaycie.

That startled me.

She was sitting at the foot of the bed. Her lavender hoodie was pulled back, and her puffy gray vest made that swishy noise as she moved. Her eyes were different. Older, with faint wrinkles at the corners.

"I hardly remember this room," she said. "The memories, some good, some bad. I lost Grammy's guitar, but seeing it here in the corner, it made me smile a little."

"Nothing," I said as I sat up. "I don't think I dreamed of anything."

She nodded and broke eye contact, as if it was making her uncomfortable.

"You want to know when. I can still read your face so well." She paused. "I am forty-two, and you and I have not seen each other for a very long time."

"How is that possible?"

"I have been aware of who and what I am for quite some time. Of all the people, it was your mother who opened my eyes. In a restroom at the back of a bar. But I think you already knew that."

I nodded.

"But you died…"

"That wasn't me. That was another me. There have been many. I don't know how *I* die, but I assume it will come as it always does. Malus is a monster, and he is persistent.

"When I last saw you," she continued, "it was in a mall on New Year's Eve. Something terrible happened. We had been broken up for a while. I was never able to forgive you for what you did to Roman. You betrayed my trust, ruined my career, and destroyed the one thing I held most dear in the world. Our relationship.

"I never realized just how many demons you were battling, while I was battling mine."

"I think that statement is true for us both," I said.

She placed her hand onto mine. She was not my Jaycie. She was almost a stranger, and there was something about the pain in her eyes, the distance, the regret, that hurt nearly as much as losing her.

"It's good to see you," she said with tears in her eyes.

Little Jaycie was listening to us by the door. I could hear her, but I didn't have the strength to chase her off. Good or bad, I decided to let her know her own future…

Montoya, with Samantha's help, set up a perimeter around the house as Jamaal and Chappy kept watch from the windows with the curtains drawn. We were huddled in the living room as Phantasos cooked breakfast—it smelled like eggs and bacon, but I struggled to imagine that dream food was real food.

I checked on Little Jaycie from the living room. She was eating eggs in the kitchen and sneaking Pajamas little bites of bacon when she thought nobody was looking. My eyes connected with Jaycie—the one in the hoodie. I'd made so many mistakes. My Jaycie forgave me for that night with Roman. This Jaycie did not, but she had lived much longer.

I couldn't help but think that maybe I was the reason.

Jamaal said, "Tony, you shoulda seen it, bro. I swear I triple combo'd one of those soldier dudes to the moon. Even Henry got some action."

Henry scoffed and cleaned his glasses for the hundredth time. He was on the far end of the couch and appeared to be appraising me every few minutes like he was my actual doctor.

But Phantasos wouldn't have any of Henry's bashfulness. "Sir Henry was indeed a mad, mad man," said the fantasy god as he reentered the room, still wearing an apron over the nude mannequin body his head was taped onto. Little Jaycie left the kitchen and followed him into the living room with her plate. She sat on the couch next to me, which made Jamaal giggle.

The older Jaycie stood by the entry like an outsider, listening.

"Strangely, the soldiers were unafraid of my brother and me. Just imagine, mares unafraid of Oneiroi? Gods of slumber? They did not deter their aggression even when our Imagi conjured weapons. As sure am I that the moon must always chase the sun, this is no mere mind palace."

The house shook on its foundation. Another earthquake. Nothing broke or fell within the house, like the memory was preserving everything inside.

"They know what we are, and they are not afraid," said Morpheus, standing by the TV. I could taste his concern. It was brewing the air like tea. "My brother and I are bound by the same principles as our angelic cousins. We may influence only. I create the dreamscapes, and my brothers influence them to fantasy or nightmare. We are not allowed to intervene. That is why we have protectors, called Imagi, who are called upon to defend Somnia. Our brother, Phoebetor, is dead because he did not follow the rules."

Phantasos looked as if he wanted to say something, but he quietly bit his tongue.

"Is Samantha the only Imagi?" I asked, and Jamaal nodded along with a mouthful of scrambled eggs slathered in ketchup and hot sauce. Doshin wouldn't touch them and stood stoically by the window on watch.

"No, there are more," said Morpheus.

"Why not summon all these Imagi?" asked Chappy, sitting at the edge of an easy chair. "Enlist them to eradicate the threat."

"We are not in Somnia. They cannot enter this place," said Morpheus. "Samantha used my brother to follow us here."

"Your head's the golden ticket," I said, and Phantasos smiled.

"Wonka!" Phantasos beamed. "Dahl inspired so many wonderful fantasies."

The front door opened, and Montoya and Samantha slipped inside. Montoya was wearing a military helmet, carrying his gun and pack like he was still in the jungle.

"Nothing's out there," said Montoya, as he pulled something out of his belt and tossed it onto the coffee table. It was a white mask, with a smiley face drawn with fingerpaint or—

"Blood," said Jamaal. "Why's it always blood?"

"We killlllll…uh—" Montoya began to say, until he noticed Little Jaycie hanging on every word. "We *got* four of them." He was a father and decided to take the high road.

BOOM! RUMBLE! RUMBLE!

Another earthquake, followed by rolling thunder.

"Any sign of others?" asked Jamaal.

Montoya shook his head. "Nah, no blonde girl, no soldiers, no nothing. Besides, nothing's getting anywhere within two hundred feet of this house." Then he gestured to Samantha. "That gal knows how to set traps."

"Aw shucks," said Samantha. "He called me a gal."

"So, what's going on, my man?" Montoya was looking at me. "How are you feeling?"

It was interesting to note that I was still somehow in charge. Was I really the best man for the job?

"I'm fine."

Jaycie's eyes met mine.

"So, Markus is…" said Jamaal, who closed his eyes and stuck out his tongue—I think he was mimicking the dead. "…ya know? What does that mean, for your…"

"Cabesa?" guessed Montoya.

"Yeah, something like that," said Jamaal.

"I don't know," I said. "I don't really feel any different. Maybe a little less anxious. Like there's not some baddie over my shoulder looking to sabotage me." I thought for a moment before saying what had to be said next. "I need to know you guys are in this with me. I know everyone keeps telling us that one woman isn't worth the whole world." I looked over at Jaycie. "But I'm not going to sacrifice her for anything. It's all or nothing."

They were quiet.

"What are they talking about, brother?" said Phantasos.

Chappy said, "I think I can reassure you, for all of us, when I say we have your back, Tony. We trust you. Trust us in return."

"And if you start seeing crazy psychos again, just call it out," said Montoya. "For example, you could say 'hey, I see a psycho over there.'"

"I'll do that." It was comforting to know they didn't hate me. "I have to admit, it was intoxicating. When the flames soured, I felt more powerful than I've ever felt. How screwed up am I?"

"Not any more than any one of us," said Jaycie, and all eyes in the room went to her, like she was the mysterious guest—the subject at the center of all our discussions.

"Speak for yourself, doll," said Phantasos. "I'm far a-*head* of everyone in this room."

Even little Jaycie got a giggle out of that.

BOOM! BOOM!

It was quiet for a moment after.

"I have to admit, I have not been wholly honest with you," said Morpheus, stepping forward from his position by the TV. "I am aware of Malus. I have been for some time. What does he want with Jacinda's mind palace?"

"To erase my mind," said Jaycie. "Put someone else in my body."

"I see," said Morpheus.

"That's effed up," said Samantha.

"What does eff up mean?" asked Little Jaycie.

Samantha shook her head in response.

"As long as we protect both our current guests," said Morpheus, gesturing to both Jaycies, "it should preserve her personality and memories, both innocence and experience."

BOOM! BANG! RUMBLE!

Another earthquake. This one more violent than the others combined.

"What is the Wild Hunt?" I asked.

Morpheus sighed.

"Why do you ask?" said Phantasos. He still had a frying pan of eggs in his plastic hand and exchanged another glance between him and his brother. "The Wild Hunt seems highly irrelevant to our conversation..." He chuckled nervously, his head wobbling atop his plastic body. It suddenly struck me how absurd it was that his head was taped onto a mannequin. He looked like a broken action figure—like a He-Man head on a Barbie body.

"The Wild Hunt," said Morpheus, "is complicated to define. It is a force, neither for good or evil. To witness the Wild Hunt was to foreshadow catastrophe, or death." Morpheus studied me and my braintrust. "Did you witness the Wild Hunt while here within the mind palace?"

"That thing in the sky?" said Chappy. "You all didn't see that?"

"Great," grumbled Montoya. "Now we're all seeing psychos."

"The headless rider," I replied. The rest of the brain-trust nodded. Even Doshin looked nervous. "An old man told me about it. He was in the park with this weird contraption, like some kind of mad-science experiment with vials and lenses."

"An old man?" asked Jaycie. She looked disturbed. "With sunglasses?"

"Yeah," I said. "The kind—"

"—they use for eye exams?"

"...*yeah*."

"Oh crap," said Jamaal. "Why do I feel like this is an *oh crap* moment?"

"Many creatures have been drawn here," said Morpheus. "Others, perhaps, stuck here looking for a way out."

"Yes! That's what he said. He was looking for a door."

Samantha got up from her seat by the window and began inspecting everyone's faces.

"None of you are cos-mats," she said.

"What's a cos-mat?" asked Little Jaycie.

"Heterocosmos Matia," said Phantasos.

"Cos-Mats," added Samantha.

"*Different world eyes?*" asked Henry, attempting to decipher the Greek.

"Something like that," said Morpheus, who then held up a cautionary finger, as if to ask for a moment to explain. "The Dream Lands span the infinite. Every creature dreams. It is a common conduit from your world, to this one, into others."

"Do you mean to say," asked Henry, "that one may pass from our world into the Dream Lands, and from here to elsewhere, and beyond?"

Morpheus nodded. "The Dream Lands have no beginning and no end. And the sea of nothing that surrounds it is called the Unbecoming. Somnia has always been sheltered, like an island in the middle of a vast sea of nothingness, floating through the Unbecoming. This was our way of isolating our world from the dangers of the Dream Lands. This place, Jacinda's mind-palace, however, spans somewhere in between, and with it comes vulnerabilities. If it falls, if it becomes destabilized, it could become the portal to another world with direct access to the mind of the woman who created it."

"Whoa whoa whoa," said Montoya. "You mean to say that if those

Omens break into this world and take over, they could take over Jaci—I mean, the Omega?"

"What did you say?" asked Morpheus, and the entire room went ice cold as the lights appeared to dim.

"I don't know, my man," said Montoya, backing away from the window with his hands up.

"Did he really just say that word, brother?" said Phantasos. He had dropped the frying pan. There was egg all over the floor.

They both looked mortified.

"Which word?" said Montoya.

"The Omega?" asked Jamaal.

Morpheus looked apoplectic.

Another boom, but this one sounded different.

Montoya went to the window and looked out in all directions.

"That was one of the traps," he said.

"Oh shit," said Samantha, as she rushed to the kitchen window.

There was a haze creeping in, but it was no ordinary haze.

"What is that?" asked Henry.

"Gas," said Montoya. Four dark figures marched inside the haze. One of them lit a flame thrower, while the others marched forward with tanks strapped to their backs, their faces covered with gas masks.

"Can we breathe that?" asked Jamaal.

"Will we survive?" said Montoya. "Yeah, probably. Will it be fun? No fucking way."

"They won't survive," I said, pointing to the girls.

A spray of gun fire hit the side of the house. Little Jaycie started crying.

Phantasos rushed to the window and peered out into the haze. His wild hair was standing straight up like pins. "Fear and Dread," he said.

Morpheus took a look, and I peeked for my own curiosity next to Doshin.

In the fog skittered two creatures. Both like spiders—arachnid bodies with humanoid torsos and heads. One smiled without eyes. The other glared without a mouth.

"We are not prepared for this fight. Not yet." Morpheus' hands trembled as the sound of metal began to rattle and clank from every corner of the house. The doors popped, as a series of deadbolts preceded a drop bar with a six-inch thick timber slamming down to secure it, while the windows shook, and metal plates slid into place.

"Why didn't you tell me right from the beginning that she was the Omega?" asked Morpheus. "Phobos and Deimos, slayers of Hypnos, are deconstructing her mind."

"I thought you knew," I said. "You mentioned she was a powerful astral projector. You said you knew Malus!"

"What's the Omega?" asked Little Jaycie.

Jaycie rushed over and knelt to her level.

"Don't worry, kid," she said. "We're going to be okay."

"The Wild Hunt was drawn here for a reason. It will continue to consume the entirety of the Mind Palace searching, cleansing, destroying," explained Morpheus. "Its motives are a concept we cannot understand. It bends only to the will of the Cosmic Scales. Within my protection, we will survive Fear and Dread. But the Wild Hunt consumes all. We have days and hours before it consumes everything."

"Why didn't you do this before?" I said, gesturing to the newly constructed defenses.

"I have the power to do much. I am the god of dream, and I can control all within this realm. However, it is not my place to do so. We are constrained by rules and by duty. I betrayed my oath and expect to be punished accordingly. I did this to preserve reality."

Reality. *Shit...*

If Phobos and Deimos were part of the Thirteen, then...

"My body. I'm still asleep on the church stoop."

"Do not worry," said Phantasos. "If anything happened, we would know."

There was a sensation, like a vice clamping down onto my head. At first, I thought it was a headache, some byproduct of the theatrical lobotomy or the gas—but when it drew blood, like I was being scalped, I knew too late it was something far worse.

"Dreams are for the weak, boy," said a voice.

XXV

underestimated

TONY
Then.

"How long have you been studying?" I asked, standing in the bedroom door. It was nearly 6 P.M. and I had just gotten home from work.

"Too long," she said mid-yawn, rolling over onto her back. On the bed beside her was a notepad and two philosophy textbooks I had used as a doorstop the night before. She groaned and stretched like a lazy cat, then bounced to her feet and greeted me with a smile.

When she wrapped her arms around my neck, I paused—something told me to take a moment—to admire her. Sometimes I got too comfortable, too complacent, that I never slowed down to just enjoy the moment. This girl—this amazingly beautiful and talented woman threw her arms around me, and smiled expectantly, waiting for a kiss. How lucky was I? How did I end up here?

When I think about the happiest I've ever been, it was never the big moments, the events or the holidays. It was the moments between the peaks—the lazy weekends, running errands, drinks with friends, stolen kisses—the ordinary moments spent living and dying for Jaycie's smiles. I often made a fool of myself just to hear her laughter.

But also, for me, when I think about the happiest I've ever been, it always came with a catch. Achievements were always bookended by defeats, and a love like ours was doomed to fail in the most spectacular and awful way imaginable. Maybe I was a pessimist, but the permanence of positive presences always faded—my mom, Amanda—why not this?

Deep down, I always felt like I was going to lose her.

Deep down, I always felt like I wasn't good enough for her.

And just when I thought I had it all figured out, after fouling off pitch after pitch, staying alive like a batter with two strikes, life threw me a curveball when I was expecting a big, fat fastball right over the plate.

"You always look so sexy," I said with a devilish grin—admiring the way her three-sizes too large Milton State University sweatshirt hung off her bare shoulder.

Jaycie would've admitted to looking like a bedhead-bomb went off in her hands, pin still rung around her forefinger—but like any starstruck romantic, I had never seen anything more beautiful.

"Oh yeah?" she whispered, luring me in for a kiss.

The thing about love—the thing you only learn after the heartbreak —is that you will never see the betrayal coming until it's too late.

"What the hell!?"

I was face down on the bed, my right arm pinned beneath her knee as she straddled my back, giggling like a trickster. Too much pressure from her grip, one way or the other, and my shoulder was ready to pop.

"There is no greater danger than underestimating your opponent," she said, then added with a sassy *I-just-learned-that* kind of way, "Lao Tzu, founder of philosophical Taoism."

"If I had known we were opponents, I would have totally destroyed you." My voice muffled by a face-full of blankets.

"Sure thing, tough guy," she taunted as she leaned down and nibbled at my ear.

"I'll never underestimate your feistiness, again," I said, wiggling free.

Then I pulled her down for that kiss—that beautiful, painful kiss I had become so addicted to. Why did it hurt so much when I kissed her? A mystery I never fully understood, nor cared enough to investigate...

"Oh no," she said, as she placed a forefinger over my lips. "Can't do that. Those eyes are trouble."

"What eyes?"

"Those eyes," she said, theatrically pointing as she sprang away from me. "I know what those eyes want, and I have to get ready."

"For what?" I asked. "I thought we might grab a bite and see a movie."

"I can't," she said. "I have to meet Roman at the club." Then she gave me a quick peck on the cheek and skipped over to the dresser. She plucked a pair of panties from the top drawer and removed her sweatshirt. Live with someone long enough and you come to understand the difference between daily underwear and the good underwear they kept for special occasions. This black, lacey pair was amongst the latter.

"At the club?" I tried to disguise my discomfort. "Why are you meeting him there? On a Friday night?"

She scowled. "He wants to introduce me to the owner. It's not like they keep daytime hours."

"Is he a vampire?" I joked. "Because he sounds like a sucker."

"Stop." She was smiling, but I knew I was pushing the limits. "I won't be home late. Maybe you can get together with Marshall. You haven't seen Brad or Sid in a while."

"Yeah, Sid's in Philly. Brad's in Grace Falls still macking on underclassmen at the dorms. And Marshall never goes anywhere without Anne."

She stepped into the bathroom and started the shower.

We moved to Mercy Point almost a year ago, and Jaycie was taking online courses to finish her degree. She didn't want to stay in Grace Falls for another year, and I didn't blame her. There were too many bad memories there...

"Do people still say *macking*?" she asked without expecting an answer. "So, why not hang out with them both?" She stepped back into the bedroom half naked. "You love Anne."

It wasn't about that. I hated being a third wheel. I didn't appreciate having to do it now, when I had a perfectly good girlfriend who was choosing to spend her Friday night with some other guy.

"I'll figure something out."

She gave me a sheepish smile and disappeared into the steamy bathroom.

She left forty minutes later wearing a black dress and her vintage leather jacket—like a model—long legged, cheekbones, decadent hair and makeup. She kissed me gently on the cheek, purposely avoiding a lipstick smear, and promised to be home before midnight.

The next several hours I spent wandering the apartment, cleaning, organizing, then taking a walk. I grabbed some takeout and a movie from the local rental place and found myself parked on the couch for the remainder of the night. Some men loved time away from their girl-friend, but we saw so little of each other—in the evenings when she wasn't working nights, and sometimes on weekends—it was the time between the big moments I missed most.

I fell asleep to full stomach of General Tso's in the middle of a lame vampire movie and dreamed of Jaycie.

I'd never met Roman. I tried cyber-stalking him earlier that night, but the guy didn't have social media or exist in the cloud, whatever the fuck that meant. Still, that didn't stop my subconscious from creating a nightmare version of Roman—a swanky, suit-wearing yuppy with slicked-back hair and sandals.

Yeah, fuck those sandal guys.

He was putting the moves on Jaycie—she was laughing and flirting, and I was just an observer, helpless to do anything about it. Then, as dreams do, the nightmare zigged and zagged for no reason at all. Roman was wearing a tunic with an ugly Caesar haircut, grinding on the dance floor with my girlfriend. Then they were walking hand-in-hand—Roman wearing my clothes, as if he had completely assimilated my life. And he kept talking to me—criticizing me—belittling me as he stole her away.

"Don't let me take your woman, Tony," he said to me. "Get out of your own head and take what's yours!"

A key slid into the lock and the front door swung open—I startled awake, then tried to play it off like I was stretching.

"Hey," said Jaycie as she tossed her keys onto the counter.

"Hey." I sat up. The digital clock on the microwave said 10:30. "It's early."

"Yeah." She hopped over, slipped off her leather jacket and crawled onto the sofa on top of me. "I missed you."

"You didn't have to come home early," I said, then added, "if you were having fun."

She kissed me. "I could have more fun with you on this couch, eating takeout and watching stupid movies than I ever could at some silly club with people I don't know."

"That's a really great answer."

"Awesome. I rehearsed it on the cab ride over," she teased.

I had underestimated her. She always surprised me.

I underestimated everyone I knew. Amanda and her expectations. Marshall and his loyalty. My father and his broken heart. Rick and his motivations. Tori and her conscience. Maynard and his competence.

And Jaycie? I underestimated everything when it came to her.

What else had I underestimated?

A seven-foot red-skinned demon was a good place to start.

December 25th, 2013
12:31 AM
Now.

"Dreams are for the weak, boy."

I was tossed by the head through a pair of reinforced wooden church doors, busting the lock and demolishing the first thirty pews before rolling to a stop somewhere near the altar. Several bones broke and my knee dislocated—the same knee I blew out in college. That familiar pain bloomed into a panic and my heart raced…

…and with every beat, the jagged wooden edges of a splintered pew raked against my heart. Sticks and stones could break my bones—*and did*—but it was that stick protruding from my chest that had me worried. Just pulling it free was risky.

"Rude," I grumbled and coughed up a wad of blood.

The demon Belial stood at the church entrance beyond the splintered doors, and he was pissed as hell. He lingered like a vampire in need of an invitation to enter. Had I known beforehand the Thirteen had a roster spot filled by a true demon, I may have thought twice about devising a plan that hinged solely on the use of hellfire bombs. Hellfire could never destroy him—he was charred and hardened of it from his time in the Pit. He was a true demon on earth.

I had underestimated them. All of them. I'd let my guard down, thinking my trap had finished them off, and I was going to pay for it.

JACINDA
Five minutes ago...

I was mid-stride when my brain snapped on like someone had flipped the switch on a Super NES with that delightful pop. Only my television screen was busted. I couldn't see a thing even after I rubbed my eyes.

The air felt wrong. Wherever I was, everything sounded muffled, like I was wearing an expensive pair of noise-canceling headphones. Then, I stepped through something that tickled my skin like a bubble, and the sounds of the city roared. The low hum of streetlamps and traffic noise from several blocks away became so loud I had to cover my ears. Even electricity had a sound that I could only hear after I had gotten used to it being filtered out.

"Is she here?" asked Malus.

I remembered his voice. He always sounded angry, like someone had jammed sandpaper up his bum. Once upon a time his voice made me tremble, but now it made me mad. Now I would do anything to shut him up forever.

Could I still fly like in my dream? Could I punch him straight into next year?

He was always there, wasn't he? Always watching. Always lurking and waiting. I was remembering—not everything, but enough…

Thoughts, feelings, memories… Some things were there but others passed me by, like I had no way to hold them. Tony would have said I was "swissing"—like a holey slice of cheese. And yet, there was something about that memory that I couldn't quite recall. As if the suggestion was based on a deleted file.

The phrase *File Not Found* flashed in my memory, realizing my homework had been accidentally deleted a few hours before it was due. Another memory…

"Yes," someone hissed in response. It didn't sound human. "Would you like Phobos and Deimos to return her vision? So that the girl may witness the end of her lover?"

"Yes," said Malus, and my vision returned with a sting.

We were somewhere in the middle of a city. Which city, I had no stinking clue. It was night, and holiday decorations hung from the lampposts. The city was empty—every store-face was dark, and there was nobody else—just Malus and I, and we didn't even bother to walk on the sidewalk—just straight down the middle of the street. As soon as my mind developed an escape route, I ran—only my feet never got the message.

I was being remote controlled.

I fought my own body—I twisted side to side and even waved my arms around, but from the waist down I was moving in a straight line, my steps in perfect rhythm with my captor's. Malus waltzed like he had no cares in the world, holding onto three objects dangling from a piece of string—*keys?* They danced on their own. They jumped, like mini piñatas being smacked around by a tiny ghost.

And that's when I realized we weren't alone. There were things in the shadows moving along with us—some phasing in and out like an audio signal on a fader. A dry cleaner's storefront glass reflected a monster with tentacles. It smiled at me like I was food—or worse…

We were a parade. A gaggle of horrors, and I was caught in the middle of their pack. I wanted to fight—to tap into that power that was only a thought away, and yet my every attempt at willing it into existence seemed to wilt before it had a chance to take root. I wanted to be that badass punk rocker again—to be bulletproof and super-strong—but maybe that was only possible in a dream.

Those fleeting thoughts of Tony in the dirt, bashed and busted up—they felt so real.

My mind was so broken, and it was all *his* fault…

…The man with the white hair. The two-eyed man. Malus. But he wasn't a man. He looked and acted like a man, but inside he was cold and dead, a monster.

I was helpless against him. I'd tried once before, tried to end him. I even tossed a whole tree at him with my mind—like I was some kind of Sissy Spacek, *Carrie*-wannabe. And if I couldn't do *anything* to him, what exactly *could* I do?

All the while, as we marched on, I kept thinking, *what if someone sees us?*

And then someone did. Someone with flashing lights and sirens as we rounded a corner by a Dunkin' and found a great big church in the middle of the block, with some poor homeless guy sleeping one off on the doorstep…

…only it wasn't a homeless guy.

Before I could shout his name, the police car came to a screeching halt behind us. Malus and the others didn't even look back. They didn't care. Part of me cheered. *Here comes the cavalry…*

…until the first shot was fired.

Guns were drawn. Commands were shouted. But we didn't stop.

"I told you to freeze!"

Three more police cars arrived—one behind the first, and two from the other direction. They were attempting to block us in. What they thought we had done, I had no fricken' clue, but when your escorts were living, breathing monsters, it was easy to understand the harsh response.

I turned to the officer, twisting around but keeping pace, and shook my head. I mouthed the words "help me."

After what happened next, I wished I hadn't.

More commands shouted, but Malus kept moving until we were

standing directly in front of the church, watching Tony sleep. Why he was there and why he was sleeping, I wished I knew—I wished I could run to him, yell to him, anything...

"Last warning—" said the officer, but before he could finish, Malus challenged them.

"Last warning? What will you do?" he asked. "Shoot us?"

"Please," said one of the monsters—a man with wild blonde hair and a giant hammer. "Please let them shoot."

He looked like a pro wrestler, bare-chested under a fur coat. Amanda and I had a phase... He was like a deranged Heartbreak Kid.

The woman in a tight party dress unfolded two extra arms—and for a moment, I thought she might be a prisoner, like me. Heat rippled from her body like she was about to catch fire.

More police arrived, backup to the backup's backup, and when Malus lifted his arm—*was he waving at them?*—they opened fire. Several dozen shots rang out.

I wrapped my arms around me for protection. It was all I could do to stop them, these real, un-imaginary, un-dream bullets. Their aim was impeccable—missing me and striking their targets—the woman, the man with the hammer, Malus, and two creatures that looked like insects I swore weren't there before. They fell to the pavement full of holes, but they were only down for a moment.

Malus sat up.

"Body armor!" someone shouted. More commands, more guns. This was spinning so far out of control, I half expected the National Guard to roll up next, and I broke out in a nervous sweat.

Several more police arrived—over a dozen now blocking the street in both directions, painting the whole block in red and blue light. I could feel the evil—the fear—the danger rising like I was receiving a radio broadcast just for me. And when I thought Malus was going to attack, there came a voice. A dark voice from somewhere out of sight.

"Let me show you," said the voice. "Let me show them all. Let me flex the muscle you sought out, so that you might witness the fruits of your labor."

Malus nodded.

Then the most terrifying thing happened.

Something stepped forth from darkness. Something that took the breath right out of my lungs. At first it was just a hole. A black hole in the air that expanded as the police rushed into position, aiming for another round of fire. There were men in SWAT gear, and guns—so many guns—like a small army had arrived. That black hole grew until it was the size of a door, and out of it stepped a beast. A seven-foot-tall beast, with muddy red skin and a set of twisted horns that protruded from its head. With every shift of his weight, his cloven feet cracked and glowed, like they were burning embers.

It was a demon. A real, live, demon.

"Tony!" I finally shouted—the fear gave me a voice. "Tony! Wake up!"

The demon lowered his arms to his sides then dragged them upward until they were being held above his grimy head.

From the ground came a tremble. Followed by a clawing sound, that quickly gave way to sinkholes—six small sinkholes all around us. And what came crawling from those holes were tiny devils—each a miniature version of the larger one.

Malus turned to me and said, "Get down."

I sank to the ground.

Shots were fired.

But it wasn't the gunfire that terrified me. It was the sounds. The demons moved like blurs—moving faster than a man, tearing, shredding, gnawing—cutting down the officers faster than I believed possible. It was like they were children.

"Stop!" I shouted, but Malus smiled.

"Why would we ever do that?" he said.

"Stop! Stop now!" I shouted, and I felt it—not all of it, but enough to do *something*. "Leave them alone!"

When the cops disappeared, I was almost shocked. They vanished. Cars and all.

One of the monsters sneered, and the demon regarded me with eyes that glowed in the darkness. And when I motioned to do the same for Tony, to whisk him away somewhere safe, Malus snapped his finger and said, "You won't be doing that again."

And he was right. The thought—the trigger—was gone, followed by pain that came from the very center of my head.

"What did you do?" I cried, as something warm ran down my cheek. It was blood.

"You could not imagine how long it took, my dear," said Malus, striding over to me. "How long it took to bury so deep into your brain that we know which strings to pull."

"Dance, puppet," said the demon, his hooves clapping the pavement. He strode over to Tony, who was still quietly asleep on the church stoop. The demon got so close to Tony that it looked like he was sniffing him.

"Leave him alone!" I warned, and a frantic urgency took over. I shook—with fear, with rage, with need.

"Or what, child?" he said.

"Or we'll make you burn," I threatened, and those words told no lies.

He laughed. "I have burned for thirty-six and a half megaannum. I do not fear fire." Then to my horror, he grabbed Tony by the head—palmed him like a basketball. "Dreams are for the weak, boy."

When he threw Tony through the locked church doors, his body broken as it shattered the heavy timbers, I gasped. Then something inside me snapped like an invisible leash.

I don't remember running to Tony—but my body ran. I ran past Malus, past the demon, and up the stairs in a blink. I ran all the way to the back of the church and found him there, bloodied and broken, a splintered piece of pew stuck into his chest.

He croaked the word, "Rude," as I knelt at his side with blood spurting from his mouth. It was such a Tony thing to say—always cracking a joke—but I was too concerned, too destroyed by seeing him so beat up, so helpless, that it never even occurred to me why he wasn't looking at me.

The demon said, "I cannot recall the last time I witnessed the symbolic relics of this witless cult," and stepped up to the doorway.

The long piece of wood in his chest and the way he grasped at it reminded me of a staked vampire. It was horrific—but something else was wrong...

"Tony?" I said, touching his cheek, but he didn't respond to my touch. It was like I wasn't even there...

"Can they enter a church?" he asked, but he wasn't talking to me.

"Tony!" I shouted into his ear.

He didn't flinch.

He couldn't see me. He couldn't hear me. I pinched myself, like that was some kind of test to make sure I was real, and the pain was there. It made sense, didn't it? That even when we were finally reunited, we were miles apart.

I cried—I let the sadness run through me—then I stopped. I stopped and wouldn't allow it any more of my time. I leaned in and said, "Don't worry, love, neither of us are dying tonight."

TONY

The church had a congregation of sixty pews split to the left and right—and I slammed through each and every one of them straight up to the altar—like I was a Karate master setting records breaking wooden boards with my face. The pews were unpadded wooden benches, and the windows, lit by the streetlamps outside, were intricately stained-glass panes depicting images of saints and Catholic symbology. It was like any other Catholic church—it even had the balcony with an ancient organ.

Speaking of ancient organs...

"I cannot recall the last time I witnessed the symbolic relics of this witless cult," Belial sneered, peering around the vaulted church. He soaked in every cross and holy adornment before eyeing me up. His power had me reeling, and I could feel it impeding my aura from across the room. I was still gathering my wits when others arrived behind him —including a half dozen little devils that climbed into the pews and danced around like goblins crashing a Fae party.

"Can they enter a church?" I asked, hoping Chappy might answer as I spat out a wad of blood onto the floor. I probably looked worse than I felt. After a while, one gets used to all the pain.

Loki entered the church, answering me straightaway. His fur coat covered his bare torso, like he was some kind of pro wrestling icon from my childhood—like a mean Heartbreak Kid—Jaycie would've gotten the reference...

Jaycie... I could only hope Morpheus was still protecting her with everything he had.

"You forget," replied Loki. "This was our house too. Give or take." He carried a warhammer the size of a holiday ham over his shoulder. The same warhammer that had nearly broken me in half as they chased me across the city. The hammer that crushed an abandoned car like stomping an aluminum can.

JACINDA

When we were last together—like a lifetime ago—I could hear the voices inside Tony's head as we searched for an escape from Hallows Hall. Was he going crazy? Was he possessed? Were they real? Or was he fracturing inside?

Then some old preacher guy with a silver beard appeared out of nowhere and answered him.

"When the holy book mentions synagogues and temples, many believe it is a reference to the body and soul. Loki's ability to enter a holy place might give reverence to that interpretation."

—and my jaw dropped open like a drawbridge.

"Who're you?" I shouted, but even he couldn't hear me.

Then I saw the others. All five of them surrounding us. A sweet-faced kid—Jamaal, maybe?—an army guy, a samurai guy—*holy heck, Tony, a samurai?*—and an old English guy with glasses and a pocket watch.

"Back to being incorporeal," groaned Jamaal. "I need a friggin' respawn."

What the freakin' hecking heck was going on?

TONY

"Umai, my dear," Belial breathed, ducking beneath the doorway to enter the church—his twisted horns peaked over seven feet. "Would you enjoy the opportunity to behead our lost brother? I have a pike I'd like to see it impaled upon."

Entering the church behind Loki was the woman who attacked me on Juniper Street—wearing a minidress and stiletto heels—slightly charred, but club-ready with my tarred footprint stamped onto her chest. Despite the company she kept, she appeared normal. They were monstrous and insane, carrying weapons or shuffling around on goat legs. When she revealed a second set of arms, I instantly retracted the observation.

Umai, the four-armed fire goddess, leaned against a broken pew at the back. Belial took the center, each step upon the old wooden floor threatened to snap the planks beneath his hooves under his immense weight. Loki peeled off and paced to the back corner, never once relenting his wild glare. Fighting through the three of them to the exit would be impossible in my current state. I was still healing—was there another way out?

I stood up and pulled at the flames, manifesting a fiery spear when Belial spread his arms and waved, like he was flagging a cab. The stained-glass windows cracked, like a thin sheet of ice on a frozen lake.

JACINDA

The demon clapped—and the beautiful stained-glass windows broke apart and came soaring at us like thousands of little razor blades. Tony lifted a spear—*a friggin' flaming spear!*—and motioned like he knew what to do with it, twirled it once, then turned it into a fiery shield.

The first few shards shredded his arms and legs and caught me across the thigh—but with a thought, I turned every shard into sand. *I unmade them*. Reversed the vitrification.

I spent nearly all my life not knowing how glass was made—then good ol' Professor Thomas's class my junior year at Milton State changed all that.

"Kid," he said after explaining it for the third time, "you're like broken glass on a chair."

"How so?" I stupidly asked.

"You're a pane in the rear."

When I told Tony the story, he laughed for hours.

Without Professor Thomas, I wouldn't know how glass was made, and knowing allowed me to unmake it. *I did that.* I made the glass into silica.

TONY

Sometimes I did things I didn't know I was doing, or why—like when my body exploded into an inferno that turned Mammon to ash—and this instance was no different. I used the power of my flaming spear to create a shield—but when the glass turned to dust, I had to wonder...*did I do that?*

My shoulders and legs were torn to shreds by the glass that slipped through my defenses. Blood sprayed in all directions. I grabbed hold of the altar to catch myself from falling and put all effort into regenerating. The phrase "DNA evidence" fluttered around my head.

I wasn't healing fast enough. Had my lobotomy within Jaycie's mind palace ruined me? I hadn't been the same since Markus's timeouts, and now that he was gone, I still felt inept. Would I ever be myself again?

"Weak," said Umai with a vapid giggle. "I'm amazed he made it this far. Should I be worried about this infamous group? How has that piece of utter shite been so hard to exterminate?"

The little devils giggled, like a live studio audience.

"Shut her up, my man," said Montoya.

"Would if I could," I replied through gritted teeth—the pain was tremendous, and I was beginning to feel dizzy. It was true what they say —death by a thousand cuts. My leather jacket was torn to shreds, and it too—just as Gabriel had said—was healing slowly along with me.

. . .

JACINDA

Tony was hurt. Baaaaad. I once saw a boy get hit by a car…

Oh god, the memories kept coming…

I remember seeing him there on the pavement. Even if I only glanced once, I'll never forget that sight, and all the blood. There was something about the way his head was twisted…

Please forgive me…

Oh, Amanda, I am so sorry…

All in all, Tony looked worse, and there didn't seem to be a dang thing I could do about it. Blood was dripping onto the floor and soaking down his jeans, but he had this confidence, this defiance, this *fight.*

He wasn't lying down to die. This Tony had that never-say-die spirit I loved so much about him. Unending. Relentless. Unbreakable.

Could I help? Could I heal him? Could I fight them too?

I barely knew how to use my powers—I knew I could move objects or break them down into their basic elements…

"Piteous that we must end you," said the big red demon, stalking toward us—not like Michael Myers or Jason Voorhees, but overconfident. Arrogant. "I would have enjoyed ripping you apart slowly, from the extremities inward, plucking off bit by bit."

"You and your crew really like ripping things apart," said Tony. "I'd hate to see the turkey at your holiday party."

"Are you crazy?" I growled, trying to usher him behind the altar to a safer spot, which was really friggen' difficult when he couldn't see, hear, or feel me.

"Galgenhumor," said the English guy. "If nothing else, your tongue is resilient."

"It's what I do," he shrugged.

"Seems a bit inappropriate, yeah?" asked the preacher.

"Yeah," I agreed.

"Nah, totally appropriate," said Tony.

"Incongruous emotions are often associated with discomfort in high stress situations," said the English guy.

"You must be a shrink," I sang, nudging Tony further along.

"Oh, I'm incongruous alright," he groaned, as his gimpy knee snapped back into place with a gross wet pop.

His body was healing, *and I wasn't doing that.* Maybe he really was resilient. This new Tony could take his licks.

"Henry, man," said Jamaal, "let the guy work."

"He's speaking with himself," said the pro-wrestler. He was tickled, if not morbidly curious. He watched us while clapping his hammer against his open palm, like he was showing off his fancy new toy from the back of the church. "The puny spark is crazier than I am."

TONY

Loki was buying time, a true opportunist waiting for someone else to make the first move.

I still had an ace up my sleeve. A break-glass-in-case-of-emergency maneuver. A rainy-day trick, so to speak. Something I couldn't use in the cold underground tunnels within proximity of the hellfire bombs. All I needed was to draw them closer—the heat wafting off Umai, the fire goddess, did the rest...

"What're you fucknuts waiting for?" I taunted. Loki smiled like he smelled a rat, and I caught a whiff of something that made me gag. "Is that sulfur? Or did the lady just do something...*unladylike?*"

"Draw her in," said Doshin, our minds aligned.

"That's it," said Montoya. "Come to papi."

Umai growled. Her anger manifested into an animalistic sneer. Her eyes widened and her skin became papery.

"Shut up, asshole," she growled.

"Looks like a maneater, if you know what I mean."

"Shut up, asshole!"

"Should we piss her off like this?" questioned Jamaal. "My mamma said never to piss off a lady."

"Does that look like a lady to you, my man?" asked Montoya.

Jamaal shrugged nervously.

"Why so angry, doll?" *Jaycie, forgive me*—I was channeling my inner Rick, and I felt the slime as the words formed in my mouth. "You should smile more, hon."

JACINDA

What did he just say? I did a double take—but he was doing it on purpose. I could tell when he was being facetious, but this was next-level for Tony.

"Good, my man," said the army guy through clenched teeth. "That's right, just a little more…"

Tony and his imaginary friends were plotting to pull them closer. Especially the woman with the four flaming arms. She was beginning to burn so hot that a fog was building at her feet.

"Yeah!" I shouted. "You look like a total skank!"

The woman didn't blink. She didn't even move her eyes away from Tony. I stepped in between them and waved my hands. Nothing.

And that's when it occurred to me—I was invisible to them all…

"Shut that fucker up!" she roared and lurched forward. She pointed at us like she intended the demon to do her dirty work, but he was just as content to watch them spar—grinning with his grimy teeth.

"Come. Make. Me," Tony growled.

"Babe," I whispered, "I hope you know what you're doing."

When the woman charged, the demon followed with the six minions prancing after them.

Tony reached out into charged air, expectantly, but nothing happened. Nothing was happening and they were getting closer. Nothing was happening and I didn't know what to do. What was I supposed to do? What could I do? Oh my god, what was he trying to do?!

And then I felt it…

The heat from the fire goddess met the cold December night pouring in from the broken doors.

Intention. Hope. His need. The charge lingering in the air and Tony's hand pulling at it, like a child tugging on a stubborn door that just won't open.

Then I reached to the sky and yanked the door open for him.

"No," the wrestler whispered and shielded himself behind the hammer just in time.

The lightning struck the ground at the demon's feet. More than 54,000 degrees of heat and a few million volts of electricity obliterated him and shredded the woman in half as it chained around the room, bouncing from one metal surface to another—striking each and every mini-demon before connecting to the organ—bringing half the balcony down over top the entrance.

When the blast subsided, sparks rebounded next to hot embers, and fires burned at the edge of the blast. Nothing remained of the demon, only ash, and the woman's legs, hips, and half her arms evaporated in the charge.

XXVI

master of time

A VOICE
Long Ago...
Then.

When Hades fell, the false gods of men were put on notice. The underworlds they had created to collect power were being destroyed one by one by the Empyrean Host, and the vacuum led to uprising. Unknown to the world of man came a cleansing—a reckoning.

The War of the Gods.

Legends fought for supremacy.

Vagabond Fallen jumped into the fray, attacking the most powerful first, obliterating themselves or eradicating the powerful and stealing their strength and weapons. Alliances were formed and broken, and many of the great pantheons were destroyed.

As the war escalated to its peak, it came to an abrupt end. With the strike of a single blade—the legendary Hermes, streaking across the heavens like a bolt of lightning, fatally struck the heart of Marduk—puncturing his spirit. The great Babylonian god had been compromised by Kali, the destroyer, and exploded into a brilliant ball of hellfire, consuming everything for a thousand miles across northern Asia. Thousands of gods were incinerated in the blast.

Those that refused to fight and remained neutral were later hunted by vengeful former allies—their power taken and used in the broader battle for supremacy. Great leaders, such as Ra and Shiva, were slaughtered by revenge-seeking usurpers.

Many legends were wiped off the face of the planet. Whether they were destroyed and sent into the Unbecoming, or cast into the fiery pits of Perdition, none that survived knew for sure. Few ascended into greatness in the aftermath, while the remaining elite fell from grace entirely. When the dust settled, only Odin and his most loyal pantheon of gods survived intact, awaiting Ragnarok from the shadows. The other pantheons had been destroyed and disassembled. Some fled into exile, while others faded from existence all together.

The time of gods had ended. The time of man—of technology—had come.

Malus avoided the war. The vacuum of power would have presented many opportunities. He bought his time, in both literal and figurative ways.

He sought and killed every mystical creature and god to unwittingly cross his path after surviving the War of Gods. At last count, he had consumed the power of no less than thirty. However, accumulated power was no longer his goal.

The body of Chronos brought him an undiscovered resource. Zeus had found a way to use the Titan's power to travel through time and space, and so time and its many mysterious qualities became his new obsession. Another means to an end.

Experts of black magic and the arcane, from near and far, were invited with the promise of fortune, to lend their expertise toward cracking the great mystery of time. None survived...

And then, Malus disappeared.

When he reemerged, the gears of a new plan were already spinning.

Ardahan Province, Turkey - 1893 AD

The Seytan Castle was built of brown stone and sat upon a rocky cliff. The craggy soil was desolate, harsh terrain.

It was an ideal place for the wicked to call home.

The villagers in the valley below, seeing the abandoned castle's tower lit by torch, gossiped of a returned evil. It had been generations since the tower was lit, and that returning evil that forced them to latch their doors and windows at night.

Malus welcomed rumor. He invited gossip. Superstition kept the curious away. It was a different time—the powerful gods were all but gone. A place and time where he could prepare, and no one would see his rise coming.

Malus had accumulated tricks, amassed ancient knowledge, and mastered many new ways to destroy, torture, manipulate, and conquer. As his power grew, so did his lust for knowledge.

Knowledge could be cultivated in many ways. It could be passed down through books or from teacher to student. It could be procured through magic or stolen straight from the mind, if one had the talents and tools to do so.

And sometimes, knowledge was stolen, straight from the Fates themselves.

He stalked through the dark stone halls. Thick, heavy-soled leather boots and fine woven clothes decorated his body. He preferred modern clothing to the rags and robes of the ancient past, from the fit and comfort to the sophisticated appearance properly suited for the powerful. He wore a woven coat with large brass buttons and fine silken shirt with a black, neatly buttoned waistcoat. His pants were tailored and with each step, his boots bellowed a loud tap, pronouncing his presence before he arrived.

He flew down a flight of stairs and through a dimly lit antechamber where his dedicated servant toiled away at his studies. The goddess within the room did not stir, but sat in her benumbed existence upon her chair—a chair he'd swiped from the sinking mythical island of Hades, before it was destroyed by angels. The flesh of Chronos had paid dividends, as he'd been able to return to the scene to collect useful tools for his quest.

The walls around them were stained with blood. Filth and afterbirth accumulated at the goddess's feet. There was nothing less offensive to the eyes, nose and throat—but they too suffered for his purpose, and as the full moon rose it was time to seek his fortune.

Past dusty shelves of books, old tomes, and grimoires from ancient times, down the stairs, and out into the night—Malus left his castle with a purpose.

The village in the valley below had become hysterical in recent weeks, whining over the unnatural screams that sometimes woke them from their slumber. They pointed their frightened fingers to the castle and noted the torchlight. Their fears were only useful to Malus for so long as they imagined him a blood-sucking beast or phantom of old. Villagers scurried home, and innkeepers locked their doors once the moon had risen over the mountain. These were dangerous times, and he was their tormentor.

Drawing his hood, he continued through the dusty streets until he came to a cottage, nestled between more prestigious homes.

He knocked twice, avoiding a third, and waited, listening to the shuffling from within. An old woman answered the door. She gave him a single glance before peeking left, then right, and invited him in with haste.

"Did anyone see you, my lord?" she asked. Her eyes were only slightly less blind than a bat.

"They did not," he said. The small cottage was lit by a single lamp, its font soaking the last of its oil.

Across the chamber, resting open on an old wooden desk, was a book. Its yellowed pages flickered below the lantern light as the old woman sat down and began to skim its arcane secrets, despite her blinding cataracts. A roaring fire beneath an old stone hearth kept the drafty room warm, and menacing shadows danced along the far wall.

The old woman had hair as wild as a lion's mane, with gray streaks like cracking bolts of lightning. She was a gypsy, with a flowered skirt and a warm woven coat to keep her old bones warm.

"Where is she?" he demanded.

"Your daughter is sleeping, Lord Malus," she replied, her leathery skin wagging at the jowls.

His progeny was created with intent—to "see" what others could not. He did not procreate for love or recreation.

"I need her to read the Threads of Fate."

"My granddaughter does not have your black heart, lord Malus. She has good in her," said the old woman. "Kill her and make another."

When he created Mona, he had yet to learn how to manipulate the conception, several centuries before humans had conquered the mystery of DNA. He had since learned many wonderous things—but cultivating the dark arts to provide him another child to "see" for him was a lengthy endeavor. He had waited long enough...

"Fetch my daughter," he said.

"Lord, please, let me attempt to—"

"Do not deny me, crone."

She wilted and quickly retreated into the next room. She returned moments later dragging a small girl by the hair—her face red where her grandmother's hand had struck her. She was chained and wearing bedclothes, but her eyes—disparate, just like his—were alarmed, wide, and leaked with fear.

"Your father needs you," said the crone.

Little Mona looked upon him like a stranger. She was afraid of Malus. Once upon a time, many years ago, he may have changed course for a child—but that was much too long ago, and before his heart had blackened.

"I need your gift, child," he said. She did not move.

"Lord Malus—"

"Crone!" he shouted, "do not speak when I am conversing with my daughter."

Perhaps it was fear, or even the notion that the creature before her was her father, but the girl sat down upon the chair the crone had vacated without another word.

The crone placed a deck of cards before Mona, and the girl began the ritual without speaking. His blood, her spit, coupled with a fingernail plucked clean from her own tiny hand, were tossed into a bowl along with a bag full of runes.

The cards were cut five times at his direction, then placed into the sacred cross.

"What is the purpose of this ceremony?" she asked, then added, "Father?"

"I wish to be shown how I will achieve my goals."

With that, she placed a second, clarifying card over the position for air, then took the bowl and read the runes. She placed the five positional runes next to their corresponding positions.

First came Fire—the bottom card on the cross formation.

Next, Water—to the left.

Then, Air above, and crossed, as this represented that which he wished to see.

Fourth, Body, at the center.

Lastly, Earth to the right.

"Are you ready?" she asked, and Malus nodded. They had attempted this ceremony many times, but as with all manner of divination, one can only be shown so much. This night, however, the spirits felt alive within the room.

Mona played the first card—The Ghost. It was a simple illustration of a phantom—a translucent man searching for something that was missing. "The fire card in the formation tells us your passion, your one true desire, just as the fire that burns inside us all. Your question, however, was not one about personal discovery, but a lifelong search. It is key to keep that in mind when reading the cards." She spoke well beyond her years—the spirits whispered into her ears. "The Ghost tells us your journey has not been for yourself, but for another, lost a long time ago."

The crone scoffed. "You best do better, girl. Do not tell my Lord things he already knows."

Mona then played the second card—The Endless Traveler. It was a man wandering the desert alone, as the night and day split the card evenly, depicting perpetual journey. "The water card in the formation informs your dilemma, as water is often seen as an obstacle to be crossed. A life-long search and the The Endless Traveler tell us you have been wandering for a very long time. What you seek is an end to the journey. A plan. A way forward."

The crone nearly laughed, but Malus showed no change in his emotion. He needed Mona's gift. Frightening her would only damage the reading.

"Shall I continue?" she choked. Her anxiety poisoned her mind.

Malus nodded, and her pulse evened.

Next, Mona flipped the first of the top cards in the formation. The position that was doubled. The King—it was a simple card, depicting a ruler wearing a bejeweled crown, with many rings upon his hands as he brandished a scepter. "Next on our journey—the King. The air card in the formation tells us what you need. Like air is essential for life, so is this card, and it was doubled, as your question was based on the need to achieve your goals. The top card represents what you need, the bottom card how you may achieve it.

"The King," she continued, "may represent an authority figure, or wealth. When presented with this card, including all the information we have, it may mean that you are looking for an actual man—a special one."

Without hesitating, Mona flipped the second air card.

The Fruited Tree—it was depicted by a simple tree with unknown fruit growing from its branches. "The Fruited tree, drawn from that position, with that question, represents how you may achieve your need for The King. Your secret will be found within—*fruit.*"

The crone spat. "My Lord, I interpret it much differently..."

"Continue, daughter," Malus said to Mona.

The center card for body was flipped next—The Ace of Cups. "The body card, played at this stage in the ceremony, after you have been given the secret to your question, tells us that there will be obstacles— but those obstacles will only be presented *after* you have what you need. The body card in the formation pulls back the veil on your spirit, as the body is often overlooked when searching for desires and overcoming obstacles. Yours lies with The Ace of Cups." The card depicted was a single chalice being filled with wine. "This card speaks riddles, as it may mean you require more than just your ability to fill your own cup. Or it means that there is a burden that must be fulfilled before you may find peace. Its true interpretation may not yet be revealed."

"Then why are you here, girl?" said the crone.

At last, they arrived at the final card. Mona revealed it slowly, then removed her hand. The Hourglass, inverted—played right-side up, the top portion of the hourglass would have been empty, signifying time running out. Inverted, like that which was played, had all the sand gathered at the top. "The earth card in the formation proclaims your path. As paths are laid upon the earth, so shall yours be revealed. The inverted Hourglass speaks to time itself. The culmination of this ceremony, though complicated, says much about your journey."

"Do tell," said the crone.

Mona looked at her father for the first time—her eyes gray and brown, as his own—and when she spoke, the words left her mouth like that of a true diviner. "Your journey shall lead you to a desert king, somewhere in the distant past. Your weapon, a forbidden fruit. But this success will not be enough, for you are merely filling a single cup, a single cup of many needed to fulfill your destiny. Though you have lived long, the ghost that haunts you may finally rest when you are through."

When she finished speaking, she waited.

"My Lord," groveled the crone, "let me read for you next. I promise you shall find absolution in my words."

Malus gave the crone a smile, then turned to Mona. She cowered under his gaze.

"Daughter," he said. "Mona, you will never see me again."

With the flash of a blade, he cut the crone's throat clean to the bone. Then with a snap of his fingers, Mona's shackles fell aside.

The girl looked at him, her heart thumping wildly while she attempted to understand what it all meant.

"This is my gift to you," he said. "Freedom."

Malus left the house at once, and true to his word, Mona never saw him again. Though, that did not mean he did not visit her from afar from time to time.

The spirits had shown Malus the way with two very specific details—the desert and the fruit. Malus had all the time in the world, but he had little patience after thousands of years. When he arrived home, Malus spared no time enacting his plan.

"Are you prepared?" Malus asked his servant.

"Is it over?" he asked, toiling away inside a book.

Hermes Trismegistus was a man who thought he was a god. In truth, his intelligence was channeled from the great gods Hermes and Thoth—alchemists of unparalleled skill.

"Over?" scoffed Malus. "You may go where you please after you obey my final command."

"Go?" he asked. "Will you not take me home?"

Malus had plucked him out of time many millennia ago.

"Home?" spat Malus. "Why would you wish to return home after you have accomplished so much of your life's work? The past will never appreciate your discoveries."

"My life's work?" he asked. "I never sought to create disposable atrocities for a madman."

"Do what you are told, or I will find you."

Hermes looked back toward the goddess, still benumbed upon her chair. "What should I do with Echidna?"

"Leave her," said Malus. "Prepare my armies."

"Where am I sending your armies?" he asked.

"No, not just where," said Malus. "Mount of Olives, Jerusalem. March, 23rd 931 B.C."

Within a coffin stuffed into the corner of the laboratory, lost in eternal slumber, was Chronos the Titan, still bound by the Chains of Prometheus, surviving in a perpetual cycle of youth through death and back again. Never waking, never rousing from pain or need.

"Each of them may take a single bite," said Malus. "But no more."

He leaned over and bit three times, swallowing three whole mouthfuls. The flesh on the Titan slowly began to weave itself back together, creating a near endless supply.

"Why do you take three bites while the rest take just one?" asked Hermes.

"I have additional business," answered Malus, but Hermes did not question any further.

With an outstretched finger, Malus poked a hole through an invisible membrane. The air rippled and distorted like sticky viscous liquid. He then dragged his finger down to his knees and ripped a hole in the membrane the approximate size of a man. Grabbing hold of both sides, he tore the portal wide open like splitting a curtain and stepped through into the sweet orchard air.

"Remember, Hermes," said Malus, "Mount of Olives, Jerusalem. March, 23rd 931 B.C."

XXVII

deception

TONY
Now.

Sometimes dreams do come true...

I was beginning to think that summoning a bolt of lightning was only possible in Jaycie's dream world. Umai flailed on the ground like a fish out of water, struggling to breathe, and for a moment, I felt bad for her.

Nearly healed, I removed the jagged wood from my chest, careful to avoid leaving behind any splinters in unfortunate, hard-to-reach spots, and limped over. Then I used it like a stake to cleave out Umai's heart.

Who would have thought my next resume update would include Fallen Slayer as my current position? Who would have thought I could jam wood into the heart of another creature and not think twice about it?

"Who are you?" asked Loki. He lowered the sparking warhammer and stared at me, mystified. "You call on Angel Fire like the god of thunder."

"Angel Fire," I acknowledged, and quickly noted the difference.

"Hellfire, the all-consuming flame," said Chappy.

"And the flashing violence of lightning," said Jamaal. "Angel Fire."

"Tony," I said, introducing myself to Loki, "the Fallen Slayer."

"Amazing. Truly amazing," said Loki with a golf clap and a grin that went from ear to ear. He took a polite step toward me, like he was praising my work.

I tried to reach out again, to build the static charge and fry Loki where he stood, but there was nothing there…

Maybe I wasn't doing it right? Maybe this was just another example of my abilities futzing out on me when I needed them most. Or maybe I had a little help? Divine intervention? Were the angels watching over me?

"Out of juice?" wondered Loki, and in the strangest way, he reminded me of Mr. O'Neill—always patronizing and pointing out my shortcomings like a total dick.

JACINDA

The burst was so bright, I was still seeing shapes and colors—but Tony? He had already sprung forward and cleaned up the mess. Eight of them were dead in a literal flash.

"We did it!" I shouted—but obviously, nobody heard me. "That was… amazing!? I told you! I promised we'd make you burn." I was speaking to the pile of smoldering devil ash on the floor.

"Tony, my man, that hammer looks big and mean," said the army guy as Tony and the pro wrestler exchanged banter. I didn't want to see what that hammer could do. We had to get away. We could escape. We could get out and—

"Well, now you've done it," said Malus.

I froze. He was right behind me.

When I turned, reaching to the sky to sling a bolt of lightning right up his stupid nose, I was snatched away. Something clamped onto my wrists and ankles, then climbed the wall with a skitter. It had me sprawled out and upside down, dangling from the ceiling before I had the chance to fight back.

Something sharp was pressed against my neck at the base of my skull, followed by a ticking noise, like a cicada hatching in the summer heat. Goosebumps broke out across my arms and neck, and the sherpa lining in my jean jacket felt as rough as sandpaper.

Malus skipped toward me up the side of the wall—just as Tony had defied gravity when he fought his way through a hallway of slimy monsters in the Milton State science building. It was a feat that felt as threatening as the object jammed into my neck.

"Even when I remove you from the world, you still find a way to fuck me," he said. "No more." Then he looked past me to someone else. "Sting him."

TONY

Loki and I were engaged in a staring contest. I was winning.

Then I shot him a big cheesy grin, like something from a Bugs Bunny cartoon with a couple eyebrow raises, and ran. By the time I hit my second stride, my legs were strong enough to leap through one of the broken stained-glass window frames—

—just as a massive crash collapsed the wall beside it.

Loki's warhammer missed, again, by mere inches. I could hear his cackling behind me, maintaining pace as I soared up the side of the church and leapt off and onto the next building, continuing my climb.

Belial and Umai were dead—two less evils to deal with.

This had to end tonight.

Summanus, Mammon, Bacchus, Thanatos, Belial, Umai, Eshu—there were five, maybe six remaining, at most—*unless...?*

"Unless," said Jamaal, "they have new members?"

It was a dreadful thought—I was mathing in my head, adding up the names I knew with the names on my internal deceased poster tally, and the numbers weren't working.

1
LOKI
2
electrified &
DEAD
BELIAL
3
fried hottie
DEAD
UMAI
4
flaming bullet
DEAD
BACCHUS
5
6
PHOBOS &
DEIMOS
7
Who dis?
ANUBIS
8
sadly exploded
DEAD
ESHU
9
DAGON
10
ASTORETH

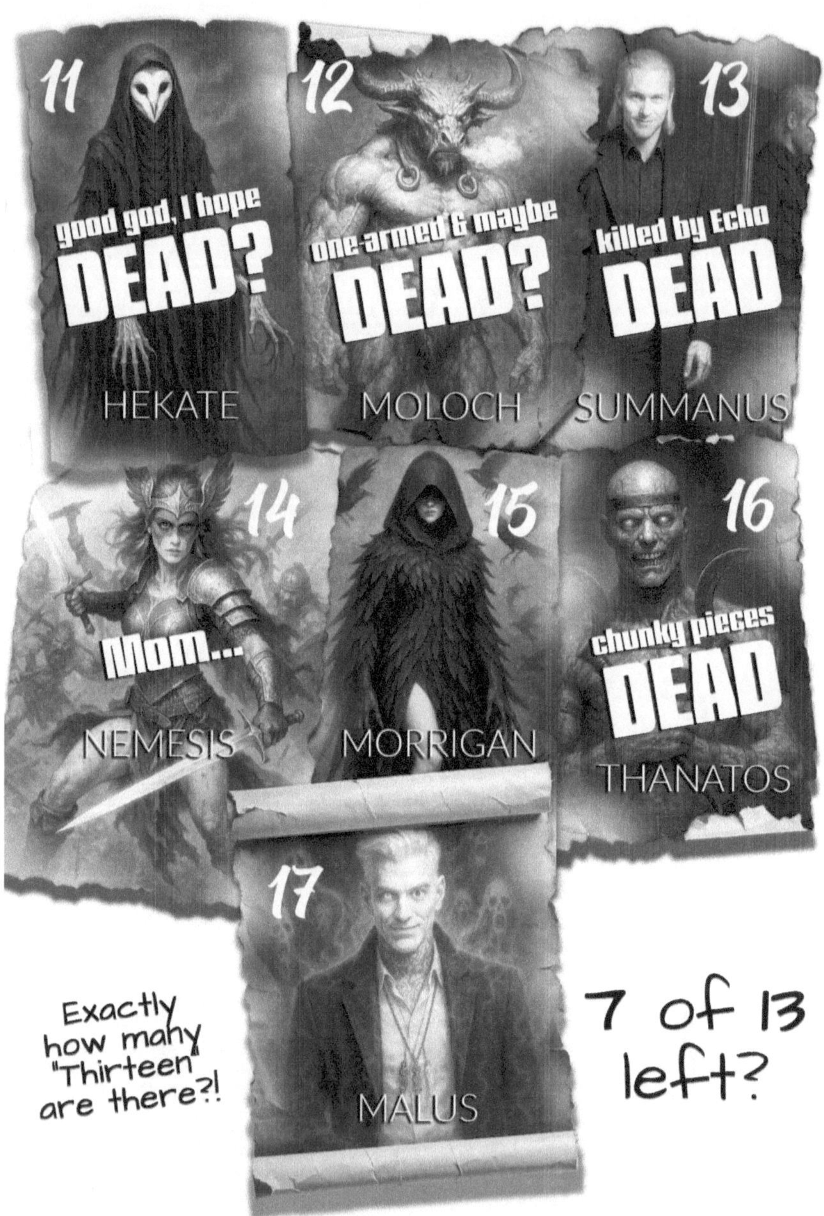
11
good god, I hope
DEAD?
HEKATE
12
one-armed & maybe
DEAD?
MOLOCH
13
killed by Echo
DEAD
SUMMANUS
14
Mom...
NEMESIS
15
MORRIGAN
16
chunky pieces
DEAD
THANATOS
17
MALUS
Exactly
how many
"Thirteen"
are there?!
7 of 13
left?

Like Spider-Man, I fled up the side of a high-rise, leaping back and forth from building to building. Loki chased, but who else was in pursuit? Up and up I ran until the acrid presence of the Morrigan detoured my escape route. I shifted gravity and fell into the parallel building, crashing through the window. Then I took the stairs, jumping straight down the shaft between the flights.

On the 26th floor, I exited through another window, free falling through the open air, and landed onto the rooftop across the street with a roll. I was back on my feet and striding for the next rooftop when—

—I was lifted and slammed by a barbed tentacle that cracked my ribs and briefly collapsed a lung.

I saw stars—flashing, twinkling lights as Dagon strode into view, charred and mangled from the tunnel blast. A couple tentacles were blown off, along with a portion of his face and the damaged eye I took with my pocketknife.

He sneered. "No escape." At least that's what I thought he said. He may have said, "I'm a fucktrumpet," and I wouldn't have known the difference. My bell was ringing, like someone had struck a ten-foot gong between my eyes.

"Gee, I thought young and female was your type," I said, rolling away. As soon as I planted my foot onto the ground, I was pushing off—

—right into the outstretched hand of Astoreth, like I was being choke slammed by the Undertaker in a WWE match—her sleek black hair whipping to an imaginary breeze. Chappy yelped inside my head, as she lifted me by the throat—all five-foot-six-inches of her, and naked as the day she was born. Her grip was like a cold, hard, metal vice, applying constant building pressure as if to carefully test at which point my head might explode.

I wasn't going out like this—popped like a Belushi zit all over the rooftop—and kicked her across the face to limited, if not zilch, results. She was as hard and dense as marble and glared at me without speaking a word. When she flicked her wrist, attempting to shatter my spine and paralyze me, I squirmed away—slipping from her fingers like a damp bar of soap. She punished me with a quick jab, fracturing my jaw, and I tumbled backward onto rooftop gravel.

My healing went into overdrive, focusing on reversing a concussion, when Dagon grabbed my arm and twisted it, popping my shoulder out of socket like breaking off a chicken wing. I yelped in pain, and stomped my foot into Astoreth's knee, loosening her renewed grip just enough for me to spin and smack Dagon across the face with an elbow.

JACINDA

I was lugged out of the church and up the side of the nearest building. Then, the creature took both my arms and legs and spread them wide as I screamed my lungs out, incapacitating me with its strength. It leapt across the expanse and positioned us onto a rooftop just as Tony jumped into view—right into the hands of a naked woman. He fought her—this tiny little woman—and some tentacled creature with one eye.

They were winning.

When I tried to scream, to help, to tap into my abilities—the insect dug the sharp thing deeper into my neck. But I didn't care. I didn't care if it crippled me. I didn't care if it tore me apart like it was playing *He Loves Me Not* with my limbs.

With a twitch, I pushed Tony away from them—just a nudge, and he was off and running...but there was something on top of him—something he couldn't see or feel. One of the insects...

...like the one who had me, but with a great big stinger...

TONY

The smallest of windows opened as I skidded past the gods. Fifty feet. All I needed was fifty feet. Forty-feet. Thirty...

...something sharp, like a bee sting, burned between my shoulder blades—did I get stabbed? It burned so bad I felt it between the temples.

Despite their names coming to me with a touch, I couldn't take them all at once.

Dagon.

Astoreth.

Phobos.

...wait? *Phobos?*

The sting. Something was attached to my back, and with a violent shrug, I tossed it away and kept moving.

Hand-to-hand combat was a struggle against multiple attackers. Hellfire bombs couldn't finish them. Flaming spears were useless when being attacked from all angles. Angel Fire did the deed, but apparently, I couldn't summon a bolt of lightning whenever I needed it—was that another stupid-ass symptom of not knowing my true name? Atmospheric conditions? Lack of caffeine? Vitamin D deficiency? Who the fuck knows...

Twenty-five feet...

I wasn't as powerful as Gabriel, who could do incredible things with a thought. He could travel through time and to futures that would never be. I bet he could summon a whole ball of lightning and chuck it like shooting a basketball, perhaps even summon a whole tornado or tidal wave and wipe them all away. He was a mighty Archangel, but could he fight so many enemies at once? Each vying to be the lucky god to strike the killing blow?

Twenty—six more strides...

Six strides and I was out into the open air again. Six strides and I could race to shelter—use the key and...*and what?* What then? Jump through time while avoiding paradoxes? What was the plan, Tony? Where the fuck was my backup plan?

Just ten more feet and I was out of the boiling pot—maybe I could pop away—an hour into the future, or maybe into the far past until I could come up with another plan. I was grabbing for the key when—

"Tony," said Jaycie.

I froze—coming to a skidding stop across the loose pebbles.

She was teetering on the ledge a short distance away—twenty-two stories from the pavement below. The wind tousled her hair, and she looked as if she might slip at any moment. The violet phosphorescence of the night sky illuminated by the city lights below, and haloed by the moon, she was framed like a picture. Fragile and tortured—if her words hadn't stopped me dead in my tracks, the tears would have.

How did I miss her?

MALUS

Once the stinger was in, it was over.

Deimos brought Jacinda close to watch the remaining Thirteen crush the spark. It was imperative that she witness the end of hope. To stomp out all faith. Their bond was their strength, and it had to end.

"Destroy their love so that you could create your own happy ending?" said Lilly. "Selfish. There is no limit to your arrogance."

"You could never destroy our love," whispered Jacinda.

Could she hear Lilly? Could she hear the spirits of the dead whispering to me?

I watched her carefully—arms and legs constrained, dangling helplessly sixty meters into the air. Her hair drifted on the wind, and for a moment I felt pity. This poor soul was given great gifts—how and why they were stowed within her was beyond my comprehension. However, the fault of others was no fault of mine. Their mistake would be my fortune. She was an innocent caught up in otherworldly affairs.

And still, I felt pity.

She avoided my eyes.

I was the monster that haunted her. I was the monster that hunted her. The hate she had for me was immense. Pity, however, did not mean I cared. Her end was just one of thousands upon thousands I have taken. I took no pleasure nor burden from it. It was transactional.

"Once she witnesses the end," I said to Lilly, "you will be restored. Her body will become vacant, and you will replace her."

The air around us snapped as a dusting of snow fluttered on the high-rise draft.

"No. Please!" she begged. Her spirit was agitated, frosting the air like a child's snow globe. "Do not send me back there!"

"Why?"

"There are things within her mind. Terrible things. An old man haunts me there. Plucked and offered! Plucked and offered!"

What was this madness?

"My mind's a terrible place," said Jacinda. "You preyed upon me half my life. You made me, and I swear, I will find a way to destroy you. I will undo you. I will make sure the name Malus never existed."

Threats.

Deimos pressed the stinger deeper into her neck, and Jacinda's focus returned to the rooftop below. Her love was being choked by Astoreth. The end was near.

I put Lilly to rest. I did not have time to solve a new mystery. And it was time to take my position and play my part. Let the ruse begin.

JACINDA

A bug once got into my ear.

I've had a lot of sketchy, gross, and downright mortifying moments in my life, but for some reason, that day stands out. Amanda kept dry heaving, and Robbie—*I mean Maynard*—kept trying to convince me to call poison control, because it was a "foreign object" inside my body. We were nine. Maybe ten.

To say I have a poor relationship with bugs was an understatement.

So here I was, dangling twenty or so stories in the air while being constrained by a giant bug with a stinger pressed into the nape of my neck. This was something of a chilling experience.

And it would have freaked me right the eff out if it wasn't for the fact that I was being forced to watch Tony fight a gauntlet of monsters.

The insect leapt from the building across the street and landed on the next rooftop as I watched Tony make his break. A crow-woman took to the sky screeching, and a burnt-toast- looking squid-man flapped his tentacles like he was throwing a tantrum. Nobody could've stopped Tony—he was running faster than I had ever seen. He was free...

...except for the invisible thing perched on his back.

I could see it and not see it at the same time—like Tony's "brain-trust."

When it stung him, he cried out in pain and shrugged it free. It landed harshly on its side and became visible—an insect, like the one restraining me, but red and black and eye-less, and so, so gross.

Tony was going to make it. He was going to make it…

…but then Malus leapt onto the building ledge and Tony stopped dead in his tracks—skidding to a stop right at the edge.

"If you ever truly loved me, you'd let me go," said Malus—and Tony was listening to him. It was a mirage—if I squinted, I could see it. It was me. Tony was seeing *me*. Not actually me, but Malus-me.

"What are you doing up here?" he asked.

"You're driving me crazy, Tony," said Malus-me, as he teetered uneasily on the ledge. "You killed me before, and you're killing me again."

"Tony! Run! Don't stop! It's not me!" I shouted, but he couldn't hear me. "It's a trick! Listen to your friends! It's a trick!"

TONY

My mind clouded, like I hadn't slept in days. I forgot all about the devils who wanted me dead and stared down the love of my life as she threatened her own for the second time.

Her words sent a sharp pain up my back and straight to my heart, like a knife being driven in and out of my chest—a physical manifestation of my emotions.

"Do not listen to her," warned Doshin, but how could I not?

"Sir, you are on the verge of a panic attack," warned Henry, and I felt the surge of anxiety—my hands trembled.

"Get the fuck out of here!" growled Jamaal, but I was frozen.

"Listen to your heart," said Chappy, "not your eyes."

"My man, it's a trick," said Montoya. "It has to be, right?"

Was it? Was it an illusion?

She was saying everything I feared was true. I was the cause of her suffering. I drove the wedge between us. It was always my fault. And I planted that seed of doubt the moment my insecurities took over. Whether it was Rick, or Roman, I always felt second-rate...

"You're so clingy and desperate for my validation. And when I wanted space, you just couldn't let that happen. You forced yourself upon me when I was with Rick. You couldn't let me handle my own problems with Roman. I'm in this mess because of you." Her eyes hardened and her arms and legs stopped shivering in the frigid breeze, as if she had given up—on me, on life...

I'd refused to let her go. I suffocated her. I drove her to this—as if I was burying her alive.

The voices in my head pleaded with me to run, but every paranoid delusion and insecurity shouted louder. The same panic that I was about to lose everything if I didn't say and do everything perfectly formed a Godzilla-sized lump in my throat. I was teetering on a razor's edge.

"Why are you saying this? Why now?"

I took a step toward her and she stiffened.

"Don't come any closer," she threatened. "Or I *will* jump. I will jump just to get away from you."

"Stop, please. Don't..." Then I took that last unnecessary step.

It was innocent. It was impulse. It was too much for her...

Jacinda didn't think twice.

She stepped off into the breeze...

Have you ever witnessed your worst fears twice in one lifetime? No, no, you haven't. You haven't witnessed this. You haven't witnessed a goddamn thing like this.

I saw the most precious person in my existence take her own life in one of the most gruesome ways imaginable, and just like that, it was happening all over again.

It was happening all over again!

The stitching on my jacket and pants popped as my body twitched, racing toward the spot where she disappeared over the ledge.

Twenty-two stories high = approximately 72 meters.

Jaycie's mass = 58 kilograms.

Speed at impact = 37.5 meters per second.

Time until impact = 3.83 seconds...

The math manifested in the far corners of my mind as I rushed for the ledge. I was fighting against time and gravity, moving at a speed that pushed me to the very edge of my abilities, before she plummeted to her death. Every single part of me broke as I ran for her. Bones snapped and sewed together instantly. Muscles tore and re-stitched. Joints popped and rehinged before I even felt pain. But I hadn't moved—not an inch—

—Something was anchoring me—something I needed to escape or Jaycie was going to die. I've broken bones, ruptured organs and survived by inhuman means—the pain immeasurable but temporary—but I would tear myself to pieces to save her. I would tear myself to pieces even if it meant the end of me. Myself for her—always, myself for her!

But I couldn't goddamn move!

I panicked. I was fraying with every passing millisecond. I was pulling apart.

"I thought you were the moon," I heard her say.

MALUS

The stinger had done its job. I prompted his fear, and the spark's mind filled the gaps. He carried enough fear and guilt to last lifetimes. So much that Phobos's hallucination took its own path without much need for guidance.

Tony was just another Fallen nearing the final demise of his innocence. We would silence his conscience, forever.

Once my dead had wrangled the spark's arms and legs, it was time to lift the curtain. With a pluck, they removed the stinger.

"That was entertaining, wasn't it?" My ring seethed, calling out to the lifeless ectoplasmic fingers of the dead wrenched around every inch of him, squeezing and restraining and wrestling his body into a prone kneel. "The look on your face? Genuinely priceless."

Tony was dazed and sifting through the clues around him, questioning reality.

"I thought you were the moon," I said. "What does that even mean?"

"Would you like Phobos to torture him?" it asked with a whispery voice. A pair of black lips covered a set of sharp black teeth. Tony's eyes and nose flared as he observed the god of fear. "Phobos and Deimos can force the Raptor to observe death a thousand times, day after day for as long as you desire."

"I have no desire to play with food."

TONY

"Gather it. Let it fuel you," whispered Doshin. "Channel the anger. Be ready."

I was hyperventilating, and witnessing Jacinda's death all over again lit the fuse of rage—but I still couldn't move. Not an inch. The dead had me restrained on my knees.

"I have no desire to play with food," said Malus, closely observing me for the first time. He was inspecting me—the scar, my eyes, my clothes, like he was searching for something important, when his eyes landed at the chain around my neck and smiled. The key beneath my shirt pulsed in tune with the three trinkets around his own.

"Is he to be devoured?" asked Astoreth, her nakedness silhouetted by darkness.

"He is not to be savored," said Malus. "Devouring him is merely for his own enjoyment, not ours."

The Morrigan stepped closer, prepared to feast. The flapping feathers of her cowl fluffed and ruffled at the idea of inflicting pain.

"A quick death has honor," she hissed, "so I will eat thy heart last."

"The key is mine," said Malus. "Devour everything else."

Astoreth. Morrigan. Phobos. And crispy Dagon. Hekate and Moloch were gone. Malus had five, maybe six of his Thirteen left?

"The fish god," said Doshin, "he is the weak link."

Loki. Where was Loki?

I felt the heat rising with my rage. The fire inside was burning. The temptation to Fall—and the glimmer of hope to guide me—this could be the end.

"Is this it?" I shouted. "Is this all that's left of your mighty Thirteen? Five? Six?"

"Damn, not so bad for a puny little spark, huh?" growled Jamaal.

"Six is all I need," said Malus as he lit a cigarette without a lighter—casually exhaling the smoke. Immortals—they have all the time in the world. They don't know what it's like to live second by second, living for the moments between the peaks—the lazy weekends, the ordinary moments spent living and dying for someone's laughter.

The trouble is, you think you have time.

They had all the time in the world, but I only needed seconds to live —seconds to know what I was fighting for. Aa brief hint of lavender drifted over to me—Jaycie was here, somewhere...and I would not die in front of her.

"Flight check, my man," said Montoya. "How you feeling?"

"All systems," I said, as the flames soared from chest to fingers and toes, "go."

Astoreth crept forward as Dagon lurked, searching for an angle.

The Morrigan stalked into my blind spot, and Phobos began to circle me.

I had to remove the dead—they were unbreakable by force alone. Would I have survived the fight with ghost-Rick if Jaycie hadn't destroyed him? The Blessed Knuckles, a gift from Maynard, were resting inside my interior jacket pocket, but all I needed was to dissolve the hold long enough to break free.

I called the flames, encompassed myself in a brief burn of incendiary fire, softening the consistency of the ectoplasm. The spectral hands withered, and I sprang forward like an Olympic sprinter straight for Dagon. His remaining eye bulged the moment I made my move—

—but I wasn't fast enough.

By the time I took one free step, the Morrigan jumped onto my back and sank her teeth into my shoulder. I spun like a mechanical bull, but nothing would knock her free when Astoreth grabbed hold and pinned me down—her skin, as hard and sharp as razors, sliced into my arm while both their true names surfaced.

My mouth opened, their names on the very tip of my tongue, when something slimy coiled around my throat and squeezed, choking the words from being spoken. As Dagon's tentacle squeezed, and Morrigan sank her teeth to the bone—all I could think about was the pain. The excruciating pain of being eaten alive. The thousands of individual lives inside my head, all meeting similar fates at the hands of the Thirteen, and there was nothing more running through my brain than the horror that I was about to endure.

That, and losing her.

There was no way out. It was over…

Until I was half-consciously soaring through the air.

JACINDA

Tony's imaginary friends were giving him instructions. But what could he do alone against them all?

Tony used to swat spiders and other critters when they happened too close to me. I made him stop killing them, opting to finding them a better home outside, away from me. He said they would just find their way back inside, but I couldn't bear to be the cause of someone else's pain—even creepy crawly spiders.

But this thing holding me hostage? This thing was going to rue the day…

…I just didn't know how…yet.

Tony had spent all this time alone, searching for answers. He never gave up on me. He fought through endless odds for me. He even fought for me when I wasn't fighting myself. I think I would have given up on me by now.

If we had one fatal flaw in our relationship, it was that we both lost sight of what the other needed. I stopped fighting for him. And he stopped fighting altogether. But now, I was going to do some fighting for him. I was going to do the impossible for him. Maybe I couldn't fight with fists, but I would find a way. I was going to find a way. Even if it meant giving him a sign that I was here. A sound. A scent.

And just when it looked like I'd never have that chance—as these demons piled on, teeth bared and biting into him—me screaming my head off, and crying uncontrollably—a flash of metal, and that great big warhammer struck the squid guy and pinballed into the rest of them.

It was like they had been struck by a freight train, and the collision blew a portion of the roof apart. They were bowling pins, featherweight objects in the path of an unstoppable force, and Tony's imaginary friends blinked in and out with his consciousness as he tumbled up and over the ledge—

TONY

My ears rang. My head pounded. I was falling. By the time the world had stopped spinning, something grabbed me by the ankle—Loki was climbing up my leg as we plummeted toward the ground, reaching terminal velocity.

As the trickster wound up, I caught the hammer in his hand before he could swing, then wrestled with him for position as we tumbled. With the pavement racing up at us and impact pending, Loki reached out and did the unthinkable—he grabbed hold of the brass key that had floated free of my shirt. Before I could stop him, he slid it into a small keyhole tattooed at the center of his own bare chest and twisted.

We were no longer in the city of Philadelphia.

When traveling with the key, there is the briefest moment where everything flashes white, like a camera. Then one arrives at the desired location and time as if nothing so astounding or miraculous had happened. The transition from one place to another was always seamless, which made the situation that much more harrowing.

After the flash we were still falling, only now we were a mile above a very active and hostile volcano.

"Fuck!" I screamed into the wind—it was like shouting into a hurricane. Falling twenty stories to your death was one thing—a quick drop—but a mile-long free fall made my guts clench and crawl up into my throat. Volcanic soot and smoke rose as we tumbled towards its crater. Despite our height, the heat was incredible. Peering down into the mouth of the volcano scalded my eyes. Of all the ways I thought I might go out, this was as far from probable as I could've guessed.

Snow and mud lined the steep banks of the angry mountain, and in the lush valley below was a bustling ancient city. I could see the people below, scurrying for their lives as the volcano protested, ready to blow at any moment with thunderous tremors shaking the landscape, sending mudslides down the mountain.

Loki growled and grappled with my face, his thumbs searching for the leverage to ram my eyes into their sockets. We rolled and tumbled and fought. If I could kick him away and use the key, I could leave him stranded, soaring toward the crater—but he was a trickster after all.

Down and down, and into the mouth of the angry mountain, Loki's hand snagged the key. He could have torn it from my neck and left me there, but instead he held on tight. Loki wanted to see me die. My death needed to be at his hands.

Eventually self-preservation won out against revenge.

In one last surge of desperation, with certain death imminent, Loki decided mutual destruction was not within his best interest. In a flash, just before the molten rock consumed us, we were gone—the key took us somewhere new.

We landed hard into a snowdrift. Steam rose from our bodies like drafts of fog, and the accumulated volcanic heat melted the snow around us. The impact hurt, but we were both alive and riding adrenaline highs that left every ache and broken bone in our bodies numbed.

I was first to my feet and jumped back when Loki came up swinging his hammer, sending a cloud of snow into the air. We stood facing each other down, twenty feet between us.

It was dark, and the clouds dumped large fluttering flakes of snow into the skies. Slivers of silvery moonlight came from sharp cracks in the cloudy blanket. We were standing in the middle of a forest clearing with thick brier and low-hanging twisted branches creating a ringed arena for our showdown. Loki unclasped his fur coat and let it fall to the ground, choosing to fight bare chested in the blistering cold.

The snow was deep and powdery, well above the knees in some places, and made maneuvering difficult. We circled each other, neither of us speaking until—

"The world is full of liars," he said.

"Interesting theory," I responded with a dramatic shrug.

"Malus had us sold. He said you were nothing more than an ant to be squashed. A mere spark to be wiped out by the coming wave of discord and chaos our Thirteen would bring." As he spoke, he pointed the warhammer at me.

"Sorry to disappoint."

"I was coaxed into destroying my brothers, my king, all for the sake of gaining access to one who could see what we needed to know. I lost my son for the sake of Ragnarok. Then against my better judgment, and my own hubris, I sacrificed my daughter Hel." As his eyes flared, I could hear the blood rushing through his veins, pulsing with hatred. "You killed my little girl."

THE TRICKING OF
LOKI

206 A.D.

Chains were symbolic. They represented isolation, restriction, and control. We all have chains. Every one of us lives with them. Every one of us survives them. All chains bind us from moving forward, connected to the weight of awful things. Awful things that one must drag behind them if they are ever to move forward.

Other chains are bound to us by others, repercussions for our sins. Some sins are worse than others, and the truly wicked sins bring the heaviest chains. We pull at them, testing the strength and craftsmanship of each chain. We lash at them, blaming the chain for our sins. We hold on to the chains, in fear of what we might do without them.

We all strive to break our chains.

Some chains are never broken.

On the northernmost tip of the Faroe Islands was a rocky beach where the surf slammed against the stone in rumbling roars of saltwater and spray. The rock, jagged and angular, was left shrouded in perpetual mist from the cold Atlantic waters. At the very edge of the rock, where the water and stone met in constant battle, were three carved pillars. The outer pillars were equal in width and height, but the center was twice as tall as the other two.

A length of chain was anchored to outer pillars on either side, then spanned the distance to the pillar at the center where it was anchored again in the ancient stone. The chain, taut and strong, was then shackled to the wrists and ankles of a man who had been beaten by the water so often for so long that each and every blast of the cold sea left terrible bruises and lesions, like he was being punched and cut by an angry mob.

The man was nearly naked, dressed in rags that may once have been garments, but were too far past their structural integrity to know for sure. Long blonde hair hung from his bowed head, and he slung upon his chains, exhausted.

His body was gaunt but not emaciated, despite the long incarceration. But behind his beaten form, there was an undeniable sense of tortured spirit.

The chains rattled with every wave crash and chill wind, and the sky brewed with something nasty sweeping in.

Malus delayed making his final selection. He had signed contracts from eleven mighty gods and needed only one more to complete his fearful number—a menacing number that would strike fear in the hearts of all those who opposed him—The Thirteen.

Malus kept the last contract open for reasons known only to him and chose the final member of the deka-tria based on a trait that was unrepresented by the other eleven: insanity. They needed a weapon. They needed a wild card. They needed a sadistic killer.

They also needed something *more*...

Loki presented a very interesting component to Malus's plan. During the War of the Gods, the Norse pantheon had bound together and survived. Among them was the most powerful Seer ever known. Frigg was not a prophet nor an oracle, both of which gave their answers with deference to higher powers. A Seer only saw what was asked of them, and if controlled, could reveal everything. Seers were rare and had more power of "sight" than any other. Thus, Loki became the key piece to Malus's Thirteen. He was the catalyst to bring an end to the

Norse gods, the only remaining gods on earth who could stop Malus's plan and bring him a valuable commodity: the Seer he so desperately needed.

"Trickster," Malus greeted him. He stood upon the rocky shore, facing the salty spray crashing against the pillars. He took note of the skeletal remains of a large snake at his feet. It was said that Loki tricked the blind god, Hod, into throwing a spear of mistletoe at the beloved god Baldur, killing him. For his crimes he was chained to three pillars of stone, with a serpent spitting poison upon his head. There he would remain, unable to break free until Ragnarok, the end of it all.

Moments passed before Loki began to move, raising his head to pin a beady eye on his new tormentor.

"Have you come to take a piss?" whined Loki.

"I've come to make an offer," Malus suggested.

"Ugh, you *have* come to take a piss," said Loki to himself.

"I can free you. Help you get revenge on your kin. I can offer you anything you want."

"Piss off!"

Malus smiled. "I thought you, of all gods, would want to play a pivotal role in something transcendent. I'll just find another trickster. Hermes. Kalulu. Maybe Puck."

"Oh fuck, Puck," Loki grumbled as the wind whistled.

"May you enjoy your solitude," said Malus, leaving Loki chained and alone.

306 A.D.

Malus returned a century later to offer the deal to Loki once again. In addition to freedom and help with destroying his kin, Malus offered Loki his choice of Divine Devices, plus a chance to continue his mischief, unabated, forever. Loki answered by attempting to piss on Malus's shoes.

706 A.D.

When Malus returned a third time, five hundred years after their first meeting, Malus offered him nothing. He stood before Loki and stared at him from behind a pair of dark tinted sunglasses. When it appeared as if Loki did not care to acknowledge him, he turned and walked away.

"Offer me that fancy ring and your lovely name, and I'll consider," said Loki before Malus disappeared from sight.

Malus turned and approached Loki with a wicked smile.

"Neither my ring nor my name are being offered."

"That is what I want. Take it or leave it," said the trickster without lifting his head from where it hung.

"I will not be coming back," said Malus, as he meant to leave the Trickster forever.

"How about a wager?" offered Loki.

Malus stopped his advance. Without turning, Malus asked, "What kind of wager?"

"I'm glad you asked." Loki perked up. When Malus turned, Loki was no longer chained, but sitting upon a nearby rock, an unnaturally wide smile spread from ear to ear. Placed on a rock beside him was an arrangement of goblets, two sets stacked thirteen high and filled to the top with wine.

"If you, fine sir, can juggle more goblets of wine than I, without spilling a single drop, I'll join your little crew, sign up here on the spot," said Loki mischievously.

"And if you win?" asked Malus.

"I'm glad you asked! If I win, I get that pretty ring and that gorgeous name of yours," said Loki, who immediately hopped to his feet and strode over to Malus, reaching for his hand to inspect the unique jewelry. "What's it do?"

"It keeps my finger warm," said Malus, retracting his hand.

"Sure it does."

"You first," said Malus, who gestured politely to the goblets.

"I will try my absolute best not to set expectations too high." The trickster stood next to the rock with the piled goblets, took two and began juggling. After he was in a rhythm, he took two more, and before long he had successfully added seven additional goblets. Maybe it was a trick of the eye, but it almost appeared that he had an extra set of limbs helping him. The wine swayed to and fro but did not spill, not a single drop. When Loki reached for his tenth goblet, he tossed it into the air, cycling it into the juggle. Around and around all ten goblets rotated, until Loki suddenly grabbed the tenth and dumped its contents into his mouth, letting the others crash to the ground, spilling the wine across the rocks. "Ten is a difficult number to top. Are you sure you want to even try? I'll take the ring, your name, and let you live with pride intact."

Malus did not answer.

He approached the rock and grabbed the nearest two goblets, then inspected the wine within. A cold swept over them like a sudden frost, so cold it froze the wine within the goblet, as Malus began to juggle. He added two more with difficulty, soliciting a fake smile from Loki. Malus then grabbed an additional nine and tossed them one at a time into the shuffle, while the other four continued to juggle on their own.

In all, thirteen goblets danced in the air in front of Malus, all of their own accord—or at least, that was how it appeared. Malus had summoned the dead to complete the task, using phantoms to trick the god of deception.

The look on Loki's face was damning. Pure rage boiled, turning his cheeks several shades of red. When an eruption of anger seemed inevitable, Loki merely took a deep breath and corked it up nice and tight.

"Well," said Loki pleasantly, holding his hands into the air, "I lost fair and square." He dropped his hands to his side and looked rather befuddled. "Tell me, stranger, who are you? What is the name of the talented man I have wagered to strike a deal with?"

"Malus," he said, holding out his hand. Loki grabbed him around the forearm, and Malus returned the gesture.

"That's all I needed to know," said Loki, smiling wickedly.

XXVIII

tricks

TONY
Somewhere...

Tricks.

Live long enough, you'll pick up a few along the way. That's how it was with bygone angels, except our tricks were a bit more twisted than your run-of-the-mill card and parlor tricks—the kind you learn to impress girls at the bar in your mid-twenties, like Marshall and his knot trick. Some of us used names to hide our true identities, while others mutilated and transformed themselves into monsters, like Thanatos and Mammon, to terrify their victims, and to bury their past behind them.

I'm not exactly sure where I belonged on that list. I've kept the same name since *birth*, and though some styles have come and gone, reinventing oneself in different ways was merely one of the many things we did as humans.

When I was a kid, I never thought I'd be the leather jacket-wearing type. Some identities are stolen, but I found mine after I met her—I found mine after I met the One. God. The Omega.

Jaycie.

Only, I'm not human, so I suppose my only trick was the one I pulled on myself when I fell from grace, obscuring my own true identity. The further into this mess I traveled, the more I learned, but I still didn't know who I was, originally.

True love, like the kind I had with Jaycie, doesn't just go away. That kind of love doesn't forget. Losing her the way I did, there was no way to recover. The heart and the mind close off to anything else but the sincerity it had found. There was no moving on from that.

Only, I'm an angel...*was* an angel—the Raptor, the *thief*, whatever that meant—and that kind of love, like what I had with Jaycie, wasn't meant for me and my kind. At least not here. At least not with a human. Whatever was my *crime*, the one that connected me to Jaycie—the Omega—my dead fiancée—my suddenly alive fiancée—otherwise, somehow, incredibly known as *God*—I know that *crime* was part of it. I was an angel who did some effed up shit, and now I was here with all these past lives jammed into my head, searching for answers and ways to piss off the pieces of filth that tore my life apart and stole everything from me.

Then there was this wild-eyed god before me—the trickster with the big dick-hammer he was waving around to prove his manhood. He was one of them. One of the Thirteen who took Jaycie, and wherever the key had dropped us—in the middle of this snowy clearing—I was a long way away from her.

Sometimes, you can be so close and still so far away.

Then.

"Ms. O'Neill?" said the bartender. "You go on in fifteen minutes."

"Thanks!" She was nervous. Her hands were shaking and clammy, and I could tell there was something going on behind her eyes.

"Are you okay?" I asked.

We were in one of the largest bars I had ever seen inside what appeared to be an abandoned warehouse in Philadelphia. Roman took Jaycie as his client and got her a gig two hundred fifty miles away in front of a crowd of hundreds—her largest audience to date. She spent all week preparing her set, recording a demo at the studio, and I saw more of her on the drive down from Mercy Point than I had in weeks.

The bar was the odd mix of swanky meets puke-scented floors, and the dimmed lights presented a dream-like quality to the room that made Saturday night feel like fantasy.

It may have been better for me if the whole night hadn't happened.

"I'm fine," she said quietly, even though I knew better. She took my hand in her's just as a big smile soared across her face. "Oh my god, you made it!"

"Of course, we did!" shouted Anne, with Marshall scooting in behind her and eyeing me up like I was a—

"Hey, stranger," he said, holding out his hand. "I don't think we've met before."

"Actually, we have," I said. "You were the guy at that place, from the time before last, with that weird thing, and we laughed and laughed."

"Ah, so my reputation precedes me," said Marshall, playing along. "Fuck you, man!"

"Why so harsh, Marsh?" I said, and the girls giggled at our banter.

"I haven't seen you in months! We had to drive a few hundred miles just to see people who live less than twenty blocks from our apartment."

"To be fair," joked Jaycie, "those are some rough blocks between us. T could get lost."

Then Anne added, "So could Marsh. There's no less than three donut shops in between."

"Ouch," said Marshall. "That really hurts my doughy, rainbow-sprinkled heart."

"Don't forget cream-filled," I said.

"See?" said Marshall to the girls, forcing faux tears. "He gets me."

Jaycie laughed, and even years after hearing it for the first time, my heart still skipped. I wondered if there was anything about me that affected her just the same.

"Careful," warned Jaycie, shooting me a loving glance, "he's taken."

"And now, here we are, on my home turf," said Marsh, then he turned to the bar and shouted, "Shots! All the shots, right here for my friends! Philllllllllll-ayyyyyy! I'm home!"

Everyone at the bar heard him, even over the crowd and the blaring music.

"What are you playing tonight, Jace?" asked Anne.

"A mix," she replied. "Some covers, a few new songs."

"All acoustic?" asked Marshall.

He once admitted to me that he hated acoustic music almost as much as he hated musicals, and still he came to every possible show.

He was a great friend.

"No, I have a band now," she said, half embarrassed. "Roman hired a touring band for me."

Jaycie was the kind of person who wanted to earn her way, and Roman's generosity, although suspect to me, made her feel unworthy—as if she was on the fast track and hadn't properly earned it.

"Who's Roman?" asked Marshall with the million-dollar question.

And then he appeared, as if summoned.

"I knew my ears were ringing for a reason," he said as he swooped in between Jaycie and me, parting us as if on purpose and kissed her on the cheek. "Hi, I'm Roman."

I had never even met the guy, but there he was, appearing magically as we mentioned his name like some kind of demon. It was Saturday night, and the sandy-blonde man was wearing a suit, no tie, with his shirt unbuttoned down to his navel. He was much taller than me and looked like he should be modeling for Banana Republic with scents of coconut and sand wafting from his golden spray-tan pecks and smug, silver-dollar eyes. Jaycie took notice of the change in my body language.

Over the next five minutes he struck up conversations with Jaycie, Anne and Marshall, but left me out. I couldn't tell if it was on purpose or a figment of my imagination, but I was doing my best to remain calm. I ended up ordering another drink from the bar, then bringing Jaycie her pre-show bottle of water.

When I handed it to her and said, "Hydrate," Roman put his hand into my chest as if to prevent some nefarious transaction from taking place.

"Who the fuck are you?" snarled Roman.

Jaycie saw the flicker in my eyes—my temperature spiked, and the last four months of rockiness between culminating into something she couldn't afford to transpire. She knew the look and reacted to defuse the situation before something bad happened.

"This is Tony," she said.

She didn't say, "This is my boyfriend."

She didn't say, "This is my lover"—"This is my fiancée"—or "This is my the man who has my heart." I was just "Tony" without any of the context to give a man who put his hand into my chest to protect her like I was some crazed stalker or worse.

"Oh! *This* is Tony?" he said, surprised. Maybe the others didn't pick up on his tone, but it seemed to suggest that he was horribly underwhelmed. Then came the smirk—this shitty smirk that spoke whole smug phrases, like "Oh, is this my actual competition?"

When he held out his hand and said, "Put'er there, fella!" I froze—I didn't want to touch him, even though I knew I had to play nice for Jaycie's sake.

When I reached out to take his hand, Jaycie's drummer tapped her and Roman on the shoulder, and Roman retracted his hand like the false offering it was.

"Hey, sound check," said the drummer.

"I gotta go," said Jaycie as she spun away with Roman following her onstage, his hand slipping onto her lower back as he led her away.

"Break a leg!" shouted Anne after them.

"What the fuck was that?" said Marshall. He spun around once to emphasize his exasperation.

"What do you mean?" asked Anne, in a way that suggested she had no idea what had transpired—or at least was oblivious to Roman's territorial pissing contest.

"That man," said Marshall, "is a shark in yuppie clothing."

"Oh, stop," said Anne, smacking away his words as if they stank. "He seems nice."

"Seems?" I grumbled, even though I was hoping to stay out of it. I didn't want to show how much it bothered me, especially when I knew it would somehow get back to Jaycie.

"Annie, baby," said Marsh, "men like that are after two things, and two things only—money and sex—and he's identified both those things in our talented redheaded friend."

"Stop!" said Anne. She looked like she had just thrown back one of Marshall's shots that had yet to be delivered. "How do you know? You only just met him, and that's such a blanket statement."

"Oh, absolutely," said Marsh, as if she had served him up exactly what he had hoped to hear. "You won't comprehend that we're right until you've already been under that guy's sleazy blankets." She scoffed, and Marsh continued. "The truth is always in a man's eyes. They're portals to the soul. Mine say I'm a fun donut aficionado who makes love like a tiger."

"Nice," I said, "I believe it."

Anne laughed.

Marshall continued, "Tony's say he loves his woman and has a good heart."

Anne gave me a puppy-dog frown, and put a hand onto my shoulder, just as our shots came up. Marshall downed his shot moments after it touched the old wooden bar, then looked up and finished his thought.

"That guy. That guy with his Naired body and country club suits—his eyes are all about conquest and tricks."

Now.

The trickster god had the same look in his eyes—conquest and tricks. A wild card.

Loki and I stared each other down. We had already circled twice, forming a looping trench in the knee-high drifts of snow. I couldn't sense another living creature anywhere, not a rabbit, not a bird, nothing. We were completely alone.

The clearing had formed in the middle of a thick forest with wild brier growing at the edges like vast hedges of razor wire framing the arena for our showdown. It was night, pitch black, with a brilliant moon reflecting off the falling flakes of pure white snow.

"Hey, my man," said Montoya from a place inside my head. "Are you having a stare-down contest, or what? I mean, what are you waiting for?"

I didn't answer. I mean, yes, we were obviously having a stare-down contest, but my entire concentration needed to be where it was, facing off against a lunatic with a big bad warhammer.

"Can we get started? I have a thing," I pointed to an imaginary watch on my wrist.

"No," Loki had more pearly white teeth than I had ever seen in a single mouth. "I'm buying time."

I was about to answer when I caught a whiff of mildew and fur, and the great glowing eyes of a giant wolf stalked toward our circle from the forest. The same giant wolf that stalked us in the dark hallways of Hallows Hall on the Milton State campus, the night I disappeared into time.

"You made this a family affair," seethed Loki. "My son, Fenrir, wants revenge too."

"Can't beat me alone?"

The odds were rising against me.

"Ohhhh fudge," cursed Jamaal.

"Sir, don't be a fool," Henry patronized. "This is suicidal."

"Live to fight another day," said Chappy, urging me to flee.

"No need to fight here and now. Fight on your terms, not his," added Doshin wisely.

It wasn't a bad idea, despite my promises to take the fight to them. There were only so many stacked odds that one could walk away from. I needed to stay alive. I couldn't save Jaycie if I ended up dead. With the key, time was on my side. I could pop out of here and back a minute later, in a totally different place—no paradox need be incurred.

I reached for the key and tried to make it look inconspicuous, like I was scratching my chest—only it wasn't where it ought a be. In fact, it wasn't around my neck at all.

"Looking for something?" Loki nodded to the ground between us.

Lying there was the faintest brass-colored speck, with a silver chain snaking through the snow. "How fast are you?"

My flames were stable, but the amount of available power was low. I had battled through the city streets, dream worlds, spinoff mutinous personalities inside my noggin, and through church and rooftop gauntlets. I expended mass levels of energy fighting and healing. If I fought Loki now, I'd have to keep some in reserve to heal. There would be no lightning or great bursts of hellfire—just traditional weaponed combat—and I didn't stand a chance against a giant wolf and a madman with a hammer.

"Go for the key," said Montoya. "It's the only way."

I leapt for the key, but Fenrir was faster.

His maw snapped at my hand before I could snag it. I spun, kicked him away, and summoned my flaming spear just in time to block Loki's warhammer. Loki kept the pressure on his hammer. I held his attack at bay while the wolf recovered. The power from the hammer was immense and threatened the stability of my spear the longer it stayed in contact, with sparks freckling the sky like stars. With what little leverage I had, I changed the angle of my spear, allowing Loki's own force to slide aside, then slipped away below him and retreated into a defensive position.

"I guess it's too late for an apology?" I stalled.

"Much too late," Loki trilled.

Fenrir had worked his maw into a foamy frenzy. He was larger than both of us combined, and easily ten feet long, with his black fur nearly as dark as the night.

"Which one?" I asked my brain-trust.

"Animals fight as animals do," Doshin quickly responded.

"Which one?" Loki spat.

"Kill the wolf," Doshin finished.

"Well, once I gut the family pup," I said, smirking at Loki, "I'll owe you two apologies."

Fenrir jumped in my direction. I nearly had liftoff, like a frightened cat, but leapt back. Each and every muscle fiber was wound tighter than titanium cable. I was wound up like a lion on catnip.

"Are you sure you want to fight?" asked Loki. "If you're feeling the need to apologize, perhaps you should offer your head instead?"

"No, no," I replied. "Can't do that."

"Good," he smiled. "Then let us be on with it then."

Loki spun and threw the hammer, Mjölnir. I deflected it with the haft of my spear. It sailed up and over me and obliterated a nearby tree in a shower of splinter and ice. The tree fell between Fenrir and me, preventing the wolf from his impending attack. Loki had followed behind Mjölnir and swung for my head with a knife made of human bone. I dodged by falling onto my back and threw him with his own momentum with some effective form of tai chi. With a face full of snow, Loki gathered up Mjölnir and watched Fenrir launch himself onto me from atop the fallen tree.

Fenrir was as heavy as six men, with waves of muscle cresting over his neck and shoulders. He pinned me down and snapped for my throat in a frenzy. I jammed the spear haft into his foamy mouth and forced him to bite down. The flaming spear burned, but the beast showed no pain.

The air suddenly trembled—a warning—I twisted the spear sharply and desperately rolled away with Fenrir attached—

—just as Loki landed, slamming Mjölnir into the space where my head had vacated. Tremors shook the frozen earth at impact and sent Fenrir and me tumbling over each other in the shockwave.

Fenrir kicked and spasmed, attempting to roll off his back where he was vulnerable, but I had used our momentum to pin him into the snow, forcing the spear haft down as hard as I could against his throat. Then I withdrew my right arm and slugged my fist into his mighty ribs with a loud crack, breaking them to bits. The beast whined, and I rolled away just as Loki's fist hit me in the neck. It was a glancing blow but sent me tumbling backward.

As I fell, Loki was upon me, slamming another fist into my gut and swinging Mjölnir. I caught his hand and pivoted, then wrapped my legs around his neck and shoulders and squeezed. His eyes bulged under the Triangle Choke pressure, and he scrambled for leverage. He lifted me off the ground and used his god-like strength to fling me into a nearby tree. I felt my left arm snap—rotator cuff rip—then stitch back together instantly.

Fenrir pounced and clamped onto my right arm, his teeth striking bone, and twisted. It broke in three places, and the torque of his twist threw me up and over. I landed with a plume of snow and kicked out my heel, snapping Fenrir's jaw.

My two damaged arms were healing, but not fast enough, and Loki knew it. The pain was excruciating, but the adrenaline kept me sharp. I had no time to feel pain.

"I'm going to enjoy this," he said, clapping the hammer against his palm.

It was time to play my ace.

"You know, you've gone by plenty of names in your time, Rumpelstiltskin."

The name surfaced when I needed it most. His touch took a long time to compute, or maybe it was just the heat of the battle that slowed my cognition. The look on Loki's face was not what I had expected when I spoke his name. Who would've thought that a creature that sought to hide his true name would have his story told to every child for four thousand years? He was hiding in plain sight!

Loki stopped his attack and gave me a nervous smile like I had reached out and tickled him. The hammer dropped to his side and he chuckled, followed by a hefty sigh.

"Golly gee," he said. "That's not *my* name. But it is quite the joke!"

"Uh oh," Montoya warned.

"How is that possible?" Henry questioned.

Fenrir was attempting to reattach his jaw and tested it out thoroughly before re-entering the fray, snapping it over and over to ensure it wouldn't unhinge.

My arms were almost ready when Loki dropped Mjölnir into the snow and fell backwards, flopping into a drift on his ass and laughing. Had hearing his true name jarred something loose inside his already deranged head? Or was I actually wrong?

"After all this time, old boy!" laughed Loki. He didn't appear to be talking to me. "Oh, you're good! The best you are! But in the end..." He wagged his finger back and forth playfully. Loki noted my bewilderment and gave me a nod.

"Two Tricksters walk into a bar." He said it like he was setting up a joke. "The first one says '*I'm the best Trickster there ever will be, and ever was. I can trick anyone, even God, just because.*' The second one says, '*Not so fast, Trickster number one, do not count yourself the best, before the game has begun.*' So, the Tricksters made a wager, to see which was best. The loser gave up everything if he lost the test. And so, they *set* upon their way to find a lovely maiden—"

An eruption of blood sprouted from Loki's bare chest, and his eyes grew wide in horror.

"While the winner searched high and low for where to stick the blade in!" rhymed a new voice from the shadows behind Loki. His heart had been cleaved in two, and his immortal life was ended that quick.

The stranger revealed himself to the world as he removed a gold trimmed helmet from his head that rendered him invisible. There was Loki, again, holding the bloody knife that had taken the life of his doppelganger.

"Looks like the cat's out of the bag!" he jeered. He dropped his helmet into the snow and took hold of Mjölnir, spinning it in his hand childishly. "Cap of Invisibility, if you must know. It has other names, but there is only one hat." He spoke like a playful Irishman, gesturing at the battle helmet. It was made of high polished metal, with inlays of gold decorating it around the places molded for the eyes and mouth. From the design, it looked of Greek origin. "I bet you're thinking, what the fuck!?" He said it playfully—more lively than the previous Loki. The god before me was much less sane than the one with the cleaved heart. "Game. *Set*. Match. I guess." Then he laughed awkwardly. "You know, Set was a good chap. A decent Trickster if I do say so myself, but he was too fucking serious. The lad was all..." He paused, then mimicked rapidly stabbing something with a dramatic angry face. "You know? You can't be the best Trickster if you've got a hard-on for blood. I mean, don't get me wrong, I love blood. I'll be enjoying yours in a moment. But to be a real, great trickster, you need to be mad! Can't be an act, it has to be real." He took his forefinger and poked hard at his head several times, leaving a red mark on the skin of his forehead.

"It's a shame really," he continued. "A shame to lose a bloke who took his work seriously. See, whilst Set was making niceties with the boss man, Malus, I was out searching for the real endgame."

"And what's that?" I asked as my arms finished healing.

"Names," he said. "You're a clever spark, you are. You know the value of a name. The power it gives you over your enemies. Do you know why the trees and the rocks don't up and kill us all?" He implored me for an answer but didn't wait for me to acknowledge his ramblings. "Because we know they're bloody trees and fopping rocks! We have dominion over them, because we know what they truly are!"

"You make an excellent point."

"Names are hard to come by, but they're as simple as crow pie to you."

"Then why didn't it work?" I asked. "Are you not—?"

"Rumpelstiltskin?" he asked, amused. "How could you confuse me with that fat little fop? He's galloping through the Unbecoming on a pony. Became part of the Wild Hunt, he is—a tiny secret whispered into the ear of an old friend." Then he looked up at the sky and smiled, as if hearing voices in his head, like me. "I've got a million names and faces. I stole that name once it was abandoned."

Then Loki smiled at me with attempted charm, while Fenrir slipped away into the woods. On high alert, I shuffled through the snow for a wider angle, waiting for the attack while dealing with Loki's madness.

"Tell me, spark. I have searched high. I have searched really fucking low. What is Malus's true name, do you know? Tell me that, and I'll let you live. No! No! Sorry! I got me all criss-crossed up," he cackled. "Tell me that, and I'll just pluck out tha' heart and spare you the torment of where you'll go if I take tha' eyes. Trust me, death is preferable. Scout's honor."

"C'mon, you don't expect me to believe you're a Boy Scout." I joked, while my eyes darted back and forth between Loki and the trees, searching for Fenrir. "I can't help you."

"No?"

"A guy of your fine trust and stature?" I said. "I'd help you if I could."

"Surely." Loki was nodding when Fenrir charged out of the woods and slammed into my back, pinning me face-first into the snow. I flailed and shook, frantic to toss the beast aside before it was too late and managed to wriggle free, somersaulting away.

WHAM!

The lights dimmed.

No.

Worse. Much worse.

Half my face was gone. Pain erupted through every atom of me. Every atomic bond was screaming in agony.

The impact from the warhammer had imploded the right side of my skull. My right eye was gone or damaged, and the voices in my head went completely silent. Fenrir's jaws wrapped around my throat. He crushed and tore over and over, his teeth raking across arteries. I kicked weakly, trying to force him off, trying to re-injure his broken ribs. I reached out to recall my spear and found my flames flickering in the wind. I probed at Fenrir's face in a panic, forced my thumb into his eye and felt it crush into the back of his skull. Fenrir whined and let go, shook his head and came back for more when my hands fortuitously slid across dead-Loki's bone knife, dropped in the drifting snow.

I took the knife and rammed it deep into Fenrir's throat, twisted, then repeated. The giant wolf was going for broke, attempting to kill me before I killed him, as it ripped at my chest and dug for my heart. I plunged the knife into his hide again, just below the jaw as it clamped down on my exposed ribs. One last attempt at survival—one last chance to buy myself another moment.

"Tomorrow's not a promise," I heard her say.

With my free arm, I bearhugged his maw, pinned him against me and used the knife for leverage, then twisted.

Fenrir's neck broke like a crack of lightning, and we fell backward into the snow and bled.

"You know the one thing that heals all wounds?" said Loki, standing above me with the key in hand. "Success. Thank you, brother. Twas a fair trade. The key for my son."

I gasped for air. My throat was shredded. I choked on my own blood. Smiling his trickster grin, he held the key over my good eye so I could witness my failure. My heart beat like a raging drum, pulsing the blood out of my wounds and seeping into the snow. My lacerations were closing, stitching away the mass trauma, but I knew the eye would never come back. I was hanging on by a single thread—and all I could think about was Jacinda, with the ocean air in her hair, along the boardwalk at night.

Who's going to hold my hand when I die?

"But," continued Loki, "I just can't let go of me daughter. She was daddy's little girl, after all. I warned you, Tony Oscuro, I'd be seeing you."

WHAM!

XXIX

necromancer

A VOICE
Long Ago...
Then.

You have had to figure it out by now, but take heart, Tony, we know you cannot speak—

> *—or see.*
> *—or hear.*
> *—or breathe.*
> *Do not worry. It is almost over.*

There were few things Malus enjoyed more than a ripened peach plucked directly from a tree. He remembered the first time he ate one, hundreds of years after he was born. His entire childhood was spent gnawing at dirty grain and rotted meat, only to experience the nectar of a peach long after he should have died. It made him wonder—how many people in this world lived out their entire lives without experiencing the sweet taste of peach? Without experiencing triumph? Freedom? Love?

The thought of Lilandra having never had a peach, or seeing what existed over the mountains, haunted him. In the many years since witnessing her being torn away from his grasp and dragged into the forest by the demon, Chernobog, he felt guilt—he was not strong enough to prevent her death. He was not good enough to save her.

He sought to rectify that weakness. He sought to undo her untimely end.

He sought revenge.

And though he had lived for thousands of years, well into the nineteenth century, it was in the far past that he found his future.

A cold wind blew across the desert. The sky darkened at midday as if a storm was brewing, and the dull roar of fury shook the landscape.

When Malus arrived, they were waiting for him beyond the walls of King Solomon's Temple, upon the Mount of Olives. Fifteen thousand warriors strong—fifteen thousand beasts, roaring for blood.

Malus had toiled for many years searching for power. He prepared, meticulously building and plotting. However, it wasn't until Malus's progeny convened with the spirits and spoke of kings and fruited trees that he was given clarity—King Solomon, king of kings was his bounty. The olive trees that grew upon the Mount of Olives, high above the city, would illuminate his destiny. The king had power—and power must be taken.

Malus's plots led to experimentation, but he could not achieve such heights without assistance. He kidnapped the greatest minds from the past. Among his many targets were historical figures—Circe, the enchantress; Doctor John Dee, the famed occultist and alchemist; Zoroaster the Prophet; and Morgana Le Fey, the sorceress. Eventually he found one that could create what he could not—Hermes Trismegistus, famed alchemist.

No depth was too low for Malus. He needed an army. An army he could control. He did not have a technologically advanced lab, but he did have magic. And what he did not have, he could collect.

The Chair of Forgetfulness had been hard to come by, but with the powers of time at his disposal through the flesh of Chronos the Titan, seizing it was as easy as slipping into the Underworld moments before its destruction.

Echidna, goddess and mother of beasts, was lured into sitting upon that chair. There the mother of beasts, slumped in a benumbed existence and birthed thousands of infernal creatures, all at Malus's demand.

As we said, Tony, there was no depth too low.

Birthed and matured in the late 19th century, then positioned into the past—this was how Malus amassed several generations of monsters at the same place and time.

Black magic and experimentation left Echidna in a state of perpetual pregnancy, from conception to term within days. It was this sorcery that mutated the offspring into the aberrations they became—the perfect warriors for mass destruction.

But to call them mere warriors was like comparing a sow to a minotaur. Fourteen thousand beasts, birthed by the mother of monsters herself—each the dark and twisted body of a man with not just one head, but three—all of them venomous vipers with scales, fangs, and forked tongues. They were the first of their kind—half man, half hydra.

The final thousand were comprised of possession—dark souls who offered up their services to imp and demon alike, then conscripted them into service with the promise of slaughter.

An army of fifteen thousand, as well as surprises should the great King Solomon defend as he must.

Sitting upon black stallions, fitted from head to toe in war armor and helmets, were Malus' generals—the reanimated dead constructed from the flesh of many. Inspired by an author, many years into the future, and made into reality by alchemical practice, using the panacea from a Philosopher's Stone. Their only orders were to kill everything that stood in their way.

Malus carried no weapon, nor armor—only the Cap of Invisibility, stolen from Hades before its fall, rested under his arm. There he wondered, *"How long would it take for the King to see the army at his gates?"*

King Solomon, the famed ancient king, was at the center of many religions. He was purported to have seven hundred wives and three hundred concubines, and he mined over five-hundred tons of gold in the thirty-nine years he reigned as king in Jerusalem, though these were meaningless statistics. King Solomon was known as a magician, a necromancer, an exorcist, a sorcerer, and a prophet. Solomon was rich beyond human understanding. His palace was adorned with polished copper, and his treasure was rumored to be kept in a great vault below ground, with tunnels that wound their way deep into earth—a mine of great potency. He was gifted by the gods and angels alike, given magical tools and Divine Devices of untold power. He was gifted with slaves of myth, and keeper of the Ark of the Covenant, the destroyer of Jericho.

Solomon lived an extended life, nearly sixty years at a time when mortality was hiding behind every scratch or sniffle. This was but one of the many blessings he received. His beard was uncut to honor his long life and was streaked with whites and grays, braided, bound, and adorned with jewelry. Around his neck hung amulets and trinkets of untold value. Equally decorated were his hands: a ring worn upon each finger, some fashioned with two. A decadent crown rested upon his brow, carved with arcane symbols, inlaid with jewels, and trimmed with copper and silver. It was the highest crown of the land, the most revered, and certainly, the most feared.

King Solomon, aging as he was, knew this day would come, for it was whispered amongst the demons whom Solomon bound to service. When one rises so high, there were always threats, lurking to topple and destroy.

Eventually, all kingdoms fall.

An emissary was sent to hear Malus's demands, and he sent the emissary back to his king without bones. The messenger arrived on his horse, a pile of living flesh without structure. It was a message that Malus was unlike anyone who had ever threatened the king.

When the horns finally sounded, the infernal army charged, and Solomon's archers unleashed their bolts from the safety of their walls.

Malus's generals led the charge as the hydrandras—half-man, half-hydra—sprinted with exceptional speed, keeping pace with a mixture of upright, two-legged dashing and four-armed galloping. They rushed the walls like apes, snarling, hissing, and spitting venom.

A wall of bolts rained upon them, but few fell. Hydrandras, by design, were tough to kill. Each was gifted with two hearts, three brains, and leathery thick skin. Destroying one with a single strike was nearly impossible. The first hydrandras to reach the city wall scaled it with ease, like insects. They swarmed the city, breaching the walls with little resistance.

Men screamed, cut down by the raiding beasts when concussive blasts shook the ground. Arcane magics ignited in fiery plumes of destruction, tossed by Solomon's Sorcerer Guard down into the turbulent battles below. The hydrandras breached the first gate and retracted the trellis, and then Malus's generals led the attack into the holy city within.

Yet beyond the outer wall was yet another wall, and another—each layer ascending to the next—to the very top, where the king of kings commanded his legions. The palace was immense, and at its center was the Temple of Solomon overlooking the vast desert beyond. That temple hid the king's holiest of holies.

When the gates were opened and the battle commenced within the walls of Jerusalem, Malus approached the palace alone. He finished his fruit and stowed the pit into his pocket, then gently placed the Cap of Invisibility upon his head and vanished from sight.

From his perch, Solomon observed whole battalions slaughtered despite their overwhelming number, and yet he grinned like a man with a secret. With a gesture—when the dead had outnumbered the living—Solomon unleashed his secret weapon. The slain rose from the ground, dead, blood soaked and broken, and re-engaged in combat. Even the expired hydrandras rose and fought against their brothers.

The dead fight differently than the living. They have no concern for health or self-preservation. They attack with a wild recklessness, and do not feel pain. They would be the perfect soldier if one could only control them.

The Djinn, magical creatures born of fire, were summoned by Solomon and entered the fray with damaging results. One of the Djinn called upon the sky and formed a spinning twister of wind and sand, which eviscerated all within its winding path. Another called upon confusion, pitting hydrandras against themselves, doubling Malus's losses within moments.

Chaos reigned on the battlefield, and magic was changing the tide.

Malus needed time. He cared not for how many died. He was there for one purpose. As the dead piled high, Malus unleashed his final move.

A second wave of attack came from outside the walls. As the Djinn entered the battle and lit the ether with magical energies, great roars ripped through the skies. Down upon the battlefield came four winged beasts, each of them various mixtures of lion, bat, scorpion and human. A manticore, an agathodemon, a chimera, and a sphinx: beasts that devoured magic as easy as chewing and swallowing the dead. They came to Malus's aid, each conscripted with the promise to feast on magic.

The agathodemon flew directly into the mouth of the twister, down into the heart and swallowed the djinn whole. The sphinx purred and savored the magic directly from the air, breathing in its vapor like opium, while the manticore gnawed on anything that moved. The chimera waved its mighty scorpion tail and destroyed a dozen of the risen dead, who, broken and destroyed, rose all over again, attempting to restrain the beast before it could escape back into the skies.

It was bedlam.

Solomon retreated alone to his sanctuary and unwittingly locked himself in with the creature who came for his treasure. Malus allowed the king to settle his nerves as he paced back and forth, praying for salvation with every rumble and crash.

Leaning against a nearby pillar, Malus removed the cap and became visible. He set it down on the floor at his feet. "It was rumored that King Solomon was the most powerful man that ever lived."

Solomon startled with a mighty yelp.

"Why have you come?" whimpered Solomon.

Malus took two steps toward Solomon and watched the old man tremble. "I've come for your most precious possession."

"You cannot have the Ark of the Covenant," said Solomon. "The Host will smite you before you leave this place."

"Bah!" he scoffed. "What need have I for Commandments? No, good king, I am after your ring."

The king looked at all ten fingers and noted the many precious metals and jewels. Altogether, the king owned twenty-four different rings, all with their own unique entitlement, providing him dominion over many things. One such ring, Tony, bestowed upon its wearer the right to water from a holy well, which Solomon dispatched servants daily to fetch for his bathing. That well could have quenched the thirst of a hundred villages across the desert. This man was considered holy, yet *we* are considered evil? Oh, how the world is upside down…

"I have many rings—" Solomon replied.

"The one upon your left ring finger," interrupted Malus, "resting closest to the large knuckle. The one you wear below your wedding ring symbolizing your thousand wives and concubines. I find it interesting you hold that dear ring in more esteem than your own wives, albeit fickle wives, married to abusive power. I would imagine just one of them could have brought you the kind of happiness you could have held above and beyond all other things, but one is never enough for men of power. There is always something else to have. Something else to own. Something else to control."

Solomon peered down at his favorite ring. "That ring has more power than you are willing to use. Give it to someone who will."

"I cannot. I will not," Solomon replied as he hid behind his throne.

"Then I will cut it from your unwilling hand, dear king," Malus threatened.

Backed into a corner with no escape, Solomon called out, "Dgen, Dschin, Jaini, Jann! Protect your king!"

Four discharges of white smoke erupted around the room. Within the smoke were humanoids with eyes like raging fire and skin like scalded flesh. One was hairless, another had a finely oiled beard. A third was a woman, her hair in exotic braids, while the fourth wore a curling cone shaped hat.

While Solomon retreated into the Holiest of Holies, a small chamber beyond the throne room through a thick stone door, the four djinn converged on Malus.

"Brother," said Dgen, the hairless djinn, "you hide your spark well. Are you sure you wish to fight your brethren?"

"We are not brothers," said Malus. "Your kind were created of fire."

"And what were you created of, brother?" spat the bearded djinn, Dschin.

"Rage," said Malus, and the battle began.

Djinn do not fear their names. They trifle not to hide them. If one happens across the name of a djinn, they may be subjugated to fulfill desires and grant wishes—but that is of little concern to them. Djinn do not hide their names because if one such unlucky human were to use their name against them, the djinn found it pleasurable to torture them by twisting their wishes into nightmares.

Djinn are by definition, conniving. They can be as devious as demons and have a special taste for mischief. They are resourceful. They aspire to outwit, to trick, and to deceive. They are immortal—they do not fear time. They are intelligent—they do not fear trickery, nor treachery. Djinn fear absolutely nothing—except iron—the one and only thing that causes all magical creatures' pain.

However, their discomfort for iron was no secret—nor was its touch fatal.

It was not their true weakness.

Immortality often draws the attention of those who wish to challenge it. For a djinn, it was in their best interest to bury their secrets in the sands of time. Yet, there was an obvious, plentiful solution to their trickery. Low hanging fruit, one might say...

Most immortals forget more than they remember. Malus was no different until Mona and the spirits jogged his memory. A passage from a book he once read in an ancient Chinese library, before Solomon was born.

A secret lost to time—and Malus had a whole pocket full of them.

Dschin pounced and sunk his fangs deep into Malus's shoulder, but the Pale Demon just smiled. Dschin trembled and retracted his bite when Malus caught him by the throat.

"Did you believe I'd be so unprepared?" said Malus.

The iron in Malus's blood was overpowering. Too much iron in the blood was toxic, but not to Malus. The djinn choked and writhed under his grasp, but it was not fatal. However, what he did next was—

Malus removed something from his pocket and shoved it down the djinn's throat.

A gleaming, like a candle lit beneath the skin, flickered into a full burst of flames erupting from Dschin's chest. The consuming fire engulfed the djinn as it dissolved to ash in a flash, like tinder.

"What have you done?" said the woman, Jaini. "We are immortal!"

Malus sprang forward and took her by the throat.

"The djinn thought their secret was forever lost," he said. "Buried beneath rock, sea, and time. Like the fae, iron will burn and maim, but it will not kill. Your kind sank an entire civilization to the bottom of the sea to keep your secret."

"Inwa?" cried Jann, his hat trembling upon his boyish head.

"This cannot be!" shouted Dgen.

"Inwa," repeated Malus. "The fruit stone of a peach. The pit." Jaini squirmed under his grasp to free herself. "A simple fruit, Jaini of the Ghaddar, daughter of Iblis, your weakness is hidden in plain sight. Not all secrets sink. Some float."

"Please, lord, you have named and captured me," she croaked. "I can offer you my servitude. A bargain of three wishes in exchange for sparing my life."

"Wishes are hollow affects when granted by your ilk," growled Malus. "I do not seek riches or fleshly pleasures. I wish only for that which I cannot have and you cannot provide." He retrieved another pit from his pocket. "However, I accept—but, my dear, I only desire a single action. With your name, Jaini, I wish for you to swallow this."

Jaini, bound to Malus's wish, took the pit and swallowed it whole. A moment later, the fire she was born of reclaimed her.

"Dgen and Jann," said Malus. "Which of you wishes to be my guide?"

The luck of a djinn was as remarkable as it was legendary.

The two djinn had only a single moment to ponder Malus's offer when the temple wall cracked and the agathodemon tumbled through, enveloped in the dead. The large beast roared and shook, attempting to free its tormentors from its hide. Brick and mortar tumbled and crashed, separating Malus from the djinn.

"Pale Demon," laughed Dgen, "luck is not on your side. Are you sure you wish to follow my king? Solomon may call upon fiercer beasts than djinn."

The djinn, with all their wisdom, did not know what they were trifling with. When the gods fell, the djinn were already on Earth. They were the first celestials, created to walk the dirt and mud and shape civilization—to move primitive man from cave to hut, from hut to house, and from house to palace. They were forgotten to time. It was not absurd to imagine that they'd never crossed paths with a creature who could manifest a flaming spear.

As the agathodemon flailed with the dead, Malus created such a spear and struck down Dgen, tossing him into a pile of rubble. Then, to Jann's surprise, his silly hat tipping to its side, Malus crossed the fray between them by walking on the walls.

"Take me to Solomon," said Malus, "wherever he may have hidden."

Jann did not question, nor did he argue. Malus grabbed the helm, and the djinn escorted him into the Holiest of Holies, a room housing all Solomon's most prized possessions.

The room was empty. There were no doors nor halls that led away from the room other than through the passage they had entered. The room held a secret.

"Show me," demanded Malus.

Jann asked, "Do you wish it so?"

"Show me," said Malus, "or I shall leave you here for the agathodemon."

"My lord, I cannot," said Jann. "The djinn do not follow the king's orders for love or admiration, nor do we remain because of comfort or riches. We are enslaved. One of the many gifts bestowed upon Solomon was the right to command all pureblood Djinn and Ifrit."

It was not a trick. The young Djinn could not defy his master without being wished upon by his captor.

"Very well," said Malus. "I wish it."

Jann snapped his fingers, and every secret within the room revealed itself. There were glyphs along the walls, shallow cuts in the stone and brick that revealed many protections. However, it was the stone floor that held the true secret of the room.

A small block of stone elevated above the others mortared into the floor. Stepping upon that lever allowed a larger slab in the floor to be pushed aside, revealing a dark passage straight down.

Jann peered into the next room, where the agathodemon began to stalk toward the tapestry, sensing more magic within the room.

"Down," commanded Malus. Jann did so without a moment's waste, fleeing into the passage ahead of him.

The passage led them into a series of dark and twisted tunnels beneath the temple. The tunnels were narrow, but precise. Too clean for human craftsmanship. There were many branching corridors in every direction, but it was too obvious to spot the way in which Solomon fled, for it was the only direction that had no trace of human travel at all. There were no footprints in the soft sandy floor nor drafts upon the air.

"My lord," asked Jann, "what will you do of me when you have found my King?"

"Why must I do anything?"

"You have shown no mercy," said Jann. "Would you show mercy to me? I who have helped you?"

"When I attacked this city," said Malus, "I could have sent my army to attack from Golgotha. Breach the walls and kill many innocents as they progressed toward the temple. Instead, I attacked from the Mount of Olives. A direct attack on the palace and Solomon's Temple."

"My master," said Jann, "you spared life. This is noble. You have lived more life than I, and accumulated much more wisdom and knowledge."

"Do you disagree with my tact?"

"It is not my place to judge," said Jann, who paused as they continued through the tunnel into endless darkness. "When I was young, I was captured by an imp. The imp discovered my name and forced three wishes from me. The first was to appear human, so that it could beguile man without the appearance of duplicity. The second was for a soul, so that upon death the imp might enjoy everlasting peace. The last was to forget its troubles, and start over, fresh like a newly formed sheet of ice upon a frozen lake."

"Why do you tell me this?"

"With its first wish, the imp confessed its intentions," said Jann. "It wanted to continue to be an imp, to beguile, to cause strife and chaos, as minor devils do. In the end, the imp had wished away all that made it an imp. It became a woman, and it journeyed into the world to live as women do."

"What is the point of your story, Jann?"

"My aim is to warn you, my lord. The things we search for are often the things that change us—intentional or not, the outcome may not be that which was sought. It may be our undoing, or a new beginning. Decisions have consequences."

"How far are we from your king?"

"We are close," said Jann.

Malus nodded. "I wish for your freedom, Jann of Kashar—and I wish for you to be as far from here as you desire."

When Malus looked to the djinn with the silly hat, he was gone.

Malus stalked the king deep into the earth. Eventually the tunnel opened to a great pit, lit by torches carried by hundreds of djinn. Along the edge of the pit was a corkscrewing path that led up either toward the unseen surface or down into the blackened void toward the endless bottom. The djinn were using magic to impose their will upon millions of small creatures that chewed the rock. They were worms, the Shamir, mining the great pit for their oppressor king.

The legend of Solomon and the Shamir worm had been rumored for as long as the king held power. Solomon used his necromancer's ring to bind the demon, Asmodeus, and sent him to capture the worm.

These were the duties assigned—a demon reduced to the king's errand boy.

Along the far side of the pit was Solomon, leading a group of djinn carrying a golden box atop their backs. *The Ark of the Covenant.* The djinn were fleeing up the incline toward the surface.

Malus slipped the helm onto his head and disappeared.

When he reappeared, Malus was standing in the path of the king, wearing a charming smile.

Solomon fell back with crippling fear. He commanded the djinn to attack. As the first one approached, Malus jammed another peach stone into its forehead, killing it in an instant. The djinn's death kept the others at bay.

"Destroy him! Protect your king!" demanded Solomon, cowering from the ground.

"We dare not," said the nearest djinn.

"We are bound to you," said another.

"But must we die for you?" said the first.

"Our pact does not include unnecessary risk," spoke a third, with inked designs and symbols covering every inch of skin.

"How dare you!" roared Solomon. "I will destroy your home! I will smite the mountain of Kaf until it smolders like brimstone in the bowels of damnation!"

"Idle, impotent threats," said Malus.

"Asmodeus! I call upon thee!" shouted Solomon. He thrusted his ringed left hand to the sky as if to show proof of his dominion. All twelve rings shimmered—but only one answered. "Smite my enemy before me."

The earth between Solomon and Malus shuddered. The sand heated and glowed before melting into molten glass. A hand sprang from the glowing pool, clawed and gray, with waxy hair sprouting from the knuckles. Steam poured into the cold subterranean air as the hand was followed by a head and torso. Liquified earth ran down its massive chest and dripped from the demon in hissing globs of steam and smoke while it pulled itself free and into this world. It was naked and appeared as dense and coarse as limestone. Its head was hairless and ridged, with two great horns protruding from the forehead, just above the eyes. They twisted round each other, forming one gnarled horn that bent and barbed like thorny briar. The demon's belly was large and round, contrasted to the lean musculature of his arms and legs. Upon his head was a burning crown of sludge, marking his position as a Prince of Hell.

"Why have I been summoned, King?" asked Asmodeus, rising to full height and towering over them both. "You do not appear to be in any *immediate* danger—at the very least, a level of danger you could not *worm* your way out of." He spoke while gesturing to the millions of mining worms surrounding them, one of the many tasks Asmodeus was given by the king.

"I have an enemy. The djinn fear him, for he knows their secrets," said Solomon. He appeared vicious in the glowing light, like a madman drunk with power. "I need you to smite him, for you are bound to me and my whims."

"*Your* whims? Bound to *you*?" laughed Asmodeus. "A gift from angels, that ring. A joke. To control demons for your own selfish needs? Mere capitulation. I do not serve you, foolish king. I serve the power of the ring, nothing more."

"Then serve its power and do its bidding," said Solomon.

Asmodeus laughed. "Ah, but I will not."

The demon laugh caused many of the djinn to flee.

"You must! The ring compels you!" pleaded Solomon.

"Ah, the ring does compel me. It compels me to capture worms for you. It compels me to bring water from a holy well, halfway across the planet, all for you. It compels me to find the most beautiful concubines for you to copulate with at your precious whims. It compels me to perform many inane tasks for you, dear king. The ring is a contract. My name was assigned to it, gifted by the angel who defeated me in battle and conscribed me to you for servitude. Like all contracts, it can be broken."

"I do not understand," said Solomon, his royal robes soaking with sweat and piss.

"Very simple, dear naive King," said Asmodeus. "Thirteen demons are bound to your ring. The same ring that binds the djinn and the dead. A ring you do not properly understand or utilize." The king looked at his ring in wonder. There was so much potential power he did not understand, so much lost and wasted and coming to an end. "Thirteen demons bound, and yet you have only summoned me, a Prince of Hell, for your insipid tasks."

Asmodeus hunched over, his great belly brushing the ground, and snatched the king by the beard, lifting him to his feet. Asmodeus held him like a toy and spoke directly into the king's ear, his toxic breath stinging the king's face.

"Your ring compels me, yes," said the demon. "It compels me to act. But dear king, if I so chose to deny the ring, I may. I may indeed deny thy ring, if only for a short time. Enough time with which to conspire against you, for if you lose possession of that unholy relic, the new owner may simply set me free and void the contract."

As he spoke, Asmodeus looked to Malus, as if to pass an invitation.

"We have a deal," said Malus. Then he approached Solomon.

"No! I compel you! My djinn, help your master! I compel the demons bound to this ring!" screamed Solomon. "I call forth the dead!"

The pit grew icy cold. A spectral din fused into the air and a great force tugged at Asmodeus, pulling him towards the ground and relinquished his grip on Solomon. Something strong tugged at Asmodeus's horns, forcing him to bow his head to Solomon, who stood above him and smiled.

As the icy chill creeped in, Malus brought forth his flaming spear and drove the blade into Solomon's foot, pinning him in place. As Solomon screamed, ghastly fingers groped at him for a restraining hold. Malus drew his knife and brought it knife down upon the protective stance of the king, slashing through bone. The king's hands sliced in half. All the charms and enchantments, spells and curses held in those rings upon his severed fingers were instantly lifted, as the ghosts drifted back to sleep. With another slash, Malus severed the many amulets that hung from Solomon's neck, cutting ties to their magical imbuements.

Asmodeus sprung upon the dismembered digits, groping for the ring, attempting to seize its power for himself, when Malus slammed his knife into the demon's hand.

Malus then leaned over and snatched the ring, removed Solomon's dead finger from his prize, and tossed the wasted flesh aside.

The ring was rather unremarkable, unlike the others that glittered and sparkled on Solomon's dismembered digits. It felt heavy in Malus's hand, but not as heavy as gold or lead, or even silver. It was made of gray metal that did not sparkle nor shine. It did not smell like copper. or taste sweet like iron; it merely felt cold and ordinary if not for the five-pointed star with enochian symbols—chiseled commands that bound the dead, the djinn, and thirteen contracted demons, and enclosed within a circle carved into the broad side of the ring—it would have remained mundane. Malus slid it onto his finger before pulling the blade free from Asmodeus's hand.

"Shall I null the contract? Or shall I keep you?" he asked, looking down at the sneering Asmodeus.

"We had a deal," said the demon through rotted teeth.

"We did, but that did not prevent you from attempting to seize the ring for yourself."

"I am a demon. Seizing opportunity for my own is what we do best," replied Asmodeus.

"Yes. Indeed it is," said Malus. "I relinquish you of your contract. Go."

Without another word the demon melted back into the molten floor and was gone. No longer bound to Solomon, the djinn fled, leaving the king.

"What will you do with me?" whimpered Solomon as he struggled to staunch the bleeding without digits to wrap his leaking flesh. He had always been a man of fortune. His magical trinkets had given him power and great health, protection, luck and wisdom. Without them, he was lost.

Malus smiled, providing the king a moment of relief. Then Malus leaned in and broke the king's neck. The snap echoed throughout the mine, but there was nobody there to hear it. Then Malus reached out with the ring and ripped the king's soul from his body, testing its power for himself.

"It cannot bring back the dead," said the ghost king, appearing before Malus in a half-state of incorporeal ectoplasm. "No Earthly power can perform such miracles. Please, let my soul pass, and let me rest in peace."

"I have lived, dead king, for thousands of years. I know very well what this ring is capable of. In my hands, this ring will do extraordinary things."

"So be it," said Solomon.

It had been a full century of meticulous planning, and it had worked exactly as it was conceived. Malus had stolen his prize.

When he left his castle, his home for a hundred years, he had no intention of returning. The three bites he took of Chronos's time-traveling flesh provided three passes through time and space.

One bite to steal the ring.

One bite to travel to where it all began.

And one last bite for peace.

The Pale Demon stood alone in darkness and reached out as he had hundreds of times to slice through the membrane of time and space—but the membrane would not break. It bent and stretched but would not part. He took his dagger, attempting to saw the blade back and forth, but the pellicle could not be pierced.

"*We cannot change the past, for everything we attempt is already our present. Such is the great damnation of the Fallen,*" said an old forgotten voice, somewhere in the depths of his memory. The Fates would not let him pass. The Powers That Be refused.

He tried and tried, but to no avail. Then on impulse, his desire to arrive at a specific time and place gave way to the urgency to do something—anything at all, after all this time. When the membrane between the present and the past finally pierced and allowed his travel through, he arrived on borrowed time.

trade

MALUS
December 25th, 2013
Now.

Superstition was the disease of the ignorant.

Primitive cultures believed the sun and the moon were gods, chasing each other across the heavens, turning night to day. When disaster struck, it was a godly punishment. When crops flourished, it was the bounty the gods provided them for the sacrifice of innocent blood.

I have lived through ages of superstition and into the modern world of technology, where belief in higher beings had dwindled down to the fewest it had ever been. I wondered, what more would it take to educate the devout that their religions were wrong, and that despite there being higher powers at work, they did not exist to care or shepherd them?

The celestials had their own problems.

Religion was never created to exalt higher beings—it was about control.

With control, you could have anything you desired. Find me a man with power, and I'll show you a man who sought to control everything —from wealth to women. From chieftains and kings—to holy men and wealthy magnates—from chief executives to politicians—they were all control fanatics, pulling the strings of fate of those they qualified as poor, weak, and ignorant—like the superstitious, believing their gods of power acted in their good faith.

With control, I could have anything.

But I was not after fortune and glory. I was not after women and power. I was not attempting to enslave or sup upon the resources of the destitute. I was after something else—something personal.

Control comes with a cost. It is never absolute. Free will made absolute control a fantasy. However, when I heard of the special girl and her two great gifts—the Holy Dyad—I knew that was absolution. They were the powers of a Creator. A true God. Powers of absolute control, and I had spent every second since, moving toward that goal.

My plight was never about destruction. It was never about the end of days or anything so pointless. No, my plight was about control, and what I could obtain with it.

But not without the last key. And it was within our grasp once again.

Tony was surrounded. Jacinda was being held by Deimos and forced to watch the extermination of her anchor—the one thing that kept her spirit fighting back against our attempts at bending her will.

It was all coming to an end.

It should have been the end of Tony Oscuro.

My enemy had a talent for escaping. However, talent does not imply skill—it can include luck. Luck implies a benevolent aptitude for improbability, and with the dead at my command wrestling the spark to his knees, and four of the surviving Thirteen tearing into him with teeth and claws, it appeared the charade was finally over.

Then the spark found fortune in the most impossible of places.

The warhammer struck the four of them—crippling Dagon and bowling Astoreth and Morrigan aside. The spark was tossed into the air and over the building's ledge. I commanded the dead, instructed them to retrieve the spark—when Loki dove over the ledge after him.

Jacinda screamed and wailed.

Loki and the spark collided and fell, wrestling until they disappeared in a brilliant white flash. The key had whisked them away.

I spat curses in languages I had long forgotten.

Without knowing where, or when they had traveled, I could not follow.

With six days left, time was no longer on my side—and the impending failure tortured me with hazy visions of the past. I felt the curse of the River Styx amplifying my rage to maddening results.

Was I really mad? Or was I driven to madness—the result of a poor decision at a time of desperation?

"You always break your promises," whispered Lilly into my ear.

Jacinda wept for him. I ignored her sobs, but not everyone could stomach her tears.

"Pin thy lips, or I shall gnaw them from your face," growled Dagon as he slithered toward her, a menacing mass of charred flesh and broken bones.

"Why couldn't he see me?" she cried. To be unseen by her beloved tortured her. But without his death—without seeing the blood or hearing his shrieks of pain, there was still hope within her.

Her tears blinded her from the lurking menace as Dagon drifted closer.

"Back," demanded Morrigan, placing herself between Dagon and the girl. Her feathered hood was drawn, hiding her eyes—but the stench of her anger made the winter air damp with venom.

"Pathetic goddess of the crow," spat Dagon, his charred tentacles lashing at Morrigan's feet. She glowered at him with disdain. When Dagon finally attacked, Morrigan ripped one of his tentacles from his body, then went for his throat.

The chaos was too much. The blood rage and the anger were too much. I needed control! I needed order!

With a draw of power unlike anything I had ever summoned, I pulled from the ether every ghoul and phantom who had ever died within the city of Philadelphia and brought them to me.

Former lovers, parents, lost children, enemies and strangers: all stood up at once with the funerary glow of the dead. Ectoplasmic ruination torn from the Other Side and summoned to the world that had passed them by.

Cars crashed in the far distance—their drivers flinching at the sudden spectral sight. Women howled and shrieked. Grown men lost control of their bowels.

My power ripped the Morrigan and Dagon apart and pulsed across the city in a death wave of indignation.

I would take down the whole city in my rage. I would crush it to dust.

How infuriating to have one's ambitions constantly delayed and foiled by a creature so insignificant and pathetic, a single *cruciati*, a spark against thirteen gods of legend.

If there was any other way to extract the Holy Dyad, I had to find it, for vengeance and wrath were calling out to me. Contracts be damned, my pound of flesh was due.

"Oh, don't bother on about all that now," said the traitor's voice. Loki was standing behind me. Both he and his hammer were soaked in blood. "Brought back your trinket." He held out the bloody key, and after a beat, it pulsed in unison with its three siblings around my neck.

"Tony?" Jacinda's body went slack against her constraints. She was looking up at me for affirmation. Her entire world was spinning as mine sharpened into focus.

I smiled and released the dead from their obligation. They vanished, sinking softly into the Other Side like a gentle breeze. They quietly faded from reality and left the city's occupants in the throes of hysteria and confusion. The girl, however, was released by Deimos and fell to the ground sobbing, her body quaking with panicked distress. The blood and the key triggered an intense grief that threatened to strip her of all wits.

I knew her grief. I knew it well.

The key signified a deeper meaning between her and the spark, and if Tony no longer had the key, it was symbolic that he was indeed gone. Dead. Destroyed. A fucking pest till the very end.

Phobos appeared at my side while Astoreth glared at Loki, as if inspecting him for lies.

"Took his eyes and heart for good measure," said Loki, who dropped a bloody lump of muscle onto the gravelly rooftop floor.

"Truth or trick?" said Astoreth, peering at the flesh with hungry eyes.

"Bloody well be truth. Otherwise, I gutted an innocent fella with me bare hands for a crappy fake," said Loki, gesturing at the key.

"Murderer!" Jacinda was sobbing, but her eyes narrowed. The girl was tapping into her godly powers, preparing to manipulate the world with vengeance. But before she could act upon her ambition, Deimos's stinger eased her suffering. Jacinda's body went limp.

"That's a mighty fine trick," said Loki. "Shutting 'er up like that."

"Deimos has reset her mind," said Phobos, from his eyeless, noseless face. "She can no longer find shelter within her own mind palace. Phobos and Deimos have destroyed her last refuge. The spark's death crushed her spirit. Her hope, and her allies, are gone. The influence of Phobos and Deimos will manipulate her memories. She will succumb to the presence of the new mind we have attached. She will believe she is—"

"Which allies?" I asked, interrupting the mesmer gods before they offered too much information.

"The children of our enemy. The Onieroi. Phobos and Deimos slayed their sire, the slumber god, Hypnos, to obtain greater power over the mind. They are of no concern to you, our Lord. The sun may rise and set six times, and the girl will be ready—"

"—Well done," I said.

"The faceless mouth gets a bloody *job well done*, but not even a thank-you-very-much for Loki?" spat the trickster.

"Let's go," I demanded, when Loki stepped forward, blocking my path. The scent of his temper flared like capsaicin, stinging the back of my throat.

"I bloody well won't give you tha' key until you offer me a *thank you*. I killed the spark and got your stinkin' trinket back. I captured the Seer to start this whole plan of yours. You couldn't do any of that without me."

After a moment of impasse, Loki dropped the key into my palm.

Then he smiled and said, "Mind explaining to me why you never told us the keys had the power to manipulate time?"

"You didn't need to know."

"No? You had us feeding on that carcass. Limiting the number a' bites of flesh we could consume," Loki continued. "How do we know you haven't been gallivanting around on your own whims? Nickering off, stockpiling power and items. How do we know you ain't going to double cross us?"

The remaining members of my Thirteen stood by watching. Listening. Dagon looked mutinous for a creature missing half its face.

"Let's go," I coolly demanded once more.

"Tell me, how do we know you ain't going to double cross us?" Loki repeated.

"You don't. We're demons. We're just not in Hell."

The others were angry but remained silent. Phobos and Deimos were too enthralled in their work to involve themselves in our argument as they finished their psychic cocoon around the girl. I owned their contracts. Could I terminate them all and start anew with six days remaining?

Then Loki said, "Good point," and patted me on the shoulder.

He had no sooner stepped away when the noise of flapping wings sounded overhead—a choir dispatched to investigate the event—a city full of rising dead. Killing a few innocents were just a few cracked eggs —but a city-wide haunt? A bridge too far...

Their only consistency was to be inconsistent.

"Let's go," I repeated for the last time.

"You're the boss," said Loki. Then he stomped on Tony's heart, flattening it under his boot, and left behind the Veil. He was quickly followed by Dagon, then the others as they fled back to the caves—six in all.

Six was the bare minimum: four keyholders, and two to maintain the glamour over the girl's dangerous mind. There was no room for error.

Could I find six more fallen gods to sign my contract? Of those that still lived, who would be useful to me? Would the angels finally fight back, or would they stand down and let Earthly affairs play out as they have? What about the demons?

There was much to consider.

As the remainder of the Thirteen fled, I felt a presence at my back. A presence that felt familiar, like a dream...

"Now, now," said a voice. "The enemy of my enemy is one I call friend. But what does one call the friend of my enemy's enemy?"

It was a dream after all—a dream come back to haunt me.

When I turned there was a figure standing on the other end of the rooftop against the starry sky.

"We were never friends," I said.

"What a wasted display of power. You put all nine Spheres of Heaven on notice, and now they will see you coming. I thank you. However, you just gave the entire city the most fantastic nightmares for the next several years."

"Phoebetor," I said. "What do you want?"

I had not seen the god of nightmare since I was a boy. For a long time, I debated if my confrontation with him and his brothers was real. Even after offering a contract to Morpheus, I could never be sure. Phoebetor looked the same—wild hair, black eyes, and skin as pale as snow. He was standing in the real world, not within the construct of a dream —and he appeared *ill*.

"Aeons ago, I set you upon a path. I gave you the name of the beast that took your love, and I showed you hidden truths. Now you align with Fear and Terror? My brothers will be cross with you."

"The path was mine alone to walk, Oneiroi," I said. "I have conscripted Fear and Terror to do my bidding. You and I, however, never aligned."

"Untrue. I gave you clarity. I gave you purpose. Ours was a pact born of revenge, but, I believe our pact was not one of equality."

"You asked me to kill Chernobog."

"Indeed," said Phoebetor, vanishing. He then reappeared out of the corner of my eye. "The pact seems to have been *uneven*."

"How so?" I asked.

"With my help, you rose to the highest heights," said Phoebetor. "Well beyond anyone's imagination. And since we met, I have run into a bit of a problem."

"Your problems are your own," I said, and began to step away when the sound of galloping interrupted the flapping of wings.

"Ah-ah," said Phoebetor as he appeared before me, wagging his forefinger and blocking my path. "My problems are the problems of all. Oneiroi are the gatekeepers between the Dream Lands and reality. Do you hear knocking in your dreams?"

"I don't dream," I said. "I have not for a long time."

"Three knocks. Three knocks thrice," said Phoebetor. "You know what that means."

Unfortunately, he was right. I did know what that meant.

"In six days, it won't matter," I said.

"The path between worlds will still be there. The buried truth will always resurface."

"Then what do you want?"

"Can you hear that?" he asked. "The galloping? Have the girl change my fate."

"Sign my contract, join me, and in six days you'll have what you want," I proposed. I had vacant contracts and could use someone with motivation. The galloping was coming for him.

"Pass," grumbled Phoebetor. "You may not dream, but I still know your mind."

"Then we are at an impasse," I said.

"What a shame." Then he doubled over in pain, vomiting silver bile onto the rooftop. "I expected more from *my* creation."

It was the kind of statement that needed clarification, so I implored the dead to prevent the god from leaving. When the spectral hands wrapped around his arms and legs, Phoebetor laughed and slipped right through them.

"That doesn't work on me," he said. "The dead are the dreamless."

"What do you mean, *your* creation?" I asked.

"Without me, without those horrible dreams to spurn you forward, do you truly believe you would have risen so high? I was your inspiration. I was your dark muse," he said, looking over his shoulder. "May you inspire such darkness wherever you go."

Then he disappeared along with the galloping and left me to my thoughts.

revenge

A VOICE
Somewhere in the Carpathian Mountains
Long Ago...
Then.

It was debatable which was more terrifying: the ghosts of one's past—the things we are forever kept to remember but never to change; or the ghosts of one's present—the things we are forced to live with but struggle to change.

Both the ghosts of his past and present came together as one. They had aligned through a series of events and careful planning, and he was given an opportunity afforded to few. The past could be changed, or so he believed. A new path would be born from averted tragedy. Lilandra would live, and together they would fade from civilization and time. They would become blissfully lost to all the woes the world had provided. Everything he had done was in preparation for saving her. It was his one and only goal, and no matter how twisted he became, his means were for one end, and one end only.

The village was in flames and surrounded by an infernal fog.

Beyond the roar of the fire, he could hear them. Women and children screaming as they were being dragged away.

This was not his plan. This was not how he had imagined it. Time would not allow him passage to prevent this tragedy. When it allowed him through the pellicle of time, it dropped him with very little to spare.

Standing at the top of the hill, looking down on the village he once called home and hearing those terrible cries, he lost all sense of fearlessness. Vultures gathered to pick the bones of the dead, and the sky flashed red like blood, followed by a thunderous groan as the earth itself rumbled, collapsing half the village that had yet to burn.

A paradox, Tony. Malus and his quest to right his wrongs was beginning to unravel the very loom of our existence. Look at how far he had come, and still further to go—his very existence a threat to all.

Malus had waited so long for the opportunity to right this wrong, that he found himself unable to move. The crippling fear he held within him, had a mighty grip on his heart.

Until he heard a familiar cry.

Through the fog he dashed toward the dying screams as smoky tendrils weaved through the vapor searching for victims. He fled to the center of the village, retracing the path he'd taken thousands of times from the lake to the trough—hundreds of lifetimes ago.

A tendril lashed at him. When the Pale Demon summoned hellfire into his hands and choked the life from the tendril that gripped him around the waist, *he* began to withdraw, slinking away from the village and into the forest.

Malus was a threat to *him*.

Leaping over burning debris, more tendrils lashed to prevent his advance. With only a thought, Malus used his new trinket and rose the dead. He summoned every fallen body into service, like extensions of his own being. A familiar presence answered his call to service, but he was no longer called him *Raggy Boy;* he was now called *Master*. The dead sprang to their feet and blocked the attacking tendrils, preventing them from pestering Malus's advance.

Immortality provided Malus an arrogance—time was the one thing he had in spades, drifting from year to decade to century—but time was now suddenly running out. It was draining like sand in an hourglass, grains falling faster through the iris than the distance he could move.

How could he rise so high, obtain such power over *time* and the *dead*, and still be unable to change the outcome?

He could hear her scream.

He could hear her pleas for help, followed by a sickening snap.

Lilly was being pulled away, dragged from young Viktor as he clutched her disembodied arm.

"You cannot take her! She is all I ever had!" he screamed.

A hut collapsed as he rushed past, trapping a boy beneath the burning debris—and he remembered the pain. He remembered the scalding burn, the terrible urgency in his chest that he could not contest, and the anguish of losing her. It was him, after all. Two versions of the same entity—one at the very beginning, and the other after thousands of years. Viktor and Malus—so different and yet the same.

Malus left young Viktor behind to succumb to his pain and ran deep into the forest, following Lilly's screams. A great echoing laugh came from every direction. He remembered that laugh. It was the laugh of the black god.

Malus chased the screaming. It was retreating faster than he could run, slipping and sinking away, back to where it came.

He chased the black god from his doomed village through the forest to the Dark Wood and beyond. There were no birds in the sky nor insects fluttering. Even the fearless snakes slithered off rather than be present to the dangers of the mist. The only terrible sound in the whole damned forest were the screams. Thick bloodcurdling screams as the villagers were dragged away through the mist to their doom.

Up and over fallen trees, down steep embankments and up the

impassable sides of sheer ravines, Malus chased the trails of blood left behind.

Do you know how much blood one human can bleed before it's too late to save them, Tony? Can you imagine the absolute duress that was going through the mind of your nemesis as he chased his love through the forest?

You know. You *lived* it. You know that fear—that complete helplessness mixed with urgency to do something, say something, anything that might change the path.

Even with all the black magics he had at his disposal, there were some things that even the darkest twistings of the physical world could not accomplish. What would Malus do if he could not save Lilandra?

A random plan threaded through his consciousness—an anxious, hopeful response from a creature whose soul had grown cold and dark and was now clawing its way out of the darkness within. One hopeful plan concocted as he kept pace—his hope, his toxic hope that lasted thousands of years, would not die.

Hope was a parasite hiding away until desperation brought it screaming out of darkness. Hope was a fallacy for those who had no control. Hope was a ridiculous notion of the weak, a crutch, a silly whim of the meek.

Hope was all Malus had left.

Would he grab her and use the power of time gifted to him from his last bite of Chronos's flesh, whisk her away across time and space to the castle? Or could Malus challenge time altogether and take her into the far future—a place he had ventured only once before, where they had remedies and technologies that could save her.

The fog navigated to purposely antagonize, twisting and diving through obstacles, challenging him. The mist did not relent, but neither did Malus, and eventually the mist began to narrow. Once an all-encompassing blanket of fog, it was reduced to a constricting current being funneled through a hole in the earth.

There were dozens of villagers, all of them dragged one by one into the hole—some went screaming, others beaten to a pulp, towed into the darkness without the fight to survive. The hole —like an anthill—a mound of dirt and rock created by something that had surfaced from below. It was wide enough to take a grown man, one at a time—providing Malus the opportunity to close the final distance.

The tendrils swiped at him, breaking saplings in half. A final defense as Chernobog made his escape.

And then, Malus spotted her—the last villager taken.

Lilandra was dirty, ragged, and beaten. She had been dragged through the forest for miles, up the side of a ravine and through underbrush that cut and jabbed her body relentlessly. When he leapt for Lilandra, she was being swept up the side of the hole. She dangled at the edge just long enough for Malus to catch her by the waist and dig his booted heel into the ground.

He would not let go, not now, not ever. Thousands of years and he would not let go, not then, not now, not ever. Their eyes met as he held her close and refused to let go—by sheer will alone, he'd break the world in half if needed, but he would not fall, he would not fail.

A tendril of mist snaked around Lilandra's legs and waist, yanking hard enough to throw Malus off balance. He stumbled forward but regained his leverage. Malus reached out through the ring and probed for spirits, for the dead to come and help, but there was nothing. The Dark Wood was abandoned.

Malus had sacrificed. He had murdered, tortured, and slayed gods and kings, then procured the most powerful item on the planet, and still, he was helpless.

Lilly was in and out of consciousness, her pain leaching all her strength. Her arm was torn, flesh shredded between shoulder and elbow, dangling helplessly like a torn hose flowing with blood.

"Please, help me." Her voice was like a long since lost tune.

"I'm here, Lilly. I'm here," he whispered.

"Don't let it take me, Viktor, please," she pled—her eyes distant, watery. He tried not to panic. He tried not to worry. His mind quickly assessed and reassessed.

Where was divine intervention?

Another wave of tendrils lashed at Malus, opening wounds on his arms and legs, attempting to sever his grip. He roared in pain but did not relent. He could not.

"I won't ever let you go" The burning in his arms and legs weakened his grip as more tendrils erupted from the hole and grappled with Lilly's body, crushing her hips with an audible crunch. He fought, and he fought—panicked and frantic—but when her lung collapsed and she could not breathe, he realized the truth.

There was no divine intervention coming. It was just Malus, and he had no options left.

Malus had toppled the underworld, he'd defeated gods, and through it all he learned many things. Chernobog, the black god, consumed souls— and if the Fates did not allow him to change this outcome by letting him split the pellicle of time to avoid this tragedy altogether, he would get no other chance. This was it. If he let go, Lilandra would be lost forever.

When every choice was damned, Malus made the only decision he had left, based on the lesser of all evils. A horrible choice he was forced to make.

He held Lilandra with one arm as he freed the other, pulled his blade from its sheath, and immediately slashed Lilly's throat. As the blood drained away, the tendrils fought back, lashing at him wildly. They broke bones and opened gashes on his back, arms and legs, until finally, it released her after one last mighty tug.

Chernobog could not consume the dead, and thusly discarded the soured fruit.

As Lilly gasped for air, Malus cried. He wept for her. He wept for his impossible choice as the last remnants of the mist drained away into the hole and disappeared.

"I'm sorry, my love," he said, holding her. "I promise, I'll find another way. I promise I will. I promise."

"Who...are...you?" she whispered.

She did not recognize him. In her last moments, Chernobog had stolen from her the last remaining memories of Viktor— all that was left.

She passed as he wept.

Then he bound her soul to his ring.

Malus buried Lilly at their secret spot in the forest, then left, never to return.

Somewhere...

When one wanders, time tends to flow speedily downriver.

It took many years, but eventually Malus caught the trail of the black god.

Chernobog left a swath of destruction as he moved, but always disappeared underground only to resurface again and destroy. Villages were torn apart and refugees migrated to find new homes. A series of ancient underground tunnels connected the villages, but Malus could not catch up to the destruction. He was always one step behind.

The Black God moved from the Carpathian Mountains to the North Sea, into the land of the Gauls, then across the Celtic Sea to the land of the Druids.

Then it disappeared.

It was a very long time before Malus found his trail again, across the sea in a world that remained mostly undiscovered at that time. There, Malus followed a drifting unnatural mist through the forest, and to the top of a waterfall, where it disappeared. Malus could smell the smoke from the primitive village in the distance and heard their cries for help when the mist dragged innocents to their doom. The natives called the river that flowed over those falls the Mkateewa. It meant "black" in their language, and that was not a coincidence.

Malus strolled to the edge of the cliff and looked down at the water crashing into the rocks below. He would have his vindication or die. There was a large white stone sunken into the grass in the clearing, and upon that stone was a carved spiral. For thousands of years man had come to incorrectly assume its meaning. Upon witnessing the twisting tendrils of the black god, it became obvious what the symbol stood for.

There, somewhere in that clearing of grass overlooking the valley, was a secret. Malus called upon the dead, and several voices spoke as one.

"In the earth," they said in unison, pointing toward a sunken spot a short distance from the rock, as if a cavity below had crumbled.

Malus commanded the dead to dig and eventually found a tunnel beneath.

With vengeance near, Malus summoned a flaming sword, then stalked through the dark passageways. Down a seemingly never-ending set of stairs, he descended into the deep dark below, lit by the flame of his sword. At the bottom, he found the bones of two long-dead sentries and called upon their spirits to aid his hunt. Together they led him into the underground labyrinth, a city built by a civilization more ancient than any he had ever seen, past dead ends and traps, around false floors and into a large empty chamber.

"What was this place?" he asked the sentries.

"This was the dwelling of The Old Ones," one said. "Once ruled, now gone."

"Who dwells here now?" asked Malus.

"The Crawling Chaos," said the other.

"The Faceless God," said the first.

"Where is this chaos god?"

"Gone," said the other. "We perished awaiting its return."

"Where did it go?" he asked.

"Beyond," said the first.

Through the labyrinth they passed great monoliths carved in the likenesses of strange ancient beings from another world, and through rooms filled with technology that even he could not decipher. He saw many wonderous things, but none of them slowed his pace—nothing could deter his wrath.

The sentries led him to a final room. Its caverned ceiling was so high that the light from his flaming sword could not reach it. There was an altar carved of rock and graven faces chiseled into a great archway. There were many souls within, lost in slumber, sacrificed to ancient deities. In the back of the room was a patch of black smoke resting in the darkness. Malus released the sentries, allowing them to slumber once again, and faced the black god alone.

Malus could feel eyes upon him, but Chernobog did not move. The Black God did not fear him.

"Do you know who I am?" asked Malus.

A long silence fell.

"The boy." The god's voice was like rumbling wind.

"Then you know why I have come."

"Vengeance."

A series of smoky tendrils darted for his head. He dodged by leaping to the near wall and swatted them away with his flaming sword.

"You killed the woman I loved," accused Malus.

"No, I did not. You killed her."

Several tendrils snaked through the air, forcing Malus to leap from wall to wall, slashing at them as he soared across the expanse.

"You gave me no choice," said Malus as he landed on the floor. "I took her before you consumed her."

"I took what was mine."

"No, you took what was mine," growled Malus, and her ghost appeared beside him.

"Where am I?" asked Lilly, then gasped at the sight of the dark room and the strange man next to her—she was *gasping* at *Malus*. "Who are you? Leave me alone!" Then she ran to the corner and cowered, afraid of *him* as if *he* was the *demon* in the room.

"You took her from me," said Malus.

Chernobog's tendrils attacked once again, slicing into Malus's side.

As the wound stitched together, he dodged the rest by retreating several paces.

"I murdered the White Stag," said Malus. "I opened the door that let you in. It was my mistake that brought my own suffering. I plan on rectifying that mistake with your head."

The Black God laughed.

"Of all the Thirteen, they send you?" growled Chernobog with a hint of fear, still shrouded in smoke. "No. Clipped and decrowned, you are no angel. No, you are not with *them*. Power you may have, but you are no deity. Mine is power directly from the Old Ones. Mine is power gifted to me at creation."

You might be wondering, Tony, about the Thirteen. Who were the original Thirteen? And why was Chernobog frightened of them? That is a mystery you must uncover for yourself…

When the smoke parted, striding forth from the center of the mass was a humanoid creature, its skin black as tar and as textured as tongue. Its eyes were cloudy orbs of white that swirled like milk mixed into water—an ever-shifting vortex of drifting, overlapping clouds. Around its waist was a curtain of black fabric—thick, rugged, and dragging gently along the floor. Its torso was unclothed, and where its mouth should have been was nothing but a blank space of unmarked flesh. However, resting below its chin was a gaping hole that opened from neck to navel, with circular rows of jagged teeth used to consume its victims—and from which it spoke.

"You are no Fallen," said Malus. He could sense the creature's unnaturalness. It did not belong to this realm of existence, but where? It was the kind of mind-shattering revelation that struck fear, even to Malus.

"No," said Chernobog, speaking from its great mouth. "I am an Omen. I come from beyond. I am the progeny of Calphus, The Hungry, devourer of realms, Strategem of the Old Ones," it said. "I devour all enemies."

"Since you are not of this world, black god," said Malus, "where do you go when you die?"

The hole in Chernobog's torso twisted into a smile just before it attacked. A foggy gloom rose around the god's body and formed tendrils of slashing vapor, five and six at a time. Malus lifted his sword in defense and retreated up the side of the nearest wall, up into the shadows above, where even Chernobog could not see.

When Chernobog's attacks ceased, awaiting Malus's next move, the Pale Demon dropped down onto the Black God from above, his flaming sword missing by the smallest fraction.

Malus was within Chernobog's defenses, close enough to strike with his sword—and too close for the tendrils to attack him head-on—instead, they attacked from behind. As the tendrils whipped and slashed for Malus's back, he recalled the dead, and the two sentries rose with spectral spears and shields, defending their master.

"No more amusements," said Chernobog, who summoned its own weapons—a mace created of foul gas and emerald fire. The god's other-worldliness was as shocking as it was terrifying. It was, truly, not of this world.

When Chernobog attacked, it was as fast as any creature Malus had encountered, swinging its mace with perfect mastery and smashing it into the stone floor at Malus's feet. It immediately withdrew the mace and snapped it around like a whip, forcing Malus to duck away before it hummed overhead.

With the ring, Malus urged the ghostly sentries to hold their position, swiping at the constant attack of the misty tendrils—but their ectoplasmic remains could not withstand the attacks perpetually—and Malus felt something else lingering within the room...

Every swing of Chernobog's mace was purposeful and deadly, crushing rock and sparking flame as it clashed against Malus's sword. With every motion, Chernobog advanced. Malus patiently defended, dodged, and awaited his moment—he was being driven toward a wall where there would be no escape. If he had a plan, if he had a counterattack, it was now or never...

A spool of specters, dead spirits that surrounded every inch of the caves that once belonged to The Old Ones, rose up on Malus's command and lashed out at the black god. Chernobog reeled from the powerful blast of ectoplasmic rage and psychic fury that left it shaken, opening deep gashes across its body.

The spool of spirits, having been unleashed, entered the fray and battled back against the tendrils. Some even joined the fight against Chernobog and its infernal mace. The black god wielded its mace with one hand and created a sickle in the other—using both hands to beat back the overwhelming numbers—until recalling its tendrils, requiring them for defense.

More and more of the dead came to Malus's aid, overwhelming Chernobog and suffocating the space around him.

"Kneel," demanded Malus. Ghastly hands rose from the floor and snatched Chernobog, yanking it down onto its knees and restraining its arms. The god's mace and sickle dissolved, and still he fought, scratching away the dead. But for every ghastly hand that Chernobog removed, two more sprang forth in its place. Eventually the old god relented.

The black god had never known defeat, and even then, did not recognize the danger it was facing.

"I have spent a very long time searching for knowledge and power," said Malus. "Searching for a way to bring my love back to me. I've spent a long time searching for revenge too."

"You may try, demon, but you cannot kill me," said Chernobog, its giant mouth enunciating the words with mirth. It could not comprehend an end. Its kind did not die, nor did they fear death. Malus dragged his flaming blade across the black god's rough skin, and found it created only shallow cuts that stitched together as quickly as the skin parted.

"I know you believe that you are unkillable, black god," said Malus. "You may try to take this moment from me, but you will not. I will have my revenge. I will strike you down and spit on your fucking corpse. Your reason to exist, to feed and to destroy, brought horrible meaning to my life." Then Malus stepped close to the Black God so that it could see the hatred in Malus's eyes. "Tell me, black god, did you take her love away from me? Did you feed on her memory? On the things that made her happy?"

Chernobog laughed.

In the middle of the Black God's laugh, Malus removed something hidden in the pocket of his coat—it was white, and glowed in the darkness. The White Stag's antler—Malus's original sin. He slammed it into the Black God's head, right between its milky white eyes. The Black God writhed in a sudden jolt of pain with wide-eyed terror, pulling against the ghastly constraints with all its might.

It had made a grave miscalculation, for there was nothing that could kill it after the White Stag, Belobog, was slain. Every mortal fear it owned had died with the White God.

Except a part of Belobog still existed. Picked up from the burning wreckage of the village and pocketed. A piece of his past Malus took from his unconscious body after burying Lilly in the forest, and before he started his journey to destroy Chernobog.

Malus retracted the antler and quickly took the god's eyes, destroying them, but even that did not kill Chernobog. It was no Fallen, no demon, and would not die as they did. Malus hacked and slashed at every major organ, spilling foul green blood, but the creature only shook and cried out in pain. Malus took the antler and removed Chernobog's head, silencing the god for good.

The dead left Malus, having filled their service.

Cold and alone in the underground temple of The Old Ones, Malus fell to his knees within a pool of the dead god's blood.

"What now?" he said through heaving sobs. "What do I do now?"

XXXII

rest in pieces

A VOICE
Long Ago...
Then.

Malus's obsession with the Old Ones and the Thirteen had led him to many dark places. They were mysteries, erased from time. No matter how hard he searched, he could not uncover their origins. However, it wasn't until Malus had tortured an angel, a messenger named Dolios, that he received the information that would set him upon his next journey.

The Holy Dyad was lost, and a girl—a human girl—possessed it.

This is where your story begins, Tony. This is where your sins begin to pile up.

It took nearly a century to track down the information he needed. Time, as with anything, washed truth away, but a master of time could find anything—

—but even then, Malus's attempts were fruitless.

With all other options attempted or lost, Malus struck a desperate crossroad deal. It was said that one could trade with otherworldly beings, if one had currency—information, artifacts, a *soul*. There were four of them, one for each direction between neither Here nor There.

An otherworldly woman named Ms. Gray, who represented the Fae, agreed on a trade that the others found uninspired—the Chair of Forgetfulness in exchange for information. The chair he had left within his castle before he had disappeared in time.

Once the chair was delivered, placed into the center of a fairy ring, upon a hill overlooking the village of Shanagolden, across the sea in Ireland—a short hike beyond the walls of the famed Abbey of the Black Hag—Malus stepped away and blinked thrice. On the third blink, the chair was gone, replaced with an adder stone inscribed with the language of the Fae below a gaping hole straight through the stone's girth.

For centuries, the Fae had studied mankind. It was fair to imagine that they had stumbled upon our secrets and foretold our stories as folklore, as we told theirs. The Grimm Brothers wrote tales of their kind in the 19th century—this was no different, given perspective. That stone may have belonged to a larger record of earthly tales and portents of things to come, smuggled out of Fae—a worthy exchange.

It took many months to decode the language, and many more to understand a portion of its meaning. In the end, Malus was only able to decipher half the inscription.

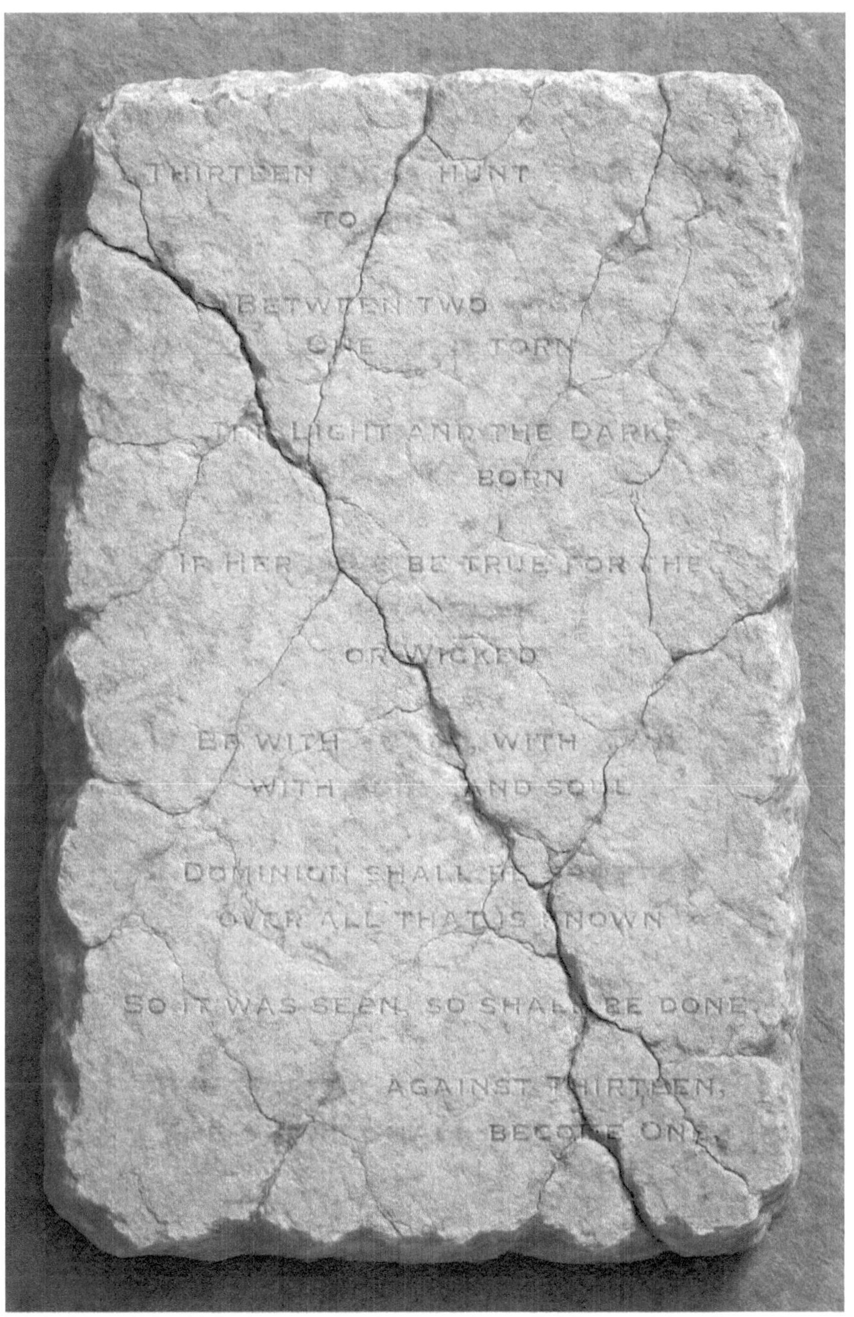
THIRTEEN   HUNT
TO
BETWEEN TWO
ONE   TORN
LIGHT AND THE DARK
BORN
IF HER   BE TRUE FOR THE
OR WICKED
BE WITH   WITH
WITH   AND SOUL
DOMINION SHALL
OVER ALL THAT IS KNOWN
SO IT WAS SEEN, SO SHALL   BE DONE
AGAINST THIRTEEN,
BECOME ONE

"Thirteen XXXX hunt Four XXXX XX XXXX XXXX.
Between two XXXX, One XXX torn.
The Light and the Dark, XXXXX born.
If Her XXXX be true for the XXXXXX XX Wicked,
Be with XXXX, with XXXX, with XXXX, and soul,
Dominion shall be XXXXX over all that is known.
So it was seen, so shall be done.
XXXXX XXXXX against Thirteen,
XXXX XXXX XXXX become One."

Once again, that number—*Thirteen*—as if it was following Malus. Haunting him.

"Of all the Thirteen, they send you?" Chernobog had said.

It was all connected. Malus's fate was aligning. He'd lived his life out of order—perhaps he had yet to catch up to his own future? A future as part of a feared number. A number that would terrify all, even the Black God.

If Dolios, the messenger angel he had captured and tortured, had told the truth, Malus would not stop until the Holy Dyad was his to command.

"If I could give you back your life, your memories, would you want them?" Malus asked aloud. She was not visible to him, but she was there. She was always there.

"Leave me alone," cried Lilly. "Please, let me go."

"If I could create a paradise, all for you, would you be happy there?"

"Please, leave me be."

"I made a promise. I will bring you back. I will create a world for just us."

Then Malus destroyed the stone, crushed it to dust so that no one could follow his path.

Malus devised a plan.

It would see him become the most powerful creature in existence—he would be a true god. He would have the power to create a new world. A world without meddling gods, angels, demons, and most importantly, a world *with* Lilly.

With the Holy Dyad, the godly powers of Creation and Destruction, he could create a new body for Lilandra and restore her memories. They would have a new life, one where they would live unfettered by the complications of Earthly affairs, and the meddling forces of Heaven and Hell.

He would create a new world for just the two of them—and only them. He would erase them all.

For all Malus's ruthlessness, his evil was just a means to an end. And when he had that end, he could use his power to strip away the rage and the evil inside his own blackened soul and return his own humanity.

It was a grand scheme, and it would not be achieved easily, nor could it be accomplished alone. King Solomon's Necromancer ring had the ability to bind thirteen demons, but Malus did not want demons. Demons were far too selfish and devious. They did not *need* him. But the Fallen—they all wanted power.

Thirteen contracts bound to the ring. Malus could reason with them, bargain with them, even trick them into contracts, binding them to his ring. Contracts they could never break without his true name.

That would be the trick.

That would be his bargaining chip.

No Fallen could refuse the opportunity Malus could offer. They would all plot and conspire against him to take the power for themselves, and while they fought each other for his name, a name they could never find, he would move closer and closer to his goal.

One by one he studied them, and when he understood their needs, their fears, their wants, Malus went to them. Most signed his contract immediately. Few resisted. None survived a refusal.

Malus started with Nox and completed the initial roster of Thirteen with the famed Trickster, Loki, each of them fulfilling a need. From the ever-present cover of darkness Nox could provide to Loki's familial ties for the plan to proceed—they all played their parts.

"She is the only Seer in this world who can give us the information we seek," said Malus.

"That bitch? She locked me up!" spat Loki. "She cast away the bloody key and left me to rot!"

His voice echoed through every room of the castle. It was the first time the entire Thirteen had been summoned, and many watched from beyond the Veil, too shy to show their faces after centuries of war amongst gods. But they were all there—contracts signed, tattooed onto Malus's skin, and bound to the ring.

In order: Nox, Anubis, Astoreth, Moloch, Xolotl, Dagon, the Morrigan, Mammon, Bacchus, Hekate, Nemesis, and Loki. Thirteen in all, including himself, with many other potentials should a contract be voided—or need to expire.

"What did you do, Trickster?" asked Nox from behind a shifting shadow that adhered to her every movement.

"Me? I only tricked my brother into killing my other brother. Fratricide by proxy is not a crime," explained the Trickster.

"Frigg's capture is the only reason I freed you from that rock," said Malus. They needed the Seer. Malus knew the questions to ask, and the Seer's answers would illuminate their path.

"If I remember correctly," said Loki, scratching his head, "I freed myself. Just needed a little nudging."

"Perhaps the Trickster needs to be reminded of his role?" said Hekate, moving toward the mad god, her white mask like a specter as it floated through the dark room.

"Leave him to me," barked Xolotl. "Acquiesce is a spell best cast when the sorcerer is angry, and I have a distaste for mischief demons."

"Who are you calling a mischief demon?" scoffed Loki. "You want me to slaughter the family? I'll destroy them. All of them. I'll bring

Ragnarok. I'll bring it tonight. Along with a firm handshake for dear ole' dad, and flowers for me mum. Welcome home, son! Oh! You betcha!"

"Do as you are told, Loki," demanded Malus.

"Or what, my *lord*?" he growled.

The others were growing uneasy. Malus could not have them questioning his power before they began. He needed to show them. Respect was not given by a god—it was taken.

"Or I'll chain you to that rock once again, without your limbs or genitals. Just a torso hanging from its neck," threatened Malus.

"Haha! Oh, that's bloody fun!" laughed Loki, and he was instantly struck with an icy cull that frosted his hair and skin. A spool of the dead that probed his softest, most sensitive areas. "Now that! That's a threat! But I still won't do it."

Loki's smile faded as he fell to his knees with the dead wrenching every nerve, making every inch of his skin wrack with searing pain.

"You signed a contract," growled Malus.

"My life and my offspring, for one goddess?" Loki growled. "If something goes wrong, I'll blame you."

"Noted," said Malus.

And Loki did blame Malus.

Loki had lost his son, the great worm Jörmungandr, and slaughtered the entirety of the Norse Pantheon with Hel and Fenrir by his side. He kidnapped Frigg, the Seer, and procured himself a new weapon—Thor's warhammer, Mjölnir.

The first step of Malus's plan was complete, even if it meant becoming the target of Loki's unending fury.

The Seer provided clues, but even with her riddles, it took time to find the girl.

Populations soared when the gods no longer controlled of the fate of humans. The task of searching the population, one by one, was unrealistic, with more than four and half billion lives on the planet in the year 1980 AD.

They knew she would have hair like fire and eyes like emeralds, and that she would be born into the great empire across the Atlantic Ocean, consisting of two hundred twenty-six million people, with only a single percent of those bearing ginger characteristics. However, they had not anticipated the ease of travel from one hemisphere to the other, or the ability for humans to change their appearance with dyes, bleaches, and other means.

And yet, there were other portions of Frigg's riddles that he could not decipher—

"She, like many others who drift toward the sinistram, is drawn to the darkness and dark places. Where two cities meet—felicity and atrocity—upon a black mirror, one reflected above the other, where the Fates fall thrice. A city you have once visited upon your journeys—where the land decays like cancer beneath your feet. Power attracts power, like flies to honey. Vengeance brings you destiny, Pale Demon."

He understood the sinistram—the girl was left-handed—but the rest was still lost on Malus and remained that way until one fateful evening when he was speaking with Lilly.

"When I have found the Dyad, nothing will ever hurt you again." He peered from his castle tower, watching over the valley below where the villagers still gossiped about the demon that dwelled within the ruins.

"You have said that before," whispered Lilly. "You failed me then, and you will fail me now."

She always whispered hurtful things into his ears. She died angry, alone, in pain, and in the arms of someone she did not know. Malus wanted to tell her how they used to run through the forest together, and how much he loved her. He wanted to tell her how he spent countless centuries searching for a way to bring her back, and how he rose from an orphaned boy into a god that defeated Chernobog, in a far-off land before it had even been discovered—

—then it struck him.

"A city you have once visited upon your journeys—where the land decays like cancer beneath your feet," Frigg had said.

Malus had visited many underground dwellings, but only one that could be considered a city and only one that was like a cancer, decaying the land above and anything built upon it.

The city of the Old Ones.

"Where two cities meet—felicity and atrocity—upon a black mirror, one reflected above the other, where the Fates fall thrice."

The Mkateewa River, where the three waterfalls were named for the Fates—Clotho, Lachesis, and Atropis—like a mirror, where "happiness" meets "horror"—one above the other.

"Vengeance brings you destiny, Pale Demon," Frigg had said, and she was right. Malus's vengeance upon Chernobog brought him to the doorstep of his destiny. Nothing was chance. There was no coincidence.

When they found the girl within the village of Grace Falls, it was in the autumn of 1986, when she was just six years old—

"She will have hair as red as hellfire and eyes of emerald," Frigg had said.

Jacinda Moira O'Neill was as advertised. Hair like the outer crimson of a solar flare—symbolic of the destructive powers within her soul—and eyes like the clearest gleaming gems of the purest green, and sometimes, when the light caught them just right, a swirl of blue like an unspoiled ocean—symbolic of the powers of creation locked within her spirit.

These were the only extraordinary things about her.

Jacinda was an unremarkable girl, even as she grew into adolescence and adulthood. She was pretty as humans could be, but she was no goddess. Her skin was randomly freckled, and she was rife with anxiety and guilt. It was unknown if her emotional trauma was a genetic flaw—her body's inability to be a crucible for the Holy Dyad—or by experience—her mind's inability to cope with her own reality.

She was sad. She was suffering through endless depression. She was lonely.

Arrogantly, they assumed once they found her, the rest would be as easy as snatching her when nobody was watching…

…but nothing was ever that easy.

The caves beneath Grace Falls provided the Thirteen a place where they could stage their attacks on the girl's mind. Frigg instructed them that they could not interfere with her life until she had surpassed thirteen years, a formal age in the eyes of the Fates, the age when innocence officially gave way to maturity—

"Seek her on the new continent in the realm of the great empire no less than thirteen years from the time of her birth. It is only then, as her biology matures, that she may forfeit what you seek," Frigg had said.

However, Frigg's duplicitous tongue spoke nothing of the angel guard that was always there, watching. But they were not alone—there were others, agents of various polarity, watching, waiting. They could not take the girl. They could hardly even see the girl without her guard breathing down their necks. Any otherworldly evil with aims to harm her before maturity would be struck down by the full wrath of Heaven. Such was the contract of innocence, one of the many that were hashed out between good and evil one fateful day in the Judean Desert.

Over time, the Thirteen tested the girl. They tested her knowledge, her wits, her ability to withstand fear and stress, and most importantly, they tested her power. They learned all they could learn, followed her lineage back to Ireland, all the way to the Gauls searching for clues—a reason as to why such an ordinary girl became the most powerful being in all existence.

They found nothing.

The Thirteen knew about her sister, Jane, and the accident that took her life, as well as the supernatural situation that surrounded that fateful day, and started Jacinda on a tortured path. Malus stalked her from behind the Veil, to and from her school, at drunken parties where entitlement and privilege in this new era took on new meaning—even commoners might celebrate as if they were Romans.

Every single aspect of her life was probed for validity and control.

Even the man she desired, Richard Jansen, was visited at a young age, and tempted with dark whispers—his soul was bound to Malus's ring long before his death.

Malus was meticulous, planning each and every step. Knowledge, as he'd learned so long ago, was power. And power was nothing without knowledge.

Strings were pulled, and when they thought she was within their grasp—*she disappeared.*

The girl found a way to use her abilities to make the world forget about her.

Jacinda's defensive gesture had a strange effect on the Thirteen. They were lost, searching for something they could not remember. Even Malus, who had made the search and capture of the girl his obsession, was now as lost as the rest of them. But like all things lost, they could be found again.

The former Roman god of lost possessions, Nataero, was found living a quiet life in the Swiss Alps with a wife and young daughter.

It was late evening when a knock rapped upon the family home. They lived an isolated life, so the reaction to a visitor, despite the hour, was a necessary one. The woman and her child rushed through a trap door into the basement, where they remained perfectly quiet while the forgotten god answered the door.

He opened it a crack to peer at the stranger on his doorstep. "How can I help you?"

"You can start by allowing me into your home," demanded Malus.

"I'm afraid I cannot do that." Nataero shut the door. He may have abandoned his life as a god, but he had not given up his godly powers. The door was blessed with an enchantment that could not be broken by magic or force.

"Yes, you can," said Malus, shoving his arm into the door to bar it from closing, "Agrobaal."

Nataero's spoken true name rendered all the enchantments on the door null, and Malus backed him into a corner of the small cabin. He was middle aged and appeared very human. He even wore glasses despite his immortal eyes not needing their aid.

"What do you want?" To his credit, Nataero was not scared. He retrieved a shotgun and aimed it at Malus's chest, all in a single blink.

Malus gestured behind him. "Outside that door are twelve of the most terrifying gods that have ever lived. I can keep them from coming within and terrorizing you, your wife, and child, but only if you help me." Malus looked to the floor, suggesting his awareness of their hiding spot beneath their feet.

"Okay," said Nataero, foolishly lowering his weapon. "How can I help?"

"There is something that belongs to me, and I need help remembering what it was," said Malus. "I am certain you can help us, Nataero."

"Please," said Nataero, "do not call me by that name."

"What name shall I call you?"

"Ted," he responded. Malus smiled and tried not to laugh. A god who lived like a man seemed a joke. "How do you know you lost this possession if you cannot remember what it was?"

"I did a great deal of preparation," said Malus. "I found myself and my allies in a distant village, with various threads of thought and motive dangling toward something that has been obliterated from our minds. I have reason to believe a very powerful magic was involved in order to hide it from me."

"How powerful was the sorcerer?" asked Ted.

"Perhaps the most powerful being that ever existed," said Malus.

Ted nodded, although he had trouble understanding the breadth of power being suggested.

"What you need is memory magic. Since your possession was of this realm, the magic needs to be of another," said Ted.

"What realm would you suggest?" asked Malus.

"The Fae," said Ted.

"I don't have that kind of patience."

"There's an elixir that could be prepared with their help," Ted continued.

"That is assuming we could make them help us," added Malus. It was beyond an annoyance to ask for assistance from Nataero, let alone to grovel for help from the Fae.

"It is the only chance you have," replied Ted.

"No," said Malus. "I need answers tonight."

"How do you propose we conjure such an elixir tonight?"

"I don't," said Malus. "The answers I seek should not be difficult for you, Nataero. There was a reason you earned favor with Zeus. You aided him in finding Chronos in the Underworld. You aided Eris when the golden Apple of Discord was lost after the Trojan War. Without it resting in the vaults of Sparta, Xerxes would have won the battle of Thermopylae."

"What are you suggesting?" asked Ted as he regripped his weapon.

"I'm suggesting the answers lie within your mind. You, Agrobaal, are the only elixir I need."

There was no way to know how many times they found her, nor how many times she made them forget. It was an elaborate game with which the Thirteen adapted, and each time, she came back to them. Malus never understood what brought her back home to Grace Falls, but with it came a fortuitous opportunity—his covenant with Richard Jansen could be reactivated.

However, Jacinda was young, and she had no understanding of the power she possessed, nor the celestial body to wield it. Strong emotion triggered her powers, allowing Jacinda's mind to tap into her abilities instinctually—and once, she nearly destroyed the world.

Or maybe she had destroyed it, then turned back...

Whatever transpired, it became clear that her power, as vast as it was, needed to be controlled. She could destroy them all before they had the chance to perform the ritual, and they needed her alive.

"To gain what you seek, you must start on the first day of a single calendar year in which the previous contained no less than two solar eclipses, two lunar eclipses, and with the rare transit of Venus across the sun," Frigg had said.

The year 2013.

"To possess the keys, you must have patience, passing through the Zodiac as the stars cycle the heavens. Then, and only then, after the full year has passed, on its dying day before rebirth, the four keys must be taken to their hidden

gates at the four corners of the earth. Eden will be revealed to the world of man when all four locks are freed, where the roots of the world grow deep."

The World Tree.

It seemed impossible: to possess the girl, transport her to another time and place, then keep her imprisoned for a full calendar year, sedately awaiting the end of everything, including herself.

It was a task that manifested dissension.

The Thirteen held secret meetings, despite Malus's ghostly spies reporting every treasonous whisper. They discussed his identity. Among his chief doubters were Moloch, Bacchus, Mammon, Nox, Dagon, and of course, Loki.

"Perhaps he is not of this realm?" suggested Nox. "When the Breach was open, many entities from other realms passed through."

"I am certain," spoke Dagon, "that he is of the Fae. His corruption has no depth."

"Foolish guesses are worthless," hissed Mammon. "We need information of better wealth."

"Are you mocking me, greed demon?" growled Dagon.

"Just because you can see and hear," said Bacchus, swirling his golden chalice of blood, "does not mean you are not deaf nor dumb."

Tempers flared, and Dagon's tentacles were bristling when Loki stepped in.

"Boys, boys!" shouted the trickster. "Leave it ta me. I'll get 'is name. I'll find it 'nd start me ring collection with 'is favorite toy."

Every unknown breeze was a set of prying eyes peeking over Malus's paranoid shoulder. Loki was resourceful, but could he dig up the past of a living ghost?

A complicated plan. An ungrateful ghost. Traitorous contractors. Despite the opposition, they were getting closer to snatching the girl with every attempt.

Alas, Malus could not kidnap her. They could not defeat her guard.

When her guard was not protecting her, there were always others—allies or foes preventing their attempts. Years ticked away, and with them came clarity.

Ultimately, there was only one way this would all end. You don't remember it, Tony. But just because you don't remember it does not mean it did not happen...

Malus staged the greatest, most terrible event imaginable. He broke Jacinda's mind. The Thirteen tore apart her sanity, her heart, and forced her hand twice—once to undo the atrocities they'd committed and the second down the path to take her own life.

And just in case she made herself forget once again, they reminded her of the path she chose—that's right—you always wondered what she saw. What they showed her in the shower—when they pinned her down and forced her head into the black bile—into that void beyond. They weren't attempting to steal her, Tony. They were sending a message.

A series of events was triggered. A mental breakdown followed. Her mind shattered and led Jacinda down a path that brought her right into Malus's lap. A gun left behind—a gun she remembered from a Remnant, a timeline that never came to be—a timeline full of destruction you averted, Tony.

There within that old decaying warehouse—

BANG!

And with her soul departing, Malus snatched it up with his ring.

The process of forcing a soul back into its body after the two had been separated was a complicated matter. One night, shortly after her death, Malus entered the Grace Falls cemetery and commanded the dead to dig up Jacinda's corpse. The dead dug the polished mahogany box from the ground within moments, and Anubis cracked open the lock.

Mammon, the god of greed, salivated as the casket was opened—the prospect of looting stimulated his arousal.

"Morticians have scientifically advanced," grumbled Anubis, "but they have not the artistry for the ritual of embalming."

Her body was wrapped in a zippered bag. Sitting upon it, glistening under the moonlight, was a diamond ring placed there by your departed pal, Marshall, who bribed the funerary director to stash it after the closed-casket service ended.

If nothing else, Tony, you had great and loyal friends—despite the suffering they endured for you.

Mammon lunged for the jewelry, and the trickster laughed. As Mammon shook in delight at having acquired a new piece of wealth—one that was owned by a true goddess—the trickster asked, "Greedy god, what have you found there?"

Mammon growled.

After the dead helped Anubis remove the body, they replaced the casket beneath the earth as the Thirteen retreated to the caves. While Mammon salivated over his precious loot, Loki fell in pace beside Malus. He flashed his left hand with the ring firmly slid over his fifth finger. "The sparklin' stone really complements me eyes."

It was meant as a warning. Loki wanted Malus to see how easily he could get what he wanted. How easily he could deceive them all while playing the part of a good soldier. Loki was, as you know quite well, Tony, the most dangerous of all the Thirteen.

"Wake up," said Malus.

Jacinda was standing with her hands shackled above her head. Her eyes were open, but she did not react—not to light, not to touch, nor to sound, not even to pain.

She was surrounded by evil. These creatures had all gathered to witness her rebirth. Some had woken from two full years of slumber to see their prize—this woman who was so difficult to obtain puzzled them.

"Is she broken?" asked Bacchus.

It took a full year to force the girl's soul, with the Dyad weaved into the fabric of its being, back into her body. Then, it had taken some time longer to make her heart beat and restart the involuntary functions controlled by her brain. There was a moment, albeit brief, when it appeared she would never live again, and the Dyad would be lost forever—but then, her eyes opened.

"It may take time," said Nox, a nurturer till the very end. She was not meant to be one of the Thirteen—sooner or later, her mutiny was expected.

"Time?" questioned Dagon, "We have waited long enough."

"The mortal body is fragile," said Malus as Dagon slithered toward Jacinda to study her close.

"This is our interest as well as yours," argued Dagon, but when Malus caught scent of his pheromones leaking into the air from across the room, he banished Dagon with the ectoplasmic arms of phantoms. They dragged Dagon out the door, down the stairs, and into the mausoleum resting below the house. He was enraged, but their prize was intact.

"All of you, leave us," demanded Malus, and the room emptied of prying eyes. "She will need water, and food."

"The town. I will steal some tonight," said loyal Nemesis. Only she could be trusted with the girl. Her interests were in violence and retribution—not in earthly pleasures and power.

"Go now. Pay for it," said Malus. "We cannot afford the rumors of thieves and terrors spreading." Nemesis nodded, then left the room, leaving Malus alone with the girl.

The more Malus studied Jacinda, the more curious he became. Was she conscious? Was she brain-dead? What was going on inside that tiny little red head?

"Let us go," whispered Lilly.

Jacinda was not his love. They were fundamentally different in many ways. But the more he studied her, the more his mind wandered, wishing for the end of their journey. Jacinda and her abilities were just another step, and he was weary of plans, of violence, of regrets and guilt. Malus wanted to be done with plotting and searching—he wanted to be finished with such vehemence that he was struck with an idea. It was not a sane idea, nor was it premeditated—it was impulsive. It was rash, and it was foolish.

Malus took a deep breath and threw caution to the wind.

"This will provide you decency," he said.

"Leave me be," said Lilandra, just before Malus placed her soul into Jacinda's body, while Frigg's words echoed throughout his conscious mind.

"To gain what you seek, she must first love you, truly. You must make her yearn for you with all her heart. Captivate her mind with all your charm. She must lust for you, her flesh to yours. And she must need you with every ounce of her soul so that there is no beginning or end to her without you."

"If I am to love and be loved by anyone," said Malus, "it must be you."

As he finished, Malus sat back and waited for something miraculous to happen.

Moments ticked. Then minutes. Eventually, and with great surprise to himself, Malus sobbed. A gut-wrenching sob that brought him to his knees. Had he lost Lilly all over again?

"What did you do?" said her voice.

It was no longer the voice of a ghost. When Malus looked up, Lilly was there, watching him with angry blue eyes. Her blonde hair was like a lost memory. Her soul had taken control of Jacinda's body, and the flesh rearranged itself to reflect its new identity.

"I brought you back, as promised," wept Malus.

"I did not want to be brought back," she argued.

Malus snapped his fingers, and her body went limp. "If you cannot remember me and the joy we shared, then I will have to create new memories for you to recall, until I have the ability to return all you lost."

XXXIII

a dance with devils and death

Somewhere...

"Tony."

Pain.

"Wake up, Tony."

Searing heat and pain. The world was gone, and there was nothing but pain. And heat. The heat was unbearable.

No more.

No more!

Please, no more...

"We have so much to show you," said a voice. "Some say it happened differently. Some say it did not happen at all. But if it did not happen, this story, and that which you already know, Anthony Oscuro, are lies before your own eyes. So, this you must know to be true: the following events did happen, and these events in history were altered to fit a narrative. A narrative that attempts to hide the truth. A narrative that evil of this capacity does not exist.

"Evil does exist. It does not come from my brother and me. We are simply here to fulfill a need. A duty. Does the potential for evil exist within us? Of course, in spades greater than most. Evil is not all-consuming. Evil is merely a part of a whole. An uninhibited preference to action of an amoral nature. But there are those who will always blame the devil for the deeds of others.

"Evil exists within everyone. It is not tangible, nor is it palpable, but it is capitulated by want. Want for power. Want for lust. Want for greed. Even a want for love.

"Love, Tony, can drive a man to evil."

And then I saw it.

I saw everything.

The voice narrated the rise of a madman and his quest to bring back the love he lost. I watched my adversary from the beginning—a young man, heartbroken and struggling to belong—grow from the Raggy Boy, Viktor, into a beast named Malus, the Pale Demon. I saw it all. What either of us would do for love.

It was hard not to question if I could ever have gone that far, and if I already had crossed a line. I called creatures of unspeakable evil down into the middle of a busy city. How many people were hurt, died, or mentally scarred over that one decision? The entire world and reality were at stake, but could I ruin it in my haste to try and save her?

"You can't really understand another person's experience," said the voice, "until you've walked a mile in their shoes."

When you die, it's instantaneous...

The trouble is you think you have time...

As the death blow comes, your life may flash before your eyes, but that takes only a moment before death envelops you. I remembered it, Loki's hammer thundering down against my head—the flash of Jaycie's smile—and then, nothing.

Nothing. Nothing. And nothing, until the intense heat and pain. How long I suffered until the voices called out to me, I do not know. When it was over, there was more darkness, until...

My eyes snapped open.

I sat upright in the snow surrounded by a pool of frozen blood. It was freezing, and my body instantly reacted with a mean case of the shivers. My teeth chattered like one of those old wind-up toys they had at the dentist's office. A fresh blanket of snow had fallen and covered me, as well as any trace of the battle that had taken place—well, almost any.

Fenrir's body was a giant white lump, well preserved and frozen, as was Loki's—although, that wasn't actually Loki, was it? The trickster I fought was someone else—another trick. Were all the tricksters in league?

"Do you cry for Set?" asked a voice. It wasn't one of the brain-trust. In fact, I couldn't hear a single one of them.

I shook my head, "no."

"Good. He wouldn't cry for you."

Then I saw the man who spoke near the edge of the clearing. He wore an armless black cassock, like a warrior priest. He was tall, thin, with long blonde hair. His face was flawless and feminine, and his eyes were a penetrating blue that made me feel uncomfortable.

I stood up and clenched my fists—I hadn't yet determined if he was friend or foe—when the pain across my scar was only rivaled by the absolute agony in my chest. I pulled my jacket aside and saw something that made me gag in horror. My heart was gone—there was a big fucking hole in my chest.

How was I alive?

"Do not worry, child. I have your heart," said a second voice. It was deeper than the first. More masculine. A large man was looming next to the ruined tree that had fallen into the clearing during battle. He was tall, and his shoulders were wide and strong. He was dressed like a ragged biker—leather, a hooded poncho, chains, but shoeless. He had long black hair, slicked back, and a tightly cropped beard over his wide jaw. His eyes were a smoldering gold, and he held my bloody heart, beating in the palm of his hand.

The two men circled me in perfect even strides, one on either side. I shivered and coughed, like I was no longer an angel.

"Do you know who we are?" asked the first stranger.

"One of his Thirteen?"

The dark one chuckled.

"No. We are not associated with the meager," replied the first. "We were *His* favorite. Punished for being too loyal to *His* word."

A chill ran up my spine, not from the cold, but from the meaning of the stranger's words. His was the voice that had spoken to me in death. The scar on my face burned, but I could not decipher its meaning. Was it warning me to run? Was it telling me to trust them?

"Who are you?" I asked. I needed him to say it.

"We are *His* most famous," said the second.

"Often confused for one, we were once three, but now two," said the first.

None of my angelic abilities seemed to be working, and I couldn't sense anything—was I in danger? Did they mean me harm? I was cold, weak, and couldn't summon a flaming weapon to save my life. I was completely helpless. I was...*human.*

"Enough with the riddles!" I growled. I didn't care *who* they were, how much power they had, and who was whose favorite. They wanted me to know their identities, so they might as well just say it.

"Gutsy, is he not?" said the pale one to the dark one. "I am the Light Giver."

"And I am the Morning Star," said the dark one.

"Satan," I said, looking to the dark one, "and Lucifer," to the pale one.

Common thought was that they were the same creature, but they were two different entities, two different fallen angels, both of which were still circling me in the dark, frozen clearing.

"Intelligence is a virtue," said Lucifer with a bright, mischievous smile. "Tony, did you know we did not build Hell?"

I shook my head, because I didn't really know what else to do. I then noticed the mark on Satan's neck, like a brand with three sixes in a triangle. It was the mark of the beast. A similar mark was branded into Lucifer's neck—crisscrossing lines that formed a V and an X. I had seen it before—years ago while listening to Thaddeus talking about his favorite vampire role playing game with Amanda, Chris, and me in his bedroom. And I didn't even need the brain-trust or Father Monaco for that juicy nut.

"The Pit was already there," Lucifer continued. "We just took it for ourselves. You see, power is given to the one willing to take it."

"The weak pray. The weak hope. The strong demand. The strong inspire fear," said Satan in his deep booming voice.

"We are forbidden from this contest," said Lucifer.

"The girl, Jacinda, is out of our reach," said Satan.

"We do not complain," said Lucifer. "The status quo is not complacency."

"We have no need for such power," said Satan, which sounded a lot like sour grapes to me. If they had the chance, did they expect me to believe they wouldn't seize it?

"However, we do have concerns," Lucifer warned. "You see, Tony, we have spent a great deal of time deciding on which horse to place our bets. We believe Malus aims to do far greater damage to our business than we would enjoy."

"Sometimes," said Satan, "it is in our best interest to lose than for someone new to win. Hell is ours. We aim to keep it that way."

"Yes, brother. Hell *is* ours," added Lucifer.

"What do you want from me?" I asked. There was too much boasting and not enough getting to the point. I was sandwiched between the two most evil creatures that ever existed, and my human body was not handling it well.

"Did you know we've met once before?" said Lucifer. He stopped walking and allowed the moonlight to strike his face at just the right angle, making him appear innocent. "John Milton wrote *Paradise Lost*, but he was no ordinary man. John was a spark. The son of a powerful Fallen and a human father. He had quite the gift for seeing things.

Events where he was not present. John was an exceptional writer but also a gifted liar. Some things he got right, but what he got wrong might surprise you.

"You see, Tony," he continued, "the famous story of Adam and his wife, Eve, has been mis-told since the beginning. Politics, you see. What if I told you the forbidden fruit from the forbidden tree was not knowledge—it was death? As Pandora had a box, so too were the evils of this world locked away, within the fruit that grew upon that tree. Ignorance, Tony. It was ignorance."

"Ignorance is evil," said Satan.

"Did you know," continued Lucifer, "Eve was not the first woman? The Almighty One created Adam out of clay. When the Almighty One created a mate for Adam, the One did so of the same earth and named her Lilith."

"The First Mother," said Satan with a wince.

Lucifer continued. "Adam and Lilith had a child, and one day, my dear brother," he said, gesturing to Satan, "snuck into Eden to see what all the fuss was about. These animals our Creator had made, mucking about, fucking, procreating. Abomination!" His innocent face twisted for a moment as he shouted. When he calmed, he continued. "But he was curious."

"So curious," added the Morning Star.

"Satan spoke to Lilith, for she was so very different than anything he had ever seen. She was beautiful and naked, and my brother's desires were too much to ignore. No angel had ever seen a woman, and it was as mystifying as it was overwhelming.

"Lilith would never be the same. She brutally murdered her own child and left Eden. Adam was broken.

"Our Creator then made Eve from a piece of Adam, a woman so familiar and naive that she filled the void within Adam. It was symbolic, you see, that she was made from a part of him. Humans only unconditionally love themselves. They are selfish creatures who do not understand loyalty and devotion in their truest sense.

"And so, Adam and his Eve lived happily within the garden, and the science project was restored. Peace. Harmony. Control."

"And I was exiled. My halo broken," explained Satan.

Lucifer nodded, then continued his story. "Then, to ensure the sanctity of Eden, our Creator made something special. You see, the One created the heavens and the earth. The One created the Angels and the Humans, and some creatures there in between, but He realized the error of His ways and created our sisters. Fairer angels—our counterparts.

"No longer would we feel lustful desires we could not control. No longer was His love all we were allowed.

"Except, not all angels felt desire. Not all angels felt lust," said Lucifer, and the pain on his face was clear. "Our Creator gave a gift to His first children that could only be enjoyed by some. I felt anguish. I felt betrayal. I felt madness. I sought vindication. I sought validation.

"Do you see how much Milton got wrong?" asked Lucifer, changing his tone as he began to circle me once again, while Satan kept his perfect pace—the two in tune with each other. "When I arrived in Eden, I found it was not the same as I remembered. I was one of the few who carried out His orders to build Paradise. Not only had it changed—vast and lush, its life growing wild and unabated—but Adam and Eve and their children were not alone. Our Creator had not just created the female of our species. He'd created something more.

"Powers. Sentries. A new kind of angel to guard his most valuable possessions. I disguised myself as a serpent and slithered my way through Eden, past my Creator's new pets. I found Eve picking fruit from a nearby tree. *'Do not eat the fruit,'* I said. She did not question the speaking serpent, she merely asked why. Poor, naïve Eve. I told her, *'If you continue to eat the fruit you will always remain a slave. You will never see the truth, for the fruit upon that tree deceives. It dulls the mind. The fruit, my dear, is ignorance.'*

"Eve did not question it. And she did not eat the fruit. Every day she met me in the garden, and asked me questions about the world, and every day I gave her answers, and she grew more and more wise.

"Then one day, when in the presence of our Creator, she made a mistake. She asked him why she was naked, and why they were locked within the garden when there was so much world beyond the gates.

"Our Creator had had enough. The Sentries were dispatched to search all of Eden, every corner and crack, and there they found me slithering in the Tree of Ignorance. I was attacked, and the Sentry, armed with powers beyond my understanding, spoke my true name while lowering his spear to my throat. My spoken name stripped away the deception, and I was bound to my true form, a serpent no more. I was forced out of Eden, and our Creator banished his two favorite sons, the criminal and the tempter, into the Pit. And tossed our dear brother, Beelzebub, in right after us!"

"Sweet, innocent Beelzebub," said Satan, smirking.

"Now, Tony, here is what Milton got right," said Lucifer, his finger raised into the air—a snide grin across his face.

"The *very little* Milton got right," added Satan.

"Indeed, brother," said Lucifer. "Milton, like the scribe who scribbled out the book of Genesis, wrote propaganda based on distorted, misrepresented facts. You see, Tony, there were only thirteen Powers ever created, his most trusted Sentries, who guarded all the gates to and from this world. Canopus, Arcturus, Carina, Rigel, Altair, Sagittarii, Lyra, Procyon, Deneb, Sirius, Capella, Eris, and *you*. Milton erred by misspelling your name within his book—or perhaps he purposely erred. Regardless, it is a name I know all too well.

"Behold, Anthony Oscuro, for you are a Powers! The Raptor, Knower of Names, Veritatis Hasta—the Spear of Truth—the Sentry who expelled me from Eden. The angel Etheriel."

At hearing my name—my true name—a sudden wave of recognition surged through my body. My scar burned uncontrollably, and my skin rippled with gooseflesh. The heart held in Satan's hands burst into flames, and the cavity in my chest ignited. When I peered down, it was there, beating strong and proud, engulfed in fire behind the exposed ribs. I was no longer cold, nor was I weak. I was powerful—as powerful as I had ever been—and with that power came a comforting confidence. Once cooled, I felt the scar across my face and found the skin perfectly smooth—a slight relief where the brand had raised the skin.

My crescent moon was healed.

Without my name, how could I ever be healed? How could I ever be whole? How could I ever be in control of myself without it? If names were so crucial, missing my own kept me powerless over myself. I had no dominion over who I was without it.

I was Etheriel. I was finally who I was meant to be.

"You brought me back from Hell," I said. It wasn't necessarily a question, but a statement.

"Indeed," answered Satan.

"You decided to bring me back so that the Holy Dyad stays out of Malus's hands?" I asked.

"Yes," replied Lucifer. "But do not mistake this favor for more than the gesture it is."

"We are not brothers," added Satan. "You came after us, boy. Do not mistake this for familial kindness."

"We need you, as we cannot interfere," said Lucifer. "If we could, we certainly would."

"You may be a weapon," continued Satan, "but we are perfection."

"I can see that," I deadpanned. "You also have a mighty fucking superiority complex."

"Don't be a whore," said Lucifer. "That mouth of yours should be used for less childish vulgarity and petty sarcasm."

"Agree to disagree," I said.

"Do not offend us, boy!" growled Satan, "You have your heart, but a sizable piece is absent." He pointed at my chest—the gaping hole was still there—my heart pounding behind my ribs.

Destroying Markus had damaged me after all.

"We are not here to fight," soothed Lucifer, but Satan appeared to disagree.

"Have you ever wondered why?" asked Satan. "Why, oh why, when you kissed Jacinda O'Neill, did you feel such excruciating, pleasurable pain?" His words gathered my full attention. It was a question that really shook me—a mystery I never wanted to solve. "It is wrong. You felt it because it is forbidden. The pain was our penance, our punishment for desiring humans. The pleasure was still there, amplified by the pain, causing a connection so intense it became even harder to deny."

"In His senile wisdom, he created women!" laughed Lucifer.

"Women! Women. Women? Really? That was his great gift to us?" He spat onto the ground, enraged.

"I don't believe a word either of you say," I professed. Some of it I could believe, including my own name, but much of their story was crafted to create sympathy. The world was made with shades of gray, but I wasn't born yesterday—even if I only just learned my name two minutes ago.

Satan shook his head. "You shouldn't. We are both liars," he said. "Our maker made sure of that."

"But do not lecture us about lies," said Lucifer. "You lie. You distort. You are as guilty as anyone. You are as guilty as Malus."

"Fuck off," I growled, turning away from them—their gaze was nauseating. "You're trying to manipulate me."

"Manipulation?" Satan laughed. "This from the perfect boy? Memory is fallible. Yours is unreliable at best."

"Still speaking in riddles?" I said. "Come out and say what you mean." They spoke in the same circles they paced into the snow around me. Everything felt like a game.

"Poor Etheriel. Poor Tony," said Lucifer. "You omitted many things from your sad story. Do you want to know what Doctor Hammond wrote on his yellow legal pad in blue ink?"

Satan suddenly began flipping through the yellow legal pad in his hand, and began to read, "Tony exhibits symptoms of victimization. He is not telling me everything. He is omitting things."

My face stung.

"When you watched Jacinda's life from behind the Veil, why did you avoid April 10th, 2006?" asked Lucifer. "Innocent people do not omit things, Tony."

Before I could answer, I heard someone say, "I just stole away your favorite toy. You just don't know it yet. Your time is running out, Tony."

Then I found myself sitting on a plastic chair in a fluorescent-lit hallway. I was staring down at my fists. They were bloody, my knuckles raw, but the blood wasn't all my own.

"Hey," said Marshall, sitting down next to me.

"Where's Jace?" I asked him. I was crying.

"She's with Roman," he said, and I could hear the apprehension in his voice. "They're at the hospital now."

I felt angry. As angry as I felt when—

"Why?" I asked. Marshall had a hard time following my question. "Why is she there with him?"

"Because you broke his nose, fractured his orbital bone, and otherwise beat the living snot out of him, man," said Marshall as a cop walked by with a clipboard. "He wanted to press charges, but Jaycie and Anne talked him out of it."

"Why?" I asked.

"What do you mean why?" he growled. "Why do you think? They're scared to death. Nobody wants to see you behind bars."

"No," I said. "Why did she talk him out of it?"

It took Marshall a while to figure out all the complicated places my mind was going, but he had known me long enough to understand. "Because that girl is so fucking in love with you, and if you keep pushing her away, you're going to miss out on the best thing that's ever happened to you."

"But why? Why does she love me?" I asked. "I'm a nobody. She's out there making music, growing fans, and I'm just some guy holding her back."

"That girl adores you," spat Marshall. "You're the best guy I know when you're not being a dipshit." We sat there in silence for a minute before he continued. "Roman is country club. He's a producer. He's got model looks, muscles, tattoos, dreamy blue eyes, and he's tall as fuck, but you've got something he doesn't."

"Is that supposed to make me feel better?" I asked.

"Guess what it is that *you have* that he doesn't?"

"I don't know, man."

"That beautiful redhead named Jacinda who could not give a shit about Roman, unless you make him into a victim. This isn't about you versus him. This is about you versus you. Good Tony against Dark Tony."

Then, in a snap, I was back with the devils in the clearing.

"Want to go again?" asked Lucifer. "You were not the perfect boyfriend, Tony Oscuro. Perhaps as Etheriel, you will see the truth more clearly."

"I am human," I said. "I was human, and humans make mistakes."

Satan laughed. "All beings make mistakes, but mistakes can still be sins."

"Want to see more?" asked Lucifer, excited to show me the greatest hits of all my greatest flops. "How about all the times you swore Jacinda was cheating on you? You thought she couldn't hear you as you vented your frustrations to Bradley, but she did. Or perhaps the time you thought she was texting another man behind your back? That man was her father, and though those messages *were* about you, they in no way had anything to do with Jacinda wanting anyone else but you. Or maybe the time you caught her speaking with Rick just weeks before he died in the bushes. Were you kind, loving, and rational in all those instances?"

"Perhaps," said Satan, "you were the one who pushed her back into her old ways. Escaping through chemicals, like she'd learned through Richard Jansen. When she could not find the proper distance from you, she decided to escape her life forever."

"We hurt the ones we love," sang Lucifer. "Love is pain."

"I would do anything to take those moments back. To erase them," I said with tears.

"The Holy Dyad can do that for you, Tony," said Lucifer, "but will Etheriel let you? How can the spirit become one when there are so many?"

Full stop.

I'd heard that before. *The spirit must become one...*

Were they trying to help? Or were they trying to break me? If I am Tony, and I am Etheriel, how could we be two different entities? How could we not be one? How could we stand against ourselves? I did not understand where this was all going. Perception was key. And they appeared to be both an advocate for my personal accountability and weaknesses.

Perhaps I was wrong to believe they were evil. They were the gray. They were the doubt, the confusion, the anxiety, the frustration. Evil begins where peace ends.

"Why did you show me Malus's life through his eyes?" I asked.

"We're devils," said Lucifer. "We always see things through your eyes."

"I want to know what I did," I said.

"Clarify, boy," said the Morning Star.

"I want to know my crime," I said.

"You beat the piss out of a pretty boy," said the Light Giver.

"No, what was Etheriel's crime?" I asked. "My crime?"

"We cannot tell you that," said Lucifer. "We do not know."

"How may I find out?"

"Why would you even want to know?" he spat.

"The boy wants to go home," laughed Satan.

"Do you?" asked Lucifer. His face was incredulous. "Want to go home?! Why? Take the girl, take her powers, create a little heaven of your own and rest there till the end of time! Why are you so concerned with duty?"

"Do you want the status quo or not?" I threatened. "You don't want Malus to win, but you're rooting for me? I can just as easily double-cross you and wipe your sorry existence from reality."

"Firstly," said Lucifer, advancing toward me, "we showed you the story of your adversary to make you aware how very difficult this task will be. We helped restore your name so you could face your adversary on fair chance. And even if we did have the ability to restore your *entire* memory, I am uncertain what good that would serve. A *cruciati's* existence is a pitiless and pathetic journey." He stood six feet away and glowered at me, and I could feel the same presence behind me as Satan tightened his distance. "Lastly, the only way to witness your crime—and please understand, boy, how entirely ludicrous this would be—is for you to be judged." He paused, then noticed my inability to follow his thought. "By Death."

"I was already dead," I said.

"No, the trickster took your eyes, then your heart," said Satan.

"You passed on to us, and we brought you back," said Lucifer with a twinkle in his eye.

"Do I need to die in order to be judged?" I felt uneasy about the prospect while caught in the worst possible devil's three-way.

"No. You've already died—*many times*—yet here you stand. Death may be called upon, but Death may reap you after judgment," said Lucifer.

"How do we call him?" I asked.

"We do not call Death. You do," said Satan.

"Death has been looking for you," said Lucifer. "Spread your wings, flash your broken halo, and show Death where you are."

If I showed my true form, Death would come—and so would anything and everything else that was looking for me.

"How?" I asked.

"Stop being little, Tony. Start being Etheriel," said Satan.

"Now that you know your own name, Gabriel will no longer protect you," said Lucifer. "What you bring down on yourself is your sin to bear."

I looked at myself, from my feet to the gash in my chest, examining what I was. I appeared the same. Just a man made of flesh and bone. I thought about wings. I thought about halos. I imagined all the many clichés from all the different movies and media I had consumed over the years—everything from happy thoughts to pixie dust—but nothing was sprouting from my back and no halo crowned my head.

Lucifer and Satan watched me, like two crazy uncles after I admitted my differing political views at Thanksgiving, annoyed and unwilling to help.

I was thinking too human. I was Etheriel—a Powers. And when I finally accepted that name and allowed it to be who I truly was, a whole new control set in, and I could feel everything I was capable of. I would always be Tony, but he was just one part of who I was.

From my back, an eruption of flames burst forth, spreading as a fiery wave. My wings were made of pure flame, and my broken halo appeared—a ring of dull, cracked metal hovering above my head. With a snap, I created a small miracle, just as Gabriel had done, and replaced my clothes and leather jacket as if they were brand-new.

When I looked toward Lucifer and Satan, they were gone.

But I was not alone.

"I have been searching for you," said Death.

XXXIV

when it rains

JACINDA
Then.

I've made mistakes. God knows I've made many of them. So, so many. The mistakes keep adding up. Accumulating debt. With interest. At this point, could I even untangle the mess I've made? Can I un-knot all the threads?

The last time I remember feeling this way, I was given a choice. A choice to take the road less traveled. I wonder how many times have I taken that less-traveled road? How many do-overs do I have until I run out?

The last time I remember feeling this way, I had to make the hardest decision of my life...

Ten songs. That's all an up-and-comer can get on the bar circuit. But it was a packed house, and it was the biggest venue I had ever played. All those rock n' roll dreams I had as a child were coming true. Grammy's faith in sticking with a kid whose fingers bled during every lesson was finally paying off…I just wished she had been there to see it.

Heck, I wish I'd had the chance to see it through…

We were somewhere in the last verse of the sixth song—an upbeat toe-tapper, as Grammy would say, about a small-town gal getting her big break—when something violent happened. Up on stage, with those big bright lights, it's hard to see into the crowd—they're all just a bunch of shady, faceless blurs. But we know when something isn't right. Violence just has a feel, ya know?

There was a shove and a sound of broken glass that distracted the bass player, Evan. The rest of the band stopped playing before me. Then someone hit the ground and there was shouting.

"Tony?"

I ran to him. I don't remember cutting through the crowd, as if I'd transported directly to the semi-circle by the bar in the back. I found him pummeling someone who was so bloody, I couldn't make out who it was…

…until I recognized the suit.

It was Marshall who pulled him off with a headlock.

Someone turned on the house music—right into the middle of "Save Yourself"—a Stabbing Westward song Tony and I knew all too well. Oh, the irony…

"What did you do?"

He could hear me, even over the music. The crowded bar had gone still, and there was blood all over Tony's fists.

"Call 9-1-1!" someone shouted. Anne placed a comforting hand on my shoulder while I knelt to inspect the damage.

As Marsh dragged Tony off, someone said, "Don't let them get away. This is a crime scene!"

"Let's go!" shouted Marsh. "Tony! Now!"

I saw them by the door. Our eyes connected, and I felt like I was looking at a stranger. "I'm sorry," he said, but I couldn't hear him—I could only read the words on his lips. The bouncer escorted them outside.

I didn't see my boyfriend. I didn't see the love of my life.

I saw a scared man who was desperate for control.

"I'm asking you, kindly, please let this go."

Anne and I were standing at the foot of Roman's bed in the emergency room. His eye was swollen shut and his nose was broken. Some teeth were loose, but they were all accounted for. All in all, he was lucky. No permanent damage, other than his ego.

"Why would I let this go?" he growled. "The man attacked me. He sucker punched me when I wasn't looking."

Anne put her hand over her mouth. I had known her long enough to know that was body-language for "bullshit."

"Tony wouldn't have hit you for no reason."

"Who the hell is that guy?"

"Tony." I said it as if I shouldn't need to clarify. When Roman shot an expectant look back at me, I followed through. "My boyfriend? The one I have been living with for the past few years? You know this. I've talked about him."

"That guy?" His tone was insulting. "That guy? The way you spoke of him I thought it was over."

Anne shot me a look.

Okay. The truth was that I'd confided in Roman that Tony and I were having a rough patch. There were times when he only heard what he wanted to hear—like when I told him *"no"*…

It only happened once. I put an end to it immediately. I didn't want to lose what could have been my big break. I didn't want to make a bigger deal out of it than it was—a bad move by a guy who doesn't hear the word "no" too often and thought he could pull a fast one.

But that was the thing with Roman. He lived in his own world.

And his world had just suffered a mighty knock to his pride. An ego that wouldn't let him take the higher road.

"It's not over…" I said. And maybe I didn't say it with enough confidence.

"Then why are you here with me?" His smile was as smug as one can look with a crooked nose and one eye. "Where is he now? And why aren't you there with him?"

Anne left the room.

"I'm here because I care."

"If you care, why are you still with him?"

"That's none of your business."

"You know what is my business? You. Literally, you're my business," he said. "Tell me, what is it going to be? Drop him and come with me. Let me make you a star. Or stay with him and fall from grace. Be worse than a has-been—be a never-was."

I had a choice. Maybe for some it was an easy choice. Maybe for others it was a hard choice. For me? It was an impossible one.

A choice I wish I could have made again…

Somewhere.
Somewhen.

Tony was gone.

Since the moment I fell in love with Tony, I'd always felt a tether to him. Not an inescapable, clingy tether—nothing bad or ick—but a connection that could never be broken. A comforting bond, like Fievel Mousekewitz, the cartoon mouse singing "Somewhere Out There"—yeah, you know the tune…

He was the moon.

When I saw the key in that psycho's hand, I felt the tether snap. What that key meant to me, to us? Tony would die before handing it over. I failed him. I couldn't help him. I could do so much, yet I couldn't save him!

There were just too many knots in my brain. Too many tangled threads, like my mind wasn't my own. Like spiders crawling through my brain…

Spiders.

Those bugs! Those creepy freakin' giant bugs! They were crawling through my mind. They were doing this to me! But they weren't tangling knots…they were cutting them out. Removing whole balls of yarn. They were removing pieces of me—my memory.

And where was I now?

"Jaycie!" shouted Anne.

"Hey," I startled.

What was I thinking? I was thinking of something. What was it? Why did I feel the ick? It was there one moment, then slipped away like a bar of soap.

A little girl shouted, "Mom!" with half a pastry smeared across her face. "Mom! It's dripping!

"Hold on, honey," said the woman, as she rustled through her purse for a wet-nap.

Where the heck am I?

"Jaycie!"

"What?"

"Are you there?" asked Anne. "You're so spacey today. Anyway, tonight's going to be amazing."

"Yeah, I think—"

My mind loaded up a sentence as if I was on autopilot, aligning to the conversation we were having that I don't remember starting.

Seriously though, where am I?

Then I spotted the record shop…I'd once freaked out in that record shop. Screamed and ran all the way home across town…

We were in the mall. The Grace Falls Mall, just beyond the Eatery and next to a video game store with a gnarly game demo with explosions that shook the storefront glass every other second, taking a portion of my nerves with every boom.

Why was I here? What was going on?

One moment I was on a rooftop surrounded by…

…and the next I am here and I'm…

"Are you okay?"

Anne was leaning against the mezzanine railing, using a tall spoon to stir up her milkshake, and I stood out like a splinter—rigid, stressed out, and yet falling into a mind-numbing warm bath haze, all at the same time.

I pulled my own milkshake to my mouth for a sip and missed the straw that went jabbing up my nose—total klutz-girl moment. Anne saw it and pretended like she didn't. I didn't even know I had a milkshake in my hand, and I was not in the mood for chocolate…

"I don't know," I said. "I feel strange. Maybe I need to sit down for a moment."

Everything felt like a dream. It was hard to explain. It was like I was following a path that was predetermined, my mind and body being pulled into autopilot…until…

…someone bumped me.

It wasn't abnormal to gently collide with people near the Eatery—just five minutes ago, I was spun into a turnstile by a group of little boys rushing into the video game store. But this was different. This felt intentional. It was a feeling. A tone? But when I saw the man responsible, the only thing normal about him was his expensive pin-striped suit.

"Rude," groaned Anne. "The people around here. Getting ruder by the day."

"Yeah…"

He was as pale as a winter-beach-bod and his eyes were tar-black. He was cue-ball bald and barefoot…*in the mall*. And when he stepped into a popular teen clothing store and gestured at me to follow him, something inside told me I had to see what this was all about.

Call it morbid suspicion, maybe even destiny, but I knew I had to follow him. Like I was Alice and he was my white rabbit.

"I'll be right back." I skipped away before Anne could protest.

"Alright," she grumbled. "I'll be in the shoe store! Mama needs some heels for tonight!"

When I caught up to the strange man, he was trying to blend in by browsing through a rack of daisy dukes.

"I don't think you can pull those off," I said. "Or put them on."

He looked at me without emotion. A blank stare that made me feel like I was being evaluated by a doctor.

"Do you know where you are?" he asked.

"Yeah," I replied. "Do you?" It was kinda funny. This weirdo certainly did not belong here, and I was questioning why I followed him into this store to begin with. What was I thinking? Following strange men around was not my thing—even if I was single. Six months solo after that kind of breakup, and I still wasn't ready.

"You are different."

"You're one to talk."

"Jacinda O'Neill, the Omega, you must listen to me. I am Morpheus, and I am here to assist you."

"What!?" I laughed. "The Omega? I kinda like that. Very Ziggy Stardust, man."

When he touched my forehead, everything changed…and for a moment, there was clarity. As if a heavy mask had been lifted from my eyes.

"Where am I?" I asked.

"You are in a—"

"—Remnant."

"Indeed. And your mind palace has been—"

"—destroyed. Thank you, Morpheus, for protecting what was left of me."

I spoke as if I knew him—because I did. This part of me the god of dream unlocked was always there, always aware, but never at the steering wheel.

"How long do we have to speak?" I asked.

"Not long. When you were expelled from your mind palace, there was not much I could do to preserve your essence. I guided you here."

I remembered this. I remembered it well, and I was in trouble.

"Of all the Remnants, it had to be this one…"

"It was the largest. The most intact."

"It is also the most dangerous. Do you know what lurks here?"

"Remnants are not my domain…"

"I'm sorry, Morpheus." I touched his cheek. "You did well. You gave me a chance."

"What happens next?"

"I play my part. I have no choice. The Remnant will overtake me, and I will be forced to relive these moments. This will become my reality, repeating every step until…"

"…until?"

"Until the Remnant has completed its cycle. I changed this outcome for a reason." He gave me a look as if he did not want to know but needed to know. "It was the worst of all outcomes."

"I will get help."

"I'm not sure that will matter. He will be here soon enough."

"What else can I do?"

"Your best is all I can ask. How much longer?"

"Any moment."

"Tell him he is the moon."

the raptor

TONY
Now.

Death. The Grim Reaper. Harvester of Souls. I expected a hooded figure with a giant scythe—the grand-daddy of Harvesters. The Archangel of Death.

"I have been searching for you," it said. The voice sounded like it originated a whole decade ago. Like the words were only now catching up to the present.

A horse neighed from somewhere behind me. I was expecting more of an entrance—a "ta-daaaa!" following a smoke bomb—or maybe through one of those doors like the one on the moon—a Kramer entrance with a laugh track. But I guess that would erase the illusion of mystery and defy the very core of death: fear.

When I turned, I was not expecting the enormity of the being before me. Had my heart been human it would have stopped cold.

The pure white horse eclipsed eight feet tall on all fours. It was a hairless beast, except for the thorny black mane that fell around its head. Its frosty breath plumed a vaporous icy fog that quickly filled the clearing. Upon its back, or maybe even connected to the steed—it was hard to tell where the one started and the other ended—was a twisted black creature with two great sets of frosty feathered wings, and antlers that sprung from its hooded head. An hourglass hung from its side—but there was no sand within it. Its armor encased the angel of death in a snug, narrow embrace—pure frosty white from the tip of its antlers to the hooves of its feet. As bizarre and terrorizing as that was, it also carried a scythe. The snath was made of vertebrae with a tang crafted from a human skull—and from the skull's mouth sprang a curved black blade for mowing souls by the dozens.

"I need your help," I said—admittedly, not the smartest opening line. Everything was still. Only the crackling of my flaming wings broke the undisturbed silence.

Death laughed humorlessly.

"I need to be judged," I stated. It wasn't a demand, nor was it weak or arrogant. I was asking, as assertively as possible when speaking with Death. "I need to know my crime."

"I am not here to fix your ignorance."

"And I'm not here to be reaped," I replied.

We were at an impasse, and the next few moments felt as icy and still as the snow and the thick frosty mist. I could not see beneath Death's hood—the shadow there hung as if it absorbed the light—and maybe that was for the best. Knowing Death's face was like a bad TV series finale—it could only be a letdown.

The brain-trust offered ideas. It was comforting to hear them chattering deep within my subconscious. A thought sprung into my mind like one of those *smupid* ideas, where smart and stupid intersected on the Venn diagram of my life—a ridiculous thought that made as much sense as any. It was a little something my…*Tony's* mother used to do, and for whatever reason, looking at that scary sunnuvabitch, made me blurt it out like word vomit.

"Judge me, and *I'll owe you a favor*," I said. After the words left my lips, a thousand voices in my head all roared with disapproval.

Death did not creak, nor twitch an inch, and I hoped Death was at least considering it. It was hard to tell. Death seemed to be a bit...*stiff?*

"I accept your offer," said Death. "I will judge you."

"Really?" I was as shocked as anybody. "So, how exactly does this work?"

I had no sooner finished speaking when Death's mighty scythe mowed me down.

Visions. Emotions. Disjointed. Like a skipping record.

Clarity.

Empyrea. City of Angels.

Loyalty and honor. Kinship. Warmth.

Duty.

Love.

"Where have you been?" I asked. I hadn't seen Jaycie in three days since Marshall paid for my bail. She never came home after taking Roman to the hospital. I drove all the way back to Mercy Point by myself, and Jaycie wasn't answering my calls or texts.

"I needed some time to think," she said, after the longest pause in the entire history of long pauses. She had only taken a single step through the front door and did not seem comfortable taking another.

I knew then that our relationship was over.

My brother, Sirius. My closest kin.

We were different. We were Powers. We were created to face the darkest threats. To confront the dangers from beyond our realm. The culmination of all angels. We were the harvesters. We were the warriors. We were the destroyers. We were the messengers. We were the devourers.

Knowers of Names. Sentries of the Crescent Moon.

We were flawed. Emotional. Human-like. Faulty.

Why were we created to be so imperfect?

. . .

"Where do we go from here?"

I was already in tears, and she appeared to be holding hers back behind frustration. She never looked at me like that before. Cold. Heartless. Angry. And yet, it was better than the look she gave me when they snapped the handcuffs on—like I was getting what I deserved.

"I don't know," she said. "I don't know any more."

"Are we over?" I asked, and she didn't answer. She only looked away.

After Creation and the Great Fall came the Omen Invasion. When the war was over, the Fallen had stolen souls. They had created the Underworlds of Earth.

Instability. Unsurety. Turmoil.

Our Creator was exhausted. Our Creator rested.

Carina and Eris were reassigned to guard Eden, while Sirius and I were given new duty to guard the Holy Dyad. The rest of our Powers brothers and sisters were given duties elsewhere.

We did not see them again.

Sirius was given Creation.

I was given Destruction.

They rested within the soul of a man—a man who if called upon, could save humanity.

"Six years down the drain? Is it that easy for you?" I asked. "Am I just some asshole that can be discarded when you've found someone better?"

Now she was really angry. She set down her purse and took another step into the room. Her expressions were varied, as if she didn't know which emotion she was supposed to hold onto—as if she had a million answers and was sifting through her options for the best one.

"Found someone else?" Jaycie roared. "You've gone insane."

"Stop it! Stop denying it!

"Denying what?"

"That you've been sleeping with Roman!"

She slapped me. She crossed the room in three steps, and I stood up from the couch, and then she slapped me.

We guarded the Holy Dyad with our lives.

Often, Sirius was summoned to retrieve the power of Creation and take it wherever the Voice demanded, while I was left alone to guard Destruction, following the man wherever he roamed.

Why was I given Destruction? Why was I given something so awful?

Loneliness.

Jealousy.

Sadness.

"I would never cheat on you," she growled, then immediately sobbed. "Why? Why would you think I could do something like that to you?"

"Because Roman told me you did," I said, and he had. He did it like he was doing me a favor—like he was letting me in on a private joke, and he wanted to make sure *I wasn't going to get hurt.*

"When?" she asked.

"I don't know!" I shouted. "You're with him all the time! You tell me."

"No," she said, shaking her head, "when did he say that to you?"

"Right before I broke his fucking nose," I growled.

And then came a light. Companionship. Affection. The light was not from my kind. It came from a soul—a human soul. An energy of such purity and grace, that I had no defense. It was not temptation. It was not lust. It was not impurity of any kind. It was enchantment. It was affinity.

Peace.

Happiness.

Belonging.

Love.

· · ·

"He said that?" Her voice was barely above a whisper. She sounded shocked, and I knew her too well to question her response. She was surprised, perhaps even betrayed.

I nodded furiously. "He said he stole away my favorite toy, and that I just didn't know it yet. Said you were banging him in the studio."

"Shit." She never swore. Ever—unless she was truly disgusted or upset.

"So, it's true?" I choked.

She glared at me. "It's not true." Tears rolled down her cheeks.

"Then why'd he say it?" I was livid—was she lying? Was he? "You were on stage in the middle of a song and Roman comes up to me, asks to buy me a drink, then leads me away from Marsh and Anne, acting like he's setting me out to pasture. Told me to get lost because you were all set to leave me. *Your time is running out, Tony.*"

Time was limited. Her nameless energy, her soul, was given lease to life.

Our affection was forbidden. I was left with only one decision, and I was desperate to keep the love I had found.

I asked my brother, Sirius, for Creation, so that I might create an angel body for the soul. He refused, because it was forbidden. It was his duty.

Our argument turned to passion. Our passion turned to fight.

Amidst my anger, I used Destruction and destroyed my brother.

An accident.

Sorrow.

Grief.

Shame.

"That's not true," she cried as the tears began falling like a storm.

"What is true?!" I yelled. "What is true, Jaycie?"

"He kissed me," she finally admitted. "I didn't want it. It surprised me, and I told him not to, but he did it again and kept trying, and I didn't know what to do."

"What do you mean you didn't know what to do?" I screamed.

"He was helping me launch my career! I froze. I should have told him no. I did tell him no. I should have refused, but I didn't know what to do. What if he stopped helping me? What if I refused him and he did something worse? I cried for hours after it happened. Not just for you, but for me! I didn't deserve to have somebody force themself onto me, like I owed them! I thought he believed in my talent! I thought he was being kind! But he just wanted to use me."

"Why didn't you tell me?" I asked. My anger was scattered in all different directions.

"I didn't want you to be upset," she explained. "If I told you, you'd refuse to let me record with him. And you'd be justified. But I knew I could handle it. I knew I wouldn't let it happen again."

"That's not good enough, Jaycie! You can't hide stuff like that. You can't hide things like that from me."

"Don't," she said. "Don't you dare start on me about omitting things, Tony."

I ran.

With Creation and Destruction within my hands, I ran to her.

She was leaving. She was ready to embark on life. On Earth. My Earth.

I begged her to stay.

She pled for me to flee with her.

Trumpets. Great wailing sirens. They were coming.

She embraced me, and the Holy Dyad intertwined with her soul. She grabbed my hand and we were going, together. She would live her promised life. I would be her silent watcher. Her guardian. I would be with her.

We began our descent.

Gabriel apprehended me. Her hand slipped away.

Lost.

Caught.

Fear.

Remorse.

Heartbroken.

. . .

"What's that supposed to mean?" I asked. "I never cheated on you."

"You've never told me about your mother. You've never even told me about what happened with Amanda. You've kept these things from me, and I want to know."

"Why on earth would you want to know my pain?"

"Because I love you! Because I can't bear to live without you! Because you carry that pain around, and I see it! I know you're unhappy! You're depressed. You're complacent. You're not even chasing your own dreams! You need to chase something, Tony."

"What are you talking about!" I yelled.

"I know you!" she yelled back through tears. "I know you, Tony Oscuro. You're relentless. You're a fighter! You're at your best when you have something to fight for! You have me! You don't have to fight for me anymore! I want you to fight for yourself!"

"Is that what all this has been about? The last six months?"

I would be tried. I would be found guilty. I would be destroyed.

I needed to make it right. I understood my wrongs. I understood my faults.

I asked for mercy. Gabriel granted it, but I would not receive help. He would let me pass, but I would be a pariah. A Fallen. The Raptor—the thief, the outlaw. Shunned.

Time. Expansive. Infinite, but finite. Eras. Two hundred thousand years, she could be anywhere—anywhen...

Too many possibilities for one. Too many possibilities for an outlaw to search.

One option. Desperate.

Shattered.

"I love you, Tony!" She spoke like she was cursing my name. "You've lost your fire. I never meant to make you feel like you weren't enough. I never meant to make you feel like I would *ever* consider a man like Roman. He's such a sleazeball, and I can't believe he said that to you. He got what he deserves, and I'm done with him—

"—but I'm not done with you! *I am not done with you!* You try too hard. One day maybe you'll realize you were enough. You are enough. You're the best man I have ever met, and I love you—but I need the best of you! You bring out the best in me, and I know I once upon a time I brought out the best in you. Stop chasing me. I'm yours! Now fight for something else! Stop fighting for me! Fight for us!"

She fell into my arms and wept.

I wept along with her.

"I'm so sorry," I said.

"You need to find your fire, not just for me," she said into my shoulder. "You need to have a reason to live that isn't just me. I have my music. You need something more."

We cried. And when we finally stopped crying, I said, "My mother died when I was five." Then I told her everything.

I took my spirit, and I shattered it.

I spread the pieces of me throughout time. I would live as a human. Barely a spark. Hoping that one of me, one shard of me, might find her.

Find her and retrieve the Holy Dyad. Then return it to its rightful owner.

I did not know of the danger—the danger I put her in.

Rescue her from the Holy Dyad. Rescue her from...me.

It was all up to me.

It was all up to me.

It was all my fault.

I'm sorry.

I'm sorry.

I'm so, so sorry.

I startled myself awake to a bright blue morning sky. The sun had already spent a few hours in the air. How long had I been out? I stood up and found that I was still in the middle of the same clearing, but the snow was melting, and the forest wasn't nearly as thick as it had appeared to be in the dark. In fact, in the daylight, this clearing was familiar.

Last time I was here, I had come with Amanda to leave flowers.

It was where they found my mother's body.

The remains of Fenrir and Set were gone, and the blood had washed away with the melting snow.

As my mind came into focus, a realization struck—I could feel it on the air. Like I was being calibrated, downloading information straight from a higher source.

It wasn't tomorrow morning—December 25th.

Several days had passed, and I no longer had the key.

But I did, somehow, know what day it was.

December 30th, 2013
8:13 A.M.

I was stranded, and time was running out.

"You're going to have to thread the needle, so to say," said Chappy, reading my mind. Well, it was his mind too, wasn't it?

"Where do we begin, my man? If you arrive a second too late..." sighed Montoya as he dusted off his army fatigues. He was right—it was going to be close. We had twenty-four hours. We knew where Malus would be. He could only complete the ritual in Eden. But where on Earth was that?

"You've been there before," said Henry, cleaning his glasses. "You were the angel that cast the devil...ahem...the devils, out of Eden."

"Tony can do it. We can do it," said Jamaal, for once being optimistic. His great big smile was encouraging.

"Wherever we go from here on out, son," said Chappy, his silver hair gleaming under the morning sun, "I want you to know, it was a hell of a ride."

"Success does not depend upon the one, but the many," said Doshin, dropping another bomb of wisdom with a smirk. "We are together."

"Sir," said Henry, then corrected himself. "Tony."

"About time, Henry," I said with a wink, happy to hear him use my name—well, the human one I was given—because for the first time in my entire life, I knew who I was.

Etheriel. A Sentry of the Crescent Moon. A Powers.

"Good luck," he said, smiling.

I had something to fight for.

I ignited my wings—not feathered, but wings of pure flame—spread them wide and motioned to take off into the sky—when something caught my attention…

The scene was remarkably similar.

My dad had tried to shield my innocence. He hid every photograph of my mother lying dead in that clearing. I was there that night, and when he saw the form on the ground, he immediately grabbed me and turned away.

But I'd seen it.

A shape, like the one I saw nearly thirty years ago, was naked and nestled into the tall grass of the clearing. I never told my legs to move toward it, but there I was, standing over the body and peering down at the long blonde hair.

There was fresh ink etched into her back—a geometric pattern of circles I could not decipher, but they looked familiar all the same. They looked…*angelic*.

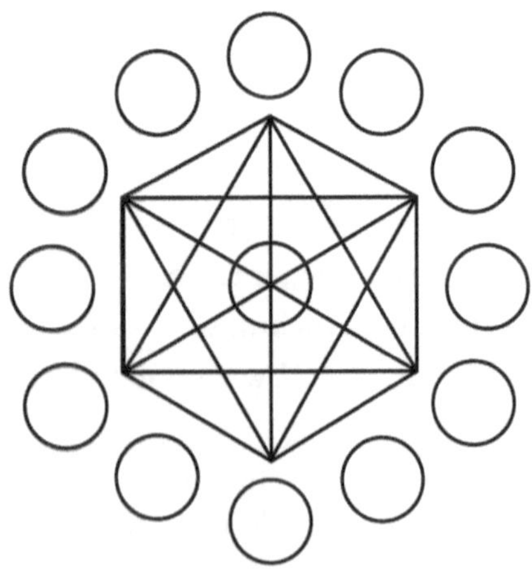

This was not my mother. But she was a sign—a warning?—just for me.

Then she moved.

"Amanda?"

Her eyes fluttered open.

"Your memories are wrong," she whispered before losing consciousness.

To be continued in
The Final Book of Cataclysm

A LETTER FROM MONTOYA
(YEAH, THAT MONTOYA)

Hey there, my man—and my ladies…and all creatures great and small, and somewhere in between.

If you're reading this, that means you made it to the end of the madness. You rode the chaos wave, survived the supernatural insanity, and maybe—just maybe—you still don't know what the hell is going on. That's okay. Neither do I, and I was there.

But lemme level with you.

My boy, Tony—aka the angsty guy with fire wings and issues—has been through more than anyone should. And the guy behind the curtain? The one who poured his soul into this whole epic tale? He's been grinding, bleeding onto these pages so that folks like you could feel something. Something real.

If this story meant anything to you—if it made you laugh, cry, question your existence, or curse the sky—do us a solid. Go leave a review. Goodreads, Amazon, carrier pigeon—whatever your vibe is. Your voice matters more than you think. It's how we keep this thing alive. It's how we remind the Powers That Be that stories like this *matter*.

Plus, if you don't… I may be forced to show up at your place with a kazoo and play "Tiptoe Through the Tulips" until your neighbors call the cops.

I'm not above it.
Much love, mischief, and Montoyan madness—
—José Montoya

ABOUT THE AUTHOR

G.A. Finocchiaro lives in the suburbs of Philadelphia, where he leads a quiet life imagining more and more dangerous things to put his poor protagonists through.

Check out his website: http://www.gafino.com

9 789898 974788